PENGUIN

# DEATH IN VENICE

THOMAS MANN was born in 1875, in the North German town of Lübeck. His father was a member of the local Hanseatic bourgeoisie, a merchant by profession and a senator on the city council, and his mother was of South American descent, part Portuguese and part Creole. His elder brother was the novelist Heinrich Mann. His early childhood and school years were spent in Lübeck, and at the age of nineteen he went to Munich, where he joined an insurance company. In his free time he studied literature and eventually attended the University of Munich. After a year in Rome he returned to Germany. He married Katja Pringsheim in 1905 and they had six children. His earlier major works include *Buddenbrooks* (1901), *Death in Venice* (1911), *Royal Highness* (1916), and *The Magic Mountain* (1924). During the 1920s Mann supported the Weimar Republic on his many lecture tours in Germany and abroad, and in 1929 was awarded the Nobel Prize for literature. With Hitler's rise to power, Mann decided to live in Switzerland and publicly dissociated himself from the National Socialist regime. He was deprived of his German citizenship in 1936. During this period he wrote the biblical tetralogy *Joseph and His Brothers.* He was visiting professor to Princeton in 1938 and wrote *Lotte in Weimar,* before settling in California, where he was in close touch with other distinguished German emigrant writers and artists. He wrote *Doctor Faustus* and *The Holy Sinner.* In 1944 he became a citizen of the United States. He revisited Germany in 1949 and in 1952 returned to Switzerland, where *The Black Swan* (1954) and *Confessions of Felix Krull, Confidence Man* (1955) were written. He died in 1955.

JOACHIM NEUGROSCHEL has translated numerous books from French, German, Italian, Russian, and Yiddish. He has won three PEN translation awards and the French-American translation prize. His most recent translations include Hermann Hesse's *Siddhartha,* Sacher-Masoch's *Venus in Furs,* and Alexandre Dumas's *The Man in the Iron Mask,* all for Penguin Classics.

PENGUIN BOOKS

# THOMAS MANN

# Death in Venice

## AND OTHER TALES

*Translated by*
JOACHIM NEUGROSCHEL

PENGUIN BOOKS

PENGUIN BOOKS

Published by the Penguin Group

Penguin Group (USA) Inc., 375 Hudson Street, New York, New York 10014, U.S.A.
Penguin Group (Canada), 90 Eglinton Avenue East, Suite 700, Toronto, Ontario,
Canada M4P 2Y3 (a division of Pearson Penguin Canada Inc.)
Penguin Books Ltd, 80 Strand, London WC2R 0RL, England
Penguin Ireland, 25 St Stephen's Green, Dublin 2, Ireland (a division of Penguin Books Ltd)
Penguin Group (Australia), 250 Camberwell Road, Camberwell, Victoria 3124,
Australia (a division of Pearson Australia Group Pty Ltd)
Penguin Books India Pvt Ltd, 11 Community Centre, Panchsheel Park,
New Delhi – 110 017, India
Penguin Group (NZ), 67 Apollo Drive, Rosedale, North Shore 0632, New Zealand
(a division of Pearson New Zealand Ltd)
Penguin Books (South Africa) (Pty) Ltd, 24 Sturdee Avenue, Rosebank,
Johannesburg 2196, South Africa

Penguin Books Ltd, Registered Offices: 80 Strand, London WC2R 0RL, England

First published in the United States of America by Viking Penguin,
a member of Penguin Putnam Inc., 1998
Published in Penguin Books 1999

THE LIBRARY OF CONGRESS HAS CATALOGUED THE HARDCOVER AS FOLLOWS:
Mann, Thomas, 1875–1955.
[Selections. English. 1998]
Death in Venice and other tales / Thomas Mann;
translated from German by Joachim Neugroschel.
p. cm.
Contents: The will for happiness—Little Herr Friedemann—Tobias Mindernickel—
Little Lizzy—Gladius dei—Tristan—The starvelings—Tonio Kröger—The
wunderkind—Harsh hour—The Blood of the Walsungs—Death in Venice.
ISBN 0-670-87424-8 (hc.)
ISBN 978-0-14-118173-8 (pbk.)
1. Mann, Thomas, 1875–1955—Translations into English.
I. Neugroschel, Joachim.   II. Title.
PT2625.A44A265   1998
833'.912—dc21        98–2803

Printed in the United States of America
Set in Bulmer
Designed by Jessica Shatan

# CONTENTS

Translator's Preface                     vii

The Will for Happiness                     1

Little Herr Friedemann                    21

Tobias Mindernickel                       51

Little Lizzy                              63

Gladius Dei                               83

Tristan                                  103

The Starvelings: A Study                 151

Tonio Kröger                             161

The Wunderkind                           229

Harsh Hour                               241

The Blood of the Walsungs                253

Death in Venice                          285

# TRANSLATOR'S PREFACE

A whole century has worn by since Thomas Mann began publishing, and both German and English have gone through tremendous changes—but obviously under very diverse circumstances and in very different directions. There is no neat parallel between these two—or, presumably, any two—languages, since the respective cultures they express and reflect are not evenly parallel. So a "retro" translation, in a "period" English that was contemporaneous with the German of a given text, may actually be a distortion.

The year 1900 or 1920 in German-speaking countries was not the same as 1900 or 1920 in England or North America. In fact, in literature, such dates are fiction. Despite the narrative past tense, which, as a metaphor, asks us to suspend our disbelief, those dates never "existed" in literature: they exist only in the present—during the action of reading. If we talk about history, we can say that the American Civil War *began* (past tense) in 1861; if we talk about fiction, we have to say that in *Gone with the Wind* the Civil War *begins* (present tense) in 1861. And if authors wish, they can juggle time and historical events; they can do what Friedrich Schiller does (did?) in his play *The Maid of Orleans* (in which Joan of Arc dies in battle), or 'what Jean Anouilh did (does?) in *The Lark* (flash back to having Joan present at the coronation of the Dauphin *after* she's burned at the stake).

Now suppose we want to evoke an earlier German era by relying on some form of English that was current in, say, 1900 or 1920. In order to draw that pseudoparallel to the German of those times, whose English should we tap? Jack London's, William Dean Howells's, Henry James's? And suppose we opt for Henry James, because he bears a seeming resemblance to Thomas Mann by way of rich vocabulary, complex hypotaxis, and intricate prose rhythms? Well, but a Johnsonian sentence in Henry James is neither historically nor stylistically equivalent to a Kantian sentence in Thomas Mann.

One reason for this lack of cross-linguistic identity is that English and German use subordinate clauses for different purposes. Modern English limits perfect tenses to the bare-bones plot and imperfect tenses to the background. German, having far fewer tenses than English and no verbal aspects, makes a *syntactical* distinction between narrative foreground and background: the plot is generally carried along by the main clauses, the background is painted in by the subordinate clauses. And since the German verb is always postponed until the end of a subordinate clause, the contrast between main clause and subordinate clause—i.e., between plot and background—is as striking as the English contrast between perfective and imperfective verbs. As a result, German narrative always has to be hypotactical, while English can easily be more paratactical. The opening verse in Amy Lowell's "Patterns" goes: "I walk down the garden path, and all the daffodils are blowing. . . ." In English, the contrast between foreground (perfective "walk") and background (imperfective "are blowing") is brought out by the verbal aspects in the two main clauses. But in German, which doesn't have verbal aspects, the second main clause would have to be turned into a relative clause—with the verb swinging in at the end.

Even within a clause, there are countless syntactical differences between English and German usage, making for very different rhythms. Take the order of adverbs. In English, place comes before time; in German, time comes before place: "I'm going to school tomorrow" versus *"Ich gehe morgen in die Schule"* (literally, "I'm going tomorrow to school").

Or take a series of parallel parts of speech—for instance, a row of adjectives. In English, you can say "a big, crooked stick" but not "a crooked big stick." Why and why not? There are two reasons. For one thing, in a chain of parallel parts of speech, the words normally fall into size place, moving from the shortest to the longest: "tall, dark, and handsome," "Tom, Dick, and Harry," "The Good, the Bad, and the Ugly," "the *Niña*, the *Pinta*, and the *Santa María*." Since German rhetoric doesn't have this gradation rule, the word order in the English translation has to be readjusted to conform to our rules of rhythm.

The "big, crooked stick" is also obedient to a second tendency in English adjectives: the more intrinsic the adjective, the closer it stands to the noun. We can apply Aristotelian categories here: "essence" overrides "accident," so that an "essential" feature is closer to the noun than an "accidental" one. "Crooked" is more intrinsic to the stick than "big" and therefore spatially closer to "stick." Indeed, this demand is so powerful that it takes precedence over the law of size place. At times, Mann's original German can easily be rendered into English: *"am Strande, in der Hotelhalle und auf Piazza San Marco"* becomes "on the beach, in the hotel lobby, and on Piazza di San Marco." No rearranging is necessary: the rhythm ascends in both German and English. But at other times, the German words have to be switched around to conform to English rhythm.

Another source of maddening dilemmas are the phonetics, the tapestries of modulated sounds: each language has its own. The vocal harmonies and disharmonies are found in even the simplest utterances: "Fee, fie, fo, fum," grunts the giant in "Jack and the Beanstalk," following a pattern of vowels that move methodically through the shaping of the lips and the positioning of the vowels in the mouth. These patterns determine all sorts of phonetic structures, including the most obvious, such as rhyme, assonance, alliteration—which are used in ordinary speech in both German and English. Thomas Mann not only draws on them as musical devices; he luxuriates in them, say, for the Wagnerian carnality in "The Blood of the Walsungs." Where possible, we can mirror them, relying perhaps on the Germanic (i.e., Anglo-Saxon and Scandinavian) portions of English vocabulary. By the same token, the meshworks of English sounds, whether harmonious or deliberately discordant, play a decisive role in the choice of words and syntax—if the translation is to exist in its own right.

The translator also has to watch out for other pitfalls. We must, for example, avoid any lineup of too many unstressed syllables, which weaken the impact of a sentence. And be careful of polysyllabic rhymes: they are an essential part of the music in German (and certainly in, say, French and Italian). Normally, however, they are used only for comic effects in English, which overwhelmingly prefers monosyllabic rhymes for serious poetry (Swinburne was a very sensual exception, a genius at drawing the most fervent effects from polysyllablic rhymes).

Thomas Mann's style evolved considerably from his early stories to his later ones, broadening in its vocabulary, more complex in its syntax, more varied in its rhythms, and more aloof—at times, disdainfully so—in its overall habitus. One of the main functions of this development was to cope with stronger and deeper emotions, especially within an erotic context, by creating an alienation effect that often draws on irony. In his depictions, Mann focused on powerful impulses, especially the outgushing of repressed feelings, the flouting of sexual taboos such as incest, homosexuality, even mixed marriage. And to face such challenges, he developed an analytical method of objectifying these factors, treating them with detachment by filtering them through his special language.

Art operates as two components of Mann's alienation approach. On the one hand, his characters sustain art as a primary reality rather than a surrogate reflection. The protagonist of "Gladius Dei" is horrified by paintings that he considers blasphemous because of their fleshly enticements; the siblings in "The Blood of the Walsungs" have sex under the impact of Wagnerian opera and its highly peculiar diction; and Gustav von Aschenbach, in *Death in Venice*, constantly sees Tadzio in terms of aesthetic allusions and references, philosophical theories and literary recollection. Mann's leading characters are often professional or would-be artists trying to grasp their existence and situation as creative people. In his fiction, experience, whether mental or physical, is sifted through art.

The second job of art in Thomas Mann is the use of language as a fairly self-contained aesthetic medium to both evoke and distance: no matter what the words may conjure up emotionally, the author's irony keeps the feelings in check, whereby his increasingly complicated syntax establishes a network of bars—but who is in the cage and who outside? Tadzio? Aschenbach? Or the reader? Or do Mann's sentences work like the beaded lead in a stained-glass window, keeping the colors apart yet holding the overall image together both physically and visually?

Intricate syntax has been a hallmark of German thinking at least since Kant, whose periods, highly elaborate, are lucid since he was a master of German style. Later epigoni cultivated hopelessly tangled sentences because they were demanded of a serious thinker, while simple speech was dismissed as simplistic—though in many cases ensnarled sentences (need it be said yet again?) disguised rather shallow and muddled thinking. Thomas Mann, however, with his very sensitive ear, obviously knew how to manipulate his syntactical entwinements, creating a personal rhythm, in which any camouflage is aimed at conceal-ing yet revealing emotions, impulses, vagaries.

To keep his diction fresh and vibrant, Mann generally avoids clichés, even idioms, in which the dormant image is so worn out that its presence would be stylistically harmful. Here, unbe-knownst to Mann, a translator is confronted with a major distinc-tion between British and American writing: Americans tend to regard set phrases (like "hand in hand") as clichés, while the British treat them as idioms—solid, traditional, and conventional in a positive sense of the term. For Americans they're too conventional—and Mann's German, in an interesting linguistic parallel, likewise avoids them most of the time.

To make up for the nearly total exclusion of idioms, Mann in-vents his own "clichés," Wagnerian leitmotifs that are attached to the characters and reiterated frequently, identifying a person by reducing him or her to a fragment—or a butterfly struggling on a pin. But unlike their operatic use, these leitmotifs never play off of one another or weave together, they are never modulated or riffed. Quite the opposite: they isolate Mann's characters or situations, disrupting the originality of his language with their recurring rigidity. These fracturing leitmotifs are part of the overall irony: caricature as characterization.

Similarly, the linking of illness, death, and sex may be derived from Wagner's *Liebestod*; but in Mann this interlacing goes through various metamorphoses in both approach and language. In "The Will for Happiness," sickness and eroticism are kept apart but then finally merge—until one partner dies. In "Little Herr Friedemann," the verbal expression (and frustration) of re-pressed sexual longings leads to suicide, in an anti-Narcissus drowning: Narcissus never realized he was in love with his own reflection, whereas Friedemann knowingly hates his own looks, his own life. He enters the "mirror" of the water.

Taking the notion of narcissism (in its modern sense) and anti-narcissism a step further, we note that both features mark some of Mann's characters, including the twins, especially the boy, in "The Blood of the Walsungs" and, in *Death in Venice*, the old reveler on the boat, Tadzio, and ultimately von Aschenbach, each of whom eroticizes his own image either through an actual mirror or through the looking glass of other people's reactions. This eroticism is expressed partly in a language that includes the realism of cosmetic details and, in some cases, the lyricism of a more sublime diction—such as an alliterative imitation of Wagnerian sex in "The Blood of the Walsungs."

This latter story involves a number of interesting language problems, including deliberate omission and revision. In describing a wealthy, assimilated Jewish family in turn-of-the-century Berlin, Mann cunningly avoids any mention of the words "Jew" or "Jewish" (just as Kafka avoided these words altogether throughout his fiction). In the manuscript, the final disdainful sentence (according to Klaus Harpprecht, in *Thomas Mann*, Rowohlt, 1995) was ultimately rewritten. The original line went: *"Beganeft haben wir ihn,—den Goy!"* "We've robbed him—the Goy!" Both *beganeft* (cheated, robbed) and *Goy* (Gentile—often pejorative) are Yiddishisms. Throughout modern German history and literature, Yiddish and unassimilated Jews were so thoroughly denigrated that German writers portrayed nice Jews as speaking perfect German and nasty Jews as yiddling. Check out Bernhard Ehrenthal, the utterly Germanized, utterly refined, utterly cultured, and therefore anything but Jewish Jew in Gustav Freytag's novel *Credit and Debit* and that sneaky, yiddling traitor Moses Freudenstein in Wilhelm Raabe's *The Hunger Pastor*. A Yiddish accent in German is still so heavily charged with negative connotations that when Max Frisch wrote *They're Singing Again* in post–World War II Switzerland, he had the Jewish survivor in this play speak straight Yiddish rather than German with a Yiddish accent. Mann patronizes his Jewish characters by letting them speak flawless German, though he hints that the twins' parents may have a Yiddish accent: "Frau Aarenhold's . . . speech was larded with bizarre and richly guttural words—expressions from her childhood dialect." Recording a Yiddish accent would have made their portraits even more degrading in German eyes—though Mann, whose wife was Jewish, whose publisher (Samuel Fischer) was Jewish, usually had few pleasant things to say about Jews (in his fiction or his correspondence). While he gently chides the Buddenbrook family and its social circle for their snobbery toward a half-Jewish family, it was not until the Fascist and Nazi era that he showed any sympathy with the Jewish plight. By then, he even recalled a historical massacre of Jews in his novel *The Beloved Returns (Lotte in Weimar)*; and he also resurrected biblical and Talmudic narratives in his Joseph tetralogy—in which, I am happy to report, the Jews, from Abraham to Joseph, all speak exquisite German.

However, Mann's portraits of the Aarenhold twins had ramifications that he himself was unaware of. Some historians claim that even assimilated Jews were distinguished in a crucial way from non-Jews in Germany and especially Catholic Austria: Jews saw aesthetics as an ethical issue, while non-Jews (especially the aristocracy and its emulator, the bourgeoisie) enjoyed art as hedonism (see Steven Beller, *Vienna and the Jews*, Cambridge, 1989). Whether or not this generalization is valid, the "Walsung" twins revel in art as the ultimate amoral pleasure, and their sexuality takes assimilation to a new and unheard-of level. Yet ironically, through this very incest, they renew their status as outsiders in the vacuum of assimilationists, who abandoned their heritage but were never accepted by the German society they so deeply yearned to join. So they turned inward. (Had this story been penned by a rabbi, it might have been subtitled "The Perils of Assimilation.")

In *Death in Venice*, the artist as outsider is one theme. On its simplest level, the story is Balzacian—and Freudian: a man who has always repressed his sexuality and sublimated it entirely into his creative duties is suddenly overwhelmed by a love that is both platonic and plutonic. His Protestant ethic and discipline both drown in his physical and spiritual hormones. He submits to a southern hedonism that proves lethal, because the author, true to his bourgeois morals, links art (even bourgeois art) and pleasure (especially erotic pleasure) to disease and death. To fight against the loss of self-control, against the overpowering libido, Mann's syntax clamps down on the sun-drenched, salt-sprayed voluptuousness that Aschenbach escapes only by dying.

The overall difficulties facing the translator of these texts, with their varying dictions, occur in just about every single word—and in between the words. Problems of rhythm and rhetoric are particularly challenging.

In rendering Thomas Mann's style, I especially had to observe its profound evolution from one story to the next: the growing richness of its lexicon, the greater intricacy of its periods, the exploration of more and more subtle rhythms. The best way, I feel, to bridge the gap between Mann's German and current American readers is to forge a special brand of English, particularly for the more complicated texts, stretching limits in order to convey the music and meaning of the original style. The gap, which is as old as these two societies, runs much wider and deeper: socially, politically, aesthetically, down to the very subject matter and its treatment, whereby each author has his melodies, each style, each language its own music—as does each translation.

*New York, October 1997*

# THE WILL
## FOR HAPPINESS

OLD HOFMANN HAD EARNED his money as a plantation owner in South America. After marrying a local girl from a good family there, he had soon taken her back to northern Germany, the place of his birth. They lived in my hometown, where the rest of his family likewise resided. Paolo was born here.

Incidentally, I never got to know his parents very intimately. However, Paolo was the very image of his mother. The first time I saw him—that is, the first time our fathers brought us to school—he was a skinny little boy with sallow coloring. I can still see him. He wore his black hair in long curls that fell, tangled, on the collar of his sailor suit, framing his narrow little face.

Since we had both been very well off at home, we were anything but satisfied with our new surroundings: the bare schoolroom, and especially the shabby, red-bearded person who was intent on teaching us our ABCs. When my father tried to leave, I held on to his coat and cried, while Paolo remained utterly passive. He leaned against the wall, motionless, his lips pressed together and his big, tear-filled eyes gazing at the rest of the youngsters, hopeful creatures who kept poking one another in the ribs and grinning callously.

Surrounded in this way by larva-like faces, we felt drawn to each other from the very start, and we were glad that the red-bearded pedagogue let us sit next to one another. From then on we stuck together, jointly laying the basis for our education and swapping our sandwiches daily.

By the way, he was already sickly back then, as I recall. Now and again he would have to skip school for longish periods, and when he returned, his cheeks and temples showed, more clearly than usual, the pale-blue veins that can be frequently noticed in delicate brunets. He always had those veins. That was the first thing I noticed when we met again here in Munich and also afterward in Rome.

Our friendship lasted throughout our school years, roughly for the same reason that had prompted it in the first place. It was the "Solemnity of Distance" toward most of our fellow students, an attitude familiar to everyone who has secretly read Heine at fifteen and, while still in high school, resolutely pronounces judgment on the world and mankind.

We also—I believe we were sixteen—took dancing lessons together and, as a result, jointly experienced our first love.

The little girl he was infatuated with was a cheerful, blond creature, and he worshiped her with a melancholy ardor that was remarkable for someone his age and at times struck me as downright lurid.

I remember one dance in particular. The little girl brought two cotillion badges, in quick succession, to another boy and none to Paolo. I watched him anxiously. He stood next to me, leaning against the wall, staring motionless at his patent-leather shoes, and suddenly he fainted. He was taken home and lay sick for a week. It turned out—on this occasion, I think—that his heart was not all that sound.

He had already begun to draw, even before this time, developing a sturdy talent. I still have a quite faithful charcoal sketch he dashed off of that girl's face, along with the caption, a quotation from Heine: "You are just like a flower! —Paolo Hofmann fecit."

I don't know exactly when it was, but we were upperclassmen when his parents left town, settling in Karlsruhe, where old Hofmann had connections. Paolo was not to change schools; instead he was sent to live with an old professor.

However, this situation was short-lived. The following incident may not have been the reason why Paolo eventually followed his parents to Karlsruhe, but it certainly contributed.

What happened was that during a religion class, the senior teacher suddenly strode over to him with a paralyzing glare, and from under the Old Testament that lay in front of Paolo, he yanked forth a drawing of a very female shape that, complete except for the left foot, presented itself unabashedly to the eyes.

So Paolo moved to Karlsruhe, and now and then we exchanged postcards, a correspondence that gradually tapered off and ended.

After our separation, some five years had passed before I ran into him again, in Munich. One lovely spring morning, while strolling down Amalia Street, I spotted someone coming down the steps of the Academy, a man who, from a distance, seemed almost to be an Italian model. When I drew closer, I saw it was he.

Of medium height, slender, his hat pushed back on his thick black hair, his sallow skin crisscrossed with tiny blue veins, his clothes elegant but casual—for instance, a few buttons were undone on the vest—his short mustache slightly twirled up, he came toward me with a swaying, indolent gait.

We recognized each other almost simultaneously, and our greetings were very hearty. As we sat on the terrace of the Café Minerva, catching up on the last few years, he seemed to be in high spirits, almost overexcited. His eyes shone, and his gestures were large and broad. Yet he looked bad, truly ill. It's easy for me to say so now; but I actually did notice it back then, and I even told him so flat out.

"Really? Still?" he asked. "Yes, I do believe you. I've been ill a lot. Last year I was even seriously ill. It's located here."

He pointed to his chest with his left hand.

"My heart. It's always been the same. But lately I've been feeling very fine, quite excellent. I can say that I'm completely healthy. Besides, at twenty-three—why, it would be sad. . . ."

His mood was really good. He spoke cheerfully and vividly about his life since our separation. He had soon talked his parents into letting him become a painter, had graduated from the

Academy some nine months ago (he had dropped in today by pure chance), had lived abroad a good deal, especially in Paris, and had settled here in Munich about five months earlier. . . .

"Probably for a long time—who knows? Perhaps forever . . ."

"Really?" I asked.

"Oh, well? I mean, why not? I like the city, I like it a whole lot! The entire ambience—you know? The people! Why—and this is not unimportant—my social status as a painter, even a totally unknown one, is exquisite; it couldn't be better anywhere else. . . ."

"Have you met pleasant people?"

"Yes—few but very good ones. For instance, I have to recommend one family—I met them during Mardi Gras. . . . The carnival is charming here! Their name is Stein. In fact, Baron Stein."

"What kind of aristocracy is that?"

"What's called a 'money aristocracy.' The baron was a stock marketeer, he used to play a colossal role in Vienna, associated with all the highnesses, and so forth. . . . Then he suddenly got into a jam and managed to extricate himself with a cool million, they say, and now he's living here, without pomp but pleasantly."

"Is he Jewish?"

"I don't think *he* is. But his wife is, presumably. All I can say, though, is that they're extremely pleasant and fine people."

"Are there children?"

"No—that is, a nineteen-year-old daughter. The parents are very charming. . . ."

He seemed embarrassed for a moment, then added:

"I'm seriously offering to introduce you to them. I'd be delighted. Are you interested?"

"Very much so. I'll be grateful to you. If only to meet that nineteen-year-old daughter . . ."

He peered at me askance and then said:

"Fine, then. Let's not put it off for too long. If it's convenient for you, I'll pick you up tomorrow afternoon around one or one-thirty. They live at 25 Theresa Street, one flight up. I'm looking forward to presenting an old schoolmate. The matter is settled."

And indeed, early the next afternoon we were ringing the doorbell on the second floor of an elegant mansion on Theresa Street. Next to the bell, the name "Baron von Stein" could be read in broad black letters.

All the way there, Paolo had been exhilarated and almost rip-roaringly merry; but now, as we waited for the door to open, I noticed an odd change coming over him. Standing next to me, he was utterly calm except for a nervous twitching of his eyelids—a tense and tremendous calm. His head stuck forward slightly. The skin on his brow was tight. He almost resembled an animal desperately pricking up its ears and listening with all its muscles tensed.

The butler, who carried away our cards, returned and asked us to be seated, the baroness would appear momentarily, and he opened the door to a medium-sized room with dark furniture.

As we entered, a young woman in light-colored spring attire got up in the alcove facing the street, and for an instant she re-mained standing and eyed us quizzically. The nineteen-year-old daughter, I thought, involuntarily glancing sideways at my com-panion. "Baroness Ada!" he whispered to me.

She had an elegant figure, but her form was mature for her age, and with her very soft and almost languid gestures, she scarcely appeared to be that young a girl. Her hair, combed over her temples, with two curls dangling above her forehead, was a shiny black, contrasting forcefully with the matte white of her complexion. With its full, moist lips, its fleshy nose, and its black almond eyes and dark, arching brows, her face left no doubt whatsoever as to her at least partly Semitic extraction, yet it was a face of a quite uncommon beauty.

"Ah—company?" she asked, taking several steps toward us.

Her voice was a bit husky. She cupped her eyes with one hand as if to see better, while she propped her other hand on the grand piano that stood against the wall.

"And very welcome company at that," she added with the same emphasis, as if recognizing my friend only now; then she cast an inquiring look at me.

Paolo walked toward her and, with the almost drowsy slowness of someone indulging in an exquisite pleasure, he bowed wordlessly over the hand that she held out to him.

"Baroness," he then said, "may I take the liberty of presenting a friend of mine, a schoolmate with whom I learned my ABCs. . . ."

She likewise held out her hand toward me—a soft, seemingly boneless hand without jewelry.

"I am delighted," she said, her dark eyes resting on me with a slight intrinsic quiver. "And my parents will be equally delighted. . . . I hope they have been notified."

She settled on the sofa, while we sat in chairs across from her. During our chat, her limp white hands rested on her lap. Puffy sleeves reached only slightly below her elbows. I noticed the soft start of her wrist.

Several minutes later, the door to the adjacent room opened, and the parents walked in. The baron was an elegant, thickset gentleman with a bald head and a gray goatee; he had an inimitable way of throwing his thick gold watchband into his cuff. There was no way of determining with any certainty whether a few syllables of his name had once been sacrificed to his elevation to the baronage; his wife, on the other hand, was a homely little Jewish woman in a tasteless gray dress. Large diamonds sparkled on her ears.

I was introduced and welcomed in a thoroughly charming way, while they shook my companion's hand as if he were a good friend of the family.

After some questions and answers about my whys and wherefores, they began to talk about an exhibition in which Paolo had a painting, a female nude.

"A truly fine work!" said the baron. "I recently stood in front of it for half an hour. The flesh tone against the red carpet is eminently powerful. Oh, yes, that Herr Hofmann!" And he patronizingly tapped Paolo on the back. "But do not overwork yourself, my young friend! For goodness' sake! You absolutely have to take care of yourself. How is your health?"

While I had given the host and hostess the necessary information about myself, Paolo had exchanged a few quiet words with the baroness, whom he closely faced. The strange, tense calm that I had previously noticed in him had not vanished by any means. Without my being able to quite pinpoint the reason, he seemed like a panther ready to pounce. The dark eyes in the narrow, sallow face had such a sickly glow that I found it almost eerie when he replied to the baron's question in a confident tone:

"Oh, excellent! Thank you so much for asking! I'm in very good health!"

When we rose after something like a quarter of an hour, the baroness reminded my friend that it would be Thursday again in two days and that he must not forget her five o'clock tea. At this point she also asked me to be so kind as to bear that day in mind. . . .

Out in the street, Paolo lit a cigarette.

"Well?" he asked. "What do you think?"

"Oh, they're very pleasant people!" I hurried to answer. "I was quite impressed with the nineteen-year-old daughter!"

"Impressed?" He laughed briefly and turned his head to the other side.

"Yes. You're laughing!" I said. "And up there it sometimes seemed as if your eyes were dimmed by . . . some secret longing. But I'm mistaken?"

He was silent for a moment. Then he slowly shook his head. "If only I knew where you—"

"Oh, please! The question for me is whether Baroness Ada also . . ."

He mutely looked down for another moment. Then he murmured with confidence:

"I believe I will be happy."

I said goodbye, heartily shaking his hand even though I could not mentally suppress a qualm.

Several weeks passed, during which I periodically joined Paolo for afternoon tea in the baronial salon. A small but very pleasant group would gather there: a young actress of the Royal Theater, a physician, an officer . . . I do not remember each and every one.

As for Paolo's behavior, I detected nothing new. Usually, despite his alarming appearance, he was in an exalted, joyful mood, and in the young baroness's proximity he always showed the same eerie calm that I had perceived in him the very first time.

Now, one day—and I happened not to have seen Paolo in two days—I ran into Baron von Stein on Ludwig Street. He was on horseback. Reining in, he held out his hand to me from the saddle.

"Delighted to see you! I hope you can drop by tomorrow afternoon?"

"If it is all right with you, then beyond any doubt, Herr Baron. Even if there were any doubt that my friend Hofmann would pick me up, as he does every Thursday. . . ."

"Hofmann? Why, didn't you know? He's left town! I would have thought that he would inform *you,* of all people."

"He didn't say a word!"

"And so utterly *à bâtons rompus* . . . That's what's known as an artist's whims. . . . Well, till tomorrow afternoon!"

He spurred his horse and left me behind, completely baffled.

I hurried over to Paolo's apartment. Yes, alas: I was told that Herr Hofmann was traveling. He had left no forwarding address.

It was clear that the baron knew of something more than an

"artist's whims." His daughter herself confirmed what I already assumed.

She did so on a stroll to the valley of the Isar River; they had arranged it, and I was invited too. We did not leave until afternoon, and on the way home, late that evening, the baron's daughter and I were the last pair following the party.

I had perceived no change in her since Paolo's disappearance. She had fully maintained her composure, never uttering so much as a word about my friend, while her parents profusely expressed their regret about his sudden departure.

By now I was walking with the baroness through this most graceful area in the surroundings of Munich; the moonlight flickered through the foliage, and for a while we listened silently to the chitchat indulged in by the rest of the company—it was every bit as monotonous as the gush of the water foaming along beside us.

All at once, she began talking about Paolo; her tone was very calm and very sure.

"You've been his friend since boyhood?" she asked me.

"Yes, Baroness."

"You share his secrets?"

"I believe I am familiar with his greatest secret, even though he hasn't confided in me."

"And I may trust you?"

"I hope you do not doubt it, dear Fräulein."

"Fine," she said, raising her head in a resolute movement. "He asked for my hand, and my parents turned him down. He's ill, they told me, very ill—but it doesn't matter: I *love* him. I can speak to you like this, can't I? I . . ."

She was confused for a moment and then went on with the same resoluteness:

"I don't know where he is; but I give you permission, the instant you see him, to repeat my words, which he has already heard from my lips, and to write them to him the instant you track down his address: I will never give my hand to any man but him. Ah—we shall see!"

That last outcry contained, along with defiance and resolution, such a hopeless pain that I could not help but take hold of her hand and silently squeeze it.

I had already written a letter to Hofmann's parents, inquiring about their son's whereabouts. I received an address in South Tyrol, but the letter I sent there was returned with the notice that the addressee had left without indicating his destination.

He refused to be pestered by anyone; he had fled everything in order to die somewhere in total solitude. For after all this, I felt a sad likelihood that I would never see him again.

Was it not obvious that this hopelessly sick man loved that young girl with the silent, volcanic, ardently sensual passion consistent with the identical first stirrings of his early adolescence? The sick man's egoistic instinct had kindled the desire for a union with radiant health; since this ardor remained unsated, was it not bound to swiftly devour his last ounce of vitality?

And five years passed without my receiving any sign of life from him—but also without any news of his death.

Now, during the previous year, I had been in Italy, in Rome and its surroundings. I had spent the hot months in the mountains, returning to town at the end of September. One warm evening I was sitting over a cup of tea at the Café Aranjo. Leafing through my newspaper, I glanced absently at the lively bustle dominating the vast, light-filled space. The patrons were coming and going, the waiters dashing to and fro, and now and then the drawn-out yells of newsboys resounded through the wide-open doors into the café.

And suddenly I saw a man around my age threading his way slowly through the tables and toward the exit. That gait . . . ? And now he turned his head toward me, raised his eyebrows, and came toward me with a joyfully astonished "Ah?"

"You here?" We shouted it in unison, and he added:

"So then we're both still alive!"

His eyes darted slightly away as he said that. He had barely changed in those five years; except that his face may have grown even narrower, with his eyes lying deeper in their sockets. Now and again he took a deep breath.

"Have you been in Rome a long time?" he asked.

"Not so long in the city; I spent a few months in the countryside. And you?"

"I was at the seashore until a week ago. You know I've always preferred it to the mountains. . . . Yes, since we last met I've seen a good bit of the world."

And while spooning up a glass of *sorbetto* next to me, he began telling me how he had spent those years traveling, always traveling. He had rambled through the Tyrolean mountains, had slowly crisscrossed all of Italy, had sailed from Sicily to Africa, and he spoke about Algiers, Tunis, Egypt.

"Finally I spent a little time in Germany," he said, "in Karlsruhe. My parents urgently wished to see me and were very reluctant to let me take off again. Now I've been in Italy for three months. I feel at home in the south, you know. I just love Rome!"

I had not spoken even one word to ask him about his health. Now I said:

"May I infer from all this that your health has significantly improved?"

He eyed me quizzically for a moment; then he replied:

"You mean because I wander about so cheerfully. Ah, let me tell you: This is a very natural need. What do you expect? I'm not allowed to drink, smoke, or love—I need some sort of narcotic, do you understand?"

Since I held my tongue, he added:

"For five years now, I've needed it *very much.*"

We had reached the topic that we had been avoiding, and the

ensuing pause betrayed our mutual helplessness. He sat leaning against the velvet cushion, gazing up at the chandelier. Then he suddenly said:

"Above all—you do forgive me, don't you, for not getting in touch with you for such a long time? . . . You do understand?"

"Certainly!"

"You're informed about my experiences in Munich?" he went on, in an almost harsh tone.

"As thoroughly as possible. And do you realize that I've been waiting all this time to deliver a message to you? A task assigned by a lady?"

His weary eyes flared up briefly. Then he said in the same dry, sharp tone as before:

"Let me hear whether it's something new."

"Hardly new; just a confirmation of what you heard from her yourself. . . ."

And I repeated for him, in the midst of the chattering and gesticulating throng, the words spoken to me that evening by the baroness.

He listened while slowly rubbing his forehead; then he said, with no sign of emotion:

"Thank you."

His tone of voice was starting to confuse me.

"But years have passed over those words," I said, "five long years that she and you, both of you, have lived through. . . . A thousand new impressions, feelings, thoughts, wishes—"

I broke off, for he straightened up and said in a voice quivering again with the passion that, for a moment, I had thought was snuffed:

"I *keep* these words!"

And at that instant I recognized, in his features and in his entire bearing, the expression I had observed on his face when I had first met the baroness: that drastic, convulsively tense calm shown by the predator before it pounces.

I changed the subject, and we again spoke about his travels, about his studies abroad. They did not seem to have amounted to much; he talked about them rather indifferently.

Shortly after midnight he stood up.

"I'd like to go to bed or at least be alone. . . . You'll find me tomorrow morning at the Galleria Doria. I'm copying Saraceni; I've fallen in love with the musical angel. Do come over, please. I'm very glad you're here. Good night."

And he went off—slow, calm, with slack, indolent movements.

I spent the whole next month roaming the city with him: Rome, that effusively rich museum of all the arts, that modern metropolis in the south, that city, which is full of loud, quick, hot, ingenious life and yet to which the warm wind carries the sultry languor of the Orient.

Paolo's behavior remained the same. He was usually earnest and silent and could at times lapse into a sluggish fatigue, and then, with flashing eyes, he would suddenly pull himself together and eagerly resume a suspended conversation.

I must mention a day when he dropped a few words that have attained their true meaning for me only now.

It was a Sunday. We had taken advantage of the wonderful late-summer morning to go strolling on the Via Appia. After walking way out on the ancient thoroughfare, we had climbed a small rise that, encircled by cypresses, offers a delightful view of the sunny *campagna* with the huge aqueduct and the Alban Hills, all shrouded in a soft mist. And now we were resting.

Paolo, half reclining, his chin propped on his hand, rested next to me on the warm turf, his weary eyes gazing vacantly into the distance. Then yet again he abruptly pulled himself out of total apathy and turned to me.

"This atmosphere! Atmosphere is everything!"

I said something in agreement, and we were silent once more. And then suddenly, with no transition, he said, his face veering toward me with a certain urgency:

"Listen, weren't you actually surprised that I'm still alive?"

Taken aback, I held my tongue, and he again peered into the distance with a wistful expression.

"It does surprise *me*," he slowly went on. "Basically it amazes me every day. Do you really know what my condition is? The French doctor in Algiers said to me, 'The devil only knows how you can still keep traveling! I advise you to go home and get to bed!' He was always so straightforward because we played dominoes together every evening.

"I'm still alive. I'm at the end almost daily. In the evening, I lie in the dark—on my right side, mind you! My heart beats almost into my throat, I'm so dizzy that I break out in a cold sweat, and then I suddenly feel as if death were touching me. For an instant it's as if everything were standing still inside me: my heart pauses, I stop breathing. I jump up, switch on the light, take a deep breath, look around, devour the objects with my eyes. Then I have a sip of water and lie down again always on my right side! I gradually fall asleep.

"I sleep very deep and very long, for actually I am always dead tired. Would you believe that if I wanted to, I could simply lie down here and die?

"I believe that during these past few years I have already seen death face-to-face a thousand times. I have not died. . . . Something is holding me. . . . I jump up, I think of something, I cling to a sentence, which I repeat to myself twenty times while my eyes greedily suck in all the light and life around me. . . . Do you understand that?"

He lay motionless and barely seemed to expect any answer. I don't recall my response; but I will never forget the impact his words made on me.

And now for that day—oh, I feel as if it had been only yesterday!

It was one of the first days of autumn, those gray, incredibly warm days when the damp, oppressive wind from Africa blows through the streets and sheet lightning flashes endlessly across the entire evening sky.

In the morning, I dropped in on Paolo to pick him up for a stroll. His big trunk stood in the middle of the room, the closet and the dresser drawers were wide open; his watercolor sketches from the Orient and the plaster cast of the Vatican head of Juno were still in their places.

He himself stood, tall and erect, at the window and kept his gaze riveted to the outside when I halted with an astonished cry. Then he briefly turned, handed me a letter, and said merely:

"Read it."

I looked at him. On that narrow, sallow invalid face lay an expression that only death can otherwise evoke, a tremendous solemnity that made me look down at the letter I had taken hold of. And I read:

Dear Herr Hofmann,

I owe the knowledge of your address to the kindness of your dear parents, to whom I turned, and I now hope that you will receive these lines in a friendly manner.

Please permit me, dear Herr Hofmann, to assure you that during these five years I have always thought about you with a feeling of sincere friendship. Were I to assume that your abrupt departure on that day, which was painful for you *and* for me, was meant to evince *anger* toward me and my family, then my distress would be even greater than the dismay and deep astonishment that I felt when you asked me for my daughter's hand.

At that time I spoke to you man-to-man, and, at the risk of striking you as brutal, I openly and honestly gave you the reason why I had to deny my daughter's hand to a man whom I—I cannot emphasize it enough—esteem so greatly in every respect. I spoke to you as a father who is intent on the *lasting* happiness of his only child and who would have conscientiously nipped in the bud any sprouting of such wishes on both sides if the thought of their possibility had ever crossed his mind!

Today I am speaking to you, my dear Herr Hofmann, in the very same capacities: as a friend and as a father. Five years have flowed by since your departure, and if I had not yet had sufficient leisure to realize how deeply rooted in my daughter is the affection that you were able to inspire in her, then an event that recently occurred has fully opened my eyes. Why should I conceal from you the fact that my daughter, at the thought of you, turned down the hand of an excellent gentleman whose courtship I, as a father, could only urgently endorse?

The passage of years has had no sway over my daughter's feelings and wishes, and should—this is an open and discreet question!—the case be the same with you, my dear Herr Hofmann, then I hereby declare that we parents will offer no further hindrance to the happiness of our child.

I look forward to your reply, for which, whatever it may be, I will be exceedingly grateful, and I have nothing to add to these lines aside from the expression of my deepest regard.

Yours devotedly,

Oskar Baron von Stein

I looked up. His hands were on his back, and he was facing the window again. All I asked was:

"Are you going?"

And without looking at me, he replied:

"My belongings have to be ready by tomorrow morning."

The day wore on with errands and packing, which I helped him with, and in the evening, at my suggestion, we took a final walk through the streets of the city.

The air was still almost unbearably sultry, and an abrupt phosphorous light flashed through the heavens at every second. Paolo looked calm and exhausted, but his breathing was deep and heavy.

Keeping quiet or conversing indifferently, we must have been wandering about for an hour when we halted in front of the Fontana di Trevi, that famous fountain that shows the god of the sea with his racing team of horses.

Once again we spent a long time contemplating and admiring this marvelously vibrant group, which, incessantly enveloped in harsh blue lightning, made an almost enchanted impression. My companion said:

"Bernini certainly delights me, even in the works of his disciples. I don't understand his enemies. Granted, if *The Last Judgment* is more sculpted than painted, then the whole of Bernini's oeuvre is more painted than sculpted. But does a greater decorator exist?"

"Do you know the story of the fountain?" I asked. "Whoever drinks from it when leaving Rome will come back. Here you have my traveling glass"—and I filled it at one of the jets of water. "You should see your Rome again!"

He took the glass and brought it to his lips. At that instant, the entire sky flamed up in a dazzling, long-lasting, fiery glow, and the thin and delicate vessel shattered to pieces on the edge of the basin.

Paolo took out his handkerchief and blotted the water on his suit.

"I'm nervous and clumsy," he said. "Let's move on. I hope the glass had no value."

By the next morning, the weather had cleared. A light-blue summer sky smiled over us as we drove to the railroad station.

Our goodbyes were brief. Paolo shook my hand wordlessly when I wished him happiness, lots of happiness.

I gazed after him for a long time as he stood erect at the broad picture window. Deep solemnity lay in his eyes—and triumph.

What else do I have to say? He is dead; he died the morning after the wedding night—almost during the wedding night.

It had to be. Was it not his will, the will for happiness alone, with which he had kept death at bay for such a long time? He had to die, die without a struggle or resistance, once his will for happiness had been satisfied; he no longer had a pretext for living.

I wondered whether he had wronged, deliberately wronged, the woman he united with. But I saw her at his funeral; she was standing at the head of his coffin. And on her face I noticed the same expression that I had found on his: the grave and powerful solemnity of triumph.

# LITTLE HERR
# FRIEDEMANN

IT WAS THE NURSE'S FAULT. When the first suspicion arose, what good did it do for Frau Consul Friedemann to urge her earnestly to suppress such a vice? What good did it do for Frau Friedemann to let her have a daily glass of red wine as well as the nourishing beer? It suddenly turned out that this girl sank so low as to drink the fuel meant for the alcohol burner. But before she could be dismissed, before a replacement for her arrived, the accident occurred. One day, when the mother and her three adolescent daughters came home, little Johannes, who was about a month old, had fallen from the nursery table. He lay on the floor, emitting a dreadfully faint whimper, while the nurse stood next to him in a daze.

The physician, who gingerly but firmly tested the limbs of the wincing, convulsing little creature, made a very, very grave face, the three daughters stood sobbing in a corner, and Frau Friedemann prayed loudly in her anguish.

Before the birth of the child, the poor woman had had to suffer the loss of her husband, the Netherlandish consul, who had been snatched away by a sudden violent illness, and she was still so broken up that she was incapable of hoping that little Johannes might survive for her. But two days later, the physician gave her hand an encouraging squeeze; he explained that the child was absolutely out of immediate danger and that, above all, the slight effect on the brain was entirely eliminated, as one could tell by the eyes, which no longer had that same vacant gape. . . . Naturally they would have to wait and see how things subsequently developed—and they would have to hope for the best, you know, hope for the best. . . .

The gray gabled house where Johannes Friedemann grew up stood at the northern gate of the old, barely middle-sized commercial town. The front door opened into a spacious hallway with a flagstone floor, where a staircase with a white wooden banister led to the upper stories. In the parlor on the next landing, the wallpaper depicted faded landscapes, while stiff-backed chairs surrounded the heavy mahogany table with its dark-red plush cover.

During his childhood he would often linger at the window, in front of which there was always a magnificent display of beautiful flowers, and he would sit on an ottoman at his mother's feet and listen to a wonderful story while gazing at her smooth gray hair and kind, gentle face and breathing in the soft fragrance that she always gave off. Or else he had her show him the picture of his father, a friendly gentleman with gray whiskers. He was in heaven, said the mother, and was waiting for all of them there.

Behind the house there was a small garden, where they would spend a good portion of each summer day despite the sugary haze that nearly always wafted over from a nearby refinery. An old, gnarled walnut tree stood in the garden, and little Johannes would often sit in its shade, on a low wooden chair, cracking nuts, while Frau Friedemann and the three daughters, now adults, gathered in a gray canvas tent. Frequently, however, the mother would look up from her needlework and with melancholy tenderness her eyes would stray over to the child.

He was not beautiful, little Johannes, and indeed, as he squatted on the footstool and cracked nuts nimbly and zealously, he presented an extremely bizarre sight with his high, pointed pigeon breast, his widely curving back, and his thin, overly long arms. His hands and feet, however, were slender and delicately formed, and he had large, fawn-colored eyes, sensitive lips, and fine, light-brown hair. Even though his face was wedged so woefully between his shoulders, it could almost have been called beautiful after all.

When he was seven, he was sent to school, and now the years passed quickly and uniformly. Every day, with the comically self-important strut that sometimes characterizes cripples, he would wander between the shops and the gabled houses and head toward the old school building with the Gothic arches. After coming home and completing his assignments, he might read his books, with their lovely colored pictures on the title pages, or else do some gardening, while the sisters ran the household for the now ailing mother. They also attended parties, for the Friedemanns belonged to the city's upper crust. Unfortunately, none of the sisters had married, for they did not have much by way of a fortune, and they were rather ugly.

Johannes likewise received occasional invitations from children his own age, but he did not really enjoy socializing with them. He could not join in their games, and since they always maintained a self-conscious restraint toward him, no genuine friendship could ever develop.

The time came when he often heard them talking, in the schoolyard, about certain experiences. Attentive and wide-eyed, he listened to their stories about crushes on this little girl or that, whereupon he kept silent. These matters, he told himself, in which the others were obviously quite absorbed, were among the things he was not cut out for, like gymnastics or throwing a ball. This was saddening at times. But then he had always been accustomed to being on his own and not sharing other people's interests.

Nevertheless, one day when he was sixteen, he developed a sudden affection for a girl the same age. She was a classmate's sister, an exuberantly cheerful blond creature, whom he met at her brother's home. He felt a strange anxiety in her presence, and he was deeply saddened by the self-conscious and artificial courtesy with which she, too, treated him.

One summer afternoon, while taking a solitary stroll on the wall outside the town, he heard whispering from behind a jasmine bush, and he peered cautiously through the branches. A bench was standing there, and that girl was sitting next to a tall, redheaded boy, whom he knew very well. The boy had put his arm around her and was pressing a kiss on her lips, which she gigglingly returned. Upon seeing this, Johannes Friedemann turned around and stole away.

His head sank deeper than ever into his shoulders, his hands trembled, and a sharp, urgent pain shot from his chest into his throat. But he choked it down and resolutely pulled himself up as best he could. "Fine," he said, "it's over. I will never again concern myself with any of that. It brings others joy and happiness, but for me it can only mean grief and sorrow. I'm done with it. Never again."

The decision did him good. He renounced, renounced forever. He went home and picked up a book or played the violin, which he had mastered despite his deformed chest.

At seventeen, he left school to become a businessman, like everyone else in his circle, and he began training at Herr Schlievogt's big lumberyard down by the river. He was treated with indulgence, and he for his part was friendly and obliging, and time went by, peaceful and orderly. However, when he was twenty-one, his mother died after a long illness.

This was very painful for Johannes Friedemann. He enjoyed it, that pain, he yielded to it as one does to a great happiness, he nurtured it with a thousand childhood memories and wallowed in it as his first powerful experience.

Is not life per se a good thing, whether or not it shapes up for us in a way that can be called "happy"? Johannes Friedemann felt that this was so, and he loved life. No one can understand with what heartfelt care this man, who had renounced the greatest happiness that life can offer us, knew how to enjoy the delights that were accessible to him. A springtime stroll through the green areas outside the town, the scent of a flower, the warbling of a bird—couldn't we be thankful for such things?

And he also understood that culture is part of the ability to enjoy—indeed, that culture is always simply tantamount to the ability to enjoy; and he cultivated his mind. He loved music and attended any and all concerts that were given in the town. He himself, though he looked uncommonly strange when doing so, gradually came to play the violin quite well, delighting in every lovely and mellow note that he managed to produce. Also, through wide reading, he eventually acquired a literary taste, which he probably shared with no one else in town. He kept up with the latest publications, both domestic and foreign, he knew how to savor the rhythmic charm of a poem, how to let a finely written novella work its intimate mood upon him. . . . Oh, one might almost have called him an epicurean.

He learned to understand that everything was enjoyable in its way and that it is almost foolish to distinguish between happy and unhappy experiences. He most readily took in each mood and sensation and cultivated them, the sad as well as the cheerful ones—and also the unfulfilled wishes, the *yearnings*. He loved them for their own sake and told himself that with fulfillment the best would be past. Aren't the sweet, vague, painful yearning and hoping of quiet spring evenings a richer joy than any fulfillments that the summer might bring? Yes indeed, he was an epicurean, that little Herr Friedemann.

But they probably did not know this—the people who greeted him in the street with that pitying and friendly air to which he had always been accustomed. With his comical self-importance, this unfortunate cripple strutted along in a light-colored overcoat and a shiny top hat (he was, strangely, a bit vain), and people did not know that he tenderly loved life, which flowed along for him gently, devoid of great emotional surges, yet imbued with a silent and delicate happiness that he created himself.

However, Herr Friedemann's chief affection, his true passion, was the theater. He possessed an uncommonly powerful dramatic sensibility, and during an intense theatrical effect, the catastrophe of a tragedy, his entire little body could start trembling. He had a seat in the front row of the City Theater, which he attended regularly, accompanied now and then by his three sisters. Since their mother's death, they ran the household for themselves and their brother in the old mansion, which they all owned together.

The sisters were, alas, still unmarried; but they had long since reached the age of resignation, for Friederike, the eldest, was seventeen years older than Herr Friedemann. She and her sister Henriette were a bit too lank and thin, while Pfiffi, the youngest, was all too short and plump. Pfiffi, incidentally, had a droll way of shaking at every word, with moisture oozing into the corners of her mouth.

Little Herr Friedemann did not concern himself overly about the three girls; but they stuck together loyally and were always of a single opinion. Especially when an engagement took place in their circle of acquaintances, they unanimously emphasized that this was indeed *very* gratifying.

Their brother stayed on with them even after leaving Herr Schlievogt's lumberyard and striking out on his own by taking over a small business, an agency or something of the kind, which did not require too much work from him. He occupied a few rooms on the ground floor of the home, so that he had to climb the stairs only at mealtimes, for he occasionally suffered a bit from asthma.

On his thirtieth birthday, a bright, warm day in June, he was sitting after lunch in the gray garden tent with a new headrest that Henriette had sewn for him; he had a good cigar in his mouth and a good book in his hand. Now and then he put the book aside, listened to the joyous chirping of sparrows in the old walnut tree, and looked at the neat gravel path leading to the house and at the lawn with its particolored flower beds.

Little Herr Friedemann wore no beard, and his face was almost unchanged, except that his features had become a bit sharper. His wore his fine, light-brown hair smooth, with a part on the side.

Once, when he lowered the book on his lap and blinked up at the blue, sunny sky, he said to himself: Now, that's thirty years. Another ten or even twenty may still come, God knows. They will come along quiet and soundless and flow by like the ones that have already passed, and I look forward to them with peace in my heart.

That July brought a change of district commandership, which set everyone aflutter. The jovial, corpulent man who had occupied that post for many years was very popular in the higher social circles, and they were reluctant to see him leave. Goodness only knew the circumstance that brought Herr von Rinnlingen of all people from the capital.

In any case, the trade-off did not seem bad, for the new lieutenant colonel, who was married but childless, rented a very spacious villa in the southern suburbs, from which it was inferred that he planned to have a household. In any case, the rumor that he was quite extraordinarily wealthy was also confirmed by his bringing along four servants, five saddle and carriage horses, a landau, and a light game cart.

Soon after their arrival, he and his wife began calling on the prestigious families, and the couple became the talk of the town. Interest, however, focused not on Herr von Rinnlingen but utterly on his wife. The men were taken aback and had no opinion for the moment; the women, however, simply did not approve of Gerda von Rinnlingen's nature and character.

"You can sense the metropolitan air," said Frau Hagenström, the lawyer's wife, when conversing with Henriette Friedemann. "Well, that's natural. She smokes, she goes horseback riding—all well and good! But her behavior is not only free and easy, it's tomboyish, and even that's not the right word. . . . Look, she's not ugly by any means; you might even find her pretty. And yet she's devoid of any feminine charm, and her eyes, her laughter, her movements, lack everything that men love. She's no flirt, and goodness knows I'd be the last person not to find that praiseworthy. But should such a young woman—she's only twenty-four—be so thoroughly lacking in natural grace? My dear, I'm not good at expressing myself, but I do know what I mean. Our gentlemen are still dumbstruck for now. But you'll see, within a few weeks they'll turn away from her in disgust."

"Well," said Fräulein Friedemann, "she's marvelously provided for."

"Yes, her husband!" exclaimed Frau Hagenström. "And how does she treat him? You ought to see it! You will see it! I am the first to insist that a married woman should have a certain degree of aloofness toward the opposite sex. But how does she behave toward her own husband? She has a way of giving him an icy look and saying 'Dear friend' to him with a pitying stress that I find outrageous! You should see *him* at such times—correct, stalwart, chivalrous, forty years old and splendidly preserved, a brilliant officer! They've been married for four years. My dear . . ."

The place where it was first granted little Herr Friedemann to see Frau von Rinnlingen was Main Street, which was lined almost exclusively with businesses, and this encounter took place in the afternoon, just as he was coming from the stock market, where he had put in a bid or two.

He was strolling, tiny and self-important, alongside Wholesaler Stephens, an unusually big and burly man with rounded sideburns and dreadfully bushy eyebrows. Both men wore top hats and had unbuttoned their overcoats because of the heat. They were talking politics while tapping their canes on the sidewalk in a regular cadence; but roughly halfway down the street, Wholesaler Stephens suddenly said:

"God damn it if that isn't the Rinnlingen woman driving this way."

"Well, that's a stroke of luck," said Herr Friedemann in his high, rather sharp voice, and he peered ahead expectantly. "You see, I still haven't laid eyes on her. Why, that's the yellow cart."

It was indeed the yellow game cart that Frau von Rinnlingen was using today, and she was personally guiding the two lean horses, while the groom sat behind her with arms crossed. She wore a very light-colored wide jacket, and her skirt was also of a light hue. From under a small, round straw hat with a leather band, her reddish-blond hair, which was combed over her ears, welled out and fell deep down the nape of her neck, into a thick knot. Her oval face was a matte white, and bluish shadows lurked in the corners of her brown eyes, which were unusually close-set. Her short but quite finely shaped nose had a small ridge of freckles, which suited her nicely; but one could not tell whether her mouth was beautiful, for her lower lip kept incessantly sliding out and then in, chafing the upper lip.

When the cart reached them, Wholesaler Stephens greeted her with extraordinary deference, and little Herr Friedemann likewise doffed his hat, while looking at Frau von Rinnlingen with large, attentive eyes. She lowered her whip, nodded slightly, and drove slowly past, viewing the houses and shop windows to the right and the left.

After a few paces, the wholesaler said:

"She's gone for a spin, and now she's driving home."

Little Herr Friedemann did not reply; he simply looked down at the sidewalk. Then he suddenly glanced at the wholesaler and asked:

"What did you say?"

And Herr Stephens repeated his astute observation.

Three days later, at twelve noon, Johannes Friedemann came home from his regular constitutional. Lunch was normally served at twelve-thirty, and he was about to spend half an hour in his "office," located to the right of the front door. But then the maid came across the vestibule and said to him:

"There is company, Herr Friedemann."

"In my apartment?" he asked.

"No, upstairs, with the ladies."

"Who is it?"

"Lieutenant Colonel and Frau von Rinnlingen."

"Oh," said Herr Friedemann, "then I'll . . ."

And he climbed the stairs. At the top, he walked through the landing and was already holding the handle of the high white door leading to the "landscape room," when suddenly he paused, stepped back, turned around, and slowly walked away, just as he had come. And though he was completely alone, he said quite loudly to himself:

"No. Better not."

He went down into his office, seated himself at the desk, and picked up his newspaper. But a minute later, he lowered it again and looked sideways out the window. And he remained like that until the maid came and announced that lunch was served; then he headed up to the dining room, where the sisters were already waiting for him, and he sat down on his chair, where several musical scores were stacked.

Henriette, ladling out the soup, said:

"Do you know who was here, Johannes?"

"Well?" he asked.

"The new lieutenant colonel and his wife."

"Really? That's nice."

"Yes," said Pfiffi, and moisture gathered in the corners of her mouth. "I find that both of them are thoroughly acceptable people."

"In any case," said Friederike, "we mustn't put off reciprocating their visit. I suggest that we call on them the day after tomorrow, Sunday."

"Sunday," said Henriette and Pfiffi.

"You *will* come with us, won't you, Johannes?" asked Friederike.

"Of course he will!" said Pfiffi, and her body shook. Herr Friedemann hadn't registered the question, and he ate his soup with a silent and anxious mien. It was as if he were listening for something, for some uncanny noise.

The following evening, the City Theater was performing *Lohengrin*, and all the cultivated people were in attendance. The small auditorium was crowded from top to bottom, humming with voices and smelling of gas and perfumes. But all opera glasses, in the orchestra and in the balconies, were focused on box thirteen, at the very right of the stage, for tonight Herr von Rinnlingen and his spouse were appearing here for the first time, and people at last had a chance to scrutinize them thoroughly.

When little Herr Friedemann, in an impeccable black tuxedo with a dazzling white, sharply protruding shirtfront, stepped into his box—number thirteen—he recoiled in the doorway, his hand moved toward his forehead, and for an instant his nostrils dilated convulsively. But then he took his seat, to the left of Frau von Rinnlingen.

As he sat down, she eyed him attentively for a while, pushing her lower lip out; then she turned to exchange a few words with her husband, who was standing behind her. He was a tall, broad-shouldered man with a brushed-up mustache and a kind, tan face.

When the overture began, and Frau von Rinnlingen leaned over the balustrade, Herr Friedemann cast a hasty sidelong glance at her. She wore a light-colored gown and was the only woman there with a slight décolletage. Her sleeves were very wide and puffy, and her white gloves reached all the way up to her elbows. Tonight there was something sumptuous about her figure, which had not been noticeable the other day, when she had worn the loose jacket. Her full bosom rose and sank slowly, and the knot of reddish-blond hair fell deep and heavy into the nape of her neck.

Herr Friedemann was pale, much paler than usual, and under the smooth, parted brown hair a few small drops beaded his forehead. Frau von Rinnlingen had stripped the glove from her left arm, which was resting on the red velvet of the balustrade, and he had no choice, he was forced to keep seeing this rounded, matte-white arm, which, like the unbejeweled hand, was traversed by utterly pale-blue veins.

The violins sang, the trumpets blared, Telramund was släin, universal jubilation swept through the orchestra, and little Herr Friedemann sat there, pale and motionless, his head drawn into his shoulders, one forefinger on his mouth and the other hand in his jacket lapel.

As the curtain dropped, Frau von Rinnlingen rose to leave the box with her husband. Herr Friedemann saw it without looking, he dabbed his forehead with his handkerchief, rose to his feet, went to the door leading to the corridor, came back, sat down in his chair, and remained there immobile, in his previous position.

When the bell rang and his neighbors returned, he sensed

that Frau von Rinnlingen's eyes were on him, and without wanting to do so, he lifted his head toward her. Their eyes met, and she did not avert her gaze; instead she continued peering at him without a trace of abashedness, until he himself, subdued and humiliated, lowered his eyes. He turned even paler, and a strange, sweetly pungent anger mounted in him. . . . The music began.

Toward the end of this act, Frau von Rinnlingen's fan happened to slip away from her, and it dropped on the floor next to Herr Friedemann. Both of them bent over simultaneously, but she got there first, and she said with a mocking smile:

"Thank you."

Their heads had been very close together, and for an instant he had been forced to inhale the warm fragrance of her bosom. His face twisted, his entire body contracted, and his heart pounded so heavily, so dreadfully that he couldn't breathe. He sat for another half minute, then softly pushed his chair back and softly went out.

He walked, followed by the sounds of the music, along the corridor to the wardrobe, picked up his cane, his top hat, and his light-colored overcoat, and walked down the stairs to the street.

It was a warm, still evening. In the light of the gas lamps, the gray gabled houses stood silent against the sky, where the stars shone bright and mild. The footsteps of the few people he encountered echoed on the sidewalk. Someone greeted him, but he did not notice; his head was deeply sunken, and he breathed so hard that his high, sharp chest quaked. Now and then he murmured to himself:

"My God! My God!"

With dismayed and frightened eyes, he peered into himself, into his feelings, which he had cultivated so gently, which he had always treated with mildness and intelligence, and now they were torn aloft, churned up, whirled about. . . . And suddenly, quite overwhelmed, in a state of dizziness, intoxication, yearning, and torment, he leaned against a lamppost and whispered, quivering:

"Gerda!"

Everything remained silent. There was no one to be seen, far or wide. Little Herr Friedemann pulled himself together and continued walking. He had gone up the street on which the theater was located and which ran down rather steeply to the river, and now he was heading north along Main Street, toward his home. . . .

The way she had looked at him! What? She had forced him to lower his eyes? She had humbled him with her gaze? Wasn't she a woman and he a man? And hadn't her strange brown eyes actually trembled with joy?

He again felt that powerless, voluptuous hatred rising inside him, but then he relived that moment when her head had grazed his, when he had inhaled the fragrance of her body, and he halted a second time, bent back his crippled torso, drew in the air through clenched teeth, and then once more murmured, completely helpless, desperate, beside himself:

"My God! My God!"

And again he walked on, slowly, mechanically, through the sultry evening air, through the deserted, reverberating streets, until he stood outside his home. For a moment he lingered in the vestibule, absorbing the cool cellar smell that filled it; then he entered his office.

He sat down at the desk, by the open window, and stared straight ahead at a big yellow rose that someone had placed in a tumbler for him. He took the rose and, with closed eyes, inhaled its fragrance; but then he shoved it aside with a sad and weary gesture. No, no, it was over! What should he care about such a fragrance? What should he care about all the things that had made up his "happiness" until now? . . . .

He turned aside and looked out at the silent street. Now and then footsteps resounded and echoed past. The stars hovered and glittered. How dead tired and feeble he was! His head was so empty, and his despair began melting into a vast, gentle melancholy. A few lines of poetry flickered through his mind, the *Lohengrin* music played in his ears, he again saw Frau Rinnlingen's figure in front of him, her white arm on the red velvet, and then he fell into a heavy, fever-dulled sleep.

Often he was on the verge of awakening, but he was afraid to do so, and each time he lapsed back into unconsciousness. When it grew light, however, he opened his eyes and looked around with a large, painful gaze. Everything was clear in front of his soul; it was as if his suffering had been completely uninterrupted by sleep.

His head was numb, and his eyes were burning; but after washing up and then moistening his forehead with eau de cologne, he felt better, and he silently sat back down in his place at the window, which had remained open. It was still very early in the day, around five A.M. perhaps. Occasionally a baker's boy strode past; otherwise no one was to be seen. Across the road, all the shades were still drawn. But the birds were chirping, and the sky was a radiant blue. It was a beautiful Sunday morning.

A sense of coziness and confidence took hold of little Herr Friedemann. What was he afraid of? Wasn't everything normal? Granted, he had had a bad seizure yesterday, but that was that! It was still not too late, he could still escape his doom! He had to avoid anything that might trigger a new attack; he felt strong enough. He felt strong enough to conquer it and stifle it altogether. . . .

When the clock struck seven-thirty, Friederike walked in and placed his coffee on the round table standing in front of the leather sofa at the rear wall.

"Good morning, Johannes," she said. "Here's your breakfast."

"Thank you," said Herr Friedemann. And then: "Friederike, dear, I'm sorry but you'll all have to pay your visit without me. I don't feel well enough to accompany you. I slept badly, I've got a headache, and in short, I have to ask you . . ."

Friederike replied: "That's too bad. You should absolutely not fail to call on them. But it's true, you do look ill. Should I lend you my menthol headache pencil?"

"No, thanks," said Herr Friedemann. "It'll pass." And Friederike left.

Standing at the desk, he slowly sipped his coffee and ate a croissant. He was pleased with himself and proud of his resolute stance. When he was finished, he took a cigar and sat down again at the window. Breakfast had done him good, and he felt happy and hopeful. He took a book, read, smoked, and squinted into the sun.

The street had become animated. Wagons were rattling, people talking, the horse-drawn trolley was jingling, and all the noises penetrated his room. Through everything, however, he could hear the chirping of the birds, and a soft, warm breeze wafted from the radiant blue sky.

At ten o'clock he heard his sisters crossing through the vestibule, heard the front door creak, and then, paying no special heed, he saw the three ladies going past the window. An hour wore by; he felt happier and happier.

A sort of exuberance began to fill him. What a day it was, and the birds were chirping! What if he took a brief stroll? And now, suddenly, with no ulterior motive, a thought arose in him with a sweet terror: "What if I went to her?" And virtually straining his muscles as he quelled all the anxious warnings inside him, he added with a blissful resolve: "I want to go to her!"

And he put on his black Sunday suit, took his cane and his top hat, and, breathing hastily, he walked all the way across town to the southern suburb. Unaware of anyone else, he fervently lifted and lowered his head at every step, completely trapped in an absent, exalted state, until he stood on the avenue of chestnut trees, outside the red-brick villa where the name "Lieutenant Colonel von Rinnlingen" could be read at the entrance.

Here he was overcome with shudders, and his heart pounded convulsively against his chest. But then he walked through the vestibule and rang the bell. The fat was in the fire; there was no going back. What will be will be, he thought to himself. He was suddenly filled with a deathly hush.

The door snapped back, the butler came toward him across the hall, took his card, and hurried up the stairs, which were covered with a red runner. Herr Friedemann stared fixedly at this carpet until the butler returned and declared that her ladyship asked him to please come upstairs.

There, next to the salon door, where he deposited his cane, he glanced into the mirror. His face was pale, and the hair stuck to his forehead over his bloodshot eyes; the hand clutching the top hat trembled incessantly.

The butler opened the door, and Herr Friedemann stepped inside. He found himself in a rather large, half-darkened room; the windows were draped. To his right stood a grand piano, and at the center of the room, armchairs upholstered in brown silk were grouped around a circular table. Over the sofa at the left-hand wall, a landscape hung in a heavy gilt frame. The wallpaper, too, was dark. At the rear, palms were standing in an alcove.

A minute wore by until Frau von Rinnlingen pushed aside the curtain on the right and soundlessly came toward him over the thick brown carpet. She wore a very simply tailored dress of red and black plaid. From the alcove, a column of light, filled with dancing dust, fell straight upon her heavy red hair, which flashed golden for a moment. She fixed her strange quizzical eyes on him and pushed out her lower lip as usual.

"Dear madam," Herr Friedemann began, glancing aloft at her, for he only reached up to her bosom, "I would like to pay my respects to you too. When you honored my sisters with your visit, I was unfortunately absent and . . . sincerely regretted it."

He could think of absolutely nothing else to say, but she stood and gazed at him relentlessly, as if trying to force him to keep speaking. The blood suddenly shot to his head. She wants to torture me and ridicule me! he thought. And she sees through me! How her eyes glitter! . . .

Finally she said in a very clear and very high voice:

"It's charming of you to come. I likewise regretted missing you recently. Would you please be so kind as to have a seat?"

She settled close to him, placed her arms on the arms of the chair, and leaned back. He sat bending forward, holding his hat between his knees. She said:

"Did you know that your sisters were here a quarter of an hour ago? They told me you were ill."

"That is true," replied Herr Friedemann. "I did not feel well this morning. I did not think I was able to go out. I apologize for my tardiness."

"You do not look well as yet," she said very calmly, her eyes glued to him. "You are pale, and your eyes are inflamed. Does your overall health leave much to be desired?"

"Oh . . . ," stammered Herr Friedemann, "I am satisfied as a rule. . . ."

"I get sick a lot too," she went on, still not removing her eyes from him, "but nobody notices. I'm nervous, and I experience the most bizarre fits."

She fell silent, dropping her chin to her bosom, and looked up at him expectantly. But he did not respond. He sat motionless, fixing his large, wistful eyes on her. How strangely she spoke, and how deeply her clear, unstable voice touched him! His heart had calmed down; he felt he was dreaming. Frau von Rinnlingen began anew:

"If I'm not mistaken, you left the theater last night before the end of the performance?"

"Yes, madam."

"I regretted it. You seemed a true devotee, although the performance was not good, or just relatively good. You love music? Do you play the piano?"

"I play the violin a little," said Herr Friedemann. "That is—it's practically nothing. . . ."

"You play the violin?" she asked; then she looked vacantly past him, lost in thought. "Well, then we can play duets together now and again," she suddenly said. "I can accompany somewhat. It would be nice to find someone here. . . . Will you come?"

"I would be delighted to be at your service, madam," he said, still as if in a dream. A pause ensued. Abruptly her expression changed. He saw her face twist into barely perceptible cruel scorn, saw her eyes focus on him with that sinister glitter, rest on him firmly and quizzically, as twice before. His face glowed red, and without knowing where to turn, utterly helpless and beside himself, he drew his head entirely into his shoulders and gazed down, shaken, at the carpet. But, like a brief shudder, a powerless, sweetish, tormenting fury surged through him. . . .

When he raised his eyes again, with a desperate resolve, she was no longer looking at him; she was gazing over his head, at the door. He arduously managed to squeeze out a few words:

"And are you quite satisfied so far with living in our city, dear madam?"

"Oh," said Frau Rinnlingen indifferently, "of course. Why shouldn't I be satisfied? Naturally I feel a bit hemmed in and observed, but . . . By the way," she promptly went on, "before I forget. We're planning to have some people over in a few days, a small, informal party. We could play a little music, chat a little. . . . We even have quite a lovely garden behind the house; it runs all the way down to the river. In short, you and your ladies will receive an invitation, needless to say, but I'd like to ask you right now to join us. Will you give us the pleasure of your company?"

Herr Friedemann had barely expressed his thanks and his acceptance when the door handle was energetically pushed down and the lieutenant colonel strode in. The two of them stood up, Frau von Rinnlingen introduced the gentlemen to each other, and her husband bowed to Herr Friedemann as politely as to her. The officer's tan face was quite shiny with heat.

While removing his gloves, he spoke in his sharp, powerful voice, saying something or other to Herr Friedemann, who gazed up at him with large, vacant eyes, constantly expecting a benevolent slap on the back. Meanwhile, the lieutenant colonel, clicking his heels and leaning forward slightly, turned to his wife and said in a perceptibly softer voice:

"Have you asked Herr Friedemann to join our little get-together, my dear? If it's all right with you, I believe we can have it a week from today. I hope the weather holds out, so we can also spend time in the garden."

"As you like," answered Frau von Rinnlingen, glancing past him.

Two minutes later, Herr Friedemann took his leave. When he bowed once again at the door, he encountered her eyes, which rested on him without expression.

He left, but he did not go back to town; instead he involuntarily struck out on a path that branched away from the avenue and ran down to the old fortification wall by the river. There were well-maintained parks here and shady paths with benches.

He walked quickly and in a daze, without looking up. It was unbearably hot, and he felt the flames leaping and falling in him, and his weary head throbbed relentlessly. . . .

Wasn't her gaze still resting on him? Not as at the end, empty and expressionless, but as earlier, with trembling cruelty after she spoke to him in that strange, silent manner? Ah, did she enjoy making him feel helpless and furious? Couldn't she, when seeing through him, pity him just a little? . . .

After walking down by the river, along the wall overgrown with green, he sat down on a bench in a semicircle of jasmine bushes. The air around him was heavy with sweet, sultry fragrance. In front of him, the sun brooded on the quivering water.

How drained and exhausted he was, and yet how anguishing the turmoil inside him! Wouldn't it be best to glance about once more and then walk down into the silent water and after brief suffering be liberated and taken across to peace and quiet? Ah, peace; it was peace, after all, that he wanted! Though not the peace in an empty, hollow void, but a gentle, sunny peace filled with good, tranquil thoughts.

All his tender love of life trembled through him at that moment, all the profound yearning for his lost happiness. But then he looked around at the silent, endlessly indifferent peace of nature, saw the river flowing along in the sunshine, saw the grass quivering and moving and the flowers standing where they had blossomed in order to wither and then waft away, saw everything, everything yielding to existence with that mute devotion—and he was suddenly overwhelmed with the sensation of friendship and rapport with the inevitable, which can make us superior to all destiny.

He pictured that afternoon of his thirtieth birthday, when, happy to be at peace, he had believed he was facing the remainder of his life without fear or hope. He had seen no light and no shadow; everything had stretched before him in the mild glow of twilight, blurring almost imperceptibly into darkness. And with a calm and superior smile, he had looked forward to the years that lay ahead. . . . How long ago had that been?

Now that woman had come, she had had to come, it was his fate, she herself was his fate, she alone! She had come, and even though he had tried to defend his peace, she had aroused everything he had suppressed since youth for fear of torture and ruin, and now it had all seized hold of him with terrible, irresistible violence and was destroying him!

It was destroying him, he felt that. But why keep struggling and torturing himself? What will be will be! Let him keep following his path and shut his eyes to the yawning abyss, obedient to fate, obedient to the drastic, agonizing sweet power from which there is no escape.

The water glittered, the jasmine breathed out its sharp, sultry fragrance, the birds chirped all around in the trees, with a heavy, velvet-blue sky shining through the leaves. But little hunchbacked Herr Friedemann sat on his bench for a long time. He sat bent forward, his chin propped in both hands.

The guests all agreed that they were thoroughly enjoying themselves at the von Rinnlingens' home. Some thirty people sat at the long, tastefully decorated table, which stretched through the large dining room. The butler and two hired waiters were already hurrying about with the ices. Dishes clattered, glasses clinked, and the warm air was hazy with food and perfume. Good-natured big businessmen with their wives and daughters were gathered here, plus nearly all the garrison officers, an old and popular physician, a few attorneys, and other persons who were considered part of high society. A student of mathematics was also present, the lieutenant colonel's nephew, who was visiting his relatives; he was engaged in the deepest conversation with Fräulein Hagenström, who was across from Herr Friedemann.

He himself sat on one of the lovely velvet cushions at the lower end of the table, next to the unattractive wife of the gymnasium principal, not far from Frau von Rinnlingen, who had been escorted to the table by Consul Stephens. It was amazing how great a change had come over Herr Friedemann this past week. It may have been partly the white incandescent gaslight filling the room that made his face so dreadfully pale; however, his cheeks were sunken, his bloodshot eyes with their dark rings had an unspeakably dismal shimmer, and his body seemed more crippled than ever. He drank a lot of wine, and now and then he addressed a remark to his neighbor.

Frau von Rinnlingen had not yet exchanged a single word with Herr Friedemann at the table; now she leaned slightly forward and called to him:

"I've been waiting in vain for you these past few days, for you and your violin."

For an instant he gaped at her quite vacantly, before replying. She wore a lightweight, light-colored gown that exposed her white throat, and a Marshal Niel rose in full blossom was attached to her radiant hair. Tonight her cheeks were slightly flushed, but as usual, bluish shadows lurked in the corners of her eyes.

Herr Friedemann looked down at his plate and squeezed out some sort of response, whereupon he had to answer the gymnasium principal's wife, who had asked him whether he liked Beethoven. But at that moment the lieutenant colonel, sitting way up at the head of the table, glanced at his wife, tapped on his glass, and said:

"Ladies and gentlemen, I propose that we take our coffee in the other rooms. Incidentally, the garden can't be bad tonight either, and if anybody wishes to catch a breath of fresh air outdoors, I'll join him."

In the ensuing hush, Lieutenant von Deidesheim tactfully cracked a joke, so that everyone got up amid cheerful laughter.

Herr Friedemann was one of the last to leave the room with his lady. After escorting her through the German Renaissance room, where the guests had already begun to smoke, he brought her to the cozy, half-darkened parlor, where he took his leave.

He was meticulously dressed: his tuxedo was impeccable, his shirt dazzling white, and his slender and delicately formed feet were in patent-leather shoes. Now and then one could see that he wore red silk socks.

He glanced out into the corridor and saw that large groups were already descending the stairs to the garden. However, he sat down with his cigar and his coffee by the door of the German Renaissance room and glanced into the parlor.

To the very right of the door, a circle of guests, with the eagerly speaking student at their center, sat around a small table. He had asserted that more than one parallel line to a straight line can be drawn through a given point. Attorney Hagenström's wife had cried: "That's impossible!" And now he proved it so irrefutably that they all acted as if they understood.

But at the rear of the room, on the sofa, next to the low lamp with the red shade, sat Gerda von Rinnlingen, conversing with young Fräulein Stephens. Frau von Rinnlingen was leaning back slightly into the yellow silk cushion, her legs crossed. She was slowly smoking a cigarette, whereby she exhaled the smoke through her nose while pushing out her lower lip. Fräulein Stephens sat upright in front of her, as if carved out of wood, and answered her questions with anxious smiles.

No one paid any heed to little Herr Friedemann, and no one noticed that his large eyes were fixed incessantly on Frau von Rinnlingen. He sat in a limp posture and stared at her. No passion was in his gaze and barely any pain; there was something obtuse and lifeless about it, a dull, powerless surrender of his will.

Some ten minutes wore by like that. Then, as if secretly observing him all that time, Frau von Rinnlingen suddenly rose, and without glancing at him, she went over and halted in front of him. He rose to his feet, looked up at her, and heard the words:

"Would you care to escort me into the garden, Herr Friedemann?"

He replied: "With the greatest pleasure, dear madam."

"You haven't seen our garden yet?" she asked him on the stairs. "It's rather large. I hope there aren't too many people there; I need some air. I got a headache during dinner. Perhaps that red wine was too strong for me. . . . We have to go out by way of this door here." It was a glass door, through which they passed from a landing to a small, cool hallway; then a few steps led outdoors.

In the wonderfully warm, clear, starry night, the fragrance welled up from all the flower beds. The garden lay in full moonlight, and guests walked along the shiny white gravel paths, chatting and smoking. One group had gathered around the fountain, where the old and popular physician was floating small paper boats amid general laughter.

Frau von Rinnlingen walked past with a slight nod and motioned into the distance, where the dainty and scented flower garden darkened toward the park.

"Let's go down the central path," she said. The entrance was flanked by two low, squat obelisks.

At the end of the very straight, chestnut-lined path they saw the river, shimmering greenish in the moonlight. Their surroundings were dark and cool. Here and there side paths branched off, probably curving down to the water. For a long time not a sound was heard.

"By the river," she said, "there's a lovely spot, where I often sit. We could chat there for a moment or two. Look—now and then a star glitters through the trees."

Instead of replying, he peered at the shimmering green surface that they were approaching. He could make out the opposite bank, the ramparts. When they left the path and stepped out on the lawn that sloped down to the water, Frau von Rinnlingen said:

"Our spot is here, a little to the right. See—it's deserted."

The bench they settled on leaned sideways six paces in front of the path and into the park. Here it was warmer than amid the broad trees. Crickets chirped in the grass, which yielded to thin reeds by the water. The moonlit river gave off a soft light.

They were both silent for a while, gazing at the water. But then he pricked up his ears, shaken, for the tone he had heard a week ago, that soft, wistful, and gentle tone, touched him again.

"How long have you had your handicap, Herr Friedemann?" she asked. "Were you born with it?"

He swallowed, for he was choking. Then he answered softly and politely:

"No, dear madam. When I was an infant, I was dropped on the floor. That's where it comes from."

"And how old are you now?" she went on.

"Thirty years old, dear madam."

"Thirty years," she repeated. "And you haven't been happy these thirty years?"

Herr Friedemann shook his head, and his lips trembled. "No," he said. "It was all lies and self-delusion."

"So you believed you were happy?" she asked.

"I tried to," he said, and she replied:

"That was brave."

A minute wore by. Only the crickets chirped, and behind them the trees rustled very softly.

"I know a thing or two about unhappiness," she then said. "Such summer nights by the water are the best remedy."

He did not respond; instead he pointed weakly to the opposite bank, which lay peaceful in the darkness.

"I was sitting there the other day," he said.

"After you left us?" she asked.

He only nodded.

But then he suddenly quivered on his seat, straightened up, sobbed, emitted a sound, a wail that was also a cry of relief, and he sank slowly to the ground in front of her. He touched her hand, which had been resting next to him, and while he clutched it, while he also took hold of the other, while this little, utterly deformed man knelt before her, trembling and twitching, and buried his face in her lap, he stammered in an inhuman, gasping voice:

"You do know ... Let me ... I can't anymore ... My God ... My God ..."

She did not resist, nor did she bend down toward him. She sat, high and erect, leaning back slightly, and her small, close-set eyes, which seemed to reflect the liquid shimmer of the water, stared tensely straight ahead, over him, into the distance.

And then suddenly, with a jerk, with a brief, proud, scornful laugh, she had wrested her hands from his hot fingers, had grabbed his arm, had hurled him sideways and sent him sprawling on the ground, had leaped up and vanished along the wooded path.

He lay there, his face in the grass, numb, beside himself, his body twitching incessantly. He pulled himself up, took two steps, and plunged to the ground again. He lay by the water.

What was actually going on in him during what now occurred? Perhaps he was seething with the voluptuous hatred he had felt when she had humiliated him with her gaze; and now, when he lay on the ground, treated like a dog by her, perhaps it was this hatred that degenerated into an insane fury, which he had to express, albeit against his own person ... a disgust at himself perhaps, which filled him with a desire to annihilate himself, rip himself to shreds, snuff himself out. . . .

He crawled along on his belly, raised his upper body, and let it drop into the water. He did not lift his head again, he did not even move his legs, which lay on the bank.

During the splash of water the crickets had paused for a moment. Now their chirping resumed, the park rustled softly, and faint laughter sounded throughout the long garden path.

# TOBIAS

# MINDERNICKEL

ONE OF THE STREETS climbing rather steeply from Wharf Way up to the central part of town is called Gray Road. About half-way along this street and to the right (if you're coming from the river) stands number 47, a drab, narrow building, utterly indistinguishable from its neighbors. The ground floor contains a grocery, where you can also buy galoshes and castor oil. If, glancing into a courtyard where cats scurry about, you cross the vestibule, a worn and narrow staircase, smelling unspeakably dank and squalid, leads to the upper stories. On the second floor, a cabinetmaker lives to the left, a midwife to the right. On the third floor, there is a cobbler to the left and, on the right, a lady who starts singing loudly the instant footsteps are heard on the stairs. On the fourth floor, the left-hand apartment is vacant, the right-hand one is occupied by a man named Mindernickel— and Tobias, to boot. And there is a story about this man, a story that has to be told because it is enigmatic and inconceivably shameful.

Mindernickel's appearance is striking, bizarre, and ridiculous. For example, if he decides to take a walk, and you see his scrawny figure, propped on a cane, trudge up the street, then he is dressed in black, and from head to foot at that. He wears a shabby old-fashioned top hat with a curving brim, a tight Prince Albert shiny with age, and equally shabby trousers, frayed at the bottom and so short that you can see the rubber inserts of the ankle boots. Incidentally, it must be said that this clothing is brushed as clean as can be. His scraggy neck seems all the longer for protruding from a low Byron collar. His gray hair is brushed smooth and deep into his temples, and the wide brim of the top hat shades a wan, clean-shaven face with hollow cheeks, inflamed eyes that seldom rise from the ground, and two deep creases that run morosely from the nose to the drooping corners of the mouth.

Mindernickel rarely leaves his home, and there is a reason for this. You see, the moment he shows up on the street, a mob of children comes running. They follow him for a good distance, laughing, jeering, singing "Ho, ho, Tobias!" and probably tugging at his coat, while people emerge in their doorways and enjoy the spectacle. But he himself, unresisting and glancing shyly around, his shoulders hunched and his head poking forward, goes off, like a person hurrying through a cloudburst without an umbrella. And even though the people in front of their doors are laughing in his face, he greets some of them with a humble bow.

Farther on, when the children stay behind, when people no longer know him and very few give him a second glance, his manner does not change essentially. His eyes keep darting about anxiously and he hastens along, cringing, as if feeling a thousand scornful stares. And if he raises his eyes from the ground, timidly and hesitantly, then you notice that, strangely enough, he is incapable of focusing on any person or even any object with a firm, calm look. Outlandish as it may sound, he seems to lack the natural and superior attribute of sensory perception, with which the individual looks at the phenomenal world. Tobias appears to feel inferior to every phenomenon, and his unsteady eyes have to crawl on the ground before people and things. . . .

What is the matter with this man, who is always alone and who seems uncommonly miserable? His vehemently bourgeois clothing as well as a certain meticulous movement of his hand across his chin seem to indicate that he absolutely refuses to be reckoned among the class of people in whose midst he lives. Goodness knows what sort of abuse he once endured. His face looks as if life itself, scornfully laughing, had punched him with all its might. . . . Then again, it's quite possible that without having experienced any hard blows of fate, he is simply no match for life. The painful inferiority and stupidity of his appearance convey the embarrassing impression that nature has denied him the measure of strength, backbone, and equilibrium that would adequately allow him to exist with his head erect.

Having taken his walk to town, leaning on his black cane, he returns to his apartment, welcomed on Gray Road by the howling children. He walks up the dank stairs to his rooms, which are squalid and austere. Only the dresser, a solid Empire piece with heavy metal handles, has value and beauty. In front of the window, whose view is hopelessly blocked by the gray sidewall of the neighboring house, there is a flowerpot full of soil but with absolutely nothing growing in it. Nevertheless, Tobias Mindernickel sometimes walks over, gazes at the flowerpot, and sniffs the bare soil. And next to this parlor lies a small, dark bedroom.

After entering the apartment, Tobias deposits his cane and his top hat on the table, sits down on the green sofa, which smells of dust, he props his chin on his hand and, raising his eyebrows, stares down at the floor. There appears to be nothing left for him to do on earth.

As for Mindernickel's character, it is very difficult to judge; but the following incident seems to speak in its favor. One day, when this peculiar man left his house and, as usual, a cluster of children formed, pursuing him with derision and laughter, a boy of about ten tripped over another boy's foot. He hit the ground so violently that blood poured from his nose and his forehead, and he lay there, crying. Instantly Tobias turned around, hurried to the fallen child, bent over him, and began commiserating with him in a mild and quavering voice. "You poor child," he said, "did you hurt yourself? You're bleeding! Look, the blood's running from his forehead! Yes, yes, how wretchedly you're lying there! Of course, it hurts so badly that he's crying, the poor child! How sorry I feel for you! It was your fault, but I'll tie my handkerchief around your head. . . . . There, there! Now just pull yourself together, now just stand up. . . ."

And after saying those words and actually tying his own handkerchief around the boy's head, he carefully helped him to his feet and trudged away. At this moment, his face and his bearing displayed a resolutely different expression than normally. His body erect, he took firm steps, and he breathed deeply under the tight Prince Albert. His eyes had widened, they were glowing and self-confidently taking in people and objects, while his mouth had a look of painful happiness. . . .

As a result of that incident, the denizens of Gray Road initially made a little less fun of him. But after a while, his surprising conduct was forgotten, and a chorus of healthy, high-spirited, and cruel throats again sang behind the unsteadily cringing man: "Ho, ho, Tobias!"

One sunny morning at eleven o'clock, Mindernickel left his house and walked up through the entire town to Lark Hill, the long, sprawling rise that offers the finest promenade in town during the afternoon. But because of the excellent spring weather, there were already a few vehicles and pedestrians here this morning. Under a tree on the large main avenue stood a man with a young, leashed hound, which he showed the passersby, his obvious intention being to sell it. The dog was a small, yellow, muscular creature about four months old, with one black ear and black rings around its eyes.

When Tobias noticed it from a distance of ten paces, he halted, rubbed his chin several times, and thoughtfully eyed the vendor and the little puppy, which was wagging its tail alertly. Thereupon Tobias started walking again, and pressing the crook of his cane against his mouth, he circled the tree on which the man was leaning. After circling three times, he stepped over to him and muttered hastily, with his eyes riveted on the animal:

"How much do you want for this dog?"

"Ten marks," the man replied.

Tobias was silent for an instant and then repeated irresolutely:

"Ten marks?"

"Yes," said the man.

Tobias drew a black leather purse from his pocket, removed a five-mark bill, a three-mark coin, and a two-mark coin, and quickly handed this money to the vendor. Then he took hold of the leash, and timidly peering about, since a few people had observed the sale and were laughing, the hunched man pulled the squealing and struggling animal along behind him. The dog resisted all the way back, digging its forelegs into the ground and anxiously and quizzically gazing up at its new master. Tobias, however, kept pulling silently and energetically, and he managed to get through town safe and sane.

On Gray Road, a tremendous uproar burst out among the street boys when Tobias showed up with the dog. But he lifted it in his arms, bent over it, and with the children tugging on his coat, he hurried through the mockery and laughter, up the stairs, and into his apartment. Here he put the still whimpering dog on the floor, stroked it benevolently, and said patronizingly:

"Now, now, you don't have to be afraid of me, animal; it's not necessary."

Then, from a dresser drawer, he brought over a plate of cooked meat and potatoes and tossed part of the food down for the creature, which instantly stopped its lament. Smacking its lips and wagging its tail, it devoured the meal.

"By the way, I'm naming you Esau," said Tobias. "Do you understand me? Esau. I'm sure you can retain that simple sound. . . ." And pointing to the floor, he commanded:

"Esau!"

The dog, perhaps expecting to receive more food, did indeed come over, and Tobias approvingly patted him on the side.

"That's right, my friend. I can praise you."

Then he stepped back a little, pointed to the floor, and commanded anew:

"Esau!"

And the animal, which had become very frisky, sprang over again and licked its master's boot.

Tobias repeated this exercise some thirteen or fourteen times, with inexhaustible delight in commanding. Eventually, however, Esau seemed tired, he apparently felt like relaxing and digesting, and he lay down on the floor in the graceful and intelligent posture of a hunting dog, stretching out his two long, finely shaped forelegs close together.

"Once again!" said Tobias. "Esau!"

But Esau turned his head aside and stayed put.

"Esau!" cried Tobias in a masterfully raised voice. "You have to come even if you're tired!"

But Esau put his head on his paws and refused to come.

"Listen," said Tobias, his tone full of dreadfully quiet menace. "Obey, or you will learn that it's not wise to annoy me!"

But the animal barely moved his tail.

Mindernickel was seized with an immense, an excessive, an insane anger. He grabbed his black cane, pulled Esau up by his scruff, and beat the screaming little animal. Beside himself and full of indignant fury, he kept repeating over and over, in a dreadfully hissing voice:

"What's that? You won't obey? You have the gall not to obey me?"

Eventually Tobias flung away the stick and placed the whimpering dog on the floor. Breathing deeply, he put his hands behind his back and, taking long steps, began to stride up and down in front of Esau. Occasionally he cast a proud and angry glance at him. After pacing like that for a while, he halted by the animal, which was lying on his back, wagging his forelegs in a pleading fashion. Tobias folded his arms on his chest and spoke, displaying the dreadfully cold and harsh glare and tone with which Napoleon addressed the company that had lost its aquila in battle:

"How have you behaved, if I may ask?"

And the dog, already happy at this overture, crawled closer, nestled against the master's leg, and looked up at him with his shiny and beseeching eyes.

For a good while, Tobias gazed down at the humble creature with wordless condescension. But then, feeling the poignant warmth of the body on his leg, he picked Esau up. "Well, I'll take pity on you," said Tobias. And when the good animal started licking his face, the master suddenly turned utterly compassionate and melancholy. He hugged the dog with painful love, his eyes filled with tears, and, unable to complete the sentence, he repeated several times in a choked voice:

"Look, you're my only . . . my only . . ." Then he carefully put Esau on the sofa, sat down next to the dog, propped his chin on his hand, and gazed at Esau with mild, silent eyes.

Tobias Mindernickel now left the house more seldom than ever, for he did not wish to appear in public with Esau. He focused all his attention on him. Indeed, from morning till evening he was occupied with nothing but feeding him, wiping his eyes, giving him orders, scolding him, and talking to him in a very human way. However, the fact was that Esau did not always behave to his master's satisfaction. When the puppy lay next to him on the sofa and, drowsy for lack of air and freedom, gazed at him with mournful eyes, Tobias was utterly content. He sat there, quiet and amiable, compassionately stroking Esau's back and saying:

"Are you looking at me in pain, my poor friend? Yes, yes, the world is sad, you're learning that too, young as you are. . . ."

At other times, the animal was tremendously frisky. Blind and crazy with desire to play and hunt, he scurried around the room, tussled with a slipper, jumped on the chairs, and rolled over and over. From a distance, Tobias would watch those movements with an ugly smile of annoyance and a helpless, grudging, and uncertain gaze. Eventually he summoned Esau in a surly tone and snapped:

"Stop being so exuberant. There's no reason to dance around."

Once, it even happened that the dog escaped from the apartment and bounded down the stairs to the street, where he promptly began chasing a cat, eating horse droppings, and joyfully cavorting with the children. But when Tobias, to the applause and laughter of half the street, showed up with a painfully twisted face, a sad thing occurred: taking long jumps, the dog dashed away from his master. . . . On that day, Tobias gave him a long, ferocious beating.

One day—the dog had already been his for several weeks—Tobias took a loaf of bread from the dresser drawer in order to feed Esau. Getting the large, bone-handled knife that he normally used for this purpose, he stooped over and sliced off small pieces, which dropped to the floor. Esau, wild with hunger and playfulness, came jumping over blindly and ran into the awkwardly held knife, which stabbed him under his right shoulder blade. He writhed on the floor, losing blood.

Terrified, Tobias threw everything aside and bent down over the injured creature. Suddenly, however, the master's expression changed, and a shimmer of relief and happiness actually passed across his face. Gingerly he carried the whimpering dog to the sofa, and no one can imagine with how much devotion he began tending the patient. He never left his side all day, and at night Tobias let him sleep on his own bed, he washed and bandaged him, comforted him, and consoled him with indefatigable joy and concern.

"Does it hurt very badly?" Tobias asked. "Yes, yes, you're suffering terribly, my poor animal! But be still; we have to endure it." When he spoke, his face was calm, mournful, and happy. But as Esau gained strength, grew cheerier, and then recovered, Tobias became more and more anxious and dissatisfied. He felt he no longer needed to worry about the injury; he would show the dog his commiseration purely through words and caresses. The healing was quite advanced; Esau had a sound constitution. He was already getting about the room. And one day, after slurping up a dish of milk and white bread, he bounded from the sofa, completely mended. With joyful yelps and as unrestrained as ever, he went scurrying through the two rooms, tugging at the bedcover, chasing a potato, and rolling over and over in sheer delight.

Tobias was at the window, by the flowerpot, with both hands sticking out, long and skinny, from his thoroughly frayed sleeves. As one hand mechanically twisted the hair that deeply covered his forehead, his figure loomed, black and bizarre, against the gray wall of the next house. His face was pale and distorted with grief, and with an envious, embarrassed, and nasty squint, he motionlessly eyed the dog as he sprang around. Suddenly Tobias pulled himself together, walked over to the puppy, stopped him, and slowly took him in his arms.

"My poor animal," he began in a woebegone voice. But Esau, exuberant and in no mood to be treated like that, snapped friskily at the hand that tried to stroke him, twisted out of Tobias's arms, executed a mischievous side leap, began yelping again, and cheerily dashed away.

What happened now was so inexplicable and frightful that I refuse to describe it in detail. Tobias Mindernickel stood bending forward, his arms dangling down his body, his lips squeezing together, his eyeballs trembling dreadfully in their sockets. Then, with a kind of frenzied pounce, he grabbed the animal, a large shiny object flashed in his hand, and with a gash running from the right shoulder and plunging deep into the chest, Esau collapsed on the floor—he emitted no sound, he simply fell on his side, bleeding and shuddering. . . .

An instant later, he was lying on the sofa, and Tobias was kneeling in front of him, pressing a cloth on the injury and stammering:

"My poor animal! My poor animal! How sad everything is! How sad we both are! Are you suffering? Yes, yes, I know you're suffering—how pathetically you're lying before me! But I, I'm here with you! I'm comforting you! I'll use my best handkerchief. . . ."

However, Esau just lay there, his throat rattling. His dimmed and quizzical eyes, filled with innocence, lament, and incomprehension, were fixed on his master—and then he stretched his legs out slightly and died.

But Tobias remained frozen where he was. He had put his head on Esau's body and was weeping bitterly.

# LITTLE LIZZY

CRITICAL LIZZY

THERE ARE MARRIAGES whose raison d'être is beyond the grasp of even the most literary imagination. You have to accept them the way you put up with unbelievable couplings of opposites in the theater, such as old dodderers and vivacious beauties—relationships that are taken for granted and that form the basis for the mathematical structure of a farce.

Now, the wife of Jacoby, the attorney-at-law, was young and beautiful, an unusually attractive woman. Some years before—let's say thirty—she had been christened with the names Anna Margarethe Rosa Amalie; but, combining their initials, people had always called her nothing but Amra, a name whose exotic flavor suited her personality like no other. Her soft, thick hair, parted on the right and combed diagonally away from both sides of her narrow forehead, was the dark brown of a chestnut. In contrast, her complexion was a completely southern dark matte yellow, and it stretched over forms that likewise seemed ripened by a southern sun. Her sensuous and indolent voluptuousness recalled the forms of a sultan's wife, and this impression, conveyed by each of her desirably lazy movements, harmonized perfectly with the fact that her common sense was most probably subordinate to her heart. And people knew that, because all she had to do was glance at someone with her innocent brown eyes and, in her peculiar way, raise her lovely eyebrows quite horizontally into her almost poignantly narrow forehead. But she herself, she wasn't naive enough not to know it. By speaking rarely and saying little, she quite simply avoided exposing her weak points; and no one can find fault with a woman who is both beautiful and silent. Yet "naive" was probably the unlikeliest word to describe her. Her gaze was not only without guile, it also had a certain lascivious cunning, and one could tell that she was not too limited to make mischief. . . . By the by, her nose may have been a bit too strong and fleshy in profile; but her full, voluptuous lips were utterly beautiful, though their only expression was sensuality.

Now, this anxiety-provoking woman was the wife of Jacoby, a fortyish lawyer—and anyone who laid eyes on him was dumbfounded. He was plump. This lawyer was more than plump: he was a veritable colossus of a man! In their column-like shapelessness, his legs, always inserted into ash-gray trousers, recalled the legs of an elephant. His arching back, round with fat, was that of a bear. And the bizarre little greenish-gray jacket that he wore over the mammoth curve of his belly was so arduously fastened with a single button that both sides of it jerked back to his shoulders the instant the button was undone. Yet this gargantuan trunk was topped, almost without the transition of a neck, by a relatively small head with beady, watery eyes, a short, stumpy nose, and overabundant, dangling jowls flanking a very tiny mouth that drooped mournfully at the corners. The round skull as well as the upper lip were sparsely dotted with hard, light-blond bristles that ubiquitously exposed the naked skin shimmering through as on an overfed dog. . . . Ah! It must have been obvious to everyone that the attorney's corpulence was not of a healthy sort. His body, gigantic in both length and width, was grossly obese without being muscular, and you could often observe a sudden torrent of blood gushing into his puffy face and just as suddenly yielding to a sallow pallor, while his mouth performed a sourish twist. . . .

The lawyer's clientele was quite limited. But since he was a man of means, partly because of his wife, the couple—childless, incidentally—lived in a comfortable floor-through on Kaiser Street and had an active social life. In all likelihood, they socialized for Frau Amra's sake, since the lawyer, who seemed to participate with only a tormented zeal, could not possibly have been happy doing so.

This fat man had the most bizarre character. No one could have been more courteous, more gracious, more obliging than he. Yet without actually articulating it, people felt that his overly friendly and flattering behavior was somehow forced, that it was rooted in timidity and insecurity, and so it got on their nerves. Nothing is uglier than a person who despises himself but who, out of cowardice and vanity, is eager to please because he wants to be liked. Nor was it, in my opinion, any different with the lawyer, who, in his almost bootlicking self-belittlement, went beyond the bounds of personal dignity. He was capable of saying to a lady whom he wanted to escort to the table, "Dear madam, I'm a revolting person, but would you do me the honor? . . ." And, with no talent for self-mockery, he would say it repulsively and in bittersweet torment.

The following incident really occurred. One day when the lawyer went for a stroll, a rude porter came along, pulling a hand wagon, and one wheel ran violently over the lawyer's foot. The porter, who hadn't stopped the wagon in time, turned around—whereupon the lawyer, pale, utterly beside himself, and with quaking jowls, doffed his hat very deeply and stammered: "Excuse me!" Such things are infuriating.

However, this bizarre colossus was plainly haunted by a bad conscience. When he and his wife appeared on Lark Hill, the main promenade in town, the lawyer would greet people eagerly, anxiously, and overzealously. Occasionally casting a shy glance at Amra, who was striding with marvelous agility, he clearly felt the need to bow to every lieutenant and apologize because he, he of all people, happened to be in possession of such a beautiful wife. And with a woefully ingratiating expression on his mouth, he seemed to be begging others not to make fun of him.

As has already been hinted, there was no fathoming why Amra had married Counselor Jacoby. He, however, loved her, and with a love so ardent as is, no doubt, seldom found in people of his physical makeup, and so humble and fearful, as was in keeping with his overall nature. Late in the evening, when Amra had already gone to bed, the lawyer would enter the large chamber, whose high windows were hung with pleated flowery curtains. He would tiptoe in so softly that only the slow shuddering of the floor and the furniture could be heard but not his steps, and he would kneel by her massive bed and take hold of her hand with infinite delicacy. Amra would then draw her eyebrows horizontally into her forehead, and while her enormous husband lay before her in the dim glow of the night lamp, she would silently gaze at him with an expression of sensual malice. His crude, quaking hands would cautiously push back the sleeve of her blouse, and his sad, chubby face would press into the soft wrist of her full, tawny arm, where the tiny blue veins stood out against the dark complexion. And he would speak in a muffled, quivering voice such as a sensible person rarely uses in everyday life.

"Amra," he would whisper, "my dear Amra! Am I disturbing you? You weren't asleep, were you? Dear God, I've been thinking all day long about how beautiful you are and how much I love you! . . . Listen to what I have to tell you—it's so hard to put it into words. . . . I love you so much that sometimes my heart convulses and I don't know where to turn. I love you beyond my strength! You probably don't understand, but you're sure to believe me, and you have to tell me just once that you are a little grateful to me for loving you, for, you know, a love like my love for you has its worth in this life. . . . And you have to tell me that you will never betray me or deceive me, even though you probably can't love me, but out of gratitude, out of sheer gratitude. . . . I come to you to beg you as fondly and devotedly as I can. . . ."

And these utterances would usually melt into soft, bitter weeping as the lawyer remained on his knees. Amra was moved by his tears; she stroked her husband's bristles and said several times, in the comforting, mocking drawl that you use with a dog who comes to lick your feet: "Yes! . . . Yes! . . . Good doggy . . ."

Amra's conduct was certainly not that of a decent woman. And it's time I unburdened myself of the truth, which I have held back until now. You see, she was, in fact, cheating on her husband—with a man named Alfred Läutner. This was a young and gifted musician, who at twenty-seven had already gained a nice reputation with his amusing little compositions. A slender man with a brazen face, loosely combed blond hair, and a very deliberate sunny smile in his eyes, he belonged to that present-day brotherhood of minor performers who make no great demands on themselves. They wish primarily to be happy and charming, using their pleasant little talents to enhance their personal charm and generally playing the naive genius in society. Consciously childlike, immoral, unscrupulous, they are smug, cheerful, and healthy enough to indulge their illnesses. Indeed, their vanity is charming so long as it is never injured. But God help these fortunate little people, these little poseurs, when a real misfortune strikes them, a sickness with which they cannot flirt, in which they cannot enjoy their own charm. They will not know how to be decently unhappy, they will not know how to "tackle" the sickness, they will perish. . . . But that is a story unto itself.

Herr Läutner came up with pretty items, mostly waltzes and mazurkas, whose gaiety might have been a bit too popular for them to be reckoned (to the extent that I know anything about it) as "music." Yet each one contained a brief original passage, a modulation, an entry, a harmonic turn, some kind of small nervous effect revealing wit and deftness, for the sake of which they seemed to have been composed in the first place. And this also made them interesting to genuine connoisseurs. Often there was something marvelously doleful and gloomy about those two lonesome measures, a melancholy that stood out against the dance-hall cheeriness of the little pieces—and then quickly and abruptly melted away. . . .

This young man, then, was the object of Amra Jacoby's inexcusable affection, and he, for his part, did not have enough moral fiber to resist her lures. They met here, they met there, and for several years now the two had been united in an illicit relationship that the whole town knew about and that the whole town discussed behind the lawyer's back. And what about him, the lawyer? Amra was too stupid to suffer from remorse and thereby betray herself. It is a foregone conclusion that the lawyer, no matter how heavy his heart with distress and anxiety, could nurture no concrete suspicion of his wife.

Now, rejoicing every heart, spring had come to the land, and Amra had an absolutely darling idea.

"Christian," she said—the lawyer's first name was Christian—"let's throw a party, a huge soiree in honor of the newly brewed spring beer—very simple, of course, just cold roast veal, but with lots of people."

"Certainly," the lawyer replied. "But couldn't we perhaps put it off just a little?"

Instead of replying, Amra promptly launched into details.

"There'll be so many people, you know, that our space here will be too limited. We have to rent an elegant restaurant, a garden, a banquet hall outside the town gates, so as to have enough room and fresh air. You can understand that. I'm leaning toward Herr Wendelin's large hall at the foot of Lark Hill. It's out in the open, and there's only a passageway connecting it to the actual eatery and brewery. We can decorate the place festively, we can set up long tables and drink spring beer. We can dance and make music, perhaps even put on a little theater—I know they've got a small stage there, something I especially value. . . . In short, it should be a highly original party, and we're going to have a marvelous time."

During this conversation the lawyer's face had turned a bit sallow, and the corners of his mouth twitched and drooped. He said:

"I'm looking forward to it with all my heart, my dear Amra. You're so skillful, I know I can leave everything up to you. Do make your preparations."

And Amra made her preparations. She conferred with various ladies and gentlemen, she personally rented Herr Wendelin's large banquet hall, she even formed a sort of committee of people who had been asked, or had volunteered, to participate in the cheerful performances that were to make the soiree more beautiful. . . . This committee was made up exclusively of men, except for Court Actor Hildebrandt's wife, who was a singer. And then there were: Herr Hildebrandt himself, a low-level civil servant named Witznagel, a young painter, plus Herr Alfred Läutner, not to mention a few students brought in by the civil servant to perform some African dances.

For a week now, after Amra had made her decision, this committee had been gathering and deliberating on Kaiser Street— that is, in Amra's salon. This was a small, warm, crowded room appointed with a thick carpet, a sofa sporting several cushions, a fan palm, English leather armchairs, and a mahogany table with cambered legs, a plush cover, and several deluxe editions lying on it. There was also a fireplace, which was still slightly heated; the black stone mantel bore several platters of dainty sandwiches, some glasses, and two carafes of sherry.

Amra, her feet lightly crossed, leaned back into the cushions of the sofa under the fan palm, and she was as beautiful as a summer night. A blouse of thin, light-colored silk ensconced her bosom, while her skirt was of a dark, heavy cloth embroidered with large flowers. Every so often, her hand would brush the billow of chestnut hair from her narrow forehead.

Frau Hildebrandt, the singer, sat next to her on the sofa; she had red hair and wore a riding habit. The gentlemen, facing the ladies, had settled in a tight half circle—in their midst the lawyer, who had found only a very low leather armchair. He looked unspeakably wretched. Now and then he took a deep breath and swallowed as if choking back his nausea. . . . Herr Alfred Läutner, dapper and cheerful in his lawn-tennis garb, had dispensed with a chair and was leaning against the fireplace, because he claimed he could not sit still that long.

Herr Hildebrandt spoke in a melodious voice about English songs. He was an extremely respectable gentleman, well dressed in black, with a thick Roman head and a self-assured demeanor—a court actor, a man of culture, thorough knowledge, and refined taste. In serious conversations he loved condemning Ibsen, Tolstoy, and Zola, who, after all, were pursuing the same reprehensible goals. Today, however, he was making his trivial point rather affably.

"Are you acquainted, ladies and gentlemen, with that delicious ditty 'That's Maria!'?" he asked. "A bit piquant, granted, but uncommonly effective. And then there's the famous . . ." And he proposed several more songs, on which they eventually agreed and which Frau Hildebrandt declared that she wanted to sing. The young painter, a gentleman with strongly sloping shoulders and a blond goatee, was to parody a magician, while Herr Hildebrandt planned to impersonate famous men. . . . In short, everything was working out splendidly, and the program already seemed complete, when Herr Witznagel, the low-level civil servant, a man with obliging gestures and with many scars left by fraternity duels, suddenly took the floor again.

"All well and good, ladies and gentlemen, the whole project does indeed promise to be entertaining. But I will not hesitate to speak my mind. It seems to me that we're still missing something—that is to say, the main attraction, the star turn, the highlight, the climax . . . something very special, quite astonishing, terribly funny, to bring the merriment to its peak. . . . I'm leaving it up to you; I've got nothing specific in mind. But my feeling is—"

"True enough!" Herr Läutner, by the fireplace, announced in his tenor voice. "Witznagel's right. We really need a star attraction to finish the performances with a bang. . . . Let's put on our thinking caps." And while adjusting his red belt with a few swift flicks of his wrist, he scrutinized the other attendees.

"Oh, well," said Herr Hildebrandt, "if you don't care to view my great men as the highlight . . ."

Everyone agreed with the civil servant. A particularly amusing star turn was desirable. Even the attorney nodded, murmuring: "Yes, yes . . . something superbly amusing . . ." They all put on their thinking caps.

And at the end of this pause, which lasted roughly a minute and was interrupted only by mild exclamations of pensiveness, the strange thing occurred. Amra was leaning back against the sofa cushions, deftly and fervently gnawing the nail of her little finger like a mouse, while her face showed a very peculiar expression. A smile lingered on her lips, an absent and almost demented smirk, hinting at a cruel and painful wantonness, and her eyes, which were wide open and quite shiny, slowly drifted toward the fireplace, where, for a second, they locked with the young musician's eyes. But then she jerked her entire torso aside, toward her husband, the attorney. Visibly blanching, keeping both hands in her lap, and peering at his features with a clinging, sucking stare, she spoke in a rich, slow voice:

"Christian, I suggest that for the final number you perform as a chanteuse; you'll wear a red silk baby dress and do some kind of dance for us. . . ."

The impact of those few words was tremendous. Only the

young painter tried to laugh good-naturedly, while Herr Hildebrandt brushed some crumbs from his sleeve with a stony-cold
face; the students coughed and were indecently noisy in using
their handkerchiefs. Frau Hildebrandt turned a vehement crimson, something she rarely did, and Witznagel, the civil servant,
simply hurried to get a sandwich. The attorney squatted in a torturous position on his low chair, while glancing around with a
sallow face and a terrified smile and stammering:

"But my goodness . . . I . . . I'm . . . hardly qualified . . . not as
if . . . forgive me. . . ."

Alfred Läutner no longer had a carefree face. He appeared to
have turned a bit red, and with a protruding head and a blank,
bewildered, and questioning look, he gazed into Amra's eyes.

Amra, however, without changing her insistent position, went
on with the same imposing emphasis:

"In fact, Christian, you should sing a ditty composed by Herr
Läutner, and he'll accompany you on the piano. That will be the
highest, the most effective peak of our soiree."

A pause ensued, an oppressive silence. But then suddenly,
something bizarre happened. Herr Läutner, infected, as it were,
excited, carried away, took a step forward and, trembling with a
kind of abrupt inspiration, began speaking quickly:

"By God, Herr Jacoby, I'm willing, I'm ready and willing to
compose something for you. . . . You have to sing it, you have to
dance it. . . . It's the only conceivable climax of the soiree. . . .
You'll see, you'll see—it'll be the best thing I've done or ever will
do. . . . In a red silk baby dress! Ah, your wife is an artiste, an
artiste, I tell you! Otherwise she could never have hit on this
idea! Please say yes, I beg you, please agree! I'll come up with
something, I'll do something, you'll see. . . ."

Now everyone relaxed and everyone livened up. Whether out
of malice or courtesy, they all began storming the attorney with
their pleas, and Frau Hildebrandt went so far as to say very

loudly in her Brünnhilde voice: "Herr Jacoby, you're usually such an amusing and entertaining man!"

And he too, the attorney, now regained his speech, and still a bit sallow but with a strong display of resoluteness, he said:

"Listen to me, ladies and gentlemen—what can I tell you? It's not up my alley, believe me. I've not been blessed with any comic talent, and aside from that . . . In short, no, I'm sorry, but it's impossible."

He dug in his heels, and Amra withdrew from the debate. She leaned back with a rather absent expression, while Herr Läutner likewise fell silent and began staring at the carpet, deeply absorbed in an arabesque. So Herr Hildebrandt managed to change the subject, and soon the group broke up, without having reached any decision on the last item.

That evening, however, when Amra had gone to bed and was lying there with open eyes, her husband trudged in, pulled a chair over to her bed, sat down, and hesitantly murmured:

"Listen, Amra—to be frank, I'm quite disturbed. If I was all too offensive to our guests, if I rubbed them the wrong way—goodness knows that wasn't my intention! Or do you earnestly believe . . . I beg you . . ."

Amra was silent for a moment, while her eyebrows slowly rose into her forehead. Then she said with a shrug:

"I don't know how to answer you, my friend. Your behavior was something I would never have expected. You said unfriendly things when you refused to support the performances with your participation, which was considered crucial by everyone, and this can only be flattering for you. To put it mildly, you disappointed everyone profoundly, and you've spoiled the entire soiree with your coarse unwillingness to oblige us, whereas it would have been your duty as host to . . ."

The attorney's head drooped, and breathing heavily, he said:

"No, Amra, I didn't mean to be unobliging, believe me. I

don't want to insult anyone or cause anyone to dislike me, and if my behavior was ugly, then I'm willing to make up for it. It's only a joke, a masquerade, an innocent prank—why not? I don't want to spoil the party; I'm willing. . . ."

The next afternoon, Amra once again left to run some "errands." She stopped off at number 78 Holzstrasse and climbed up to the second landing, where someone was waiting for her. And while she lay stretched out, dissolving in love as he pressed his head into her breasts, she whispered passionately:

"Compose it for four hands, do you hear!? We'll accompany him together while he sings and dances. I—I'll take care of the costume. . . ."

And a strange thrill, a stifled and convulsive laughter, went through their limbs.

For anybody who wishes to host a soiree, to put on a large-scale entertainment outdoors, one can most heartily recommend Herr Wendelin's premises on Lark Hill. Coming from the graceful suburban road, you pass through a high lattice gate and into the establishment's parklike garden, with the spacious banquet hall at the center. This hall, connected to the restaurant, the kitchen, and the brewery by only a narrow passageway, is made of wood painted in many cheerful colors and in a droll blend of Chinese and Renaissance styles. The building, which has big French doors that may be kept open in good weather to let in the woodland air, can accommodate a large crowd.

Today the vehicles rolling up were welcomed in the distance by the colorful shimmer of light, for the entire latticework, the trees in the garden, and the banquet hall itself were densely adorned with particolored lanterns. The interior was a truly joyous sight: underneath the ceiling hung heavy garlands with countless paper lanterns, and amid the flags, shrubs, and artificial flowers decorating the walls, a throng of electric bulbs shone forth, brilliantly illuminating the hall. At one end lay the stage, flanked by foliage plants and with a curtain on which an artist had painted a tutelary spirit. The long tables were lined up from the other end of the room almost to the stage, and Herr Jacoby's guests were helping themselves to spring beer and roast veal. These were attorneys, officers, businessmen, artists, high-level officials, together with wives and daughters—most surely over one hundred fifty people. They had dressed quite simply, in black jackets or in spring gowns that were halfway between dark and light, for cheerful informality was the rule today. Indeed, the men personally took the pitchers to the large kegs set up on one sidewall. The vast, bright, gaudy room, imbued with the sweetish, sultry festive haze of firs, flowers, people, beer, and food, was alive with the clattering of tableware, the noisy humming of simple conversation, and the loud, buoyant, and courteous laughter of all these carefree people. . . .

The attorney sat shapeless and helpless at the end of a table, next to the stage. He drank little, and now and then he arduously squeezed out a word to his neighbor, Frau Havermann, the wife of the assistant government secretary. The attorney breathed with great distaste, the corners of his mouth drooping, while his puffy, bleary, watery eyes gaped motionless and with a kind of mournful alienation at the cheerful bustle, as if there were something ineffably sad and incomprehensible about this noisy merriment. . . .

Now large cakes were passed around, accompanied by sweet wine and speeches. Herr Hildebrandt, the court actor, celebrated the spring beer in a discourse consisting entirely of classical quotations; yes, even Greek ones. Next, Herr Witznagel, the civil servant, toasted the ladies with his most obliging gestures and with the greatest subtlety by taking a handful of flowers from the nearest vase and from the tablecloth and comparing one of the ladies present to each blossom. Amra Jacoby, however, who sat opposite him in a gown of thin yellow silk, was called "the more beauteous sister of the tea rose."

She then promptly brushed her hand over the soft part in her hair, raised her eyebrows, and earnestly nodded at her husband—whereupon the fat man stood up, and he almost spoiled the entire mood by stammering a couple of wretched words with an ugly smile. . . . Only a few halfhearted bravos were heard, and for an instant the room was filled with low-spirited silence. Soon, however, the merriment won out again. The guests, smoking and quite tipsy, were beginning to stand up and pitch in, noisily moving the tables out of the hall, for they wanted to dance.

It was past eleven o'clock, and a casual atmosphere now reigned supreme. Some of the company had poured out into the gaudily illuminated garden to catch a breath of air, while others remained in the hall, gathering in groups, smoking, chatting, tapping beer, drinking while standing. . . . Then a powerful trumpet blast came from the stage, summoning everyone into the hall. Musicians—winds and strings—had arrived, settling in front of the curtain. Rows of chairs had been set up, with red programs lying on them, and the ladies took their seats, while the gentlemen stood behind them or along the sidewalls. The room was filled with an expectant hush.

Then the band played a rousing overture, the curtain opened—and lo and behold, there stood a bunch of dreadful Africans in garish costumes and with blood-red lips, baring their teeth and launching into barbaric howls. . . . And indeed, the various performances became the zenith of Amra's soiree. Enthusiastic applause broke out as the adroitly composed program offered act after act. Frau Hildebrandt appeared in a powdered wig, banged a long stick on the floor, and sang, stentoriously, "That's Maria!" A magician in a tuxedo covered with medals performed the most astonishing tricks. Herr Hildebrandt did terrifyingly lifelike impressions of Goethe, Bismarck, and Napoleon, and Dr. Wiesensprung, the newspaper editor, had agreed in the last moment to give a humorous lecture on the theme of "The Social Significance of Spring Beer." But the suspense reached its acme toward the end, for the final number was next, that mysterious act that the program announced inside a laurel frame: "*Little Lizzy*. Song and dance. Music by Alfred Läutner."

A stir passed through the hall, and eyes met when the musicians put aside their instruments. Herr Läutner, who had been leaning silently against a door, a cigarette in his indifferently pouting lips, now joined Amra Jacoby at the piano, which stood in the center of the stage, in front of the curtain. His face was ruddy, and he leafed nervously through the sheet music, while Amra, who, quite the opposite, was a bit pale, kept one arm on the arm of her chair as she peered at the audience with a lurking gaze. Then, while all necks were craned, a sharp bell resounded. Herr Läutner and Amra played a few bars of a negligible introduction, the curtain rolled up, and Little Lizzy appeared. . . .

A jolt of amazement and paralysis swept through the crowd of spectators when this sad and horribly bedizened bulk lumbered onstage like an arduously dancing bear. It was the attorney. A loose, floor-length evening gown of uncreased blood-red silk draped his shapeless body, and this gown had a décolletage that repulsively exposed the throat, which was powdered with flour. The sleeves were puffed very short on the shoulders, but long, pale-yellow gloves covered the fat, flabby arms, while the head was topped with a high coiffure of flaxen curls, on which a green feather wobbled to and fro. From under this wig, a sallow, puffy, unhappy, and desperately mirthful face peered out. Its jowls kept pitifully quivering up and down, and its small, bloodshot eyes stared laboriously at the floor without seeing anything. Meanwhile, the fat man arduously threw himself from one leg to the other, either clutching his gown with both hands or lifting both forefingers with feeble arms—he could execute no other movement. And in a strained and gasping voice, he sang a silly ditty to the tinkling of the piano. . . .

Did not a cold breath of suffering, more intense than ever, emanate from that wretched figure, killing any unabashed hilarity and pressing down upon this entire company like an inescapable weight of painful discord? . . . The same horror lay in the depths of the countless spellbound eyes glued to that picture, to that couple at the piano and to the husband up there. . . . The silent outrage must have lasted for some five long minutes.

But then came the moment that no one who was present will forget till his dying day. . . . Let us evoke what actually happened in that brief, terrible, and complicated time span.

We know the ridiculous vaudeville song titled "Little Lizzy," and no doubt we recall the lines, which go:

> *No other gal has danced the polka,*
> *Has danced the waltz the way I can,*
> *I'm Little Lizzy, holy smoka,*
> *I've won the heart of many a man.* . . .

Those are the unattractive and frivolous lines that make up the refrain of the three rather lengthy stanzas. Well, in setting those lyrics anew, Alfred Läutner had created a masterpiece by carrying his manner to an extreme, his way of astonishing the audience by abruptly inserting a sleight of hand from higher music in the midst of some vulgar and comical botchwork. The melody, in C-sharp major, had been rather pretty and quite banal during the first few stanzas. At the start of the quoted refrain, the tempo grew livelier, and dissonances ensued, which, through the increasingly vivacious emergence of a B minor, forecast a transition to F-sharp major. These disharmonies got more and more complicated until the words "I can," and after "I'm Little," which completed the realization and the tension, they were bound to dissolve into F-sharp major. Instead the most surprising thing occurred. Through a reckless twist created by a flash of genius, the key changed to F major, and this entry, which utilized both pedals on the drawn-out first syllable of "Lizzy," had an indescribable, an absolutely incredible effect! It was an utterly stunning surprise attack, a sudden tingling of the nerves that sent shivers up and down your spine, it was a miracle, a revelation, a cruelly abrupt unveiling, a ripping curtain. . . .

And at that F-major chord Herr Jacoby the attorney stopped dancing. He stood still, he stood rooted in the middle of the stage, both forefingers still erect, one a bit lower than the other, the "L" in "Lizzy" erupted from his mouth, then he fell silent. And while the piano accompaniment stopped short at almost the same time, that eccentric and horribly ludicrous figure up there, with his bestially protruding skull and his bloodshot eyes, gaped straight ahead. . . . He gaped into that bright, decorated, crowded banquet hall, where, like an exhalation from all these people, the outrage brooded, thickening into an atmosphere. . . . He gaped into all those upturned, distorted, and glaringly illuminated faces, into those hundreds of eyes that focused, with the same expression of knowledge on him and on the couple down there in front of him. . . . While a dreadful hush, unbroken by any sound, settled on everyone, his ever-widening eyes wandered slowly and eerily from that couple to the audience and from the audience to that couple. . . . A sudden burst of understanding seemed to pass across his features, a torrent of blood gushed into that face, making it bloat up as red as the silk gown and instantly leaving it a waxy yellow—and the fat man collapsed so heavily that the boards groaned.

The hush persisted for another moment. Then shouts resounded, tumult began, a few valiant men, including a young physician, leaped up to the stage, the curtain was lowered.

Amra Jacoby and Alfred Läutner, turning away from each

other, were still sitting at the piano. He, with a drooping head, seemed to be listening for his transition to F major; she, with her bird brain incapable of swiftly comprehending what was going on, glanced around with an utterly blank face. . . .

Next, the young physician reappeared in the hall, a short Jewish gentleman with an earnest face and a black goatee. As several guests clustered around him at the door, he shrugged and replied: "It's over."

# GLADIUS DEI

MUNICH WAS LUMINOUS. A radiant, blue-silk sky stretched out over the festive squares and white-columned temples, the neo-classical monuments and Baroque churches, the spurting fountains, the palaces and gardens of the residence, and the latter's broad and shining perspectives, carefully calculated and surrounded by green, basked in the sunny haze of a first and lovely June day.

The chattering of birds and furtive rejoicing throughout the streets . . . and the unhurried and amusing bustle of the beautiful and leisurely city rolled, surged, and hummed across plazas and rows of houses. Tourists of all nations climbed up the steps to museums or rode around in the small, slow droshkies, peering right and left and up the building walls in promiscuous curiosity.

Numerous windows were open, and from many of them music poured out into the streets, people practicing on pianos, violins, or cellos, sincere and well-meaning dilettantish efforts. But at the Odeon, as could be heard, people were earnestly studying at several grand pianos.

Young men, whistling the Nothung motif and crowding the back of the modern theater every evening, wandered in and out of the university or the National Library, with literary journals in the side pockets of their jackets. A royal coach stopped outside the Academy of Fine Arts, which spread its white wings between Turk Street and the Victory Gate. And at the top of the Academy's ramp, the models stood, sat, and lounged in colorful groups—picturesque oldsters, youngsters, and women in the costumes of the Alban Hills.

Casualness and unhurried ambling through all the long avenues in northern Munich . . . People were not exactly driven or devoured by the greedy craving to earn their livelihood; instead their aim was to lead a pleasant life. Young artists, with small round hats on the backs of their heads, with loose ties and no canes, carefree fellows, who paid their rent with color sketches, were strolling about to let this light-blue morning affect their moods, and they looked at the young girls, that short pretty type with brunet hair in a band, somewhat oversize feet, and heedless morals. . . . Every fifth house had studio windows blinking in the sun. At times an artistic structure stood out in the series of bourgeois buildings, the work of an imaginative young architect, a wide house with flat arches and bizarre ornamentation, full of wit and style. And suddenly, somewhere, the door in an all-too-boring facade was framed by a bold improvisation, by flowing lines and sunny colors, bacchantes, nixes, and rosy nudes. . . .

It is always a fresh delight to linger at the displays of artistic cabinetry and of the modern luxury items in the bazaars. How much fanciful comfort, how much linear humor, in the shapes of all things! Scattered everywhere are the little shops that sell frames, sculptures, and antiques; and from their windows the busts of quattrocento Florentine women gaze toward you with a noble piquancy. And the owner of even the smallest and cheapest of these stores talks to you about Donatello and Mino de Fiesole as if they had personally granted him the right to reproduce their oeuvre. . . .

But up there on Odeon Square, across from the tremendous loggia with the spacious mosaic area spread out in front of it, and diagonally across from the Regent's Palace, people were crowding around the broad windows and showcases of M. Blüthenzweig's enormous art boutique. What a joyful magnificence in the display! Reproductions of masterpieces from all the galleries on earth, mounted in costly, cunningly tinted and ornamented frames revealing a taste for precious simplicity; reproductions of modern paintings, sensual fantasies in which antiquity seemed reborn in a humorous and realistic fashion; the sculpture of the Renaissance in perfect castings; naked bronze bodies and fragile decorated glasses; elongated earthen vases that emerged from metal-vapor baths in iridescent mantles; deluxe editions, triumphs of the new art of design, works by fashionable poets, clad in a decorative and elegant splendor; in between, portraits of artists, musicians, philosophers, thespians, authors, hung out to satisfy the popular curiosity about intimate details. . . . In the first window, next to the adjacent bookshop, a large picture stood on an easel, and the crowd was congesting in front of it: it was a valuable russet photograph in a wide, old-gold frame, a sensational piece, a facsimile of the highlight of that year's grand international exhibition, at which your attendance was requested by effective, archaizing posters wedged in amid concert schedules and artistically decked-out recommendations for toiletries on outdoor pillars.

Glance around, look in the windows of the bookshops! Your eyes encounter such titles as *The Art of Elegant Living Since the Renaissance*, *The Formation of the Sense of Color*, *The Renaissance in Modern Arts and Crafts*, *The Book as a Work of Art*, *The Decorative Arts*, *The Hunger for Art*—and you ought to know that these stimulating volumes are bought and read by the thousands and that these selfsame topics are the contents of lectures given every evening to packed houses. . . .

If you are lucky, you will meet, in person, one of the renowned women whom we are accustomed to gazing at through the medium of art, one of those wealthy and beautiful ladies who are adorned with diamonds and with an artificial Titian blondness, ladies whose bewitching features have been immortalized by the hand of a brilliant portraitist and whose love life is the talk of the town—queens of artists' parties during Mardi Gras, a bit rouged, a bit painted, full of noble piquancy, coquettish and worthy of admiration. And lo and behold, there goes a great painter with his mistress, in a car driving up Ludwig Street. People point at the vehicle, they halt and peer after the couple. Many people greet them. And it would not take much for the policemen to stand at attention.

Art was in full bloom, Art reigned supreme, Art stretched its rose-entwined scepter across the city and smiled. The city was dominated by a universal and respectful participation in the thriving of Art, a ubiquitous, diligent, and devoted practice and publicity in the service of Art, an ingenuous cult of line, decoration, form, senses, beauty. . . . Munich was luminous.

A youth came striding up Schelling Street; surrounded by the jingling of bicyclists, he strode along the middle of the wooden sidewalk outside the broad facade of the Ludwig Church. If you looked at him, you felt a shadow passing across the sun or a memory of difficult hours across your mind. Did he not love the sun, which was dipping the beautiful city in festive splendor? Why did he, averted and inverted, keep his eyes glued to the ground?

He wore no hat, though not a soul was offended, given the sartorial freedom of this lighthearted city; instead the hood of his loose black cloak was pulled over his head, shading the angular protuberance of his low forehead, covering his ears, and framing his gaunt cheeks. What sorrowful conscience, what scruples, and what self-inflicted maltreatment had managed to hollow out those cheeks so deeply? Is it not dreadful to see grief dwelling in the hollows of a man's cheeks on such a sunny day? His dark eyebrows grew extremely bushy at the narrow root of his nose, which jutted, big and bulging, from his face, and his lips were strong and blubbery. Whenever he raised his rather close-set brown eyes, horizontal creases formed on his angular forehead. He gazed with an expression of knowledge and narrow-minded suffering. Viewed in profile, this face thoroughly resembled an old portrait painted by a monk and preserved in Florence, in a harsh and tiny monastic cell, from which, long ago, a dreadful and devastating protest had been uttered against life and its triumph. . . .

Hieronymus strode up Schelling Street, strode slowly and firmly, with both hands holding his loose cloak together from the inside. Two young girls—two of those stubby, pretty creatures with headbands, oversize feet, and heedless morals—who strolled past him, arm in arm and eager for adventure, elbowed each other and laughed, bent forward and laughed so hard at his hood and his face that they broke into a run. But he paid them no mind. Lowering his head, and never glancing right or left, he crossed Ludwig Street and mounted the steps of the church.

The huge wings of the central portal were wide open. Somewhere far away in the hallowed twilight, cool, dank, and pregnant with sacrificial fumes, one could make out a faint reddish glow. An old woman with bloodshot eyes rose from a prayer desk and dragged herself along on crutches between the columns. Otherwise the church was empty.

Hieronymus moistened his forehead and his chest at the stoup, knelt before the high altar, and then came to a standstill in the nave. Was it not as if his figure had grown taller inside here? Upright and immobile, with a freely lifted head, he stood there, and his big, bulging nose seemed to protrude over the strong lips with a domineering expression, and his eyes were no longer riveted to the floor but gazed bold and straight into the distance, at the crucifix over the high altar. He remained like that for a while, motionless; then, backing away, he genuflected once more and left the church.

With a lowered head, he walked slowly and firmly up Ludwig Street, along the middle of the broad, unpaved roadway, toward the gigantic loggia with its statues. But upon reaching Odeon Square, he looked up, so that horizontal creases formed on his angular forehead, and he slackened his pace; his attention had been drawn by the cluster of people at the display windows of the large art boutique, the beauty emporium owned by M. Blüthenzweig.

The people were passing from window to window, pointing out the exhibited treasures to one another and exchanging their opinions, each person peering over the shoulders of the next. Hieronymus mingled with the throng and began to view all these things himself, scrutinizing everything item by item.

He saw the copies of masterpieces from all the galleries on earth, the costly frames in their simple bizarrerie, the Renaissance sculptures, the bronze bodies and the decorated glasses, the iridescent vases, the book ornaments and the portraits of artists, musicians, philosophers, thespians, poets—he looked at everything, devoting an instant to each object. With both hands tightly holding his cloak together from the inside, he turned his hooded head in small, short twists from one object to the next, and from under his dark raised eyebrows, which became much bushier at the root of his nose, his eyes, with a dull, alienated expression of cool astonishment, looked at each thing for a time. In due course he reached the first window, the one showing the sensational picture; he looked for a while over the shoulders of the people thronging in front of him and finally made it to the front, right at the display.

The large russet photograph, framed with utmost taste in old gold, stood on an easel in the middle of the window space. It was a Madonna, a thoroughly modernist work, free of all convention. The figure of the holy birth-giver was of a bewitching womanliness, bared and beautiful. Her large, sultry eyes had dark circles, and her lips were parted in a strange and delicate smile. Her slim fingers, grouped a bit nervously and spasmodically, surrounded the hip of the infant, a naked boy of distinguished and almost primitive slenderness, playing with her breast and keeping a knowing side glance on the viewer.

Two other youths stood next to Hieronymus, discussing the picture, two young men with books under their arms, books they had gotten from or were returning to the National Library, men well versed in art and science.

"The kid's got it made, God damn it!" said one man.

"And he's obviously out to make us envious," retorted the other. "A dubious woman!"

"She'd drive you crazy! Sort of makes you wonder about the dogma of the Immaculate Conception."

"Yes, yes, she does make a pretty unvirginal impression. . . . Have you ever seen the original?"

"Of course. I was totally shaken. In full color she's a lot more aphrodisian . . . especially the eyes."

"The resemblance is really powerful."

"What d'you mean?"

"Don't you know the model? He used his little milliner. It's practically a portrait, but with a strong thrust toward sleaziness. . . . The actual girl's more innocent."

"I hope so. Life would be all-too-strenuous if there were a lot of women like this *mater amata*. . . ."

"The Pinakothek has bought it."

"Really? Imagine! But the museum must've known what it was doing. The treatment of the flesh and the flow of lines in the mantle are truly outstanding."

"Yeah, an incredibly gifted guy."

"You know him?"

"Slightly. He's gonna have a fine career, that's for sure. He's already had dinner twice with the prince regent. . . ."

They made their final comments as they began taking leave of one another.

"Are you going to the theater tonight?" asked one man.

"The Dramatic Association's performing Machiavelli's *La Mandragola*."

"Oh, bravo! That sounds like fun. I was gonna take in a vaudeville show, but I'll probably give the nod to good old Niccolò instead. See you later. . . ."

They separated, stepped back, and headed right or left. Newcomers replaced them and gazed at the successful picture. But Hieronymus stood motionless in his spot; he stood with a protruding head, and his hands, holding his cloak together from the inside, on his chest, could be seen clenching convulsively. His eyebrows were no longer drawn up with that cool expression of slightly resentful astonishment, they had descended and darkened; his cheeks, half covered by the black hood, seemed more hollow than before, and his thick lips were utterly pale. Slowly his head sank deeper and deeper, so that in the end his eyes stared up rigidly at the artwork from below. The nostrils of his big nose were quivering.

He remained in that stance for probably a quarter of an hour. The people around him came and went, but he never budged from his spot. At last he turned slowly, slowly on the balls of his feet and went away.

However, the picture of the Madonna went with him. Now, whether he was in his harsh and tiny room or kneeling in the cool churches, the picture hovered before his indignant soul, with sultry, circled eyes, with enigmatically smiling lips, bared and beautiful. And no prayer could drive it away.

But during the third night, it happened that a call and a command from on high came to Hieronymus, bidding him to take action and to raise his voice against frivolous wickedness and the brazen arrogance of beauty. In vain did he contend that he, like Moses, was of a slow tongue. God's will remained unshakable and loudly demanded that despite his faint heart he go and perform this sacrifice among the laughing foes.

And so he set out in the morning, and because it was God's

will, he made his way to the art store, to M. Blüthenzweig's huge beauty boutique. His head was hooded, and he held his mantle together on the inside with both hands as he walked.

The day had grown sultry; the sky was pale, and a storm was brewing. Once again a large throng was beleaguering the outside displays of the art boutique, especially the window containing the picture of the Madonna. Hieronymus glanced only briefly in that direction; then he pressed the handle of the glass door, which was hung with posters and art journals. "It is God's will!" he said, and entered the store.

A young girl, who had been writing in a big ledger at some desk or other, a pretty, brunet creature with hairbands and oversize feet, came toward him and amiably asked if she might help him.

"Thank you," said Hieronymus softly, and with horizontal creases in his angular forehead, he peered earnestly into her eyes. "It is not you to whom I wish to speak; it is the proprietor of this establishment, Herr Blüthenzweig."

A bit hesitant, she drew away from him and resumed what she had been doing. He stood in the middle of the store.

Things displayed as single examples in the windows were stacked up here twentyfold and lavishly spread out: a wealth of color, line, and form, of style, wit, fine taste, and beauty. Hieronymus gazed slowly in both directions, and then he drew the folds of his black cloak tighter around himself.

There were several people in the shop. At one of the wide tables cutting straight through the room, a man in a yellow suit and with a black goatee sat viewing a folder of French drawings, at which he sometimes emitted a bleating laugh. A young man whose appearance smacked of ill pay and vegetarianism was assisting him by lugging new folders for him to peruse. Cattycorner from the bleating gentleman, a distinguished old lady was examining modern artistic embroideries, huge mythical flowers in bland tones, standing vertically side by side on long, stiff stems. Another employee of the store was likewise attending to her. At a second table, an Englishman sat nonchalantly, his traveling cap on his head and his wooden pipe in his mouth. Durably dressed, clean-shaven, cold, and of an indefinite age, he was picking through bronzes that Herr Blüthenzweig was personally carrying over to him. Now the client was contemplating a comely figure of a naked little girl, who, undeveloped and with delicate limbs, held her small hands crossed upon her breasts in coquettish chastity. Holding her by the head, he scrutinized her in detail, as he slowly turned her around.

Herr Blüthenzweig, a man with a short, full brown beard and shiny eyes of the very same color, hovered around him, rubbing his hands, praising the little girl with all the vocables that he could lay hold of.

"One hundred fifty marks, sir," he said in English. "Munich art, sir. Very lovely indeed. Charming, you know. The very epitome of grace, sir. Extremely pretty indeed, winsome and worthy of admiration." Now something else occurred to him, and he said, "Highly attractive and alluring." Then he started again, from scratch.

His nose lay somewhat flat on his upper lip, so that he constantly made a slightly hissing sound, snuffling into his mustache. Sometimes he would approach the client, leaning over as if smelling him. When Hieronymus entered, Herr Blüthenzweig had casually sized him up the very same way, then promptly refocused on the Englishman.

The distinguished lady made her choice and walked out. A new gentleman came in. Herr Blüthenzweig smelled him briefly, as if to scout out the measure of his purchasing power, and then handed him over to the young female bookkeeper. The gentleman acquired only a faience bust of Piero, son of the splendid Medici, and departed. Now the Englishman also prepared to get under way. Taking possession of the little girl, he left amid Herr Blüthenzweig's bows. Then the art dealer turned to Hieronymus and stood before him.

"May I help you?" he asked, showing little deference.

Hieronymus held his cloak together on the inside with both hands and gazed into Herr Blüthenzweig's eyes almost without batting an eyelash. He slowly separated his thick lips and said:

"I have come to you about the picture in that window there, the big photograph, the Madonna." His voice was husky and unmodulated.

"Yes indeed, quite right," said Herr Blüthenzweig briskly, and started rubbing his hands. "Seventy marks including the frame, sir. It will last forever . . . a first-class reproduction. Highly attractive and alluring."

Hieronymus was silent. His head bowed in the hood, he shrank slightly while the art dealer spoke; then he straightened up again and said:

"I warn you in advance that I am in no position, indeed have absolutely no desire, to purchase anything. I regret that I must disabuse you of your expectations. I sympathize with you if this causes you any pain. But first of all, I am poor, and secondly, I do not like the things that you peddle. No, I can buy nothing."

"If not . . . well, then, not," said Herr Blüthenzweig, snuffling loudly. So may I ask . . ."

"If I know you as I believe I do," Hieronymus went on, "you despise me for being unable to buy anything from you. . . ."

"Hm," said Herr Blüthenzweig. "Not at all! Only—"

"Nevertheless, I beg you to please hear me out and to attach significance to my words."

"Attach significance. Hm. May I ask—"

"You may ask," said Hieronymus, "and I will answer. I have come here in regard to that picture, the big photograph, the Madonna, to ask you to remove it immediately from your window and never exhibit it again."

For a while Herr Blüthenzweig peered mutely into Hieronymus's face, as if challenging the youth to feel some embarrassment about his bizarre words. But nothing of the sort occurred, so the proprietor snuffled more vehemently and blurted out:

"Will you please be so kind as to inform me whether you are here in any manner of official capacity that authorizes you to dictate to me, or else advise me what it is that actually brings you here. . . ."

"Oh, no," replied Hieronymus. "I have neither an office nor a rank in the government. The power of the state is not on my side, sir. The only thing that brings me here is my conscience."

Herr Blüthenzweig, hunting for words, kept wagging his head to and fro, blasting his nose vehemently into his mustache and struggling to speak. Finally he said:

"Your conscience . . . Well, would you please be so good . . . as to take notice . . . that for us your conscience is an utterly irrelevant institution!"

Thereupon he wheeled around, hurried over to his desk in the back, and started writing. The two employees laughed heartily. Even the pretty girl giggled over her ledger. As for the yellow gentleman with the black goatee, it turned out that he was a foreigner, for he had obviously understood nothing of the conversation; instead he remained absorbed in the French drawings, from time to time emitting his bleating laugh.

"Would you deal with the gentleman," said Herr Blüthenzweig over his shoulder to his assistant. Then he continued writing. The young man whose appearance smacked of bad pay and vegetarianism walked over to Hieronymus, trying to stifle his laughter, and the other salesman likewise approached him.

"Is there anything else we can do for you?" the ill-paid man gently asked. Hieronymus kept his dull, sorrowful, and yet penetrating glare fixed on him.

"No," he said, "nothing else. Please remove the picture of the Madonna from the window, instantly and forever."

"Oh . . . Why?"

"She is the Holy Mother of God . . . ," said Hieronymus softly.

"To be sure . . . But you heard that Herr Blüthenzweig is not disposed to carry out your wish."

"One must remember that she is the Holy Mother of God," said Hieronymus, his head trembling.

"That is true. But so what? Should we not have the right to exhibit Madonnas? Should we not have the right to paint them?"

"Not like this! Not like this!" said Hieronymus, almost whispering as he pulled himself up and vehemently shook his head several times. His angular forehead under the hood was thoroughly furrowed with long, deep horizontal creases. "You know very well that it is Vice itself that a man has painted there . . . Voluptuousness exposed! There were two simple and innocent men viewing this picture of the Madonna, and with my own ears I heard them saying that it made them wonder about the dogma of the Immaculate Conception. . . ."

"Oh, if you will permit me, that is not the point," said the young salesman, with a superior smile. In his leisure hours he was writing a pamphlet about the modern art movement and was quite capable of indulging in a cultured conversation. "This picture is a work of art," he went on, "and one must apply the standard appropriate to it. It has been vociferously acclaimed everywhere. The government has purchased it—"

"I know that the government has purchased it," said Hieronymus. "I also know that the painter has dined twice with the prince regent. The populace is talking about it, and goodness knows how it interprets the fact that a man can be highly honored for such a work. To what does this fact testify? To the blindness of the world, a blindness that is incomprehensible if it is not based on shameless hypocrisy. This handiwork was born of sensual pleasure and is enjoyed in sensual pleasure . . . is that true or is it not? Answer me! You answer me too, Herr Blüthenzweig!"

A pause ensued. Hieronymus seemed in all seriousness to be demanding an answer, and his agonized and penetrating eyes kept switching between Herr Blüthenzweig's round back and the two salesmen, who stared at him, curious and bewildered. Silence reigned. It was broken only when the yellow gentleman with the black goatee, hunching over the French drawings, emitted his bleating laugh.

"It *is* true!" Hieronymus went on, with a deep indignation trembling in his husky voice. "You dare not deny it! But how is it possible for anyone to seriously celebrate the maker of this handiwork as if he had given mankind one more of the spiritual goods? How is it possible for anyone to stand in front of it, heedlessly indulge in the vile enjoyment it provides, and silence his conscience with the word 'Beauty'—nay, seriously convince himself that he is yielding to a noble and exquisite experience that is sublimely worthy of a human being? Is that wicked ignorance or depraved hypocrisy? My mind halts at this point. . . . It halts at the absurd fact that a man can reach supreme glory on earth through the stupid and sanguine deployment of his animal drives! . . . Beauty . . . What is Beauty? How is Beauty driven to reveal itself, and what does it affect? It is impossible not to know this, Herr Blüthenzweig! Yet how is it conceivable that someone can see through something so thoroughly and not be filled with disgust and sorrow? It is criminal to pursue the exaltation and blasphemous adoration of Beauty in order to confirm, strengthen, and empower the ignorance of shameless children and audaciously heedless adults, for they are remote from suffering and even more remote from Redemption! . . . 'You take a dark view,' you reply, 'you unknown person.' Knowledge, I tell you, is the deepest agony in the world; but it is the purgatory without whose purifying torment no human soul can attain Salvation. It is not audacious childishness and wicked ingenuousness that are useful, Herr Blüthenzweig, but the true knowledge in which the passions of our loathsome flesh die out and fade away."

A hush. The yellow gentleman with the black goatee let out a short bleat.

"You have to leave now," said the ill-paid employee gently.

But Hieronymus made absolutely no move to leave. Tall and upright in his hooded cloak, with burning eyes, he stood there in the middle of the art boutique, and with harsh and virtually rusty sounds, his thick lips formed inexorably damning words.

" 'Art!' they cry. 'Enjoyment! Beauty! Cloak the world in Beauty and bestow on every object the nobility of style!' . . . Get away from me, you odious ones! Do people think they can varnish the world in magnificent colors? Do people think they can drown out the moans of the tortured earth with the festive noise of voluptuous savor? You are mistaken, you shameless ones! God is nobody's fool, and your brazen idolatry of the glistening surface is an abomination in His eyes! . . . 'You revile art,' you answer me, 'you unknown person.' 'You lie,' I tell them. 'I do not revile art!' Art is no unprincipled deception that tempts and beckons you to strengthen and confirm life in flesh! Art is the sacred torch that should mercifully shine into all dreadful depths, into all shameful and sorrowful abysses of existence; art is the divine fire that ignites the world so that it may flame up and perish, together with all its sin and agony in redeeming compassion! . . . Remove it, Herr Blüthenzweig, remove the famous painter's work there from your window. . . . Indeed, you would do well to burn it up in a hot fire and scatter its ashes to the winds, to the four winds!"

His unlovely voice broke off. He had taken a vehement step back; one arm had been wrested from the shroud of the black cloak and had stretched far out in a passionate movement, and a strangely distorted hand, convulsively shaking up and down, pointed at the display, at the window containing the sensational picture of the Madonna. He remained in that domineering pose.

His big, bulging nose seemed to protrude with a belligerent expression, his dark eyebrows, much bushier at the root of the nose, were drawn so high that the angular forehead, shadowed by the hood, was covered with broad horizontal creases, and a hectic heat was blazing on the hollows of his cheeks.

But now Herr Blüthenzweig turned around. Either he was sincerely scandalized by the arrogant demand to burn the seventy-mark reproduction or else he was finally out of patience with Hieronymus's speechifying; in any case, he presented an image of strong and righteous wrath. He pointed his penholder at the door, briefly and angrily blasted his nose into his mustache several times, struggled to speak, and finally managed to exclaim, with utmost emphasis:

"If you don't get the hell out of here, you dimwit, then I'll have the mover facilitate your departure—do you understand me?"

"Oh, you will not intimidate me , you will not drive me away, you will not silence my voice!" cried Hieronymus, his fist pulling his hood together over his chest and his head shaking fearlessly. "I know that I am alone and powerless, and yet I will not hold my tongue until you listen to me, Herr Blüthenzweig! Remove the picture from your window and burn it this very day! Ah, do not burn just that! Also burn these statuettes and busts, the sight of which plunges the viewer in sin, burn these vases and adornments, these shameless rebirths of heathenism, these voluptuously decked out love poems! Burn everything that your shop contains, Herr Blüthenzweig, for it is filth in God's eyes! Burn, burn, burn it!" he shouted, beside himself as his arm performed a wild, vast, circular movement. "The crop is ripe for the reaper. . . . The insolence of this age smashes through all dams. . . . But I say unto you—"

"Krauthuber!" Herr Blüthenzweig strenuously yelled toward a door in the back. "Get in here immediately!"

What appeared on the scene in response to that command

was a massive and overpowering entity, a tremendous and exuberant human manifestation of terrifying fullness, whose swelling, welling, padded limbs melted shapelessly into one another everywhere—an unmeasurable colossus, lurching slowly across the floor and puffing heavily, nourished with malt, a son of the people, dreadfully hale and hearty! A fringelike sailor's beard and a walrus mustache were visible up there on his face, his body was swathed in a paste-smeared leather apron, and the yellow sleeves of his shirt were rolled back on his incredible arms.

"Would you open the door for this gentleman, Krauthuber," said Herr Blüthenzweig, "and if he still doesn't find it, then help him out into the street."

"Huh?" said the man, his small elephant eyes alternating between Hieronymus and his angry employer. It was a dull sound of arduously curbed strength. Then, his footsteps making everything around him quake, he plowed over to the door and opened it.

Hieronymus had turned very pale. "Burn . . . ," he wanted to say, but he already felt turned around by a terrible superior power, thrust by a body bulk against which no resistance was conceivable, and slowly and inexorably pushed toward the door.

"I'm weak," he managed to say. "My flesh will not endure violence, it will not withstand, no. . . . What does this prove? Burn . . ."

He fell silent. He found himself outside the art boutique. In the end, Herr Blüthenzweig's gigantic employee had sent him sprawling with a small shove and swing, so that Hieronymus, propped on one hand, had plunged sideways on the stone stoop. And behind him the glass door jingled shut.

He pulled himself up. He stood erect, breathing heavily, with one fist holding his hood together above his chest and the other hand dangling under his cloak. A gray pallor lurked in the hollows of his cheeks; the nostrils of his big, bulging nose flared and closed, twitching; his ugly lips were twisted into an expression of desperate hate, and his eyes, surrounded by glowing fervor, swept insanely and ecstatically across the beautiful square.

He did not notice the curious and mirthful looks focused on him. On the mosaic surface in front of the huge loggia he saw the vanities of the world, the masks and costumes of artists' parties, the ornaments, vases, jewels, and stylistic objects, the naked statues and female busts, the painted rebirths of heathenism, the portraits of famous beauties by the hands of masters, the voluptuously decorated love poems and informative writings on art—he saw them heaped in pyramids and going up in crackling flames amid the jubilant cheers of a populace enthralled by his dreadful words. . . . He looked toward the yellowish wall of clouds that had drawn up from Theatiner Street, thundering softly, and he saw a broad fiery sword standing and stretching into the sulfurous light over the joyful city. . . .

"*Gladius Dei super terram* . . . The Sword of God over the earth," his thick lips whispered, and pulling himself up higher in his hooded cloak and with a concealed and spasmodic shaking of his dangling fist, he murmured with a shiver: "*Cito et velociter!* Quick and swift!"

# TRISTAN

HERE IS THE SANATORIUM called Einfried, "Enclosure." With its long main building and its side wing, it lies, white and rectilinear, in the middle of the vast garden, which is delightfully appointed with grottoes, pergolas, and small gazebos made of tree bark. Looming behind the slate roofs, the mountains, massive, fir green, and softly rugged, tower toward the heavens.

As in the past, Dr. Leander still heads the institution. With his two-pronged black beard, which is as crisp and frizzy as horsehair stuffing, and with his thick, sparkling spectacles, he has that look of a man whom science has rendered cold and hard, imbuing him with silent and forbearing pessimism. In his brusque and taciturn fashion, this physician holds sway over the patients—all these individuals who, too weak to lay down laws for themselves and to abide by them, fork over their wealth so that they may be bolstered by his severity.

As for Fräulein von Osterloh, she runs the house with indefatigable devotion. My goodness, what a busy beaver she is, hurrying upstairs and down, from one end of the establishment to the other! She rules kitchen and pantry, she climbs around in the linen closets, she commands the staff, she plans meals with an eye toward thrift and nutrition, tastiness and graceful appearance, and she manages money with frantic prudence. However, her extreme proficiency conceals an endless reproach toward the world of men, not one of whom has so much as entertained the thought of marrying her. Nevertheless, her cheeks reveal two round, crimson spots that glow with her undashable hope of someday becoming Frau Doctor Leander.

Ozone and silent, silent air . . . For consumptives, Einfried, whatever Dr. Leander's grudgers and rivals may say, is to be most warmly recommended. And not only phthisics stay here, but all kinds of patients—men, women, and even children: Dr. Leander can boast of his successes in the most diverse areas. There are gastric cases here, like Frau Spatz, a town councillor's wife, who also has an ear disease; there are cardiac patients, paralytics, rheumatics, and sufferers of all kinds of nervous conditions. A diabetic general uses up his pension here, grumbling all the while. Several gentlemen with emaciated faces have legs that kick uncontrollably, in a way that bodes no good. A fifty-year-old lady, Frau Höhlenrauch, a pastor's wife, who has given birth to nineteen children and is no longer capable of a single thought, nevertheless achieves no peace of mind; instead, for a year now, driven by a confused disquiet, she has been wandering all over the house, leaning on the arm of her private nurse, stiff and mute, aimless and eerie.

Now and then one of the "serious" cases dies—those who lie in their rooms and never appear either for meals or in the salon—and no one, not even the patient next door, learns about the death. In the still of the night, the waxen guest is gotten rid of, and the activities in Einfried continue unruffled, the massaging, electrifying, and injecting, the showering, bathing, exercising, sweating, and inhaling in the various rooms, which are equipped with all the triumphs of the modern age. . . .

Yes, things are lively here. The institute is flourishing. The concierge, at the entrance to the side wing, bangs the big gong when new guests arrive, whereas departing guests are formally escorted to the carriage by Dr. Leander and Fräulein von Osterloh. What lives have been given asylum at Einfried! There's even a writer here, an eccentric man, who bears the name of some sort of mineral or precious stone and who whiles away his days here. . . .

Incidentally, along with Herr Doctor Leander, there is a second physician, for light cases and for the hopeless. But his name is Müller, and he's not worth talking about.

In early January, Klöterjahn, a wholesaler in the firm of A. C. Klöterjahn & Co., brought his wife to Einfried. The concierge banged the gong, and the travelers from far away were greeted by Fräulein von Osterloh in the ground-floor reception room, which, like almost the entire old and elegant mansion, is furnished in marvelously pure Empire style. Dr. Leander then promptly appeared; he bowed, and a conversation developed, for the orientation of all parties.

Outdoors, in the wintry garden, the flower beds were covered with mats, and the grottoes and isolated pagodas were snowed in. Two house employees were lugging the baggage of the new guests from the carriage, which was parked on the road, outside the lattice gate—for there was no driveway running up to the house.

"Take it easy, Gabriele," Herr Klöterjahn had said, then, in English, "Take care," then, in German, "my angel, and keep your lips closed," as he led his wife through the garden. And anyone who saw her would, with a tender and trembling heart, have to concur with that "take care"—although there is no denying that Herr Klöterjahn could have readily said it in German.

The coachman who had driven the couple from the station to the sanatorium, a rough, blunt, unaware man, had virtually kept his tongue between his teeth in powerless caution while the wholesaler helped his wife climb out. Indeed, it had seemed as if the two chestnut bays, steaming in the silent, frosty air, strenuously followed this anxious procedure with eyes rolled back and with utmost concern about so much feeble grace and delicate charm.

The young woman had a windpipe problem, as was explicitly stated in the letter that Herr Klöterjahn had sent from the Baltic shore informing Einfried's head physician of their arrival—and thank goodness it was not her lungs! However, even if it *had* been her lungs, this new patient could not have presented a lovelier and more exalted, a more enraptured and ethereal image than now, at her robust husband's side, sitting back, soft and weary, in the white-lacquered, linear armchair while following the conversation.

Her beautiful pale hands, unbejeweled except for the plain wedding band, rested in her lap, among the folds of a dark and heavy cloth skirt, and she wore a tight-fitting silvery-gray bodice with a firm stand-up collar and a dense array of very thick velvet arabesques. However, these warm and weighty materials made the ineffable sweetness, tenderness, and weariness of the little head appear even more poignant, more unearthly, and more charming. Her light-brown hair, tied in a knot deep on the nape of her neck, was combed back smoothly, and only one loose, curly lock dangled into her forehead, near the right temple, not far from the place where, above the sharply drawn eyebrow, a strange and tiny vein branched out, pale blue and sickly, in the clarity and immaculateness of her virtually translucent forehead. That tiny blue vein above the eye reigned in an unsettling way over the whole fine oval of the face. The vein protruded more visibly as soon as the woman began to speak, indeed even if she just smiled, and it then gave her expression a touch of strain, why, even distress, arousing vague anxieties. Nevertheless, she spoke and smiled. She spoke, frank and friendly, in her slightly husky voice, and she smiled with her eyes, which peered a bit arduously, in fact tended to *close* now and then, while their corners lay in deep shadows on either side of the narrow root of her nose. And she also smiled with her wide and lovely lips, which were pale and yet seemed to shine, perhaps because they had such an exceedingly pure and distinct outline. At times she would cough slightly. Whereupon she put her handkerchief to her mouth and then stared at it.

"Don't even clear your throat, Gabriele," said Herr Klöterjahn. "You know that Dr. Hinzpeter at home expressly forbade it, *darling*"—he said "darling" in English—"and it's simply a matter of pulling yourself together, my angel. It is, as we know, the windpipe," he repeated. "When it began, I honestly believed it was her lungs, and it gave me quite a scare, God knows. But it's not her lungs, no, sir, damn it—that's one thing we won't put up with, right, Gabriele, eh, eh?"

"No doubt about it," said Dr. Leander, and glared at her through his sparkling spectacles.

Whereupon Herr Klöterjahn ordered coffee—coffee with rolls and butter—and he had a vivid way of pronouncing the *c* in "coffee" deep in the back of his throat and uttering "rolls and butter" with such gusto that everyone felt pangs of hunger.

He got what he wished; he also got a room for himself and his wife, and they settled in.

By the way, Dr. Leander personally took charge of the care, without enlisting Dr. Müller.

The new patient caused an unusual sensation in Einfried, and Herr Klöterjahn, accustomed to such triumphs, was gratified to accept any homage that she was paid. The diabetic general momentarily stopped grumbling when he first set eyes on her, the gentlemen with the emaciated faces smiled and strenuously tried to control their legs when coming near her, and Frau Spatz, the town councillor's wife, instantly attached herself to the newcomer as an older friend. Yes indeed, she made quite an impact, the lady who bore Herr Klöterjahn's name! The writer who had been sojourning in Einfried for several weeks now, the weird and disconcerting figure whose name sounded like that of a precious stone . . . his face literally changed color whenever she passed him in the corridor, and he halted and stood there transfixed long after she had disappeared.

Within less than two days the entire sanatorium was familiar with her story. She was a native of Bremen (as, incidentally, could be recognized in her charming way of twisting certain sounds when she spoke), and that was where, two years earlier, she had pledged her lifelong troth to Wholesaler Klöterjahn. She had followed him to his hometown, up there on the Baltic shore, and then, some ten months ago, under highly extraordinary and dangerous circumstances, she had presented him with a child, an admirably lively and well-wrought son and heir.

However, since those dreadful days, she had not regained her strength, assuming she had ever had any strength in the first place. Scarcely had she risen from childbed, utterly exhausted, utterly destitute of vim and vigor, when she had coughed up a little blood. Oh, not much, just a trifle—but it would certainly have been better if it had not appeared. And what gave them pause to think was that the same sinister little thing recurred a short time later. Well, there were remedies, and Dr. Hinzpeter, the family physician, made use of them. Complete rest was prescribed, pieces of ice were swallowed, morphine was administered against any tickle in her throat, and her heart was kept as tranquil as possible. But no recovery ensued, and while the child, Anton Klöterjahn, Jr., a splendid specimen of a baby, conquered and maintained his place in life with tremendous energy and ruthlessness, the young mother seemed to be vanishing in a gentle and silent glow. . . . It was, as we know, the windpipe—a word that, on Dr. Hinzpeter's lips, made a surprisingly comforting, reassuring, almost gladdening impact on all minds. But even though it was not her lungs, the physician eventually felt that in order to accelerate the healing, it was urgently desirable for the mother to seek the effect of a milder climate and a stay in a sanatorium; and the reputation of Einfried and its director had clinched his opinion.

That was how things stood; and Herr Klöterjahn himself told the story to anyone who evinced any interest in it. He talked loudly, casually, cheerfully, like a man whose digestion is as fit and orderly as his wallet, and his lips swept out widely, in the broad yet rapid manner of inhabitants of the North German coast. He hurled several words out so vehemently that each sound was like a small discharge, and he laughed at it as if it were a successful joke.

Herr Klöterjahn was husky and medium-sized, he had short legs, broad shoulders, and a full, red face with moist lips, commodious nostrils, and sea-blue eyes shadowed by very pale blond lashes. His whiskers were English, his wardrobe was completely English, and he was delighted to find an English family in Einfried—father, mother, and three attractive children with their nanny, who were staying here solely because they did not know where else to stay. Herr Klöterjahn had an English breakfast with them every morning. Incidentally, he loved copious amounts of good food and drink and proved to be a true connoisseur of cuisine and wine cellars, and he entertained the sanatorium society by telling the most stimulating tales about the dinners back home in his social circles as well as describing certain choice dishes that were unknown here. As he talked, his eyes narrowed amiably, and his speech gained a palatal and nasal touch, accompanied by lightly smacking noises in the back of his throat. Nor was he fundamentally averse to other earthly joys, as he demonstrated one evening when a guest at Einfried, the writer by profession, saw him with a chambermaid in the corridor. The wholesaler was flirting quite outrageously—a small, humorous incident, at which said writer made a ridiculously disgusted face.

As for Herr Klöterjahn's wife, it was clear and obvious that she loved him with all her heart. She smiled at everything he said and did: not with the patronizing indulgence that some invalids show the healthy, but with the charming joy and sympathy that good-natured patients display toward the sanguine vital signs of people who feel just fine and dandy.

Herr Klöterjahn did not linger on in Einfried. He had escorted his wife here; but after a week, confident that she was in good hands and well looked after, he could remain no longer.

Responsibilities of equal importance—his flourishing child, his likewise flourishing business—demanded his presence; he was forced to depart, leaving his wife in the enjoyment of the finest care.

Spinell was the name of the writer who had been living in Einfried for several weeks now—Detlev Spinell, a person with a peculiar exterior. Picture a brown-haired man named Detlev Spinell, in his early thirties and of a stately stature, his hair already starting to turn perceptibly gray on his temples, his round, white, slightly puffy face, however, not showing the least trace of a beard. His face was not shaved—it might then have hinted at stubble; it was soft, blurry, and boyish, with only a meager scattering of peach fuzz. And this looked very strange. The expression in his shiny, roe-brown eyes was gentle, his nose squat and a bit too fleshy. Furthermore, Herr Spinell had an arched, porous upper lip of a Roman character, large, rotting teeth, and unusually big feet. One of the gentlemen with uncontrollable legs, a man who was a wag and a cynic, had given him a nickname behind his back: "the decomposed suckling"; but that was nasty and scarcely apt. Herr Spinell dressed well and fashionably, in a long black jacket and a colorfully stippled vest.

He was unsocial and not close to anyone. Though now and then he was struck by an affable, affectionate, and ebullient mood, and this occurred whenever Herr Spinell got into an aesthetic state, whenever he was carried away in sheer admiration for something beautiful: the harmony of two colors, a vase with a noble shape, the mountains illuminated by the sunset. "How beautiful!" he would then say, tilting his head to one side and drawing up his shoulders, while splaying his fingers and curling his nose and his lips. "My God, just look how beautiful!" And, profoundly moved at such moments, he was capable of blindly embracing even the most distinguished people, whether male or female.

The book he had written lay constantly on his table, visible to anyone who entered his room. It was a moderate-sized novel with an utterly bewildering jacket design, printed on a sort of coffee-filter paper; each and every letter in the book looked like a Gothic cathedral. Fräulein von Osterloh had read it in a spare quarter hour and found it "clever," which was her way of circumventing the verdict "unspeakably boring." It took place in society salons, in luxurious boudoirs that were full of exquisite objects—Gobelins, antique furnishings, delightful porcelains, priceless textiles, and artistic treasures of all sorts. The most loving care had been expended on describing these things, and one constantly envisioned Herr Spinell curling his nose and saying, "How beautiful! My God, just look how beautiful!"

Incidentally, it was quite surprising that he had authored no further books, for apparently he wrote with passion. He spent the bulk of each day writing in his room, and he dispatched an extraordinary number of letters to the post office, one or two almost daily, whereby it struck people as astounding and amusing that he very seldom received any mail himself. . . .

Herr Spinell sat across the table from Herr Klöterjahn's wife. For the first meal in which the couple participated, the writer showed up a bit tardily at the large ground-floor dining room in the side wing. He muttered a universal greeting and headed toward his place, whereupon Dr. Leander introduced him to the newcomers without much ceremony. Herr Spinell bowed and then, clearly a bit embarrassed, started to eat; his big, white, beautifully shaped hands, which emerged from very narrow sleeves, manipulated his knife and fork in a rather affected manner. Eventually he loosened up, and his eyes sedately alternated between Herr Klöterjahn and his wife. In the course of the meal, the wholesaler addressed several questions and remarks to him about the layout of Einfried and the local climate, whereupon his wife inserted one or two words in her charming fashion, and Herr Spinell politely responded. His voice was mild and quite pleasant, but his speech was somewhat handicapped and shuffling, as if his teeth got in the way of his tongue.

After dinner, when everyone had crossed over to the salon and Dr. Leander had personally told the new guests that he hoped they had enjoyed their meal, Herr Klöterjahn's wife asked about her vis-à-vis.

"What is the gentleman's name?" she asked. "Spinelli? I didn't catch it."

"Spinell . . . not Spinelli, dear madam. No, he's no Italian; he was simply born in Lemberg, so far as I know. . . ."

"What did you say? He's a writer? Of what?" asked Herr Klöterjahn. He held his hands in the pockets of his comfortable English trousers, leaned over with his ear toward the physician, and, as some people are wont to do, he opened his mouth when listening.

"Why, I don't know . . . he writes," replied Dr. Leander. "He has, I believe, published a book, a sort of novel . . . I really don't know."

That repeated "I don't know" implied that Dr. Leander did not hold the writer in great esteem and that he declined any responsibility for him.

"Why, that's very interesting!" said Herr Klöterjahn's wife. She had never before met a writer face-to-face.

"Oh, yes," replied Dr. Leander obligingly. "I hear that he enjoys a certain reputation. . . ." Then the writer was discussed no further.

A bit later, however, when the new guests had retired and Dr. Leander was likewise about to leave the salon, Herr Spinell held him back and made his own inquiries.

"What is the couple's name?" he asked. "Naturally I didn't catch a thing."

"Klöterjahn," replied Dr. Leander, starting to leave again.

"*What's* the man's name?" asked Herr Spinell.

"Their name is *Klöterjahn!*" said Dr. Leander, and went his way. He did not hold the writer in great esteem.

Did we reach the point at which Herr Klöterjahn returned home? Yes, he was back on the Baltic shore, with his business dealings and his child, that ruthless and lively little creature who had caused his mother a lot of suffering and a minor defect in her windpipe. She herself, however, the young wife, remained in Einfried, and Frau Spatz, the town councillor's wife, attached herself to her as an older friend. But this did not prevent Herr Klöterjahn's wife from being on friendly terms with the other guests—for example, Herr Spinell. To the amazement of all and sundry (for he had been not close to anyone else so far), he was extraordinarily helpful and devoted to her from the very outset, and she did not mind chatting with him during the spare moments left her by a rigid schedule.

He approached her with tremendous caution and reverence and always spoke to her in a carefully subdued voice, so that Frau Spatz, who had an ear problem, usually understood absolutely nothing of what he said. He tiptoed on his big feet to the armchair where Herr Klöterjahn's wife was leaning back, delicate and smiling, and he remained at a distance of two paces, keeping one leg back and bending his torso, while speaking forcibly in his somewhat handicapped and shuffling way, and always ready to retreat quickly and vanish the instant any sign of weariness or surfeit crept into her face. But his presence did not bother her. She invited him to join herself and Frau Spatz, asked him some question or other, and then listened to him, smiling with curiosity, for sometimes he came out with terribly amusing and bizarre things, such as she had never heard before.

"Why are you in Einfried anyway?" she asked. "Which treatment do you need, Herr Spinell?"

"Treatment? . . . I get a little electrified. No, it's not worth talking about. Let me tell you, dear madam, why I'm here. For the sake of style."

"Ah!" said Herr Klöterjahn's wife, propping her chin on her hand and turning toward him with exaggerated zeal, as we do with children when they wish to tell us a story.

"Yes, dear madam. Einfried is pure Empire. It used to be a castle, a summer residence, I am told. This side wing is a subsequent addition, but the main building is old and genuine. There are times when I simply cannot do without Empire, when it is absolutely crucial to me if I am to achieve even the slightest degree of well-being. It is clear that people feel one way among furniture that is lasciviously soft and comfortable and another way among these straight and linear tables, armchairs, and draperies. . . . This brightness and hardness, this cold, austere simplicity and reserved strictness, fill me with composure and dignity, dear madam. In the long run, the consequences are a spiritual purification and restoration—I am morally elevated, without question. . . ."

"Yes, that is strange," she said. "Incidentally, I do understand it if I make an effort."

To this he replied that it was not worth any effort, and then they laughed in unison. Frau Spatz also laughed and found it strange; but she did not say that she understood it.

The salon was spacious and beautiful. The high white double door was wide open to the adjacent billiard room, where the gentlemen with the uncontrollable legs and other people were enjoying themselves. On another wall, a glass door offered a view of the broad terrace and the garden. A piano stood to the side. At a green-covered card table, the diabetic general was playing whist with a few other gentlemen. Ladies were reading or doing needlework. An iron stove provided heat, but there were cozy places for chatting in front of the stylish fireplace, where lumps of imitation coal lay, with strips of fiery red paper glued to them.

"You're an early riser, Herr Spinell," said Herr Klöterjahn's wife. "Two or three times, I happened to see you leaving the house by seven-thirty."

"An early riser? Ah, but there's a great difference, dear madam. The truth of the matter is that I rise early because I actually oversleep."

"You'll have to explain that, Herr Spinell!"

And Frau Spatz likewise desired an explanation.

"Well . . . if a man is an early riser, then, it seems to me, he doesn't need to get up so early. The conscience, dear madam . . . A conscience is a terrible thing! I and my kind, we've been struggling with it all our lives and have our hands full deceiving it now and then and granting it small, wily satisfactions. We are useless creatures, I and my kind, and aside from a very few good hours, we drag around the awareness of our uselessness until we are sore and sick. We hate useful things, we know that they are common and unsightly, and we defend this truth as one defends only truths that one absolutely needs. And yet we are so thoroughly nibbled at by our bad consciences that there is not an unscathed spot left on us. In addition, the entire manner of our spiritual existence, our Weltanschauung, our work methods, have a dreadfully unhealthy, undermining, grueling effect, and that, too, makes matters worse. Now, there are small palliatives without which we simply could not endure. A certain decorum and hygienic rigor in our lifestyle, say, are things that some of us need. Early to rise, atrociously early, a cold bath, and a stroll out into the snow . . . This allows us to feel a little satisfied with ourselves for perhaps an hour. If I behaved according to my true self, I would lie in bed until the afternoon, believe me. When I rise early, it is actually hypocrisy."

"Goodness, why, Herr Spinell? I call that strength of mind. Isn't that so, Frau Spatz?"

The councillor's wife also called it strength of mind.

"Hypocrisy or strength of mind, dear madam! Whichever term one prefers. I am so sorrowfully honest by nature that I—"

"That's it. You probably spend too much time being sorrowful."

"Yes, dear madam, I am frequently sorrowful."

The good weather held out. The region and the mountains, the house and the garden, lay white, hard, and clean, in wind lulls and light frosts, in dazzling brightness and bluish shadows, and everything was domed by an immaculate, a delicately azure sky, where myriads of tiny flickering luminaries and glittering crystals seemed to be dancing. Herr Klöterjahn's wife was doing tolerably during this period; she was free of fever, almost never coughed, and ate without too much repugnance. Often, as was prescribed for her, she spent hours out on the terrace in the sunny frost. She sat in the snow, bundled up in furs and blankets and optimistically breathing the pure, icy air in order to help her windpipe. At such times she often noticed Herr Spinell, who, warmly dressed and in fur-lined shoes, which made his feet look fantastically huge, was promenading in the garden. He trudged with tentative steps, holding his arms in a certain cautious and stiffly graceful pose. Reaching the terrace, he greeted her reverently and mounted the lower steps in order to start a brief conversation.

"Today, during my morning constitutional, I saw a beautiful woman. . . . God, was she beautiful!" he said, tilting his head to one side and splaying his fingers.

"Really, Herr Spinell? Do describe her to me!"

"No, I can't. Or I'd give you an incorrect picture of her. My eyes barely grazed the lady in passing; I didn't actually see her. But that blurry glimpse was enough to fire my imagination and enable me to carry away a beautiful picture. . . . God, is it beautiful!"

She laughed. "Is that your way of looking at beautiful women, Herr Spinell?"

"Yes, dear madam; and it's a better way than grossly staring into a face and being greedy for reality and carrying away an impression of the actual defects. . . ."

"Greedy for reality . . . That is a bizarre phrase! Truly a writer's phrase, Herr Spinell! But it makes an impact on me, I tell you. There's something about it that I scarcely understand, something free and independent, which even disrespects reality, although reality is the most respectable thing in the world—why, it's respectability itself. . . . And then I understand that something exists beyond appearances, something more delicate—"

"I know only one face," he abruptly said, with a strangely joyous lilt in his voice. He raised his clenched fists to his shoulders, and his overexcited smile revealed his rotting teeth. "I know only one face whose noble reality it would be sinful to correct with my imagination, only one face that I would like to contemplate, linger upon, not for minutes, not for hours, but for the rest of my life, fully lose myself in it and forget all earthly things. . . ."

"Yes, yes, Herr Spinell. Except that Fräulein von Osterloh's ears do stick out quite far."

He fell silent and bowed deeply. When he straightened up again, his eyes rested with a look of painful embarrassment on the strange and tiny vein that branched out, pale blue and sickly, in the clarity of her virtually translucent forehead.

A quaint man, an utterly quaint and peculiar man! Every so often, Herr Klöterjahn's wife thought about Herr Spinell, for she had a great deal of time for thinking. Now whether the change of air was losing its effect or some definitely harmful influence was at work, her health had worsened. The condition of her windpipe apparently left much to be desired, she felt weak, tired, had no appetite, often ran a fever; and Dr. Leander most emphatically recommended rest, idleness, and caution. So, when she did not have to lie down, she sat in Frau Spatz's company, said little, keeping some needlework in her lap but not sewing, and followed one train of thought or another.

Yes, he gave her food for thought, that eccentric Herr Spinell, and oddly enough, not so much about him as about herself, for he somehow aroused a strange and unfamiliar curiosity about herself, an interest in her own existence. One day he had said in the course of conversation:

"Oh, my, women are an enigmatic business. . . . This is hardly a new insight, yet one cannot help looking and marveling. You find a wonderful creature, a sylph, an airy wraith, a dreamland delight. And what does she do? She goes and gives herself to some county-fair Hercules or butcher's assistant. She comes strolling along on his arm, perhaps even leaning her head on his shoulder while glancing around with an impish smile as if to say, 'Go ahead, rack your brains about it!' And rack them we do!"

This was something that Herr Klöterjahn's wife had repeatedly pondered.

On another day, to Frau Spatz's amazement, the following dialogue took place:

"May I ask you, dear madam—though I *am* prying—what your name is, your real name?"

"Why, it's Klöterjahn, Herr Spinell!"

"Hm! I know it. Or rather: I deny it. I mean, of course, your own name, your maiden name. You must in all fairness, dear madam, admit that anyone who wishes to call you 'Frau Klöterjahn' deserves to be horsewhipped."

She laughed so heartily that the tiny blue vein above her eyebrow emerged, alarmingly sharp, lending her sweet, delicate face a deeply unsettling expression of strain and anguish.

"No! Heaven forbid, Herr Spinell! Horsewhipped? Do you really find 'Klöterjahn' so awful?"

"Yes, dear madam; I've hated that name with all my heart from the very first moment I heard it. It's comical and desperately hideous, and it's a vile and barbaric custom to force your husband's name on you."

"Well, and what about 'Eckhof' [corner court]? Is Eckhof any more attractive? My father's name is Eckhof."

"Oh, now look! 'Eckhof' is an entirely different matter! There was even a great actor named Eckhof. Eckhof passes. You mentioned your father. Is your mother . . . ?"

"Yes. My mother passed away when I was little."

"Ah. Tell me more about yourself, if I may ask. If it tires you, then don't. Just rest, and I'll continue telling you about Paris, as I did recently. But you could speak very softly—yes, if you whisper, it will make everything only lovelier. . . . You were born in Bremen?" And when he asked that question, his voice was almost toneless, and his expression was full of awe and momentous gravity, as if Bremen were a city without peer, a city alive with unnameable adventure and secret beauty, conferring a mysterious sublimity on anyone born there.

"Yes, imagine!" she said involuntarily. "I'm from Bremen."

"I was there once," he remarked pensively.

"My goodness, you were *there* too? Now listen, Herr Spinell, I do believe you've seen everything between Tunis and Spitsbergen!"

"Yes, I was there once," he repeated. "A few brief hours one evening. I recall an old, narrow street, with a strange moon hovering askew over the gables. Then I was in a cellar that smelled of wine and mildew. It is a haunting memory. . . ."

"Really? Where could that have been? Yes, I was born in a gray, gabled house like that, an old merchant house with a reverberating vestibule and a gallery that was painted white."

"So your father is a merchant?" he asked, a bit hesitant.

"Yes. But besides that and really primarily, he's an artist."

"Ah! Ah! In what way?"

"He plays the violin. . . . But that's not saying much. It's the *way* he plays it, Herr Spinell, that's the thing! I've never been able to hear certain notes without tears burning so strangely in my eyes, something I've never experienced at any other time. You don't believe it—"

"I do believe it! Oh, how I believe it! . . . Tell me, dear madam: Is your family old? Many generations must have lived, worked, and passed away in the gray gabled house?"

"Yes. Why do you ask, by the by?"

"Because it is no rare occurrence for a family with dry, practical, bourgeois traditions to be transfigured by art toward the end of its days."

"Is that so? Yes, as far as my father is concerned, he is certainly more of an artist than any number of people who call themselves that and live on their fame. I only play a little piano. Now they've forbidden me to play; but back then, at home, I used to play. My father and I, we played together. . . . Yes, I have fond memories of all those years—especially the garden, our garden, behind the house. It was dreadfully wild and overgrown, and it was enclosed by mossy, crumbling walls; but that's what made it so charming. There was a fountain in the middle, surrounded by a dense wreath of irises. In the summer, I would spend long hours there with my girlfriends; we all sat on small folding chairs around the fountain. . . ."

"How beautiful!" said Herr Spinell, drawing up his shoulders. "Did you sit there and sing?"

"No, we mostly crocheted."

"Still and all . . . Still and all . . ."

"Yes, we crocheted and chatted, my six girlfriends and I. . . ."

"How beautiful! God, do you hear, how beautiful!" cried Herr Spinell, and his face was completely twisted.

"Now, what do you find so beautiful about *that*, Herr Spinell!?"

"Oh, that there were six of them besides you, that you were

not in that number, instead you stood out virtually as the queen. . . . You were set apart from your six companions. A small gold crown, quite plain but meaningful, glittered in your hair. . . ."

"No, nonsense, absolutely no crown . . ."

"Oh, but there was; it glittered in secret. I would have seen it, would have clearly seen it on your hair if, during one of those hours, I had been standing unnoticed in the shrubbery. . . ."

"Goodness knows what you would have seen. But you did not stand there; it was my husband who emerged from the bushes there one day, together with my father. I'm afraid they heard all sorts of things in our chatter. . . ."

"So it was there that you met your husband, dear madam?"

"Yes, that's where I met him!" she exclaimed cheerfully, and as she smiled, the tiny pale-blue vein protruded, strained and bizarre, over her eyebrow. "He was paying my father a business call, you know. The next day he came for dinner, and three days later he asked for my hand."

"Really? Was it a whirlwind engagement?"

"Yes . . . That is, from then on it went a bit slower. For actually my father was not in favor of the match, you must know, and he stipulated a long period for us to think it over. First of all, he preferred keeping me at home with him, and then he had other qualms. But . . ."

"But?"

"But I simply *wanted* it," she said, smiling, and once again the tiny pale-blue vein with a distressed and sickly expression ruled her entire lovely face.

"Ah, you wanted it."

"Yes, and I showed a very solid and respectable determination, as you see . . ."

"As I see. Yes."

". . . so that eventually my father had to give in."

"And so you left him then and his violin, left the old house, the overgrown garden, the fountain, and your six companions, and went forth with Herr Klöterjahn."

" 'And went forth with . . .' You do have a way of expressing yourself, Herr Spinell! Almost biblical! Yes, I left all that, for that's the will of nature."

"Yes, that's her will, I guess."

"And then it was a matter of my happiness."

"Certainly. And it came, your happiness. . . ."

"It came the moment, Herr Spinell, when they first brought me little Anton, our little Anton, and when he screamed so powerfully with his healthy little lungs, strong and healthy as he is. . . ."

"This isn't the first time that I've heard you speak about your little Anton's health, dear madam. He must be quite unusually healthy?"

"That he is. And he looks so ridiculously like my husband."

"Ah! Yes, so that's how it happened. And now your name is no longer Eckhof but something else, and you have healthy little Anton, and you have a slight problem with your windpipe."

"Yes. And *you* are a thoroughly enigmatic person, Herr Spinell, that I can assure you. . . ."

"Yes, upon my soul, you certainly are!" said Frau Spatz, who, by the way, was still present.

However, Herr Klöterjahn's wife also mulled over that conversation several times. Trivial as it was, it contained, deep down, something that nourished her thoughts about herself. Was *this* the harmful influence at work? She grew more feeble, and she often ran a fever, a quiet glow, in which she rested with a feeling of gentle exaltation, to which she abandoned herself in a pensive, precious, self-complacent, and slightly offended mood. Whenever she left her bed, and Herr Spinell, with tremendous caution, tiptoed over to her on his big feet, halted two paces off, and, keeping one leg back and bending his torso, spoke to her in a reverently hushed voice, as if gently raising her aloft in timid awe and bedding her on cloud cushions, where no shrill sound and no earthly touch could reach her . . . at such times she would recall Herr Klöterjahn's way of saying: "Careful, Gabriele, *take care* [in English], my angel, and keep your lips closed!"—a way that felt as if he were giving someone a hard but well-meaning slap on the back. But then she would quickly turn away from this memory, resting in feebleness and exaltation on the cloud cushions that Herr Spinell obligingly prepared for her.

One day she abruptly recurred to their brief conversation about her background and her earlier life.

"So it's true, Herr Spinell," she asked, "that you would have seen the crown?"

And even though that chat had taken place two weeks before, he promptly caught her drift, and he assured her in deeply moved words that when she had been sitting at the fountain among her six companions he would have seen the small crown glittering—would have seen it secretly, glittering in her hair.

Several days later, a sanatorium guest courteously asked her about the health of her little Anton at home. Glancing swiftly at Herr Spinell, who was nearby, she replied, slightly bored:

"Thank you, how else could he be but healthy? He and my husband are fine."

In late February, on a frosty day that was purer and more radiant than all the days preceding it, Einfried was bursting with utter exuberance. The cardiac patients conversed among themselves with flushed cheeks, the diabetic general warbled like an adolescent, and the gentlemen with the uncontrollable legs were absolutely wild with joy. What was it about? Nothing less than the prospect of a group excursion into the mountains, a ride in several sleighs with jingling bells and cracking whips. Dr. Leander had come up with this idea for the diversion of his patients.

Naturally the "serious" cases had to stay behind. The poor

"serious" ones! People nodded at one another, agreeing to keep mum: it generally did them good to practice a little sympathy and show consideration. But even among the people who could easily have participated in the pleasure, a few declined. As for Fräulein von Osterloh, she was excused without further ado. Anyone who was up to her ears in responsibilities, as she was, could not seriously consider going on sleigh rides. The household imperatively demanded her presence, so in short, she remained in Einfried. However, when Herr Klöterjahn's wife declared that she wanted to stay at home, it caused all-around disgruntlement. Dr. Leander vainly tried to talk her into benefiting from the ride in the fresh air; but she claimed that she was not in the mood, that she had a migraine and felt weary, and so they had to resign themselves. But the wag and cynic seized the opportunity to remark:

"Watch out; now the decomposed suckling won't go either."

And he proved to be right, for Herr Spinell announced that he wanted to work this afternoon—he liked using the term "work" for his dubious activity. Incidentally, not a soul complained about his absence, and everyone just as easily got over the fact that Frau Spatz decided to keep her younger friend company since riding a sleigh made her seasick.

Right after lunch, which today had been served around noon, the sleighs drew up outside Einfried, and the guests, in lively groups, warmly bundled up, eager and animated, trudged through the garden. Herr Klöterjahn's wife and Frau Spatz stood at the glass door leading to the terrace, and Herr Spinell stood at the window of his room, observing the departure. They watched as small fights for the best places broke out amid banter and laughter, as Fräulein von Osterloh, a fur boa around her neck, dashed from one team of horses to the next, shoving baskets of food under the seats, while Dr. Leander, his fur cap on his forehead, once again surveyed the whole business through his sparkling spectacles, then sat down and gave the signal for departure. . . . The horses began to pull, a few ladies shrieked and tumbled back, the bells jingled, the short-handled whips cracked, their long cords dragging in the snow behind the runners, and Fräulein von Osterloh stood at the garden gate, waving her handkerchief until the gliding vehicles vanished around a bend in the road and the cheery noises dwindled away. Then she returned through the garden, hurrying to her responsibilities, the two ladies left the glass door, and Herr Spinell almost simultaneously moved away from his lookout point.

Einfried lay tranquil. The expedition was not slated to return before evening. The "serious" cases lay in their beds and suffered. Herr Klöterjahn's wife took a brief stroll with her older friend, after which they returned to their respective quarters. Herr Spinell likewise kept to his room, busying himself in his fashion. Toward four o'clock the ladies were each brought a pint of milk, while Herr Spinell received his weak tea. A short time later, Herr Klöterjahn's wife tapped on the wall dividing her from Frau Spatz and said:

"Why don't we go down to the salon, Frau Spatz? I don't know what to do with myself here."

"Right away, my dear!" replied the town councillor's wife. "I just have to put on my boots, if you don't mind. You see, I've been lying down."

As was to be expected, the salon was empty. The ladies sat down by the fireplace. Frau Spatz embroidered flowers on a piece of canvas, while Herr Klöterjahn's wife did a few stitches, whereupon the needlework sank into her lap and she daydreamed away, beyond the arm of her chair. Finally she made a remark that was not worth separating one's teeth for; but since Frau Spatz nevertheless said, "Pardon?" her friend, to her mortification, had to repeat the entire sentence. The town councillor's wife once again asked, "Pardon?" But at that moment steps were heard from the vestibule, the door opened, and Herr Spinell came in.

"Am I intruding?" he gently asked from the threshold, gazing exclusively at Herr Klöterjahn's wife and bending his torso forward in a certain delicate and hovering way.

The young woman replied: "Goodness, of course not! First of all, this room is meant as a free port, Herr Spinell. And then, why should you be intruding? I have the distinct feeling that I am boring Frau Spatz. . . ."

To that he could think of no response, and so he merely smiled, revealing his rotting teeth, and before the eyes of the ladies, he walked rather self-consciously to the glass door, where he halted and peered out, somewhat discourteously showing them his back. Next, he turned halfway around, while still looking into the garden, and said:

"The sun is gone. The sky has clouded over, imperceptibly. Darkness is already setting in."

"Yes, that's right; everything is shadowy," replied Herr Klöterjahn's wife. "Apparently our day-trippers are going to encounter snow. Yesterday we still had broad daylight at this time; and now it's already dusk."

"Ah," he said, "after all these overly bright weeks, the darkness does the eyes some good. This sun is equally insistent whether illuminating beauty or baseness, and I am downright grateful to it for finally concealing itself a little."

"Don't you like the sun, Herr Spinell?"

"Well, I'm no painter. . . . One becomes more introspective without sunlight. There is a thick layer of grayish-white clouds blotting out the sky. Perhaps it portends a thaw for tomorrow. Incidentally, I wouldn't advise you to look at your needlework back there, dear madam."

"Ah, don't worry; I wouldn't do that anyway. But what should we do now?"

He had settled on the swivel stool at the piano, placing one arm on the lid of the instrument.

"Music . . . ," he said. "If only we could hear a little music!

Sometimes the English children sing their little spirituals, but that's all."

"And yesterday afternoon Fräulein von Osterloh gave us a hurried rendition of 'The Monastery Bells,' " remarked Herr Klöterjahn's wife.

"Why, but you play, dear madam," he said beseechingly, and stood up. "You used to play with your father every day."

"Yes, Herr Spinell; that was back then! In the days of the fountain, you know. . . ."

"Do it today!" he begged. "Let us hear a few bars just this once! If you only knew how I crave—"

"Both our family physician and Dr. Leander have strictly forbidden me to play, Herr Spinell."

"They're not here, either one of them! We're free. . . . You're free, dear madam! A few wretched chords . . ."

"No, Herr Spinell, it won't happen. Who knows what miracles you expect of me! And I've forgotten everything, believe me. I know almost nothing by heart."

"Oh, then play that almost-nothing! And anyway, there are some scores here, they are here on the piano. No, this is nothing. . . . But here's Chopin."

"Chopin?"

"Yes, the nocturnes. And all I have to do now is light the candles. . . ."

"Don't imagine that I'll play, Herr Spinell! I mustn't. What if it harms me?!"

He fell silent. With his big feet, his long black Prince Albert, his gray hair, and his blurry, beardless face, he stood in the light of the two piano candles, his hands dangling.

"Then I won't ask you anymore," he finally murmured. "If you're afraid of causing yourself harm, dear madam, then leave beauty dead and mute, the beauty that would like to blossom from under your fingers. You weren't always so sensible, at least not when, on the contrary, you had to take leave of beauty. You weren't concerned about your physical welfare and you showed a firmer and more heedless determination when you left the fountain and took off the small gold crown. . . .

"Listen," he said after a pause, his voice sinking even lower. "If you sit here now and play as you used to, when your father stood next to you and his violin sang those notes that made you weep . . . then it may secretly glitter in your hair again, the small gold crown. . . ."

"Really?" she asked, smiling. Her voice happened to break at that word, which came out both husky and toneless. Clearing her throat, she then said:

"Are those really the Chopin nocturnes?"

"Of course. They're open, and everything is ready."

"Well, then I'll play one of them, for goodness' sake," she said. "But only one, do you hear? Then you'll have enough forever."

With that, she stood up, put her needlework aside, and went to the piano. She sat down on the swivel seat, on which a few bound scores were lying, she arranged the candleholders and leafed through the score. Herr Spinell had pushed a chair over, and he sat next to her like a music teacher.

She played the Nocturne in E-flat Major, op. 9, no. 2. If she had truly forgotten anything, then her earlier delivery must have been one of consummate artistry. The piano itself was only mediocre, but after the first few notes she knew how to handle it with a sure sense of taste. She displayed a high-strung feel for subtleties of timbre and an almost fantastic delight in rhythmic mobility. Her touch was both firm and mellow. Under her fingers the melody sang out every last bit of sweetness, and with hesitant grace the embellishments nestled around its measures.

She was wearing the same dress as on the day of her arrival: the heavy silvery gray bodice with the sculptural velvet arabesques, which gave her head and her hands such an unearthly delicacy. Her facial expression did not change while she played, but the outlines of her lips seemed to grow clearer, with the

shadows deepening in the corners of her eyes. When she was finished, she put her hands in her lap and continued gazing at the
score. Herr Spinell remained seated without a sound or motion.

She played another nocturne, played a third and fourth. Then
she stood up, but only to seek more music on top of the piano.

Herr Spinell had the idea of examining the black, bound volumes on the swivel stool. Suddenly he emitted an incoherent cry,
and his big white hands passionately fingered one of these neglected books.

"Not possible! . . . It's not true!" he said. "And yet I'm not
mistaken! . . . Do you know what this is? What was lying here?
What I'm holding?"

"What is it?" she asked.

He mutely showed her the title page. He was quite pale; he
lowered the book and gazed at her, his lips trembling.

"Really? What is it doing *here*? Well, let me have it," she said
simply. She put the score on the stand, sat down, and, after a moment of silence, started with the first page.

He sat next to her, leaning forward, his head bowed, his hands
folded between his knees. She played the beginning with an
excessive and torturous slowness, with alarmingly drawn-out
pauses between the individual phrases. The *Sehnsuchtsmotiv,*
the yearning motif, a lonesome and wandering voice in the night,
softly utters its anxious question. A stillness and a waiting. And
lo, a response: the same timid and lonesome strain, only clearer,
only more delicate. Another hush. And now, with that muted
and wonderful sforzando, which is like passion rousing itself and
blissfully flaring up, the love motif emerged, ascended, rapturously struggled upward to sweet interlacing, sank back, dissolving, and, with their deep crooning of grave and painful ecstasy,
the cellos came to the fore and carried the melody away. . . .

The woman playing the wretched instrument was not unsuc-
cessful in conjuring up the orchestral effects. The violin passages
of the great crescendo resounded with radiant precision. She

played with precious reverence, dwelling credulously on each element and emphasizing each detail in a humble demonstrative fashion, the way a priest elevates the Most Holy Sacrament above his head. What was happening? Two forces, two entranced beings, were striving toward each other in pain and bliss, embracing in the ecstatic and delirious yearning for the eternal and the absolute. . . . The prelude blazed up and faded. She stopped where the curtain opens, and she then kept staring wordlessly at the score.

Meanwhile, Frau Spatz's boredom had reached the degree at which it distorts the human face, driving the eyes out of the head and making the features cadaverous and terrifying. Furthermore, this sort of music affected her gastric nerves, triggering fits of anxiety in her dyspeptic organism, so that the town councillor's wife was afraid she might have a seizure.

"I am forced to go back to my room," she said weakly. "Goodbye. I shall return. . . ." With that, she left.

The twilight had greatly thickened. They could see the snow falling dense and silent outside, on the terrace. The two candles shed a fickle and restricted light.

"Act Two," he whispered. She turned the pages and launched into Act Two.

The blare of horns melted into the distance. What? Or was it the rustling of leaves? The gentle gurgle of the wellspring? The night had already poured its silence through grove and house, and no pleading, no warning, could halt the sway of yearning any longer. The holy mystery was consummated. The light waned, the death motif sank down with a strange, suddenly overcast timbre, and hasty and impatient yearning fluttered its white veil toward the beloved, who came through the darkness, approaching desire with outspread arms.

Oh, rhapsodic and insatiable jubilation of merging in the eternal and abstract beyond! Rid of tormenting error, eluding the fetters of space and time, the Thou and the I, the Thine and the

Mine, fused in sublime bliss. The insidious illusion of day could divide them, but its boastful lies could no longer deceive the night-seers now that the power of the magic potion had hallowed their vision. If a human being has amorously seen the night of death and its sweet mystery, then all that remains for him in the delusion of light is a single longing, the yearning for sacred night, the true, the eternal night that blends two into one. . . .

Oh, sink, night of love, give them the oblivion they desire, enfold them fully in your bliss and remove them from the world of falsehood and separation. Lo, the final light has faded! Thought and fancy have submerged into holy twilight, which spreads across delusion, redeeming the world. Then, when the illusion pales, when my eyes dim in ecstasy: that from which the lies of day excluded me, that which the lies deceptively pitted against the unquenchable torment of my yearning—even then, oh, miracle of fulfillment! even then *I* am the world. And Brangäne, darkly singing "Be on the watch," was accompanied by that soaring of the violins that transcends all reason.

"I don't understand everything, Herr Spinell, there's a lot that I only have inklings of. What does this mean: 'Even then *I* am the world'?"

He explained it to her, softly and briefly.

"Yes, that's what it is. But why is it that you understand it so well and yet you can't play it too?"

Strangely enough, he could not endure this harmless question. He reddened, wrung his hands, and virtually shrank away with his chair.

"The two seldom go together," he finally said in agony. "No, I can't play. But *you* go on."

And on they went in the drunken singing of the mystery play. Has love ever died? Tristan's love? The love of your Isolde and mine? Oh, the strokes of death never reach eternal love! What would die for him but that which disturbs us, which deceptively sunders those who are one? With a sweet "And love has joined them both," death tore it apart; how else but with the life of one could the other by death be undone? And a mysterious duet fused them in the nameless hope for the *Liebestod,* the love-death, for the finally unsevered envelopment in the wonder realm of night. Sweet night! Eternal night of love! All-encompassing land of bliss! If someone has sensed you and seen you, how could he ever awaken without anxiety and return to the desolate day? Exile anxiety, gracious death! Release the yearners utterly from the misery of awakening! Oh, bewildering tempest of rhythms! Oh, chromatically ascending ecstasy of metaphysical knowledge! How to grasp it, how to leave it, this bliss so far from the parting pains of light? Gentle yearning without deception or anxiety, sublime and painless fading, joyfully delirious twilight in boundlessness! You Isolde, Tristan I, Tristan no more, Isolde no more—

All at once, something dreadful occurred. The pianist stopped playing, she cupped her eyes with her hands and peered into the darkness, and Herr Spinell whirled around in his chair. The door at the back, leading to the corridor, had opened, and a dark figure shuffled in, leaning on the arm of a second figure. It was an Einfried patient who likewise had been unable to join the sleigh ride and instead was using this evening hour to take one of her dismal and instinctive walks through the institution. It was the sick woman who had given birth to nineteen children and was no longer capable of a single thought; it was Pastor Höhlenrauch's wife, on the arm of her nurse. Never looking up, she trudged along the back of the room, with fumbling, wandering steps, and vanished through the opposite door—mute and gaping, rambling and unaware. Silence prevailed.

"That was Frau Höhlenrauch, the pastor's wife," he said.

"Yes, that was poor Frau Höhlenrauch," she said. Then she turned some pages and played the finale of everything, played Isolde's *Liebestod.*

How clear and colorless her lips were, and how the shadows

deepened in the corners of her eyes! Above her eyebrow, in her transparent forehead, the tiny pale-blue vein, strained and unsettling, emerged more and more sharply. Under her flitting fingers, the music surged unbelievably, splintered by that sudden, almost ruthless pianissimo, which is like a floating away of the ground underfoot and like a sinking in sublime desire. The exuberance of a tremendous dissolution and fulfillment was repeated, a stunning roar of boundless satisfaction, insatiable, again and again, was reshaped as it flooded back, seemed to be trying to wane, melded the yearning motif once again into harmony, breathed its last, perished, faded, floated away.

Deep hush.

They both listened, tilted their heads to the side and listened.

"Those are bells," she said.

"It's the sleighs," he said. "I'm leaving."

He stood up and went across the room. Reaching the door at the back, he halted, turned around, and, for an instant, shifted nervously from one foot to the other. And then it happened: fifteen or twenty feet away from her, he sank to his knees, silently to both knees. His long black Prince Albert spread out on the floor. His hands were folded over his mouth, and his shoulders heaved.

She sat, holding her hands in her lap, leaning forward, away from the piano, and she gazed at him. An uncertain and distressed smile lay on her face, and her wistful eyes stared so arduously into the penumbra that they tended to shut.

From far away the jingling of bells drew closer and closer, the lashing of whips, and the jumble of human voices.

The sleigh ride, which everyone talked about for a long time, had taken place on February 26. On the twenty-seventh, when a thaw set in, with everything softening, dripping, splashing, flowing, Herr Klöterjahn's wife was in excellent health. On the twenty-eighth she coughed up a little blood. . . . Oh, insignificant; still, it *was* blood. She also felt faint, much more so than ever before, and so she stayed in bed.

Dr. Leander examined her, and his face was stone cold. Then he prescribed what is demanded by science: pieces of ice, morphine, absolute rest. Incidentally, the next day, the head physician, being overextended, withdrew from the case and transferred it to Dr. Müller, who dutifully and meekly took it over in accordance with his contract. He was a pale, quiet, gloomy, unimportant man, whose modest and inglorious activity was devoted to the almost healthy and the hopeless.

The opinion he mainly expressed was that the Klöterjahns had been separated for too long. It was urgently desirable, he said, for Herr Klöterjahn—if his flourishing business could possibly allow it—to visit Einfried again. They could write him, perhaps send him a brief wire. . . . And it would surely make the young mother happy and strengthen her if he also brought little Anton. Besides, it would be downright interesting for the physicians to make the acquaintance of that healthy little child.

And lo and behold, Herr Klöterjahn appeared. He had received Dr. Müller's brief wire and had come from the Baltic shore. He stepped down from the carriage, ordered coffee with rolls and butter, and looked very bewildered.

"Doctor," he said, "what's wrong? Why've I been summoned to her?"

"Because it is desirable," replied Dr. Müller, "for you to be near your wife now."

"Desirable . . . Desirable . . . But is it necessary? I'm concerned about my money, sir; the times are bad and trains are expensive. It took me a whole day to get here—wasn't my trip avoidable? I wouldn't mind if it were, say, her lungs. But since it's her windpipe, thank goodness—"

"Herr Klöterjahn," said Dr. Müller gently. "First of all, the windpipe is an important organ. . . ." That "first of all" was inaccurate, because he didn't follow it with a "secondly."

Together with Herr Klöterjahn, a voluptuous woman all in red, plaid, and gold had arrived at Einfried, and it was she who carried Anton Klöterjahn, Jr., healthy little Anton, on her arm. Yes, he was here, and no one could deny that he was indeed excessively healthy. Rosy and white, fat and fragrant, in fresh, clean clothes, he weighed down on the bare red arm of his gold-braided servant, devoured tremendous amounts of milk and chopped meat, bawled, and yielded to his instincts in every way, shape, and form.

Standing at the window of his room, Spinell, the writer, had watched the arrival of young Klöterjahn. With strange, partly closed, and yet piercing eyes, he had focused his gaze on the little boy as he was conveyed from the carriage to the house, and the writer had then remained in his place for a long time, with the same expression.

From then on he did his best to avoid any encounters with Anton Klöterjahn.

Herr Spinell sat in his room, "working."

It was a room like any other at Einfried: old-fashioned, simple, and distinguished. The massive bureau was mounted with metallic lions' heads; the high wall mirror was not a smooth surface but was composed of many small, square, leaded shards; no carpet covered the stone floor, which, painted bluish, extended the stiff legs of the furnishings as clear shadows. A spacious desk stood near the window, across which the novelist had drawn the yellow curtain—probably to make himself more introspective.

In yellowish twilight, he sat hunched over the desk, writing—writing one of those countless letters that he dispatched to the post office every week and to which, amusingly enough, he seldom received any answers. Before him lay a large sheet of thick stationery, at the top-left-hand corner of which, under an intricately drawn landscape, the name "Detlev Spinell" could be read in utterly novel letters. Spinell was covering the paper with a tiny, meticulously daubed, and exceedingly immaculate penmanship.

"Dear sir," it said. "I am addressing the following lines to you because I have no choice, because what I have to tell you fills me, torments me, and makes me tremble, because the words come flooding toward me so vehemently that I would choke on them if I could not unburden myself of them in this letter. . . ."

To give truth its due, that "flooding" was not quite the case, and God only knew the vain reasons why Herr Spinell asserted it. In no wise did the words seem to be flooding toward him; for someone whose stated profession was writing, he was woefully sluggish about getting started, and anybody watching him would have had to conclude that a writer is a man who has a more difficult time writing than anyone else.

With two fingertips, he clutched one of the strange bits of fuzz on his cheek, twirling it for whole quarters of an hour as he stared into space without advancing by a single line; then he wrote a few dainty words and stagnated again. On the other hand, we must admit that the eventual result made an impression of smoothness and liveliness, although the contents had a peculiar, questionable, and often even incomprehensible character.

It is [the letter went on] my imperative need to have you see what I see, what for weeks now has been hovering before my eyes as an indelible vision, to have you view it through my eyes, in the linguistic illumination in which it looms before my mind's eye. I am accustomed to yielding to this urge, which forces me to turn my experiences into those of the world, to employ unforgettable words that are blazingly apt and accurate. And you must therefore hear me out.

All I wish to do is say what was and is: I am merely telling a story, a very brief, ineffably outrageous story, telling it without commentary, without accusation or judgment, purely in my own words. It is the story of Gabriele Eckhof, sir, the woman whom you call your own. And mark my words! It was you who experienced the story, and yet it is I whose words will first truly lend that story the significance of an experience.

Do you remember the garden, sir, the old, overgrown garden behind the gray patrician mansion? The green moss sprouted in the crannies of the weathered walls that enclosed the dreamlike wilderness. Do you also remember the fountain in the center? Lilac-colored irises bowed over its crumbling circle, and its white spurt babbled down mysteriously upon the jagged stone. The summer day was drawing to its close.

Seven maidens sat in an orbit around the fountain; but in the hair of the Seventh, the First, the One, the setting sun seemed to be secretly weaving a shimmering insignia of supremacy. Her eyes were like anxious dreams, and yet her bright lips were smiling.

They sang. They held their slender faces up toward the acme of the gush, there where, in a weary and noble curve, the water was about to fall, and their soft, clear voices floated around that slender dance. Perhaps their delicate hands enfolded their knees as they sang.

Do you remember that scene, sir? Did you see it? You did not see it. Your eyes were not made to see that, nor your ears to hear the chaste sweetness of that melody. Had you seen it, you would not have dared to draw a breath. You would have ordered your heart to stop beating. You would have had to leave, return to life, to your life, and, for the rest of your earthly existence, guard that vision in your soul as a sacred object, inviolable and invulnerable. But what did you do?

That scene was an end, sir. Did you have to come and destroy it, in order to make it continue in vileness and ugly suffering? It was a poignant and peaceful apotheosis, dipped in the evening transfiguration of decay, dissolution, and decease. An old family, too weary by now and too refined to act and to live, is at the end of its days, and its final utterances are sounds of art, a few notes on a violin, full of the knowing melancholy of the readiness for death. Did you see the eyes from which those notes drew tears? The souls of the six companions may have belonged to Life; but the soul of their sisterly ruler belonged to Beauty and to Death.

You saw it, that deathly beauty: you looked at it in order to desire it. No trace of awe, no trace of timidity, touched your heart in the presence of that poignant holiness. It was not enough for you to look; you had to possess, exploit, desecrate. How fine was your choice! You are a gourmand, sir, a plebeian gourmand, a peasant with taste.

I beg you to note that I harbor absolutely no desire to offend you. What I am expressing is not a slur but the formula, the simple psychological formula, for your simple personality, which for literary purposes is utterly uninteresting. And I am articulating this only because I feel an urge to shed a bit of light on what you do and are, because it is my ineluctable vocation on earth to call a spade a spade, to make things speak, and to illuminate the unconscious. The world is full of what I call the "unconscious type"; and I cannot stand them, all those unconscious types! I cannot stand it—all this obtuse, ignorant, and unperceptive living and acting, this world of infuriating naïveté all about me! I feel an agonizingly irresistible urge to explain, express, and make people conscious of all existence all around—to my utmost strength—heedless of whether this entails a fostering or an inhibiting effect, whether this brings comfort and solace or inflicts pain.

You are, sir, as I have said, a plebeian gourmand, a peasant with taste. Actually of a crude constitution and on an extremely low evolutionary level, you attained, through your wealth and sedentary lifestyle, a sudden, unhistorical, and barbaric corruption of your nervous system, which involves a certain lascivious refinement of sybaritic self-indulgence. It is quite possible that when you decided to make Gabriele Eckhof your own, the muscles of your esophagus began to contract with a smacking sound, as if at the sight of a delicious soup or a rare dish.

Indeed, you lead her dreamy will astray, you take her from the overgrown garden out into life and ugliness. You give her your vulgar name and make her a wife, a housewife, make her a mother. You degrade the shy, weary, deathly Beauty, who blossomed in sublime uselessness, you degrade her in the service of common everyday life and of that stupid, hulking, and despicable idol known as "Nature," and not the slightest inkling of the profound baseness of that beginning so much as stirs in your peasant conscience.

Once again: What happens? She, with eyes that are anxious dreams, presents you with a child; and to this creature, who is a continuation of the sordidness of its begetting, she gives everything she has of blood and the possibility of Life, and then she dies. She is dying, sir! And if she does not pass away in vileness, if she nevertheless rises from depths of her degradation and, proud and blissful, perishes under the lethal kiss of Beauty, then that was *my* doing. Your concern meanwhile was probably to while away your time with chambermaids in secluded corridors.

But her child, Gabriele Eckhof's son, thrives, lives, and triumphs. Perhaps he will continue his father's life, becoming a tax-paying, well-eating, wheeling-dealing burgher; perhaps a soldier or government official, an ignorant and capable pillar of the state; in any case, an inartistic, normally functioning creature, strong and stupid, confident and unfazed by any qualms.

Allow me to confess to you, sir, that I hate you, you and your child, as much as I hate the kind of life, the common, the ridiculous, and yet triumphant life, that you embody, the eternal antithesis to and deadly enemy of Beauty. I cannot tell you that I despise you. I am unable to despise you. I am honest enough to say so. You are the stronger. I have but one thing to pit against you in the struggle, the sublime weapon and tool of revenge for the weak: intellect and language. Today I have made use of them. For this letter (I am honest here too, sir) is nothing but an act of revenge, and if but a single word of it is sharp, lustrous, and beautiful enough to have struck you, to have made you feel an alien power, rattled your equanimity for even an instant, then I shall gloat.

Detlev Spinell

And Herr Spinell put this document in an envelope, applied stamps, provided it with a daintily written address, and dispatched it to the post office.

Herr Klöterjahn knocked on Herr Spinell's door. He held a large, neatly written sheet of paper in his hand, and he looked like a man who is determined to put his foot down. The post office had done its duty, the letter had gone its route, it had completed its peculiar trip from Einfried to Einfried and had duly reached the hands of the addressee. It was four o'clock in the afternoon.

When Herr Klöterjahn entered, Herr Spinell was sitting on the sofa, reading his own novel with the bewildering jacket design. He stood up and eyed the visitor, surprised and quizzical, though clearly blushing.

"Good day," said Herr Klöterjahn. "Excuse me for disturbing you when you're so busy. But may I ask whether you wrote this?" His left hand held up a large sheet of paper covered with neat writing, while the back of his right hand struck it hard enough to make it crackle. Thereupon he shoved his right hand into the pocket of his loose, comfortable trousers, tilted his head to one side, and, as some people do, opened his mouth the better to listen.

Oddly enough, Herr Spinell smiled; he smiled accommodatingly, a bit confused and half apologetic, put his hand on his forehead as if pondering, and said:

"Yes, right . . . yes . . . I took the liberty . . ."

The thing was that today he had been true to himself and had slept almost till noon. As a result, he suffered from a bad conscience and a dull mind and felt nervous and highly vulnerable. Furthermore, the spring air that had wafted in made him feel weary and somewhat despairing. All this must be mentioned to explain why he cut such an utterly silly figure during this scene.

"I see! Aha! Fine!" said Herr Klöterjahn, poking his chin into his chest, drawing up his eyebrows, and stretching his arms. Having acquitted himself of his rhetorical question, he made a number of similar preparations to ruthlessly get down to brass tacks. Delighting in his own antics, he went a bit too far: the ultimate outcome was not quite in keeping with the menacing ceremonial of this precautionary dumb show. Yet Herr Spinell was rather pale.

"Very fine!" Herr Klöterjahn went on. "Then you'll get your answer in person, my good man, and since I find it moronic to write pages and pages of letters to someone you can talk to any time—"

"Well, now . . . moronic," said Herr Spinell with a smile, apologetic and almost humble.

"Moronic!" Herr Klöterjahn repeated, vehemently shaking his head to show how unimpeachably certain he was of his cause. "And I wouldn't dignify your scribbling with a single word; it simply wouldn't even be good enough, frankly, to wrap a sandwich in, if it didn't enlighten me about certain things that I didn't previously understand, certain changes. . . . But that's none of your business, and it's not relevant to the matter at hand. I'm a man of action; I've got more important things to worry about than your inexpressible visions—"

"I wrote 'indelible vision,' " said Herr Spinell, drawing himself up full-length. It was the only moment of this scene in which he displayed a modicum of dignity.

"Indelible . . . inexpressible . . . !" retorted Herr Klöterjahn, eyeing the manuscript. "Your handwriting is miserable, my good man; I wouldn't hire you for my office. At first glance your penmanship looks quite neat, but if you hold it up to the light it's totally defective and shaky. However, that's your business, it doesn't concern me in the least. I've come to tell you that, first of all, you're a buffoon—well, I hope you realize that already. Furthermore, you're a big coward, and I probably don't have to prove that to you in detail either. My wife once wrote me that when you meet women, you don't look them square in the face, you just peep at them from the side in order to carry off a lovely inkling, because you're scared of reality. Too bad she eventually stopped mentioning you in her letters; otherwise I'd know more stuff about you. But that's the way you are. Your every other word is 'Beauty,' but basically it's totally chickenhearted and sanctimonious and envious, and that explains your brazen remark about 'secluded corridors,' which was supposed to hit me where it hurts, but I simply got a kick out of it. I got a *kick* out of it! Well, do you get the picture now? Have I now 'shed a little light' for you on what . . . 'what you do and are,' you spineless creep? Even though it's not my 'inevitable vocation,' heh-heh!"

"I wrote 'ineluctable vocation,' " said Herr Spinell; but then he promptly gave up. He stood there, helpless after being raked over the coals, like a big, wretched, gray-haired schoolboy.

"Ineluctable . . . inevitable . . . You're a low-down coward, I tell you. You see me at meals every day. You greet me and smile. You pass bowls to me and smile. You wish me 'bon appétit.' And then one day you dump this garbage on me, and it's full of moronic insults. Yes, when you write you've got courage, eh! And if it were only this laughable letter. But you plotted against me, plotted against me behind my back—I completely understand it now . . . although you needn't flatter yourself that it did you any good! If you're indulging any hope that you've put a bee in my wife's bonnet, then you're barking up the wrong tree, my esteemed friend. She's much too level-headed for that! Or if you actually believe that she greeted me any differently than normal, me and the child, when we came, then that puts the lid on your tactlessness. She may not have kissed the boy, but she was being cautious because recently the hypothesis came up that it's not her windpipe, it's her lungs, and in that case you never can tell . . . although it still really remains to be proved, incidentally, that business about the lungs, and you and your 'She dies, sir!' You're an ass!"

Here Herr Klöterjahn tried to regain his breath. He was completely beside himself; he kept thrusting his right forefinger in the air, while his left hand was maltreating the manuscript dreadfully. His face, between the blond English whiskers, was horribly red, and his clouded brow was shredded by swollen veins as if by bolts of wrath.

"You hate me," he continued, "and you'd despise me if I weren't the stronger one. . . . Yes, that's what I am, damn it; my heart's in the right place, while yours must be mostly in your pants, and I'd beat the crap out of you, together with your 'intellect and language,' you devious idiot, if it weren't illegal. But that doesn't mean, friend, that I'm simply going to swallow your invectives, and when I show that business about the 'vulgar name' to my attorney at home, then we'll see if you don't get the surprise of your life! I've got a good name, sir, and I've earned it myself. And as for whether anyone would lend even a copper penny on your name, you can debate that question with yourself, you loafer, you vagrant! They oughta throw the book at you! You're a menace to society! You drive people crazy! . . . But don't flatter yourself—you didn't get away with it this time. You back-stabbing numskull! I'm not gonna be licked by characters like you. My heart's in the right place. . . ."

Herr Klöterjahn was now really extremely angry. He kept yelling and bellowing that his heart was in the right place.

" 'They sang.' Wrong. They never sang! They knitted. Besides, so far as I could make out, they were talking about a recipe for potato pancakes, and if I tell my father-in-law about the 'decay' and the 'dissolution,' then he'll take you to court too—you can count on it! . . . 'Do you remember the scene? Did you see it?' Of course I saw it, but I don't understand why I should hold my breath and run away. I don't peep past women's faces, I look at them, and if I like them and if they want me, then I take them. My heart's in the right pl—"

There was a knock. It was instantly followed by a quick run of nine or ten knocks on the door to the room—a small, vehement, frantic drumroll that silenced Herr Klöterjahn, and a voice that had lost its hold and was about to come unstrung out of sheer anxiety said in utmost haste:

"Herr Klöterjahn, Herr Klöterjahn, oh, is Herr Klöterjahn there?"

"Stay outside," Herr Klöterjahn snapped gruffly. "What's wrong? I'm busy talking here."

"Herr Klöterjahn," said the faltering, breaking voice. "You have to come. . . . The doctors are here too. . . . Oh, it's so dreadfully sad. . . ."

He reached the door in one stride and yanked it open. Frau Spatz stood outside. She held her handkerchief to her mouth, and pairs of big, longish tears rolled into the cloth.

"Herr Klöterjahn," she managed to utter, "it's so dreadfully sad. . . . She brought up so much blood, so horribly much. . . . She was sitting up in bed very calmly and humming some music to herself, and then it came, good Lord, such a huge amount. . . ."

"Is she dead?" shouted Herr Klöterjahn. He grabbed Frau Spatz's upper arm and pulled her to and fro on the threshold. "No, not entirely, huh? Not entirely, she can still see me. . . . Did she bring up a little blood again? From the lungs, huh? I admit it may come from her lungs. . . . Gabriele!" he suddenly said, with gaping eyes, and they saw a good, warm, human, and sincere emotion erupting from him. "Yes, I'm coming!" he said, and taking long strides, he dragged the town councillor's wife out of the room and down the corridor. From a remote part of the covered walk, his words, which were dashing farther and farther away, could still be heard: "Not entirely, huh? . . . From the lungs, eh?"

Herr Spinell stood on the spot where he had stood during Herr Klöterjahn's so suddenly disrupted visit, and he gazed at the open door. At last he took a few steps and listened into the distance. But everything was still, and so he went back into the room and shut the door.

For a while he viewed himself in the mirror. Next, he went over to the desk, produced a small cut-glass carafe and a small snifter from a shelf, and drank a cognac—for which no human being could blame him. Then he stretched out on the sofa and closed his eyes.

The upper transom of the window was open. Outside, in the garden of Einfried, the birds were chirping, and these small, bold, tender sounds, fine and penetrating, expressed the entire springtime. At one point Herr Spinell murmured to himself: "Inevitable vocation . . ." Then he moved his head back and forth, drawing the air in through his teeth as if suffering from a violent nervous pain.

It was impossible for him to relax and compose himself. A man isn't made for such gross experiences! Through a spiritual process, whose analysis would lead us too far afield, Herr Spinell reached the decision to stand up and get a little exercise, go for a stroll outdoors. So he took his hat and left the room.

As he emerged from the house and the mild, fragrant air swirled around him, he turned his head. His eyes slowly glided up the building to a window, a curtained window, where his gaze lingered for a while, firm, dark, and earnest. Then he put his hands behind his back and strode along the gravel paths. He strode in deep thought.

The flower beds were still covered with mats, and trees and shrubs were still naked; but the snow was gone, and the paths showed moist traces only here and there. The vast garden with its grottoes, pergolas, and small pavilions lay in splendid colors of afternoon illumination, with intense shadows and mellow golden light, and the dark branches of the trees stood sharp and delicately articulated against the bright sky.

It was the hour when the sun takes shape, when the formless light mass turns into the visibly sinking disk, whose richer, milder glow is tolerated by the eyes. Herr Spinell did not see the sun; the path ran in such a way that for him the sun was covered and concealed. He walked with a lowered head, humming a strain of music to himself, a brief passage, a rising figure, anxious and lamenting, the yearning motif. . . . Suddenly, however, heaving a short, convulsive sigh of relief, he jerked to a halt, spellbound, and from under violently contracted eyebrows his widened eyes gawked straight ahead with an expression of horrified repugnance. . . .

The path twisted; it now led toward the setting sun. Streaked by two narrow, luminous strips of clouds with golden linings, the sun loomed large and slanting in the sky, setting the treetops aglow and pouring its yellow-reddish brilliance over the garden. And in the midst of that golden transfiguration, someone stood with the tremendous gloriole of the sun around her head, stood tall and straight on the path, a sumptuous woman dressed all in red, gold, and plaid, her right hand propped on her swelling hip, her left hand gently rocking a graceful little carriage to and fro. And in that carriage sat the child, sat Anton Klöterjahn, Jr., sat Gabriele Eckhof's fat son!

He sat in the pillows, wearing a white woolly jacket and a large white hat, chubby-cheeked, splendid, and well-wrought, and his merry eyes unswervingly encountered Herr Spinell's eyes. The novelist was about to pull himself together; he was a grown man, he was strong enough to march past this unexpected, lustrous manifestation and continue his stroll. But then the horrible thing happened. Anton Klöterjahn began to laugh jubilantly; he shrieked with such inexplicable pleasure that it became downright eerie.

Goodness knows what had set him off, whether his wild hilarity was triggered by the sight of that black figure or whether he was seized with some fit of animal well-being. He held a bone teething ring in one hand and a tin rattle in the other. Exultantly he stretched both these objects up into the sunshine, shook them, and banged them together as if ridiculing someone and shooing him away. His eyes were almost shut in delight, and his mouth gaped so wide that it exposed his entire rosy palate. He even tossed his head to and fro as he exulted.

Herr Spinell spun around and walked off. Followed by little Klöterjahn's jubilation, he walked over the gravel, holding his arms with a certain caution and stiff grace, and his steps were hesitant, like those of a man trying to hide the fact that he is mentally running away.

# THE STARVELINGS

## A STUDY

THE MOMENT CAME when Detlef was profoundly over-whelmed by a sense of his own superfluousness, and so he let himself be swept away, as if unexpectedly, by the festive swarm, vanishing from the sight of those two people without saying goodbye.

Abandoning himself to a torrent that carried him along one wall of the sumptuous theater auditorium, he offered no resistance and gained no solid foothold until he knew that he was far away from Lilli and the short painter. Near the stage, leaning against the thickly gilded arch of a proscenium box, he stood between a bearded Baroque caryatid with a neck bent by his burden and a female counterpart who thrust a pair of swelling breasts out into the auditorium. Convincing or not, Detlef assumed the posture of a complacent observer, occasionally lifting his opera glass to his eyes, which, when scanning the theater, avoided only one spot in the radiant circle.

The party was in full swing. In back of the protruding boxes, people were dining and drinking at covered tables, while at the balustrades, gentlemen in black or colored tuxedos, sporting gigantic chrysanthemums in their buttonholes, bent over the powdered shoulders of women who were clad fantastically and coiffed extravagantly. The chatting gentlemen pointed down at the exuberant bustle, which broke up into groups, gushed along, clogged, whirled, eddied, and then thinned out into a swift blaze of colors. . . . Propped on long staves, the women, clad in flowing gowns and in hats like poke bonnets, with grotesque bows under their chins, peered through lorgnettes with long handles, while the men's puffed sleeves towered almost to the brims of their gray top hats.

Loud jokes soared up to the tiers and were toasted there by raised glasses of beer or champagne. Craning their necks, the merrymakers thronged in front of the open stage and shrieked vividly at some outlandish performance. Then, when the curtain rustled to a close, they pushed back, laughing and cheering. The orchestra surged up. People strolled and milled chaotically. And throughout the lavish space, all eyes shone with a golden-yellow light that was far brighter than day, while everyone, breathing rapidly with promiscuous desire, sucked in the warm, arousing smells of wine and flowers, of food, dust, powder, perfume, and festively heated bodies. . . .

The orchestra broke off. People stood still, arm in arm, looking mirthfully at the stage, where something new was happening amid squawks and sighs. Four or five people in peasant costumes, playing clarinets and twangy stringed instruments, were lampooning the chromatic struggle of Wagner's *Tristan*. . . . For an instant, Detlef closed his burning eyes. His mind was such that he had to catch the passionate yearning for unity that spoke from those notes even when mischievously warped. And suddenly it swelled up in him again, the suffocating melancholy of the lonely man who has lost himself in jealous love for some radiant and ordinary creature.

Lilli . . . His soul formed the name out of pleading and tenderness; and now he could no longer stop his eyes from darting secretly to that distant spot. . . . Yes, she was still there, still standing back there, in the same place where he had left her. And at times, when the crowd thinned, he viewed her full-length in her milky-white, silver-studded gown. With her hands behind her back and her blond head at a slight angle, she leaned against the wall, chatting with the short painter, staring teasingly into his eyes, which were as blue as hers, as open and undimmed. . . .

What were they talking about, just what were they still talking

about? Oh, that chitchat, pouring so easily and effortlessly from
the inexhaustible wellspring of harmless, unpretentious innocence and liveliness; and he did not know how to participate, for
he had been rendered slow and earnest by a life of reverie and
knowledge, by paralyzing insights and the tribulations of creativity! So he had gone off, had stolen away in a fit of despair, defiance, and magnanimity, leaving the two creatures to their own
devices; but from a distance, choking with jealousy, he spotted
their smiles of relief and approval upon being rid of his intrusive
presence.

Why had he come, just why had he come here again today?
What drove him to torture himself by mingling with this unin-
hibited mob, which surrounded and agitated him without ever
actually taking him in? He knew that longing so well! "We lonely
ones," he had once written somewhere, in a moment of hushed
confession, "we solitary dreamers, disinherited by life and
brooding our days away in an icy and artificial world that is aside
and apart . . . we who spread a cold breath of indomitable alienation around us the instant we appear among living creatures, our
foreheads bearing the mark of knowledge and despair . . . we
poor ghosts of existence, who are met with timid respect and
who are left to ourselves as soon as possible so that our hollow
and knowing eyes may no longer blight the festivities . . . we all
nurture within ourselves a secret and degenerative yearning for
the harmless, the simple, the lively, for a little friendship, devotion, intimacy, and human happiness. 'Life,' from which we are
excluded, never presents itself to us, the unusual ones, as something unusual, as a vision of utter grandeur and wild beauty; instead we yearn for what is normal, decent, and kind, the things
that make up life in its seductive banality. . . ."

He glanced over at the chatting couple, while throughout the
auditorium good-natured laughter interrupted the clarinets,
which were distorting the sweet and heavy melos of love into
shrill sentimentality. . . . "You people are life," he said to himself.

"You are warm, sweet, foolish life, the eternal antithesis to the intellect. Do not think that the intellect despises you people. Do not think that it reveals even a glance of disdain. We sneak after you, we deep fiends, we demons mute with knowledge; we stand far away, and our eyes ogle you greedily, burning with a lust to be like you.

"Is pride stirring? Would it deny that we are lonely? Is it boasting that the works of the intellect assure love a higher fusion with the living everywhere and evermore? Ah, but with whom? With whom? Why, only with our own kind, with the poor, who yearn and suffer, but never with you, the blue-eyed people, who never need the intellect!"

The stage performances were over, and now the merrymakers were dancing. The orchestra blared and crooned. On the smooth floor, the couples slid and swayed and curved. And Lilli was dancing with the short painter. How daintily her sweet little head rose from the calyx of the stiff collar with its silver embroidery! Gliding and turning sedately and buoyantly, the couple moved around the narrow area; his face was toward hers, and in restrained obeisance to the sweet triviality of the rhythms, they continued chatting and smiling.

All at once, the lonely man felt as if his hands were reaching out, were gripping and shaping. "The two of you are mine all the same," he said to himself, "and I am above you! Don't I see through your simple souls and grin? Don't I notice and preserve with sarcastic love every naive stirring of your bodies? When I watch your heedless activities, don't I feel the tense strength of language and irony inside myself so that my heart beats with a pleasurable sense of power, a lust to emulate you playfully and to let the light of my art expose your ludicrous happiness to the feelings of the world? . . ."

But now his edifice of defiance collapsed and left nothing but weary yearning. Oh, to be a human being instead of an artist just once, on a night like this! To flee, just once, the curse that states unswervingly: "You cannot be, you must look; you cannot live, you must create; you cannot love, you must know!" Oh, to live, love, and laud just once and experience frank and forthright emotions! To be among you, just once, be in you, be you, you living beings! To lap you up, just once, in delightful sips—you bliss of normality!

He winced, turned away. He felt as if an expression of inquiry and repulsion would emerge on all these flushed, pretty faces, were they to become aware of him. All at once, he was overcome with an irresistible wish to quit the field, to find stillness and darkness. Yes, leave, retreat completely, without saying goodbye, just as he had retreated from Lilli's side—go home and place his wretchedly hot and intoxicated head on a cool pillow. He strode toward the exit.

Would she notice? He was so familiar with this action, this kind of departure, this proud, silent, desperate withdrawal from a room, a garden, from some place of convivial cheer—and always he secretly hoped that he would thereby briefly darken the thoughts of the radiant object of his desire, cause her a quick moment of bewildered reflection, of compassion. . . . He halted, stealing another glance. He mentally pleaded. Should he linger, endure, remain with her, though at a distance, and await some sort of unexpected happiness? No use. There was no approach, no communication, no hope. Go, go into the darkness, bury your head in your hands and weep, if you can, if there are tears in your world of petrifaction, of ice, bleakness, intellect, and art! He left the auditorium.

His chest was filled with a burning, quietly piercing pain and also a senseless, irrational expectation. . . . She had to see it, had to understand, had to come, follow him, if only out of pity, had to stop him in his tracks and say: "Stay here, be cheerful, I love you." And he sauntered very slowly, even though he realized, was laughably certain, that she would never come—little dancing, chatting Lilli. . . .

It was two A.M. The corridors were deserted, and the wardrobe women were nodding drowsily behind their long tables. No one aside from him dreamed of going home. He shrouded himself in his coat, took his hat and his cane, and left the theater.

Out on the square, in the whitish fog of the illuminated winter night, the carriages stood in a long row. With drooping heads, the blanketed horses waited in front of the vehicles, while groups of bundled-up coachmen stamped their feet on the hard snow. Detlef hailed one of them, and while the man prepared his animal, Detlef lingered in the doorway of the bright lobby, letting the cold, bracing air play around his throbbing temples.

The stale aftertaste of the bubbly wine made him hanker for a smoke. Mechanically he drew out a cigarette, struck a match, and lit up. And at that instant, as the tiny flame went out, something happened to him, something that he did not grasp at first, something that left him perplexed and aghast, with dangling arms, something that he could not get over, could not forget. . . .

As his eyesight, blinded by the small flame, recovered, a haggard, dissipated, red-bearded face emerged from the darkness, its horribly inflamed, red-rimmed eyes gaping into Detlef's eyes, glaring wild and scornful, and greedily scrutinizing him. . . . A mere two or three steps away, his fists buried in the deep pockets of his trousers, the collar of his ragged jacket turned up, the owner of this woebegone face slouched against one of the lampposts flanking the entrance to the theater. His gaze wandered over Detlef's entire figure, over his fur coat with the hanging opera glass, down to his patent-leather shoes; then the stranger's gaze bored into Detlef's with that lecherous and greedy probing. One single time the man let out a brief and scornful snort. . . . And then his body shuddered in the frost, his slack cheeks seemed even more haggard, while his lids trembled shut and the corners of his mouth twitched down, both malignant and careworn.

Detlef stood there, petrified. He struggled to understand. . . .

He suddenly grew conscious of the air of ease and luxury with which he, the partygoer, had walked out of the lobby, hailed the coachman, and removed the cigarette from his silver box. Involuntarily he raised his hand in order to bang it on his head. He stepped toward the man, he took a deep breath in order to speak, to explain. . . . But then he wordlessly mounted the waiting carriage, almost forgetting to tell the coachman his address. He was beside himself, rattled by the impossibility of clearing things up.

What a mistake, my God! What a dreadful misunderstanding! That destitute outcast glowered at him greedily and bitterly, with the tremendous scorn caused by envy and yearning! Hadn't he virtually flaunted himself—that starveling? Weren't his shivers, his careworn and malignant grimace, supposed to bring him, the arrogantly happy man, a moment of gloom, bewildered reflection, and compassion? You're wrong, friend, you've missed the mark: your pitiful sight is no terrifying and humbling warning from an awful, alien world. *We are brothers, after all!*

Is it located here, friend, here above the chest, and does it burn? I know it all too well! And why have you come? Why don't you remain in the shadows, proud and defiant? Why do you stand under lit windows, listening to the music and the laughter of life behind them? Don't I, too, know that morbid longing that has driven you here to nourish your misery, which can just as easily be called love as hate?

Nothing is alien to me in all the misery you're imbued with, and you thought you could shame me! What is intellect? Playful hatred! What is art? Creative desire! We are both at home in the land of the betrayed, the land of the starvelings, the accusers, the deniers, and we also share the treacherous hours of self-hatred, hours that we waste in disgraceful love, that we lose to life, to foolish happiness. But you did not recognize me.

Wrong! Wrong! . . . And how thoroughly this pity filled him, and deep, deep down he felt a both sweet and painful inkling. . . . Is that man the only one who's mistaken? Where does the mistake end? Isn't all yearning on earth a mistake—most of all my yearning, for simple and instinctive life, mute life that is not transfigured by art and intellect, not redeemed by language? Ah, we are all brothers, we creatures of a will that suffers without peace; and we do not recognize one another. We need a different love, a different love. . . .

And at home, while sitting among his books, paintings, and silent, gazing busts, he was moved by these mild words: "Children, love one another. . . ."

# TONIO KRÖGER

# CHAPTER ONE

THE WINTER SUN was only a meager glow, milky and matte behind layers of clouds above the cramped town. The narrow streets lined with gabled houses were wet and windy, and sometimes a kind of soft hail fell, not ice, not snow.

School was out. The troops of liberated children poured across the cobbled courtyard and through the barred gate, dispersing and hurrying right or left. With dignity, tall schoolboys held their packs of books against their left shoulders, rowing against the wind with their right arms as they headed toward their lunches. Young boys trotted off cheerfully, splattering the slush all around, while the paraphernalia of knowledge rattled in their sealskin satchels. But now and then, with awe-filled eyes, all the students yanked off their caps in deference to the Wodin hat and Jupiter beard of a gravely striding teacher. . . .

"Are you coming, Hans?" said Tonio Kröger, who had been waiting and waiting in the street. With a smile, he moved toward his friend, who emerged through the gate, conversing with schoolmates and about to take off with them. "What do you mean?" he asked, looking at Tonio. "Oh, that's right! Okay, let's walk a little."

Tonio clammed up, and his eyes dimmed. Had Hans forgotten, had he recalled only now that they had planned a little stroll this afternoon? And Tonio had been looking forward to it almost incessantly ever since making the appointment!

"Yeah. So long, guys!" Hans Hansen said to his chums. "I'm

taking a little walk with Kröger." And the two boys turned left, while the others sauntered to the right.

Hans and Tonio had time for strolling after school because both their families did not have lunch until four in the afternoon. Their fathers were prominent businessmen, who held public offices and had great clout in the town. For generations the Hansens had owned the vast lumberyards down by the river, where huge power saws hissed and snarled as they sliced up tree trunks. Tonio, however, was the son of Consul Kröger, whose grain sacks, bearing the name of the firm in broad black letters, could be seen rolling through the streets day after day; and his big, ancient ancestral home was the lordliest mansion in town. The two friends had to keep doffing their caps because they had so many acquaintances—indeed, some adults even anticipated the fourteen-year-olds in their greetings. . . .

Both had slung their satchels over their shoulders, and both were dressed well and warmly: Hans in a short peacoat, with the wide blue collar of his sailor suit turned out on his back and shoulders, and Tonio in a gray belted topcoat. Hans wore a Danish naval cap with short ribbons, from which a shock of his bright-blond hair welled out. He was extremely handsome and well built, broad in his shoulders and narrow in his hips, with keen steel-blue eyes, set far apart. Tonio, however, was dark, with a sharply chiseled, entirely southern face and dreamy eyes in delicate and gloomy shadows, with overly heavy lids, peering a bit timidly from under his round fur cap. His mouth and chin had unusually soft outlines. His walk was careless and uneven, while Hans's slender legs strode along in their black stockings with a steady, buoyant rhythm. . . .

Tonio held his tongue. He was in pain. Drawing his somewhat diagonal eyebrows together, puckering his lips to whistle, and tilting his head, he gazed askance into the distance. This posture and expression were peculiar to him. All at once, Hans, looking at him from the side, slipped his arm into Tonio's, for he was quite aware of what was going on. And even though Tonio remained silent during their next few steps, he suddenly felt quite mellow.

"I didn't forget, you know, Tonio," said Hans, staring at the sidewalk. "I just figured it wouldn't work out today because it's so wet and windy. But that doesn't faze me, and I think it's fabulous that you waited for me all the same. I figured you'd gone home already, and I was annoyed. . . ."

At these words, everything in Tonio surged and bounded in sheer jubilation.

"Yes, so then let's go by way of the walls!" he said in a trembling voice. "Over the Mill Wall and the Holstein Wall, and I'll walk you home, Hans. . . . I'll go back alone, but that doesn't matter at all—next time you'll walk *me* home."

Basically he didn't have much faith in what Hans had said, and he knew very well that Hans cared only half as much about their walk as Tonio. But he did see that Hans regretted his forgetfulness and was intent on reconciling. And Tonio had no intention whatsoever of delaying their reconciliation.

For you see, Tonio loved Hans Hansen and had already suffered a great deal because of him. The person who loves more is the underdog and has to suffer: life had already taught this harsh and simple lesson to Tonio's fourteen-year-old soul, and he was the sort of person who registered such experiences, wrote them down mentally, as it were, and somewhat enjoyed them, without, of course, drawing any practical benefit by acting on them. His makeup was such that he found these lessons far more crucial and far more interesting than the knowledge forced upon him at school. Indeed, during instruction under the Gothic vaults of the classroom, he usually occupied himself with feeling such insights to their very depths and thoroughly mulling them over. And this process gave him a satisfaction similar to the one he experienced when he moved around his room with his violin (for he played the violin), producing the notes as softly as he possibly could and blending them into the splashing of the fountain, where the jet of water spurted and capered under the branches of the old walnut tree.

The fountain, the old walnut tree, his violin, and the faraway sea, the Baltic, whose summer dreams he could listen to during vacation—these were the things he loved, and surrounded himself with, living his inner life among them. These were things that can effectively be named in poems and that actually kept recurring in the verses that Tonio Kröger occasionally penned.

He preserved these writings in a notebook, whose existence leaked out through his own error, causing him a great deal of trouble among his schoolmates as well as his teachers. On the one hand, Consul Kröger's son felt it was stupid and nasty of them to be scandalized, and so he detested both his schoolmates and his teachers; he was also offended by their ill breeding, and he saw through their personal foibles in an uncommonly penetrating way. On the other hand, Tonio Kröger himself felt that it was wanton and really inappropriate to write poems, and to a certain extent he had to agree with all the people who regarded it as a disconcerting pursuit. But these qualms did not prevent him from going on.

Since he frittered his time away at home and was slow and inattentive at school, thereby displeasing his teachers, he kept bringing home the most dreadful report cards, which greatly troubled and angered his father, a tall, impeccably dressed gentleman, who had pensive blue eyes and always wore a wildflower in his buttonhole. However, Tonio's marks were of no consequence to his mother, his beautiful black-haired mother, whose first name was Consuelo and who was altogether different from the other women in town because his father had brought her here from way below on the map.

Tonio loved his dark and fiery mother, who played the piano and the mandolin so wonderfully, and he was glad she didn't fret about his dubious position in the world. But then again, he felt that his father's anger was far more dignified and respectable, and, though scolded by him, Tonio at bottom fully agreed, whereas he found his mother's indifference a bit wanton. At times he thought more or less: It's quite enough that I am what I am and that I won't or can't change, that I'm negligent and unruly and think about things that no one else thinks about. And so they're right to scold me and punish me, rather than ignoring it with kisses and music. After all, we're no Gypsies in a green wagon, we're decent people, Consul Krögers, the Kröger family. . . .

And sometimes he also thought: Just why am I so strange and in conflict with everyone, on bad terms with the teachers and alien among the other boys? Look at them, the good pupils and the ones who are solidly mediocre. They don't find the teachers ludicrous, they don't write poems, and they think only things that people normally think and that they can express out loud. How proper they must feel, in agreement with everything and everyone! That must be nice. . . . But what's wrong with me, and how will it all end?

This practice of mulling about himself and his relationship to life played an important role in Tonio's love for Hans Hansen. He loved him first of all because he was beautiful; but then because he was Tonio's opposite and counterpart in all respects. Hans Hansen was an excellent student and also lively and breezy: he rode horseback, did gymnastics, swam like a star athlete, and was extremely popular. The teachers liked him almost tenderly, addressed him by his first name, and helped him along in every way, while his schoolmates vied for his favor. In the street, ladies and gentlemen would stop him, grab the shock of bright-blond hair welling out from his Danish naval cap, and say: "Good day, Hans Hansen, with your pretty shock of hair! Are you still first in your class? Say hello to Papa and Mama, my splendid lad. . . ."

That was Hans Hansen, and ever since first meeting him,

Tonio Kröger had felt a yearning whenever he looked at Hans, an envious longing that burned above his chest. To have such blue eyes, thought Tonio, and to live in such orderly and happy conformity with the whole world as you do! You're always occupied with something wholesome that's respected by everyone. When you've done your homework, you take riding lessons or work with your fretsaw. And even during vacation, you're busy rowing, sailing, and swimming, while I lie in the sand, idle and lost, staring at the mysterious changes that flit across the face of the sea. But that's why your eyes are so clear. To be like you . . . .

He made no effort to be like Hans Hansen, and his wish may not even have been very earnest. But Tonio painfully desired to be loved by him just as he was, and he courted his love in his own way, a slow and affectionate, a devoted, suffering, and melancholy way—a melancholy that can burn and devour more deeply than any sudden blaze of passion that might be expected of someone with Tonio's exotic appearance.

And his courtship was not fully in vain. For one thing, Hans respected a certain superiority in Tonio, his verbal fluency, which enabled Tonio to express difficult thoughts. Altogether, Hans realized that Tonio had an unusually strong and tender feeling for him; Hans showed his gratitude and made Tonio happy by responding somewhat—but Hans also caused pangs of jealousy and frustration in Tonio, who made futile attempts to create a mental and spiritual rapport with him. For oddly enough, while Tonio envied Hans Hansen for his mode of life, he constantly tried to draw him over to his own, succeeding at best for moments at a time and then only superficially. . . .

"I've just read something wonderful, something incredible. . . ," said Tonio. They walked along, eating from a bag of fruit drops that they had bought for ten pfennigs at Iwersen's shop on Mill Street. "You've got to read it, Hans—it's Schiller's *Don Carlos.* I'll lend it to you if you like."

"Oh, no," said Hans Hansen. "Don't bother, Tonio, it's not

for me. I'll stick to my horse books, you know. They've got fabulous pictures, I tell you. I'll show them to you the next time you come over. They're high-speed photos, and you see the horses trotting and galloping and hurdling, in all positions, which you can never see in real life because it all happens too fast. . . ."

"In all positions?" Tonio said courteously. "Yes, that's fine. But *Don Carlos* is unbelievable. There are passages—you ought to see them. They're so beautiful they give you a jolt; they practically explode—"

"Explode?" asked Hans Hansen. "What do you mean?"

"Well, for instance, there's the scene where the king cries because he's been deceived by the Marquis de Posa. But the marquis has deceived him only for the sake of the king's son, you understand, because the marquis is sacrificing himself for the prince. And now the news comes from the king's private cabinet to the antechamber: The king has wept. 'He's wept? The king has wept?'

"All the courtiers are horribly embarrassed, and it's totally overwhelming, because the king is always so terribly stiff and stern. But you can easily understand why he's cried, and I feel sorrier for him than for the prince and the marquis combined. The king is always so alone and without love, and now he believes he's found someone, and that man betrays him. . . ."

Hans Hansen looked sideways at Tonio's face, and something in its expression must have won him over, for he suddenly slipped his arm back into Tonio's and asked:

"How does he betray him, Tonio?"

Tonio geared up.

"Well," he began, "you see, all letters to Brabant and Flanders—"

"Here comes Erwin Jimmerthal," said Hans.

Tonio fell silent. He can go to hell, Tonio thought, that Erwin Jimmerthal! Why does he have to come and bother us? If only he doesn't join us and talk about riding lessons all the way home! . . .

For Erwin Jimmerthal also took riding lessons. He was the son of the bank president, who lived out here, beyond the town gates. With his bowlegs and slanting eyes, he walked toward them along the avenue; he had no schoolbag by now.

"Hi, Jimmerthal," said Hans. "I'm walking a little with Kröger."

"I have to go downtown and get something. But I'll walk with you a ways. . . . Those are fruit drops, aren't they? Yeah, thanks, I'll have a couple. Tomorrow we've got another lesson, Hans." He was referring to their riding lesson.

"Fabulous!" said Hans. "Y'know, my parents are giving me a pair of leather gaiters because I got an A on my composition."

"You don't take riding lessons, do you, Kröger?" asked Jimmerthal, and his eyes were a pair of shiny slits.

"No. . . ," replied Tonio with a faltering inflection.

"You should ask your father to let you take lessons too, Kröger," Hans Hansen remarked

"Yes. . . ," said Tonio, his voice hasty but indifferent. He choked for an instant because Hans had addressed him by his last name; and Hans appeared to sense this, for he explained:

"I call you Kröger because your first name is so crazy, you know. I'm sorry, I just don't like it. Tonio—that's no kind of name. Oh, well, it's not your fault, God knows!"

"No; they named you that because it sounds so foreign and it's something special," said Jimmerthal, trying to act friendly.

Tonio's mouth twitched. He pulled himself together and said: "Yes, it's a stupid name. God knows, I'd much rather be called Heinrich or Wilhelm—believe me. But it's because I was christened after my mother's brother, who's named Antonio. My mother's from overseas, you know. . . ."

Then he fell silent, letting the other two boys discuss horses and leather gear. Hans had slipped his arm into Jimmerthal's, and he talked with a glib fervor that could never have been aroused in him by *Don Carlos*. . . . From time to time, Tonio felt an urge to cry prickling in his nose, and he had a hard time controlling his chin, which kept trembling.

Hans didn't like Tonio's name—what could be done? He himself was named Hans, and Jimmerthal was named Erwin. Fine, those were familiar, ordinary names, which put no one off. But "Tonio" was something foreign and special. Yes, there was something special about him in every way, like it or not, and he was alone and excluded from normal and orderly life even though he was no Gypsy in a green wagon but a son of Consul Kröger, of the family of Krögers. . . . Yet why did Hans call him Tonio so long as they were alone but act ashamed to be with him whenever anyone else joined them? Sometimes Hans was close to him and on his side. "How does he betray him, Tonio?" he had asked, and slipped his arm into Tonio's. But then, when Jimmerthal had come, Hans had breathed a sigh of relief, had deserted Tonio and readily reproached him for his foreign name. How badly it hurt to see through all this! . . . Hans Hansen basically liked him a little when they were alone—Tonio knew that. But if anyone else came, Hans was ashamed and sacrificed him. And Tonio was alone again. He thought of King Philip. The king has wept. . . .

"Damn it," said Erwin Jimmerthal. "I really have to get downtown! So long, guys, and thanks for the fruit drops!" He jumped up on a roadside bench, vaulted over it with his bowlegs, and trotted off.

"I like Jimmerthal!" said Hans emphatically. Spoiled as he was, he had a self-confident way of proclaiming his likes and dislikes, graciously doling them out, as it were. . . . And then, since he was warmed up, he continued talking about the riding lesson. By now they weren't all that far from Hans's home; it didn't take that long to go by way of the walls. Clutching their caps, they bent their heads into the strong, damp wind that moaned and creaked in the bare branches of the trees. And Hans Hansen talked, while Tonio sometimes inserted a perfunctory "Ah" and

"Oh, yes"; nor did he enjoy the fact that Hans, talking himself into a state of excitement, had again slipped his arm into Tonio's, for this was only a sham closeness, without significance.

They left the wall not far from the railroad station and watched a train puff by, lumbering officiously. To while away the time, they counted the cars and waved at the man who, swaddled in fur, was perched way up on the final car. They halted on Linden Square, outside the mansion belonging to Herr Hansen the merchant, and Hans demonstrated how much fun it was to stand on the bottom rail of the garden gate and swing back and forth, making the hinges shriek. But then he said goodbye.

"Well, I have to go in. So long, Tonio. Next time I'll walk *you* home—count on it."

"So long, Hans," said Tonio. "It was nice, walking."

Their hands, when they shook them, were very wet and rusty from the garden gate. But when Hans looked into Tonio's eyes, something like rueful awareness came over his pretty face.

"Listen, I'll read *Don Carlos* very soon!" he quickly said. "That business about the king in his cabinet must be fabulous!" Then he slipped his satchel under his arm and ran through the front garden. Before vanishing inside the house, he nodded.

And Tonio Kröger walked away, cheerful, utterly transfigured. The wind carried him along, but that was not the only reason he moved so easily.

Hans would read *Don Carlos*, and then they'd have something to share that neither Jimmerthal nor anyone else could participate in! How well they understood each other! Who could tell—Tonio might even get him to write poems too. . . . No, no, Tonio didn't want that! Hans was not to be like Tonio; he was to remain as he was, clear and strong, the way everyone loved him, and Tonio most of all! But it still wouldn't hurt if Hans read *Don Carlos*. And Tonio walked through the old, squat town gate, along the waterfront, the wet, windy streets, and up the steep road lined with gabled houses to his parents' home. Back then, his heart was alive; it felt yearning and mournful envy and a wee bit of scorn and a very chaste bliss.

## CHAPTER TWO

BLOND INGE, INGEBORG HOLM, the daughter of Dr. Holm, who lived by the marketplace, there where the Gothic fountain stood with its many tall spires—it was Inge whom Tonio Kröger loved when he was sixteen years old.

How did it happen? He had seen her a thousand times; then one evening he saw her in a certain light, saw her laughing and talking with a girlfriend, saw her tossing her head to the side with a certain exuberance; he saw her hand touching the back of her head in a certain way, her white gauze sleeve sliding back from her elbow—and her girlish hand was by no means particularly slender, by no means particularly fine. He heard her stress a word, an indifferent word, in a certain way, with a warm resonance in her voice—and a rapture took hold of his heart, a rapture far stronger than what he had sometimes felt upon looking at Hans Hansen when Tonio had been a stupid little boy.

That evening he carried away her image: the face with the thick blond braid, the elongated and laughing blue eyes, and the delicate ridge of faint freckles on her nose. He couldn't fall asleep because he kept hearing that resonance in her voice, kept trying to imitate softly the way she had stressed that indifferent word, and he shuddered. Experience had taught him that this was love. He knew very well that love was bound to bring him a mass of pain, distress, and humiliation, that it also destroyed your peace of mind, flooding your heart with melodies, giving you no calm leisure to bring something to fruition, no serenity to forge something into a whole. Nevertheless, he joyfully welcomed love, surrendered to it entirely, and cultivated it with the strength of his mind and soul; for he knew that love makes you rich and alive, and he longed to be rich and alive instead of serenely forging something into a whole.

It was in the salon of Consul Husteede's wife that Tonio Kröger was overwhelmed by his feelings for cheerful Inge Holm; the room had been cleared of furniture, since it was Frau Husteede's turn to host the dancing class this evening. It was a private course, open solely to members of the best families, and the participants gathered at each parental home in turn to take lessons in dancing and etiquette. And for this purpose, ballet master Knaak would come every week, all the way from Hamburg.

François Knaak was his name, and what a figure he cut! *"J'ai l'honneur de me vous représenter,"* he would say. *"Mon nom est Knaak. . . .* And one says those words not while bowing but subsequently, after straightening up again, and they are pronounced softly yet distinctly. To introduce oneself in French is not a daily requirement, but if one can do so correctly and impeccably in French, then one will certainly avoid any faux pas when doing so in German."

How wonderfully snugly his silky black Prince Albert clung to his fat hips! How sharp the creases with which his trousers dropped to his patent-leather shoes, which were adorned with wide satin bows! And his brown eyes looked around with languid happiness about their own beauty. . . .

Everyone was in awe of his excessive assurance and decorum. He walked (and nobody had a walk like his, elastic, swaying, swinging, majestic) toward the lady of the house, then bowed and waited for her to hold out her hand. Upon receiving it, he murmured his thanks, stepped back buoyantly on his left foot, snapped his right foot sideways from the floor while pressing down the tip of his shoe, and walked off with swaying hips.

When exiting from a social function, you walked backward to

the door, executing bows all the while. You moved a chair not by clutching one leg and dragging the chair over the floor; rather, you carried it, lightly holding its back, and you set the chair down noiselessly. When standing, you did not fold your hands on your belly and stick your tongue into the corners of your mouth; if you did, then Herr Knaak had a way of mimicking you so vigorously that you were left with a lifelong disgust at such a posture.

That was etiquette. And in dancing, Herr Knaak possessed an even higher degree of mastery—if that was possible. The gas flames of the chandelier and the candles on the mantelpiece were burning in the salon, which had been cleared of furniture. The floor was strewn with talcum powder, and the participants stood about in a mute semicircle. But beyond the portieres, in the adjoining room, the aunts and the mothers sat on plush chairs, training their lorgnettes on Herr Knaak, who, bowing while holding each tail of his Prince Albert with two fingers, was demonstrating the individual steps of the mazurka on buoyant legs. And if he desired to flabbergast his audience completely, he would suddenly leap into the air for no compelling reason, twirling his legs with bewildering rapidity, virtually trilling them—whereupon he landed on the earth with a thud that, albeit muffled, shook everything to its very foundations.

What an unbelievable monkey! Tonio Kröger thought to himself. But he did see that Inge Holm, cheerful Inge, often observed Herr Knaak's movements with a self-oblivious smile; and that was not the sole reason why all this marvelously controlled physicality elicited something like admiration from Tonio. How calm and unflappable Herr Knaak's eyes were! They did not penetrate to the depths of things, they did not see the sadness and complexity; his eyes knew only that they were brown and beautiful. But that was why his bearing was so proud! Yes, you had to be stupid to strut about like that; and then you were loved, for you were lovable. Tonio understood so well why Inge, sweet, blond Inge, gazed at Herr Knaak the way she did. But would no girl ever gaze at Tonio like that?

Oh, yes, it did happen. There was Magdalena Vermehren, Attorney Vermehren's daughter, with her gentle lips and big, dark, shiny eyes, which were deeply earnest and dreamy. She often fell down when dancing, but she did come over to him during ladies' choice. She knew he wrote poems, she had asked him twice if she could see them, and she often stared at him from afar, lowering her head. But why should he care? He—he loved Inge Holm, blond, cheerful Inge, who most certainly reviled him for writing poetic stuff. He looked at her, looked at her narrow blue eyes, which were filled with joy and scorn, and his chest burned with an envious yearning, the harsh, urgent pain of being excluded from her and forever alien to her. . . .

"First couple, *en avant!*" said Herr Knaak, and no words can possibly describe how wonderfully the man enunciated the nasals. The class was practicing a quadrille, and to Tonio Kröger's utter dismay, he found himself in one and the same square with Inge Holm. He avoided her as much as he could, and yet he kept finding himself near her; he prevented his eyes from approaching her, and yet his gaze constantly alighted upon her. . . . Now she came gliding and running along, hand in hand with red-haired Ferdinand Matthiessen; she tossed back her braid, took a deep breath, and stationed herself across from Tonio. Herr Heinzelmann, the piano player, thrust his bony hands into the keys, Herr Knaak issued his orders, the quadrille commenced.

She moved to and fro in front of Tonio, backward and forward, stepping and turning. At times he caught a fragrance wafting from her hair or her delicate white frock, and his eyes grew dimmer and dimmer. I love you, dear, sweet Inge, he said mentally, and he imbued these words with all the pain he felt because she was dancing so eagerly and cheerfully and ignoring him completely. He thought of a wonderful poem by Theodor

Storm: "—to sleep, but you long, you have to dance." Tonio was tormented by the absurdity and humiliation of having to dance although loving someone. . . .

"First couple, *en avant!*" said Herr Knaak, for a new figure was coming. "*Compliment! Moulinet des dames! Tour de main!*" And no words could capture how gracefully he swallowed the silent *e* in *de*.

"Second couple, *en avant!*" Tonio Kröger and his partner were next. "*Compliment!*" And Tonio Kröger bowed. "*Moulinet des dames!*" And Tonio Kröger, with a lowered head and gloomy eyebrows, placed his hand on the hands of the four ladies, on the hand of Inge Holm, and he moulineted.

All around, people sniggered and laughed. Herr Knaak struck his ballet pose, which expressed a stylized horror. "Oh, dear!" he cried. "Halt! Halt! Kröger has joined the ladies. *En arrière,* Fräulein Kröger, back. *Fi donc!* Everyone else has understood, but not you. Whoosh! Away! Back with you!" And producing a yellow silk handkerchief, he shooed Tonio Kröger back to his place.

They all laughed—the boys, the girls, and the ladies beyond the portieres—for Herr Knaak had turned the incident into something hilarious, it was as entertaining as the theater. Only Herr Heinzelmann kept his dry, businesslike mien, waiting for the signal to continue playing, for he was inured to Herr Knaak's antics.

Then the quadrille resumed. And then came a recess. The parlormaid entered jingling through the door with a tray of glasses of wine jelly, and the cook followed suit with a cargo of plum cake. But Tonio Kröger stole off, sneaking into the hall. There, his hands on his back, he stood at a window with a lowered blind, heedless of the fact that one could not see through the blind, so that it was ridiculous standing in front of it and pretending to look out.

Actually, he was looking inside himself, where there was so

much sorrow and yearning. Why, why was he here? Why wasn't he at home in his room, by the window, reading Storm's *Immensee* and occasionally gazing out into the twilit garden, where the old walnut tree ponderously creaked? That was his place. Let the others dance and do a fresh and skillful job of it! . . . But no, no, his place was here after all, here where he knew he was near Inge, even though he stood alone and far away, trying to make out her voice amid the humming, jingling, and laughing—a voice resonant with warm life. Your elongated and laughing blue eyes, you blond Inge! People can be as serene and beautiful as you only if they don't read *Immensee* and never try writing anything of their own; that's what's so sad about it. . . .

She had to come! She had to notice he was gone, she had to sense his state of mind, had to slip after him, if only out of pity, put her hand on his shoulder, and say: "Come on in and join us, be cheerful, I love you." And he listened for any sounds behind him, waiting in irrational suspense for her to come. But she did *not* come. Such things did not occur on earth.

Had she laughed at him too, like all the others? Yes, she had, much as he would have preferred to deny it for both their sakes. And yet it was purely his self-oblivion in her presence that had made him join her *moulinet des dames*! But what did it matter? Eventually they might stop laughing! Hadn't a magazine recently accepted a poem of his, even though the magazine had gone under before his poem could be printed? The day was coming when he'd be famous, when everything he wrote would be published, and then they'd see whether it wouldn't make an impression on Inge Holm. . . . It would make *no* impression, none—that was the problem. Though it *would* make an impression on Magdalena Vermehren, who always kept falling down— yes, Magdalena. But it would never impress Inge Holm, cheerful, blue-eyed Inge. So why even bother?

Tonio Kröger's heart convulsed painfully at this thought. It hurts deeply to feel wonderful, playful, and mournful energies stirring inside you and yet to know that the people you long to be with are cheerfully inaccessible to those forces. But though he stood excluded, hopeless, and lonely at the closed blind, pretending, in his grief, to look through it, he was happy all the same. For back then his heart was alive. It beat warmly and sadly for you, Ingeborg Holm, and in blissful self-denial, his soul embraced your blond and radiant, your exuberantly normal little personality.

More than once, with a flushed face, he stood in lonesome places barely reached by the sound of music, the scent of flowers, the clinking of glasses, and he tried to make out your resonant voice in the faraway festive din, and he stood there in pain because of you and yet he was happy all the same. More than once he was upset because he could talk to Magdalena Vermehren, who always kept falling down but who understood him and laughed with him and was earnest with him, whereas even when he sat next to blond Inge, she seemed remote and foreign and alienated, for his language was not her language. And yet he was happy all the same. For happiness is not, he told himself, being loved; that is only a nauseating satisfaction of the ego. Happiness is loving and perhaps snatching brief moments of deceptive closeness to the object of your love. And he mentally noted that thought, mulled it over thoroughly, and felt it to its very depths.

Be true! thought Tonio Kröger. I will be true to you and love you, Ingeborg, as long as I live! He was so well-meaning. And yet a quiet fear and grief whispered to him that he had already forgotten all about Hans Hansen, even though he saw him every day. And the ugly and wretched truth was that this quiet and slightly gloating voice turned out to be right, that time wore by and the day came when Tonio Kröger was no longer so absolutely ready to die for cheerful Inge, because he felt the wish and the strength to achieve, in his own way, a host of noteworthy things in the world.

And he cautiously circled the sacrificial altar where the pure, chaste flame of his love was blazing; he knelt before it and stoked and fed the flame in every way because he wanted to be true to it. And yet after a while it went out all the same, imperceptibly, without a flurry or a murmur.

But Tonio Kröger stood at the cold altar for a time, astonished and disappointed because it is impossible to stay true to someone in this world. Then he shrugged and went his way.

# CHAPTER THREE

HE WENT THE WAY HE HAD TO GO, a bit negligent and irregular, whistling to himself, tilting his head to the side and staring into space; and if he went astray, it was because for some people there is no right way. If he was asked what in the world he wanted to be, he would supply different answers, for he was in the habit of saying—and had already written—that he bore within himself the possibilities of a thousand different ways of life, together with the secret awareness that they were all impossibilities.

Even before he left the cramped town, the clips and threads holding him there had quietly loosened. The old Kröger family had gradually started declining and disintegrating, and people had good reasons to count Tonio Kröger's life and lifestyle as symptoms of this condition. His father's mother, the head of the family, had died, and she was soon followed into death by his father, that tall, pensive, impeccably dressed gentleman with the wildflower in his buttonhole. The huge Kröger mansion was put up for sale, together with its stately history, and the firm closed down. Tonio's mother, however, his beautiful, fiery mother, who played the piano and the mandolin so wonderfully, and who was indifferent to everything, remarried within the year; her new husband was a musician, a virtuoso with an Italian name, whom she accompanied into the blue yonder. Tonio Kröger found this a bit wanton, but was it up to him to forbid it? He wrote poems and couldn't even answer when asked what in the world he wanted to be. . . .

And so he left his hometown with its crooked streets and the damp wind whistling around its gables, he left the fountain and the old walnut tree in the garden, the confidants of his youth, he left the sea, which he loved so much, and he felt no pain when leaving. For he was grown up and smart, he had realized what he was all about, and he was full of mockery for the coarse and base existence that had held him so long in its midst.

He surrendered entirely to the power that he considered the most sublime on earth, that he felt destined to serve, and that promised him honor and exaltation: the power of intellect and language, the smiling power that rules over mute and unconscious life. He surrendered to it with his youthful passion, and this power rewarded him with everything it could give, and it relentlessly took from him everything that it normally takes as its fee.

This power sharpened his eyes so that he could see through the grand words that puff up people's chests; it revealed other souls to him and his own soul; it made him see clearly and showed him the interior of the world and every last thing that exists behind words and deeds. And what he saw was this: comedy and misery—comedy and misery.

Then, with the torment and arrogance of knowledge came loneliness, for he could not stand being among the innocuous, with their cheerfully murky minds, and they were bewildered by the mark on his forehead. However, his delight in language and form grew sweeter and sweeter, for he was in the habit of saying—and had already written—that the knowledge of the soul was bound to make us melancholy if the pleasures of expression did not keep us awake and alert. . . .

He lived in big cities and in southern Europe, hoping that its sun would foster a more luxuriant ripening of his art; and perhaps it was his maternal blood that drew him there. But since his heart was dead and without love, he plunged into adventures of the flesh, wallowing deep in lechery and hot guilt, suffering unspeakably. Perhaps it was the legacy of his father—the tall, pensive, neatly dressed man with the wildflower in his button-hole—that made him suffer so terribly in the south, sometimes evoking a feeble, yearning memory of a spiritual delight that had once been his and that he did not find in any of his current pleasures.

A hatred of the senses took hold of him, a disgust at them, and a craving for purity and decent peace of mind, yet he breathed the air of art, the sweet, warm, deeply fragrant air of an endless springtime, which stirs and brews and sprouts in the secret bliss of procreation. And so, unsteadily hurled back and forth be-tween crass extremes, between icy intellect and the devouring heat of the senses, he managed to lead an exhausting life amid pangs of conscience, an exceptional, extravagant, extraordinary life that he, Tonio Kröger, utterly despised. What a labyrinth! he sometimes thought. How was it possible for him to get entangled in all these eccentric adventures? After all, by nature I'm no Gypsy in a green wagon. . . .

But while his health weakened, his artistry intensified, became fastidious, exquisite, precious, refined, hypersensitive toward ba-nality and supremely intuitive in questions of tact and taste. His very first publication was joyfully and vociferously acclaimed by the relevant people, for he had presented a well-crafted thing full of humor and the knowledge of suffering. And in no time at all, his name—the same name with which his teachers had once scolded him, with which he had once signed his early poems to the walnut tree, the fountain, and the sea, this name that coupled south and north—his exotically tinged bourgeois name became synonymous with excellence. For the painful thoroughness of his experiences was joined by a rare, tenacious, and ambitious zeal that, in its torturous struggle with his fastidious, his hyper-sensitive taste, produced an uncommon oeuvre. He did not work like someone who works in order to live; rather, he worked like someone who wants nothing but to work because he considers himself nothing as a living person, wishes only to be regarded as a creative being, and otherwise goes about gray and inconspicu-ous, like an actor who has taken off his makeup and is nothing so long as he has nothing to portray. He worked in silent and invisi-ble seclusion, disdainful of those small-minded people for whom talent was a social asset, who, whether rich or poor, went about wild and dilapidated or lived high on the hog with very individu-alistic neckties, who were devoted to their charming and artistic lives and unaware that good works can emerge only under the pressure of a bad life, that the person who lives does not work, and that an artist must virtually die in order to be fully creative.

## CHAPTER FOUR

"AM I INTRUDING?" asked Tonio Kröger at the threshold of the studio. He held his hat in his hand and even bowed slightly, although Lisaveta Ivanovna was his friend, to whom he told everything.

"For pity's sake, Tonio Kröger, come on in and don't stand on ceremony!" she replied with her lilting intonation. "We all realize that you're well bred and know what's proper." She stuck her brush into the palette in her left hand, held out her right hand, and looked into his face, laughing and shaking her head.

"Yes, but you're working," he said. "Let me see. . . . Oh, you've made progress." And his eyes moved back and forth be-tween the large painting and the color sketches leaning on chairs at either side of the easel; on the gridded canvas, the first dabs of pigment were starting to emerge in the confused and wraithlike charcoal draft.

All this took place in Munich, several flights up in a rear building off Schelling Street. Outside, beyond the broad window that let in the northern light, the sky was blue and sunny, birds were chirping, and the air was alive with the young, sweet breath of spring, which poured in through an open vent, blending with the smell of fixative and oil paints that filled the large work space.

Unhindered, the golden radiance of the lustrous afternoon flooded the vast bareness of the studio, freely exposing the slightly defective floor, the unframed studies on the unpapered walls, and, under the window, the rough-hewn table covered with jars, tubes, and brushes. The radiance brightened the torn silk screen that stood near the door, closing off a small, stylishly appointed nook for living and relaxing. The radiance also glowed on the work developing on the canvas, and it illuminated the painter and the writer in front of the easel.

She was probably around his age—a bit over thirty, that is. In her stained dark-blue smock, she sat on a low footstool, propping her chin on her hand. Her brown hair, firmly combed and slightly graying on the sides, covered her temples in short waves, framing her dark features: her utterly likable Slavic face with its snub nose, high, sharp cheekbones, and small, shiny black eyes. Tense, leery, almost grumpy, her eyes squinting at an angle to the easel, she scrutinized her work. . . .

He stood next to her, his right hand on his hip, his left hand swiftly twirling his brown mustache. His clothing was extremely meticulous and dignified—a calm gray suit in a reserved cut. With his slanting eyebrows in a dark and arduous frown, he whistled softly to himself as usual. His dark hair had an extraordinarily simple and correct part, below which his labored forehead twitched nervously. The features of his southern face were already sharp and distinct, as if traced out by a hard stylet; yet his lips seemed so gently outlined, his chin so softly shaped. . . . After a while he ran his hand over his forehead and his eyes and turned away.

"I shouldn't have come," he said.

"Why shouldn't you have, Tonio Kröger?"

"I've just gotten up from my work, Lisaveta, and on the inside my head looks exactly like that canvas. A skeleton, a pale draft smudged by revisions, plus a few splotches of color, yes. And now I come here and I see the same thing. And I also find the same conflict and antithesis here," he said, sniffing the air, "that tortured me at home. It's bizarre. If you're haunted by a thought, then you find it expressed everywhere; you can even *smell* it in the wind. Fixative and the aroma of spring, right? Art and—yes, what's the other? Don't say 'nature,' Lisaveta; nature is not exhausting. Oh, no, I ought to have taken a walk instead, though I question whether it would have made me feel any better. Five minutes ago, not far from here, I ran into a colleague, Adalbert, the short-story writer. 'God damn the spring!' he said in his aggressive style. 'It's always been the worst season of the year! Can you come up with a sensible idea, Kröger, can you calmly work on the tiniest climax or effect, if your blood is prickling indecently and you're harassed by a swarm of inappropriate sensations, and the moment you examine them, they turn out to be a lot of absolutely trivial and totally useless junk? As for me, I'm going to the café; that's neutral territory, untouched by the change of season, you know. It virtually constitutes the sublime and enraptured literary sphere, where you're capable only of noble ideas. . . .' And he went to the café, and perhaps I should have joined him."

Lisaveta was amused.

"That's good, Tonio Kröger. That 'indecent prickling' is good. And he's right in a way, because it's really not all that easy working in the spring. But now listen. I'm going to do this little thing here all the same—this little climax and effect, as Adalbert would say. Then we'll step into my 'parlor' and have tea, and you can unburden yourself. For I can see very clearly that you're brimming over today. Meanwhile, arrange yourself somewhere— for instance, on that crate, if you're not worried about your fancy clothes. . . ."

"Oh, leave my clothes alone, Lisaveta Ivanovna! Would you rather I ran around in a torn velvet jacket or a red silk vest? An artist is always enough of an adventurer on the inside. So on the outside, he should dress well, damn it, and behave like a respectable person. . . . No, I'm not brimming over," he said, watching her mix some pigments on her palette. "You can tell that what I have on my mind, the thing that's interfering with my work, is a problem and a conflict. . . .

"Yes, what we were just talking about? About Adalbert, the short-story writer, and what a proud and solid man he is. 'Spring is the most horrible season,' he said, and went to the café. A man has to know what he wants, doesn't he? Look, the spring is making me nervous too; I'm just as confused by the sweet triviality of the memories and feelings it arouses. Except that I can't get myself to scold it and despise it. For you see, I'm shamed by it, I'm shamed by its pure naturalness and its victorious youth. And I don't know whether to envy Adalbert or look down on him for knowing nothing about that. . . .

"People work poorly in the spring, granted, and why? Because they feel. And because only a botcher believes that a creative person is allowed to feel. Every genuine and sincere artist smiles at the naïveté of that bungler's mistake: his smile may be melancholy, but smile he does. For the main thing can never be what you say; it has to be the basically indifferent raw material from which the aesthetic work is to be fashioned in sedate and playful mastery. If you care too much about what you have to say, if your heart beats for it too warmly, then you can look forward to a complete fiasco. You wax grandiloquent, you become sentimental—something gawky, awkwardly serious, uncontrolled, unironic, unspiced, boring, and banal emerges from your hands—and ultimately your audience feels nothing but indifference, and you yourself feel nothing but disappointment and misery. . . . For that's what it is, Lisaveta: feeling, warm, deep feeling, is always banal and unusable, and only the irritations and cold ecstasies of the performer's corrupted nervous system are artistic. You have to be some kind of nonhuman and inhuman thing, you have to have a strangely distant and neutral relationship to the human, in order to be able, to be even tempted, to play it, to play with it, to depict it effectively and tastefully. The gift of style, form, and expression already presupposes the existence of this cool and finicky relationship with human beings— why, it even implies a certain impoverishment and desolation of your own humanity. For a strong and sound feeling has no taste—and that's that. An artist stops being an artist the instant he becomes human and starts feeling. Adalbert knew this, and that's why he went to the café, to the 'enraptured sphere'—yes indeed!"

"Well, God bless him, *batushka*," said Lisaveta, washing her hands in a tin basin, "but you don't have to follow him."

"No, Lisaveta, I won't follow him, but only because now and then I'm capable of feeling slightly ashamed when I'm confronted with the spring, ashamed of being an artist. Look— sometimes I get letters from strangers, from my readers, praising me and thanking me, admiring letters from people who've been deeply moved. I read their words and I'm touched by the warm and awkward human feelings that my art has evoked. I'm overcome by a kind of sympathy for the enthusiastic naïveté of the lines, and I blush at the thought of how this honest person would sober up if he caught even a glimpse behind the scenes, if, in his innocence, he ever understood that a healthy, upright, respectable man will never write, act, compose. . . . None of which prevents me from using his admiration for my genius in order to improve myself and stimulate myself. And none of it prevents me from taking that admiration very seriously and making a face like a monkey playing the VIP. . . . Oh, don't say a word, Lisaveta! I tell you, I'm often utterly exhausted from depicting what's human without participating in it. . . .

"Is the artist really even a man? Ask a woman! It strikes me that we artists all vaguely share the fate of those specially treated papal singers. Our singing is so poignantly beautiful . . . and yet—"

"You ought to be a little ashamed of yourself, Tonio Kröger. But come and have some tea. The water's almost boiling, and here are some *papirosi*. You were talking about singing soprano; so please continue. But you really ought to be ashamed of yourself. If I didn't know how proudly and passionately you're devoted to your calling—"

"Don't talk about a 'calling,' Lisaveta Ivanovna! Literature is no calling, it's a curse—just so you'll know. And when does this curse make itself felt? Early on, terribly early. At a time when one should be living in peace and harmony with God and man. You start feeling marked, in an enigmatic antithesis to others, the ordinary people, the respectable ones. The gulf of irony, skepticism, conflict, knowledge, emotion that separates you from other people yawns deeper and deeper. You're lonely, and there is no more communication with others. What a fate! Assuming that your heart is still alive enough, loving enough, to feel how awful that is! . . . Your self-awareness is intensified because you feel the mark on your forehead among thousands of people and you sense that it escapes no one's notice.

"I once knew a brilliant actor who, on a human level, had to struggle with a pathological self-consciousness and instability. He was so hypersensitive, and when he wasn't acting, when he had no role to play, this consummate thespian became an impoverished human being. An artist, a real one—not one whose middle-class job is art, but one who's predestined and damned—

you don't need such a sharp eye to make him out in a human throng. There's a look of being separate, of not belonging, in his face, a sense of being recognized and scrutinized, something both royal and embarrassed. You can detect something similar in the face of a prince wearing mufti as he walks incognito through a crowd of people. Except that no amount of mufti can help, Lisaveta! Disguise yourself, camouflage yourself, dress like an attaché or a guards lieutenant on furlough: but no sooner do you peer into the world and utter a single word than everyone knows you're not human, you're something alien, alienating, something different. . . .

"But *what* is an artist? No other question has so thoroughly exposed human laziness and intellectual sluggishness. 'That's a gift,' decent people say humbly when they're affected by an artist. And because, in their kindhearted opinion, serene and sublime effects absolutely have to have serene and sublime causes, no one suspects that this may be an extremely bad, extremely dubious 'gift.' . . . We know that artists are easily hurt—well, and we also know that this usually isn't true of people with a clear conscience and solid self-esteem. . . . Now, speaking intellectually, Lisaveta: deep, deep down, I nurture a *suspicion* of the artist as a type—the extreme suspicion that each of my honorable and respectable ancestors up north, in that cramped town, felt toward any mountebank or adventurous performer who entered their home.

"Listen to this. I know a banker, a gray-haired businessman, who has the gift of writing stories. He makes use of this gift in his idle moments, and a couple of his stories are excellent. But despite—I say *despite*—his sublime talent, this man is not entirely irreproachable; quite the contrary, he once served a long prison term, and for very sound reasons. Indeed, it was behind bars that he first became aware of his gift, and his experiences as a convict are the main theme in all his writings. We could therefore quite rashly assume that one would have to make one's home in some kind of penitentiary in order to be a writer. Yet must we not suspect that this man's artistry has its roots and sources not so much in his prison experiences as in *what sent him to prison in the first place*? A banker who writes stories—that's a rarity, isn't it? But a noncriminal banker, a respectable and irreproachable banker who writes stories—*there's no such person.* . . .

"Yes, now you're laughing, and yet I'm only half joking. There is no problem, indeed nothing in the world, that is more tormenting than the issue of art and its effect on humanity. Take the most marvelous opus by the most typical and therefore most powerful artist—take such a morbid and profoundly ambiguous work as *Tristan and Isolde*—and observe the effect it has on a young, healthy person of utterly normal sensibilities. You will see exaltation, encouragement, warm, upright inspiration, and perhaps he will even be stimulated to produce his own 'artistic' creation. . . . The good dilettante! However, we artists are utterly different from what he may imagine with his warm heart and honest enthusiasm. I have seen artists cheered and adored by women and adolescent boys, while I *knew* the truth about them. . . . In regard to the origins of being an artist, in regard to the accompanying phenomena and conditions, I keep discovering the strangest things."

"In other people, Tonio Kröger—excuse me—or not only in other people?"

He fell silent. Drawing his slanting eyebrows together, he whistled to himself.

"Let me have your cup, Tonio. The tea isn't strong. And have another cigarette. Incidentally, you know very well that you look at things in ways that they don't necessarily have to be looked at. . . ."

"Why, that's Horatio's answer, dear Lisaveta. ''Twere to consider too curiously, to consider so'—isn't that true?"

"I'm saying that one can consider those things just as accurately from a different angle, Tonio Kröger. I'm only a silly painting female, and if I can argue with you at all, if I can defend your vocation a little against you, then what I have to say is certainly nothing new—I'm merely reminding you of what you yourself already know very well. For instance: the purifying, sanctifying effect of literature, the quelling of the passions through knowledge and language, literature as a path to understanding, to forgiveness, to love, the redemptive power of words, the literary spirit as the very noblest manifestation of the human mind, the litterateur as the perfect human being, as a saint—would considering things in *that* way mean considering them not curiously enough?"

"You have the right to say such things, Lisaveta Ivanovna, especially in regard to the works of your writers. After all, Russian literature deserves our admiration, it truly constitutes the sacred literature that you're talking about. However, I'm not ignoring your objections; they are part of what's on my mind today. . . . Look at me. I don't seem excessively alert, do I? A little old and tired and with sharp features, right? Well, to get back to 'knowledge': we could imagine a person who acts in good faith, who is by nature gentle, well-meaning, a bit sentimental, and we could picture him being quite simply ground down and destroyed by his clear psychological vision. Not to be overpowered by the sadness of the world; to observe, register, integrate even the most tormenting things and, incidentally, to remain in high spirits, feeling deeply a moral superiority over the dreadful invention of Being—yes indeed! Yet at times it all gets a little too much for you, despite the pleasures of expression. To understand everything is to forgive everything? I don't know about that. There is something that I call 'the disgust at knowledge,' Lisaveta: the state in which a person has only to see through a thing in order to feel lethally nauseated (and in no way reconciled)—the case of Hamlet the Dane, that typical litterateur. He knew what it meant to be called upon to know without being to the manner born. To see clearly through the tears veiling the emotions, to recognize, register, observe, and, smiling, put your observations aside in moments when hands entwine, lips find one another, where human eyes, blinded by feelings, break . . . It's dreadful, Lisaveta, it's despicable, outrageous—but what use is outrage?

"Then, of course, there's another side, which is no less charming: a person is blasé and indifferent to all truth, he feels only an ironic weariness about it—just as it's a fact that nothing in the world is more mute and hopeless than a group of brilliant people who know all the tricks of the trade. They find all knowledge old and boring. Articulate a truth that you may have conquered and taken possession of with a certain youthful joy, and people will respond to your coarse enlightenment with a very terse snort. . . . Ah, yes, literature is tiring, Lisaveta! I can assure you that if you are utterly skeptical and refrain from voicing your opinion, human society may regard you as stupid—whereas you are merely arrogant and lacking in courage. . . . So much for 'knowledge.'

"As for 'words': are they perhaps less a means of redemption than a tool for getting emotions out of harm's way, putting them in cold storage? Literary language gets rid of feelings in a very quick and shallow fashion, and there's really something very icy and outrageously presumptuous about that process. If your heart is too full, and you're all too deeply moved by a sweet or sublime experience—then nothing could be simpler! You go to a litterateur, and everything is taken care of in a jiffy! He will analyze and formulate your problem, identify it, articulate it, make it speak—he will rid you of the entire matter for good, neutralize it, and not accept any gratitude. And you will go home relieved, cooled off, cleansed, and you will be amazed that this issue could have ever upset you with such sweet tumult. And you seriously want to champion this cold and conceited charlatan? His motto is: Anything that's articulated is taken care of. And if the whole world is articulated, then it's taken care of, redeemed, eliminated. . . . All well and good! But I'm no nihilist."

"You're no . . . ," said Lisaveta. Holding her spoonful of tea near her lips, she paused in that posture.

"Come on, come on, Lisaveta! Just think about it! I'm no nihilist, I tell you, in regard to living emotions. Look, the litterateur basically doesn't understand that life may want to go on living, that life is not ashamed to do so after being articulated and 'taken care of.' Yet lo and behold, despite all redemption by literature, life keeps sinning wildly and without letup; for all action is a sin in the eyes of the intellect. . . .

"I'm just about done, Lisaveta. Listen to me: I love life. That is a confession. Take it and preserve it—I haven't made it to anyone else. People have stated, they have even written, have said in print, that I hate life or fear it or scorn it or despise it. I enjoy hearing that, I am flattered; but that doesn't it make it any less wrong. I love life. . . . You're smiling, Lisaveta, and I know why. But I beg you, don't take what I'm saying as literature! Don't think of Cesare Borgia or some drunken philosophy that praises him to the skies! He's nothing to me, that Cesare Borgia. I have absolutely no regard for him, and I will never, never comprehend how anyone can revere the demonic and extraordinary as an ideal. No, life is the eternal antithesis to intellect and art—and it's not as a vision of utter grandeur and savage beauty, it's not as something unusual, that it presents itself to us, the unusual beings. No, the normal, the decent, the lovable, are the realm of our yearning: they are life in all its seductive banality! A man is anything but an artist, my dear, if he ultimately and profoundly worships the refined, the eccentric, the satanic, if he never longs for what is simple, harmless, and alive, for a little friendship, devotion, intimacy, and human happiness—the furtive and devouring yearning, Lisaveta, for the bliss of the ordinary! . . .

"A human friend! Would you believe that it would make me proud and happy to have a friend among human beings? But so far my only friends are demons, ogres, dreadful fiends, and ghosts that are dumbstruck by knowledge—that is, literati.

"Sometimes I end up on some podium or other, I find myself in an auditorium, facing people who have come to hear what I have to say. And then, you see, it happens: I observe myself checking my audience, I catch myself secretly peering around the hall, wondering in my heart who it is who's come to me, whose applause and gratitude are reaching me, with whom my art is creating an ideal fusion here. . . . I do not find what I'm seeking, Lisaveta. I find the flock and the parish that I'm so familiar with—a gathering of the first Christians, so to speak: people with awkward bodies and refined souls, people who keep falling down, so to speak. They understand me, and for them poetry is a gentle revenge on life—always just suffering people and yearning people and poor people, and never any of the others, the blue-eyed people, Lisaveta, who do not need the mind! . . .

"And if things were otherwise, wouldn't it ultimately be a regrettable lack of consistency to be glad? It's nonsense loving life and yet focusing all your strength on winning it over, gaining its support for all the finesse and melancholy, the whole morbid aristocracy of literature. The kingdom of art is growing, and the kingdom of health and innocence is shrinking on earth. We should gather any remnants of the latter kingdom and meticulously preserve them, and we should not try to inveigle people into reading poetry if they prefer books about horses, illustrated with high-speed photos.

"For after all, what would be a more lamentable sight than life trying its hand at art? We artists despise no one more thoroughly than the dilettante, the man who lives life and who believes that he can also be an artist on occasion. I assure you, I have personally felt such scorn. I find myself at a party in a respectable home, people are eating, drinking, and chatting, they're getting along gloriously, and I feel glad and grateful to be spending a little time with harmless and regular people, losing myself among them as one of their own. All at once (and this has happened to me), an officer stands up, a lieutenant, a dashing and handsome man, whom I would never have expected to conduct himself in a manner unbecoming his honorable uniform. In all candor, he asks for permission to read aloud some verses that he has composed. This permission is granted with stunned smiles, and he goes through with it: pulling out a scrap of paper hidden in his coat-tail pocket, he reads his text to us, something about love and music—in short, something both deeply felt and worthless. Now I ask you: a lieutenant, of all people! A man of the world! He really doesn't need this . . . Well, the consequences are unavoidable: long faces, silence, a bit of strained applause, and profound malaise all around.

"My first psychological reaction that I become aware of is a sense of my complicity in the distress that this unthinking young man has brought upon the group. And no doubt about it: even though *he* has poached on *my* territory, people ogle me derisively and somewhat resentfully. And then my second reaction is that this man, for whose person and being I nurtured the most honest respect, is now suddenly going down in my esteem, down, down. . . . A benevolent pity takes hold of me. Along with several other brave and kind gentlemen, I go over to him and reassure him. 'Congratulations, Herr Lieutenant,' I say. 'What a lovely talent! Why, that was absolutely charming.' And it wouldn't take much for me to clap him on the back. But is benevolence the right emotion to show a lieutenant? . . . He had no one but himself to blame! There he stood, utterly embarrassed, atoning for his error: he had falsely assumed that you can pluck a tiny leaf, a single tiny leaf from the laurel tree of art and not pay with your life. No, here I'd go along with my colleague the criminal banker. . . . But don't you find, Lisaveta, that I'm being as garrulous as Hamlet today?"

"Are you done, Tonio Kröger?"

"No. But I'll say no more."

"And it suffices. Do you expect an answer?"

"Do you have one?"

"I should think so. I've listened to you carefully, Tonio, from start to finish, and I will give you the answer that fits everything you've said this afternoon, and it will solve the problem that has unsettled you so deeply. Here it is: The solution is that as you sit here you are quite simply a burgher."

"Am I?" he asked, drooping.

"That really hurts, doesn't it? As well it should. And that's why I'd like to soften my verdict a little, which I can do. You are a burgher who's gone astray. Tonio Kröger—a lost burgher."

Silence. Then he stood up resolutely and reached for his hat and his cane.

"Thank you, Lisaveta Ivanovna. Now I can go home in full confidence. *I've been taken care of!*"

## CHAPTER FIVE

TOWARD AUTUMN, Tonio Kröger said to Lisaveta Ivanovna:

"Well, I'm taking a trip, Lisaveta: I need some fresh air. I'm heading out, out into the wide world."

"And where to, *batushka*? Are you deigning to revisit Italy?"

"Goodness, don't get me started on Italy, Lisaveta! I'm so indifferent to Italy that I practically despise it! It's been a long time since I imagined I belonged there. Art—right? Velvety blue sky, hot wine, and sweet sensuality. In short, I don't like it. Thanks, but no thanks. That whole *bellezza* business makes me nervous. And I can't stand all those horribly vibrant people down there, with their black animal eyes. Those Latins have no conscience in their eyes. . . . No, I'm going to spend a little time in Denmark."

"Denmark?"

"Yes. And I feel it'll do me good. It happens that I've never gotten up there, even though I was so near the border throughout my youth, and yet I've always known and loved that country.

I probably got this northern bent from my father; my mother really leaned more toward *bellezza,* so far as she wasn't indifferent to everything, you know. But take the books that are written up there, these deep, pure, humorous books, Lisaveta—there's nothing I like better; I love them. Take the Scandinavian meals— those incomparable meals, which can be digested only in strong, salty air. I have no idea whether I can still endure them; I became a bit familiar with them at home, for those are the only kinds of meals that are now eaten back there. And take just the names, the first names that adorn the people up there—and by now there are a lot of those names in my hometown. A set of sounds like 'Ingeborg'—a stroke of the harp producing the most pristine poetry. And then the sea—they've got the Baltic up there! . . . In a word, Lisaveta, I'm heading north. I want to see the Baltic again, I want to hear those names again, I want to read those books right where they were written. I also want to stand on the terrace of Kronborg, where the 'ghost' appeared to Hamlet, bringing anguish and death to the poor noble young man. . . ."

"How are you traveling, Tonio, if I may ask? What route are you taking?"

"The usual one," he said, shrugging and noticeably reddening. "Yes, I'm touching my . . . my point of departure, Lisaveta, after thirteen years, and that might be rather comical."

She smiled. "That's what I wanted to hear, Tonio Kröger. And so bon voyage and God be with you. And don't forget to write me, do you hear? I'm looking forward to a letter bursting with your experiences on your trip to . . . Denmark."

# Chapter Six

AND TONIO KRÖGER WENT NORTH. He traveled in comfort—
for he used to say that someone who has a much harder internal
life than other people has a just claim to a little external ease.
And he did not rest until the turrets of the cramped town where
he had started out loomed before him in the gray air. He had a
brief, bizarre visit. . . .

A dreary afternoon was thickening into evening when the
train pulled into the narrow, smoky, and so peculiarly familiar
station. The smoke still coagulated under the dirty glass roof,
drifting to and fro in tattered strips, as in the past, when Tonio
Kröger had gone forth from here with nothing but scorn in his
heart. Now he saw to his luggage, had it sent to his hotel, and left
the station.

Outside, waiting in a line, stood the town's black two-horse
hackneys, immoderately high and wide. He hailed none of them;
he merely looked at them as he looked at everything—the narrow
gables and pointed turrets greeting people over the nearest
roofs; the blond, casually coarse people all around him, with
their broad yet rapid pronunciation—and a nervous laughter
arose in him, a laughter secretly akin to sobbing. He went on
foot; with the damp wind blasting incessantly into his face, he
slowly crossed the bridge with the mythological statues standing on its parapets and he then ambled along a stretch of the
waterfront.

Good God—how tiny and crooked it all seemed! Had the narrow streets lined with gabled houses been climbing all this time,

so droll and steep, up to the town? In the wind and the twilight, the masts and smokestacks of the ships rocked softly on the dreary river. Should he go up the street, that one, to the house he was thinking of? No, tomorrow. He was so sleepy now. His head was heavy from the trip, and slow, foggy thoughts drifted through his mind.

At times during those past thirteen years, when he'd had an upset stomach, he had dreamed that he was home again in the old, echoing house on the steep road; that his father was there too, jumping down his throat about his dissolute lifestyle, and Tonio had always found each scolding to be quite proper. Nor did this present moment differ in any way from any of those deceptively concrete phantasms in which you wonder if this is a dream or reality, and you are forcibly convinced that this is real, but in the end you do wake up after all. . . . He strode through the drafty and almost deserted streets, bent his head into the wind, and virtually sleepwalked to the hotel where he planned to spend the night—the best hotel in town. Ahead of him, a bow-legged man, holding a pole with a tiny fire burning on its end, swayed along like a sailor, lighting the gas lanterns.

How did Tonio feel? What were all those things gleaming so dark and painful under the ashes of his fatigue, without bursting into clear flames? Hush, hush, not a word! No words! He would have wanted to keep going and going through the wind, through the dreamy familiarity of the twilit streets. But everything was so cramped and close together. He was almost there.

The upper part of town had arc lamps, and they were just lighting up. There was the hotel, and there, reclining in front of it, were the two black lions that he had feared as a child. They still glared at each other as if they were about to sneeze; only they seemed to have shrunk a lot. Tonio Kröger passed between them.

Having come on foot, he was received without much fuss. The desk clerk was joined by a very fine person in black, who did the honors, his little fingers constantly thrusting his cuffs into his sleeves. The two men scrutinized Tonio, examining and investigating him from crown to boots, blatantly striving to identify him socially, to determine his standing, fit him into the hierarchy, and allocate a rank for him in their esteem. But failing to reach any satisfactory conclusion, they opted for a moderate courtesy. An attendant, a mild-mannered person with bread-blond sideburns, a tuxedo shiny with age, and rosettes on his soundless shoes, led the guest up two flights to an immaculate room with old-fashioned furnishings. In the twilight, the window offered a picturesque and medieval view of courtyards, gables, and the bizarre bulk of the nearby church. Tonio Kröger lingered at this window for a bit, then he sat down on the spacious sofa, crossed his arms, drew his eyebrows together, and whistled to himself.

Light was brought, and his luggage arrived. At the same moment, the mild-mannered attendant placed the registration form on the table, and Tonio Kröger, his head tilting to the side, scrawled something that looked like his name, his profession, and his home address. Next, he ordered a small supper and then stared into space from his corner of the sofa. When the food was placed in front of him, he left it untouched for a long while, eventually took a few bites, and spent an hour pacing up and down the room, occasionally halting with closed eyes. At last he slowly undressed and went to bed. He slept for a long time, amid confused dreams with strange yearnings.

Upon awakening, he saw that his room was filled with bright daylight. In his grogginess, he quickly recalled where he was, and he stood up to draw the curtains. The slightly pale blue of the late-summer sky was crisscrossed with thin shreds of wind-tattered clouds; but the sun shone over his native town.

He dressed more fastidiously than usual, washing and shaving meticulously, making himself fresh and immaculate, as if about to visit a proper and respectable household where he had to make an attractive and irreproachable impression; and while fiddling around with his clothes, he listened to the anxious pounding of his heart.

How bright it was outdoors! He would have felt better if yesterday's twilight were filling the streets; but now he had to walk through the clear sunshine, before the eyes of the people. Would he bump into acquaintances, would they stop him, quiz him, would he have to account for the way he had spent these past thirteen years? No, thank goodness, there was no one left who knew him, and if any people did remember him, they would not recognize him, for he had certainly changed a little. He studied himself closely in the mirror, and suddenly he felt more secure behind his mask, behind his face, which had been thoroughly molded at an early point and now looked older than his years. He ordered breakfast, ate, and went down, walked through the lobby, past the assessing glances of the desk clerk and the fine gentleman in black, then between the lions and into the open.

Where was he going? He scarcely knew. It was like yesterday. No sooner was he again surrounded by this peculiarly dignified and thoroughly familiar cluster of gables, turrets, arcades, and fountains, no sooner did he again feel the wind blasting into his face—the powerful wind that brought along a delicate and bracing aroma from faraway dreams—than his senses were swaddled in veils and foggy phantasms. . . . His facial muscles relaxed; and with calm eyes he gazed at people and things. Perhaps he would wake up after all, there, at that corner. . . .

Where was he going? He felt as if the direction he was taking were connected to his sad and strangely rueful dreams of the previous night. Passing under the arched vaults of the town hall, he went to the marketplace, where butchers with bloody hands were weighing their wares: the marketplace, where the Gothic fountain stood with its many high spires. There he halted outside a house, a plain and narrow house that looked like so many others, with a curving, openwork gable, and he stared at it, completely absorbed. He read the nameplate on the door and he gazed awhile at every window. Then he slowly turned to leave.

Where was he going? Home. But he took a detour, strolling out beyond the town gates, for he had time. He walked along the Mill Wall and the Holstein Wall, clutching his hat, bucking the wind, which creaked and rustled in the trees. He left the wall not far from the railroad station and watched a train puff by, lumbering officiously. To while away the time, he counted the cars and waved at the man who was perched high up on the final car. Tonio Kröger then halted on Linden Square, outside one of the lovely mansions, peered into the garden and up at the windows for a long time, and finally he hit on the idea of swinging the garden gate to and fro, making the hinges shriek. For a while he studied his hands, which had become cold and rusty. And then he walked on, walked through the old, squat gateway, along the waterfront, and up the steep, drafty road lined with gabled houses, to his parental home.

It stood, gray and solemn, as it had stood for three centuries, closed in by the neighboring houses, its gable towering above them; and Tonio Kröger read the pious, blurring motto over the entrance. Then he took a deep breath and went inside.

His heart beat anxiously, for as he moved past the ground-floor doors, he expected his father to emerge from one of them, in his office smock and with his pen behind his ear; he expected his father to take him to task for his dissolute lifestyle, and Tonio found that scolding perfectly in order. However, he managed to get past those doors unscathed. The outside door wasn't shut but was merely ajar, which he found reprehensible, while he felt as if he were dreaming a certain kind of flimsy dream, in which obstacles recede of their own accord and you can forge ahead unhindered, favored by marvelous luck.

The wide vestibule, its floor covered with large rectangular fieldstones, echoed with his footsteps. Opposite the silent kitchen, the strange, rough, but immaculately painted wooden rooms leaped forth from the wall, as they had done since time immemorial, reaching a considerable height; these were the maids' rooms, and they were accessible only through a kind of exposed staircase running from the vestibule. However, the huge cupboards and the carved chest that once been here were now gone.

The son of the household mounted the tremendous stairway, leaning on the white wooden openwork banister, raising his hand with every step and gently dropping it at the next step, as if shyly testing whether he could restore his former intimacy with this old, solid banister. . . . But then he halted on the landing, at the entrance to the mezzanine. On the door, a white sign with black letters said: "Public Library."

Public library? Tonio Kröger thought to himself, for he felt that neither the public nor literature had any business being here. He knocked on the door. Someone called, "Come in!" and he obeyed. Tense and gloomy, he gazed at the results of a highly unsuitable transformation.

The mezzanine was three rooms deep, and the connecting doors were open. The walls were covered, almost to the ceilings, with long rows of uniformly bound books standing on dark shelves. In each room a shabby man sat writing at something like a counter. The farthest two men only turned their heads toward Tonio Kröger, but the closest one jumped to his feet, propping both hands on the countertop, thrusting his head forward, pursing his lips, raising his eyebrows, and scrutinizing the visitor with eagerly blinking eyes.

"Excuse me," said Tonio Kröger, without averting his gaze from the many books. "I'm a stranger here; I'm sightseeing. So this is the public library? Would you permit me to have a look at the collection?"

"By all means!" said the librarian, blinking even more vehemently. "Certainly; it's open to everyone. Please look around. . . . Would you care to see the catalogue?"

"No, thank you," said Tonio Kröger. "I'll find my way." Then he began walking slowly along the walls, pretending to study the titles on the book spines. Eventually he pulled out a volume, opened it, and stationed himself at the window.

This had been the breakfast nook. The family had always breakfasted here and not up in the large dining room, where white statues of gods had stood out against the blue wallpaper. . . . The second room had been the bedroom. His father's mother had died there, struggling long and hard—old as she was—for she had been a pleasure-lover, a woman of the world, who had clung to life tenaciously. And later on, his father himself had breathed his last there—the tall, correct, pensive, and slightly wistful gentleman who always had a wildflower in his buttonhole. . . . Tonio had sat at the foot of the deathbed, his eyes hot, all of him yielding honestly to strong and mute emotions, to love and grief. And his mother, too, had knelt by the bed, his beautiful, fiery mother, utterly dissolving in hot tears; after which she and the southern artist had headed toward the blue yonder.

However, the smaller room back there, the third one, now likewise crammed with books guarded by a shabby man, had for many years been his own room. That was where he had returned after school, after a stroll, like the one he had just taken; and his desk, where he had kept his first, ardent, and awkward verses in the drawer, had stood against that wall. The walnut tree . . . a piercing melancholy cut through him. He peered sideways through the window. The garden lay overgrown, but the old walnut tree stood where it had always stood, ponderously creaking and rustling in the wind. And Tonio Kröger's eyes darted back to the book he was holding, an outstanding literary opus that he was familiar with. He gazed down at the black lines and sentence clusters, briefly followed the stylish flow of the diction, as its shaping passion rose to a climax and an effect and then strikingly subsided. . . .

"Yes, that's well done," he said, replacing the book and turning around. Now he saw the librarian still standing there, his eyes blinking with officious and pensive misgivings.

"An excellent collection, I see," said Tonio Kröger. "I've gotten a general idea. I'm very grateful to you. Good day." With that, he went out the door; but it was a dubious departure, and he clearly felt that the librarian, quite unsettled by this visit, would stand there for several minutes, blinking his eyes.

Tonio Kröger felt no desire to press on any further. He had been home. Up there, strangers were living in the large rooms behind the columned hall—he could tell because the top of the stairs was closed off by a glass door that had not been there in the past, and a nameplate was on it. He went off, down the stairs, and left his parents' home. Lost in thought, he consumed a rich and heavy meal in the corner of a restaurant, and then he returned to the hotel.

"I've finished," he said to the fine gentleman in black. "I'm leaving this afternoon." And he asked for his bill and ordered a carriage to take him to the waterfront, to the steamer for Copenhagen. Then he went to his room and sat down at the table, sat still and erect, propping his cheek on his hand and gazing blankly at the tabletop. Later, he settled his bill and packed. The carriage was announced on schedule, and Tonio Kröger went down, dressed in his travel outfit.

At the foot of the stairs, the fine gentleman in black was waiting for him.

"Forgive me!" he said, and his little fingers thrust his cuffs back into his sleeves. "Forgive me, sir, but we have to trouble you for a minute. Herr Seehaase—the proprietor of the hotel—would like a word with you. A formality . . . He is back there. . . . It is *only* Herr Seehaase, the proprietor of the hotel."

And, his gestures underscoring his invitation, he led Tonio Kröger to the back of the lobby. And indeed, there stood Herr Seehaase. Tonio Kröger knew him by sight from long ago. He was short, fat, and bowlegged. His trimmed whiskers had turned white; but he still wore a low-cut tuxedo jacket and a velvet cap with green embroidery. Incidentally, he was not alone. Next to him, at a tiny desk attached to the wall, stood a helmeted policeman, his gloved right hand resting on the desktop—specifically on a document covered with particolored writing. With his honest soldierly face, the policeman gaped at Tonio Kröger as if expecting that his gape would make the earth swallow him up.

Tonio Kröger's eyes darted back and forth between the two men, and he restricted himself to waiting.

"You're coming from Munich?" the policeman finally asked in a clumsy and good-natured voice.

Tonio Kröger said yes.

"You're going to Copenhagen?"

"Yes, I'm en route to a seaside resort in Denmark."

"Resort? Yes, well, you'll have to show me your papers," said the policeman, pronouncing the word "show" with particular gratification.

"Papers? . . ." He had no papers. He pulled out his briefcase and peered into it; but aside from a few banknotes, all it contained were the galley proofs of a short story, which he planned to correct at his destination. He didn't like dealing with officials, and so he had never applied for a passport.

"I'm sorry," he said, "but I don't carry any papers."

"Really?" said the policeman. "None at all? What is your name?"

Tonio Kröger told him.

"Is that true?" asked the policeman, straightening up and suddenly opening his nostrils as wide as he could.

"Completely true," replied Tonio Kröger.

"What do you do?"

Tonio Kröger swallowed and then announced his profession

in a firm voice. Herr Seehaase lifted his head and peered inquiringly into Tonio Kröger's face.

"Hm!" said the policeman. "And you allege that you are not identical with an individgil named . . ." He said "individgil" and, reading the document covered with particolored writing, he spelled out a quite intricate and romantic name that seemed to blend haphazard sounds from diverse races and that Tonio Kröger had forgotten a moment later. ". . . of unknown parentage and unknown residence," the policeman went on, "who is being sought by the Munich police on various charges of fraud and other felonies and is probably fleeing to Denmark?"

"I'm not just alleging it," said Tonio Kröger, his shoulders moving nervously. His response made a certain impact.

"What? Oh, I see—well, of course!" said the policeman. "But you have no papers to show!"

Herr Seehaase tried to mediate and propitiate. "The whole thing is a mere formality," he said, "that's all! You must realize that the officer is simply doing his duty. If you can somehow prove your identity . . . a document . . ."

They all fell silent. Should he put an end to this situation by identifying himself, by revealing to Herr Seehaase that he was no confidence man without a primary residence, that by birth he was no Gypsy in a green wagon but the son of Consul Kröger, of the Kröger family? No, he had no desire to do so. And weren't these representatives of public safety vaguely doing the right thing? To some extent he fully agreed with them. . . . He shrugged and held his tongue.

"What do you have here?" asked the policeman. "Here in your briefcase?"

"Here? Nothing. These are galley proofs," replied Tonio Kröger.

"Galley proofs? What do you mean? Let me see."

And Tonio Kröger handed him his work. The policeman

spread the galleys out on the desk and began reading them. Herr Seehaase likewise came closer and read along. Tonio Kröger peered over their shoulders and saw where they were. It was a good moment, a climax and an effect that he had worked out marvelously. He was satisfied with himself.

"Look!" he said. "There's my name. I wrote this, and now it's being published, you see?"

"Well, that suffices!" said Herr Seehaase resolutely. He gathered the sheets together, folded them, and handed them back. "That should suffice, Petersen!" he tersely added, furtively shutting his eyes and shaking his head by way of ending the matter. "We mustn't hold up the gentleman any longer. The carriage is waiting. Please excuse this minor inconvenience, sir. The officer was only doing his duty, but I told him right off that he was on the wrong track."

Really? thought Tonio Kröger.

The policeman did not appear fully convinced; he objected, muttering something about an "individgil" and "show." But Herr Seehaase, reiterating his regret, led his guest back through the lobby, escorted him between the two lions, brought him to the carriage, and asserting his great esteem, he personally closed the carriage door behind Tonio Kröger. And then the ridiculously high and wide hackney, clanging, rattling, and lumbering, trundled down the steep roads to the waterfront. . . .

That was Tonio Kröger's bizarre visit to his native town.

# CHAPTER SEVEN

NIGHT WAS FALLING, and the moon was already drifting up with a silvery glow, when Tonio Kröger's ship reached the open sea. He stood by the bowsprit, bundled up against the wind, which was blasting harder and harder, and he peered down into the dark surging and wandering of the waves, which were strong, smooth bodies, swaying around each other, crashing into one another, shooting apart in erratic directions, and suddenly foaming and glowing. . . .

He was overcome by an agitated mood of silent delight. He had felt a bit depressed because they had wanted to arrest him back home as a confidence man, yes—although to a certain extent he had found it in order. But then, after boarding ship, he had watched the loading of the cargo (as he had sometimes done in his boyhood, together with his father). Shouting in a mixture of Danish and Low German, the men had now filled up the deep belly of the steamer, and Tonio saw them lowering not only the bales and crates but also a polar bear and a Bengal tiger, in densely barred cages; the animals, which were probably coming from Hamburg, were meant for a Danish menagerie. And all this had taken his mind off things.

By the time the ship then slowly glided downstream between the flat riverbanks, he had forgotten all about Officer Petersen's interrogation; and everything preceding it had intensified in his soul: the sweet, sad, rueful dreams at night, the walk he had taken, the sight of the walnut tree. And now that the sea was widening out, he saw the faraway beach where during his boyhood he had listened to the summer dreams of the sea, he saw the flashing of the lighthouse and the lights of the resort where he had stayed with his parents. . . . The Baltic! He bent his head into the strong, salty wind that came blasting in, free and unhindered, shrouding his ears, causing a slight dizziness, a dull stupor, which blissfully and sluggishly dissolved the memory of all evil, of torment and vagary, of wishes and efforts. And in the roaring, crashing, foaming, and moaning that surrounded him, he thought he could hear the rustling and creaking of the old walnut tree, the shrieking of a garden gate. . . . It was growing darker and darker.

"The stars, my God, just look at the stars," a voice suddenly said in a thick, heavy North German singsong that sounded as if it were coming from inside a barrel. He knew that voice. It belonged to a simply dressed man with reddish-blond hair, inflamed eyelids, and a dank appearance, who looked as if he had just bathed. He had dined next to Tonio Kröger in the cabin, where, with timid and modest gestures, he had devoured amazing quantities of lobster omelettes. Now, next to Tonio Kröger again, he leaned on the railing, peering up at the sky, his chin clasped between thumb and forefinger. He was plainly in one of those extraordinary moods of solemn introspection in which the barriers between people drop, in which the heart opens up to strangers and the lips utter things from which they otherwise bashfully retreat.

"Just look at the stars, sir," the man went on, in his thick North German accent. "They hover and glitter there—why, the sky is chock-full of them. And now I ask you: when you look up at them and think that lots of them are supposedly a hundred times bigger than the earth, how does that make you feel? We human beings have invented the telegraph and the telephone and so many modern achievements—yes, that we have. But when we look up there, we have to realize and understand that we're basically worms, miserable worms, and that's all—am I right or am I wrong, sir? Yes, we're worms!" He answered his own question, nodding humbly and contritely toward the firmament.

Ow . . . no! He has no literature in his body! thought Tonio Kröger. And he promptly recalled something he had recently read, an essay by a famous French writer about the cosmological and psychological view of the world: it had been a truly fine bit of gobbledygook!

He gave the young man some response or other to his deep-felt remark, and then they went on conversing, leaning over the railing and peering into the skittishly illuminated and turbulent evening. It turned out that the fellow passenger was a businessman from Hamburg, who was spending his vacation on this pleasure trip.

"You oughta," he said in his thick North German accent, "go 'n' take the steamer to Copenhagen, I says to myself, and now here I am, and it's been fine so far. But those lobster omelettes, that wasn't the right thing, sir, you'll see, 'cause it's gonna be a stormy night—the captain said so himself—and it's no fun having food in your stomach that's hard to digest."

Tonio Kröger listened to all this trusting fatuousness, feeling a secret rapport.

"Yes," he said, "the food up north here is too heavy. It makes you lazy and wistful."

"Wistful?" the young man repeated, giving him a perplexed look. "Are you a stranger here, sir?" he suddenly asked.

"Ah, yes, I come from far away!" replied Tonio Kröger, warding off the question with a vague wave of his arm.

"But you're right," said the young man, in his thick North German accent. "You're right, God knows, right about being wistful! I'm almost always wistful, especially on evenings like this, when the stars are in the sky." And again he propped his chin between thumb and forefinger.

I'm sure he writes poems, thought Tonio Kröger, profoundly sincere businessman's poems. . . .

The evening wore on, and the wind was blasting so violently that it drowned out their words. So they decided to turn in and said good night to each other.

Tonio Kröger stretched out on his narrow bunk but was unable to sleep. The severe wind and its tangy aroma triggered a strange agitation, and his heart was skittish, as if anxiously looking forward to something sweet. He was also horribly nauseated by the quaking of the ship, which kept sliding down mountains of waves while the propeller whirled spasmodically outside the water. He got fully dressed again and went out into the open air.

Clouds were rushing past the moon. The sea was dancing.

These were no round and even waves coming here in an orderly way. Instead, far and wide, in pale, flickering light, the sea was lashed up, churned up, shredded up, it licked and leaped in sharp, flaming giant tongues, scooped out foam-filled chasms and threw up jagged and improbable shapes, and it seemed to be playing a wild game with tremendous, powerful arms that hurled the spindrift every which way.

The ship was having a hard passage: pitching, swerving, and groaning, it lumbered through the tumult, and sometimes the tiger and the polar bear could be heard roaring in the hold, suffering from the rough sea. A man in an oilskin, with the hood on his head and a lantern strapped to his body, arduously managed to keep his balance as he straddled up and down the deck. And back there at the stern, bending far over the railing, stood the young man from Hamburg—he was in wretched shape. "God," he said in a hollow, faltering voice upon spotting Tonio Kröger. "Just look at the uproar of the elements, sir!" But then he was interrupted and he hurriedly turned away.

Tonio Kröger held on to some taut rope as he gazed into the untamable exuberance. Exultation surged up in him, and he felt as if it could outshout the storm and the waves. A song to the sea, inspired by love, resounded in him: You wild companion of my youth, / Once more we're joined together now. . . . But then the poem stopped. It was not completed, not rounded off, not calmly forged into a whole. His heart was alive.

He stood like that for a long time; then he stretched out on a bench by the pilothouse and gazed up at the sky, where the stars were flickering. He even dozed a little. And when the cold foam sprayed into his face, it was like a caress in his light sleep.

Sheer chalk cliffs, ghostly in the moonlight, heaved into view and moved closer: that was the island of Møn. And again he nodded off, doused by showers of salty spray that bit sharply into his face, stiffening his features.

By the time he was fully awake, it was already day, a fresh, light-gray day, and the green sea had calmed down. At breakfast he again saw the young businessman, who blushed violently, probably for having uttered such embarrassing poetic things in the dark. Twirling up his small reddish mustache with all five fingers, he greeted Tonio with a brisk military exclamation and then anxiously kept out of his way.

And Tonio Kröger landed in Denmark. He arrived in Copenhagen, tipping anyone who looked as if he had a claim to a gratuity. From his hotel room, he wandered through the city for three days, holding his small guidebook open and conducting himself altogether like a well-bred tourist who wishes to broaden his knowledge. He perused the King's New Market and the "horse" in the center, he gazed deferentially up the columns of the Church of Our Lady, stood for a long time in front of Thorwaldsen's noble and lovely sculptures, climbed the Round Tower, viewed castles, and spent two lively evenings in the Tivoli Gardens. But none of this was what he actually saw.

With their curving openwork gables, the houses often looked exactly like those in his native town, and on the nameplates he saw names that were familiar to him from long ago, hinting at something delicate and precious, yet containing something like a reproach, a lament, and a yearning for a lost past. He inhaled the damp sea air slowly, pensively, and everywhere he saw eyes so blue, hair so blond, faces shaped and fashioned like the ones he had seen in the strangely painful and rueful dreams he had dreamed that night in his native town. Out in the street, a glance, a sonorous word, a burst of laughter, might cut him to the quick.

He couldn't stand the hectic city for long. He was haunted by a sweet and foolish restlessness, half memory and half expectation, and he longed to lie quietly on a beach somewhere rather than play the eager, urgent tourist. So on a dreary day, when the sea was black, he set sail once again, heading northward up the Zeeland coast to Helsingör—Elsinore. From there he rode a carriage for three-quarters of an hour, along the highway, always slightly above the sea, until he reached his true and final destination, the small white resort hotel with green shutters and a wood-covered turret; nestling in a cluster of low cottages, it faced the sound and the Swedish coast. Here he got out and took possession of the bright room that they had held for him; he filled the shelves and the wardrobe with what he had brought, and he prepared to stay awhile.

# CHAPTER EIGHT

SEPTEMBER WAS ALREADY ADVANCING; not many guests were left in Aalsgaard. The unmarried proprietress officiated at meals, which were served in the large ground-floor dining room, with ceiling beams and with lofty windows that faced the glass veranda and the sea; an elderly woman with white hair, faded eyes, delicately rosy cheeks, and an unsteady, twittering voice, she always tried to arrange her red hands a bit advantageously on the tablecloth. There was also an old gentleman here, with a short neck, an ice-gray seaman's beard, and a dark, bluish face; a fish dealer from Copenhagen, he spoke German. He seemed thoroughly congested and apoplectic, for he breathed in short spurts, and from time to time he lifted his ringed forefinger to one nostril, squeezing it shut and blasting through the other nostril, trying to clear a passage for a little air. Nevertheless, he continually did full justice to the bottle of aquavit that stood in front of him at breakfast as well as at lunch and supper.

The only other guests were three big American teenagers with their tutor or chaperon, who kept silently adjusting his eyeglasses and played football with them during the day. They had reddish-yellow hair, parted down the middle, and long, immobile faces.

"Please pass me that wurst there!" said one.

"That's not wurst—that's schinken!" said another.

And that was all that they and the tutor contributed to the conversation, for normally they sat still and drank hot water.

Tonio Kröger would not have wished for any other sort of company at meals. He enjoyed his peace and quiet, listened to the Danish gutturals, the bright and dark vowels in which the fish dealer and the proprietress sporadically conversed. Now and then Tonio Kröger and the fish dealer would exchange a simple remark about the barometric pressure, and Tonio would then stand up and again walk across the veranda to the beach, where he had already spent long morning hours.

Sometimes the beach was still and summery. The sea lay smooth and sluggish, with blue, bottle-green, and reddish streaks, with silvery reflections flashing and glittering over them; the sun was drying the seaweed into hay, and the jellyfish lay there, evaporating. The air smelled a bit rotten, with a whiff of tar from the fishing boat that Tonio Kröger was leaning against in the sand; he sat in such a way that he could view the open horizon rather than the Swedish coast. However, the quiet breath of the sea wafted across everything, pure and fresh.

And gray, stormy days came. The waves lowered their heads like bulls and they charged furiously into the beach, flooding it high up and covering it with shiny wet sea grass, shells, and driftwood. Between the long, long hills of waves, the valleys stretched foamy and bluish green under the overcast sky; but a whitish patch of velvety radiance lay on the water when the sun lingered behind the clouds.

Tonio Kröger stood wrapped in wind and in roaring, absorbed in this heavy, deafening, eternal frenzy, which he loved so dearly. When he turned and set off, the air around him suddenly felt calm and warm. But he knew the sea was behind him; it called, beckoned, and greeted. And he smiled.

He went inland, following meadow paths through the solitude, and soon a forest of beeches enfolded him, stretching far across the hilly region. He sat down in the moss, leaning against a tree, so that he could make out a strip of water between the trunks. Sometimes the wind brought him the crashing of the surf, which sounded like faraway boards clattering on one another. Above the treetops, there was a cawing of crows—hoarse, bleak, and forlorn. . . . He held a book in his lap, but he didn't read a single line. He enjoyed a profound oblivion, a relaxed floating over space and time, and only occasionally did a pain shoot through his heart, a brief, sharp jab of longing or regret; he was too sluggish and too absorbed to ask for its name and origin.

That was how day after day wore by; he would not have been able to say how many days, nor did he wish to know. But then a day came on which something occurred; it occurred while the sun was in the sky and people were present, and Tonio Kröger wasn't even extraordinarily astonished.

The very start of this day was festive and delightful. Tonio Kröger awoke very early and quite suddenly, jumping out of his sleep with a fine and hazy terror: he believed he was witnessing a miracle, a bright, ethereal enchantment. Through its glass door and its balcony, his room faced the sound, and a thin white gauze curtain divided the space into a living room and a bedroom; the wallpaper had a delicate tinge, and the furniture was bright and simple, so that the room always looked friendly and radiant. But now his drowsy eyes saw it lying before him in an unearthly transfiguration and illumination, dipped in an unspeakably sweet and fragrant rosiness that gilded the walls and furnishings and lent the gauze curtain a mild red luster. . . . For a long time Tonio Kröger was unable to grasp what was happening. But when he stood at the glass door and peered out, he saw that it was the sun coming up.

The weather had been dreary and drizzly for several days, but now the sky stretched like taut, pale-blue silk, shimmering clearly across land and water; and crisscrossed by fiery red and gold clouds, the sun rose festively over the flickering, rippling sea, which seemed to shudder and brighten under the rays. . . . That was how the day began, and Tonio Kröger, dazed and happy, threw on his clothes, breakfasted down on the veranda before anyone else, swam from the small wooden cabana some distance out into the sound, and then walked along the beach for hours. When he returned, several omnibus carriages were parked in front of the hotel, and from the dining room he noticed that the adjoining parlor (which contained the piano) as well as the veranda and terrace were crowded with people. Dressed in petty-bourgeois style, they sat at round tables, excitedly talking while consuming beer and sandwiches. These were whole families, older people and younger ones—even a few children.

During the late-morning snack (the table groaned under a smorgasbord of smoked, salted, and baked delicacies), Tonio Kröger inquired what was going on.

"Hotel guests!" said the fish dealer. "From Helsingör: excursionists and people coming for the ball. Yes, God help us, we won't get any sleep tonight! There'll be dancing, dancing and music, and I'm afraid it's gonna go on for a long time. It's a family get-together, a country outing and a reunion—in short, a subscription or something of the kind, and they're taking advantage of the beautiful day. They've come by boat or by carriage, and now they're having their big breakfast. Later on, they're going cross-country, but they'll be back this evening, and then they're gonna dance here in this room. Yes, God damn it, we won't get a wink of sleep. . . ."

"That's a nice change of pace," said Tonio Kröger.

After that no one spoke for a while. The proprietress arranged her red fingers on the table, the fish dealer blew through his right nostril to get a little air, and the Americans drank hot water and made long faces.

Then all at once it happened: *Hans Hansen and Ingeborg Holm passed through the room.*

Tonio Kröger, pleasantly weary after his swim and his swift walk, was leaning back in his chair, eating smoked salmon on toast; he was facing the veranda and the sea. And suddenly the door opened, and the two of them came in, hand in hand, tranquil and unhurried. Ingeborg, blond Inge, was dressed in light colors such as she had worn for Herr Knaak's dance classes. Her thin flowery dress reached down only to her ankles, and around her shoulders she wore a broad white tulle fichu with a pointed décolletage that exposed her soft, supple throat; her hat dangled from her arm by the knotted ribbons. She may have been a bit more grown up, and her wonderful braid was looped around her head. Hans Hansen, on the other hand, was exactly the same as ever. He was wearing his naval jacket with the gold buttons, and the wide blue collar lay on his back and shoulders. His dangling hand clutched the short ribbons of the sailor cap, swinging it to and fro in a carefree way. Ingeborg kept her narrow eyes averted; perhaps she was slightly embarrassed by the people gazing at her from their tables. Hans Hansen alone, defying all the world, turned his head straight toward the buffet table, his steel-blue eyes somewhat scornfully challenging one person after another. He even let go of Ingeborg's hand and swung his cap more vehemently in order to show what kind of man he was. And so, against the background of the still sea, which grew bluer and bluer, the two of them passed Tonio Kröger, strode the full length of the room, and vanished through the opposite door, into the parlor.

That took place at eleven-thirty A.M., and while the hotel guests were still eating, the throng next door and out on the veranda got up, avoiding the dining room, and left the hotel through the side entrance. The guests heard them joking and laughing as they mounted their carriages, and they heard one vehicle after another grinding off and rumbling away. . . .

"So they'll be coming back?" asked Tonio Kröger.

"That they are!" said the fish dealer. "And God help us.

They've hired a band, you oughta know, and I sleep right over this room!"

"It's a nice change of pace," Tonio Kröger repeated. Then he stood up and left.

He spent this day as he had spent the previous days: on the beach and in the forest, holding his book in his lap and blinking into the sun. His mind had room for only one thought: They were coming back and they would be dancing in the dining room, as the fish dealer had promised. And Tonio Kröger could only look forward to it, with a sweet and anxious joy such as he had not experienced in all these long, dead years. Once, through some association of ideas, he vaguely recalled a very casual acquaintance, Adalbert, the short-story writer, who had known what he wanted and had headed for the café to escape the springtime air. And Tonio shrugged at that memory. . . .

They ate lunch earlier than usual, and supper, which likewise took place ahead of time, was served in the parlor, because the dining room was already being transformed for the ball: it all resulted in a festive disorder. Then, when it was dark, and Tonio Kröger was sitting in his room, the highway and the hotel livened up again. The excursionists were returning; yes, and new guests were arriving from Helsingör by bicycle or carriage, and downstairs a violin was warming up and a clarinet was practicing twangy runs. . . .

By all indications, the ball would be dazzling.

Now the small band launched into a march: the muffled music welled upward in a steady beat; the ball was opening with a polonaise. Tonio Kröger sat in his room awhile, listening silently. But when he heard the march tempo pass over into a waltz rhythm, he stood up and soundlessly slipped out.

From the corridor outside his room, one could take the back stairs to a side entrance of the hotel and then reach the glass veranda without cutting through a single room. He took this route, quietly and furtively, as if stealing along forbidden paths, and groped his way through the darkness, irresistibly drawn by that silly and blissfully swaying music, which already sounded clear and unmuffled in his ears.

The veranda was empty and unlit, but its glass door was open to the dining room, where the two big kerosene lamps, equipped with giant reflectors, were shining brightly. Tonio Kröger sneaked over on soft soles, and his skin prickled with his illicit delight in standing here in the dark and listening, unseen, as the people danced in the light. He glanced around hastily and eagerly, trying to spot the couple he was looking for. . . .

The merriment was in full swing by now, even though the festivities had begun scarcely half an hour before; but the guests had already been warm and excited upon arriving here, after spending the whole day together, carefree and happy. In the piano room, which Tonio Kröger could survey by venturing a bit farther forward, several elderly gentlemen had gathered to smoke, drink, and play cards; others sat with their wives, either in front of or along the walls of the dining room, and they watched the dancing from their plush chairs. Their hands rested on their spread knees, and their cheeks were puffed up with an expression of opulence, while the mothers, their parted hair in bonnets, their arms folded under their bosoms, their heads tilted sideways, peered into the hurly-burly of the young people.

A platform had been set up on the longitudinal wall, and there the musicians were playing for all they were worth. They even had a trumpet, which blew with a certain hesitant caution, as if scared of its own voice, which nonetheless kept cracking and breaking. . . .

Swaying and swirling, couples moved around one another, while a few strolled through the room arm in arm. There was no formal attire; they were dressed merely as if spending a summery Sunday outdoors: the gentlemen in small-town suits that were plainly handled with kid gloves all week, and the young girls in bright, airy frocks, with nosegays of wildflowers tucked into their

belts. There were also a few children here, dancing with one another in their own way, even during breaks in the music. A long-
legged man in a short swallowtail jacket—a provincial lion with a
monocle and frizzed hair, a postal clerk or something of the sort,
a comical figure who looked as if he had stepped straight out of a
Danish novel—appeared to be the supervisor of the ball and also
the master of ceremonies. Assiduous, perspiring, and devoted
heart and soul to the business at hand, he was everywhere at
once, wiggling and bustling about the room. Skillfully thrusting
down on his toes and intricately crossing his feet in their
smooth, pointed military ankle boots, he flung his arms in the
air, gave instructions, called for music, clapped his hands, and
all the while, he kept fondly turning his head toward the huge,
colorful bow that was attached to his shoulder as a sign of his
rank, with its ribbons fluttering behind him.

Yes, there they were, the two of them, the couple who had
passed Tonio Kröger in the sunlight today, and he felt a frightened joy upon recognizing them almost simultaneously. There
stood Hans Hansen, very close to him, right by the door; bent
slightly forward on straddling legs, he was gingerly consuming a
large piece of pound cake, cupping his palm under his chin to
catch the crumbs. And there by the wall sat Ingeborg Holm,
blond Inge, and the postal clerk came wiggling over in order to
ask her to dance: he accompanied his invitation with an exquisite bow, placing one hand on his back and gracefully slipping the
other into his chest. But she shook her head, indicating that
she was too out of breath and had to rest a little; whereupon the
postal clerk sat down next to her.

Tonio Kröger looked at the two of them, whom he had loved
painfully so long ago—Hans and Ingeborg. It was they not so
much because of individual features and similar clothes, but because they were of the identical race and type—that radiant
breed with blond hair and steel-blue eyes, evoking an image of
purity, harmony, serenity, looking plain and proud, standoffish

and untouchable. Tonio gazed at them, gazed at Hans Hansen, as bold and well shaped as in the past, broad in his shoulders and narrow in his hips, standing there in his sailor suit. Tonio looked at Ingeborg laughing and tossing her head to one side with a certain exuberance, touching the back of her head in a certain way with her not particularly slender, not particularly fine girlish hand, whereby the airy sleeve slid back from her elbow—and all at once the nostalgia shook his chest with so much pain that he automatically backed farther into the darkness, to keep anyone from seeing him wince.

Had I forgotten you? he wondered. No, never! Not you, Hans, nor you, blond Inge! After all, you were the ones I was writing for, and whenever I heard applause, I furtively peered around to see if you, too, were clapping. . . . Did you finally read *Don Carlos*, Hans Hansen, as you promised me at your garden gate? Don't do it! I no longer ask you to read it. Why should you care about the king who weeps because he's lonesome? You should not dim your bright eyes or dull them with dreams by staring at verses and melancholy. . . . To be like you! To start all over again, grow up like you, upright and cheerful, plain, proper, and orderly, and in agreement with God and the world, to be loved by the innocent and happy, to take you as my wife, Ingeborg Holm, and have a son like you, Hans Hansen—to live, love, and laud, free of the curse of knowledge and the torment of creativity in blissful normality! . . . Start all over again? But it wouldn't help—it would all turn out the same, everything would come again the way it has come. For some people are bound to go astray because there is no such thing as a right way for them.

Now the music stopped; there was a break, and refreshments were provided. The postal clerk dashed about personally with a tray of herring salad, serving the ladies; and upon reaching Ingeborg Holm, he actually knelt on one knee before her as he handed her a small dish, and she blushed with joy.

Some of the guests were beginning to notice the spectator behind the glass door, and flushed, attractive faces peered quizzically at the outsider; but he stood his ground all the same. Ingeborg and Hans likewise glanced at him almost simultaneously, with that utter indifference that verges on scorn. Suddenly, however, Tonio Kröger realized that somewhere, someone was staring at him very intently. . . . He looked around, and instantly his eyes met those that he had felt upon him. Not far from him stood a girl with a fine, pale, slender face, which he had noticed earlier. She hadn't danced much—the gentlemen had paid her little attention—and Tonio had seen her sitting at the wall, alone, her lips severely pursed. And she was standing alone now too. Her frock was bright and airy like the others, but her bare shoulders glistened sharp and meager through the transparent cloth, and her skinny neck was thrust so deep between those wretched shoulders that this silent girl looked almost a bit deformed. She held her hands, in thin half-gloves, on her flat bosom, so that the fingertips grazed one another. Her head lowered, she stared up at Tonio Kröger with black, liquid eyes. He turned away. . . .

Here, very close to him, sat Hans and Ingeborg. Hans had joined her, and perhaps she was his sister. Surrounded by other red-cheeked people, they ate and drank, chatted and enjoyed themselves, teased each other in sonorous voices, and laughed loudly into the air. Couldn't he get a little closer to them? Couldn't he say something amusing to him or to her, some flash of wit that they would at least have to smile at? It would make him happy; he longed to do so. He would then return to his room more satisfied, knowing he had established a little rapport with the two of them. He pictured what he might say to them; but he couldn't find the courage to say it. Besides, it would be the same as always: they wouldn't understand him, they would be disconcerted by what he might say. For their language was not his language.

Now the dancing appeared to resume. The postal clerk unfurled a vast range of activity. He dashed about, asking everybody to join in; with the waiter's help, he put the chairs and glasses out of the way; he issued orders to the musicians; and with his hands on their shoulders, he pushed along a few awkward people who had no idea what they were doing. What was in the offing? Sets of four couples were forming squares. . . . A horrible memory made Tonio Kröger redden. They were going to dance a quadrille.

The music struck up, and the couples bowed, curtsied, and wove in and out. The postal clerk was in charge: he commanded in French, by God, emitting the nasals in an incomparably distinguished manner. Ingeborg Holm was dancing right near Tonio Kröger, in the square immediately by the glass door. She moved back and forth in front of him, up and down, striding and turning, and at times he caught a fragrance wafting over from her hair or from the delicate cloth of her frock, and he closed his eyes, feeling an emotion he was long familiar with; during the past few days he had sensed its aroma and pungent appeal, and now it imbued him again with its sweet distress. Just what was it? Yearning? Tenderness? Envy, self-hatred? . . . *Moulinet des dames?* Did you laugh, blond Inge, did you laugh at me when I danced the *moulinet* and made such a wretched fool of myself? And would you laugh again today, now that I've become sort of famous? Yes, you would, and you'd be absolutely right! And if I, all by myself, wrote all nine symphonies, penned *The World as Will and Conception*, and painted *The Last Judgment*, you would still be forever right to laugh at me.

He looked at her, and he recalled a line of poetry that he hadn't thought about for a long time, and yet it was so familiar and so close to him: "I long to sleep, but you—you have to dance." He was so intimate with it—the northern melancholy, the heartfelt awkwardness and ponderousness that it expressed.

To sleep . . . To yearn for the chance to live simply and fully for the feeling that is sweet and sluggish and self-contained and not duty-bound to become deed and dance—and yet to have to dance, alert and nimble, to do the hard, hard, and dangerous dance of knives that is art, though never completely forgetting the humbling conflict of having to dance while loving . . .

All at once, the party turned into a wild and reckless torrent. The squares had broken up, and everyone was springing and sliding about; the quadrille was ending with a gallopade. The couples flew past Tonio Kröger to the raging beat of the music, dashing, sashaying, outrunning one another, with short spurts of breathless laughter. One couple came hurrying along, swept away by the flood, whirling and zooming forward. The girl had a fine, pale face and thin shoulders that were too high. And suddenly, right in front of Tonio Kröger, they were tripping, slipping, plunging. . . . The pale girl fell down. She fell so hard and heavy that it seemed almost dangerous, and her partner fell with her. He appeared to be so grossly hurt that he forgot all about his lady; pulling himself only halfway up, he grimaced and began rubbing his knees; while the girl, who seemed utterly stunned by her fall, was still lying on the floor. Now Tonio Kröger stepped forward, gently took hold of her by both arms, and helped her to her feet. Panting, muddled, and wretched, she peered up at him, and suddenly her delicate face turned a dull red.

"*Tak! O, mange tak!* Thank you! Oh, thank you!" she said, looking up at him with dark, liquid eyes.

"You probably shouldn't dance anymore, miss," he said gently. Then he looked about for *them,* for Hans and Ingeborg, and walked away, left the ball and the veranda and went up to his room.

He was intoxicated with the party which he hadn't joined, and he was weary with jealousy. It had been the same as always, the same as always! With a flushed face, he had stood in a dark spot, painfully yearning for you, you blond, lively, happy people, and had then gone away in his loneliness. Someone had to come now! Ingeborg had to come now, she had to notice that he was gone, she had to slip after him, put her hand on his shoulder, and say, "Come on in and join us! Be cheerful! I love you!" But she did not come. Such things did not occur. Yes, it was the same as always, and he was happy as he had been long ago. For his heart was alive. But what had happened during all the time in which he had become what he now was? Petrifaction; bleakness; ice; and intellect! And art! . . .

He undressed, lay down, put out the light. He whispered two names into the pillows, a few chaste Nordic syllables that designated his intrinsic and original way of loving, suffering, and being happy—designated life, simple and intimate emotions, his homeland. He looked back at the years that had flowed by till now. He recalled the wild adventures of his senses, nerves, and thoughts, he saw himself chewed up by irony and intellect, ravaged and paralyzed by knowledge, half ground down by the frosts and fevers of artistic creation, shaken by inner distress, precariously hurled to and fro between crass extremes, between holiness and rutting, refined, impoverished, and exhausted by cold and artificially heightened exaltations, confused, devastated, agonized, sick—and he sobbed with regret and nostalgia.

Around him the night was still and dark. But from below came the muted and swaying sounds of the sweet and trivial three-quarter beat of life.

# CHAPTER NINE

TONIO KRÖGER SAT UP NORTH, writing to his friend Lisaveta Ivanovna, as he had promised her:

Dear Lisaveta, down there in Arcadia, where I will soon return [he wrote]. Here now is a letter of sorts, but it will probably disappoint you, for I plan to keep it rather general. Not that I have absolutely nothing to tell you, and not that I haven't experienced a thing or two in my own way. In fact, I nearly got arrested at home, in my native town. . . . But you'll hear about that in person. I now have days on which I prefer saying something general in a good way rather than telling stories.

Do you still remember, Lisaveta, that you once called me a burgher, a burgher who's gone astray? You called me that at a time when I—led astray by other admissions that I had let slip—confessed my love for what I call "life"; and I wonder if you realized how close you came to hitting on the truth of how profoundly my bourgeois condition and my love of "life" are one and the same. This trip has prompted me to mull this over.

My father, you know, had a Nordic temperament: pensive, thorough, puritanically correct, and with a wistful bent; my mother, who was of indeterminate exotic blood, was beautiful, sensual, naive, both careless and passionate, and impulsively wanton. There is no doubt whatsoever that this was a blend containing extraordinary possibilities—and extraordinary perils. And this was the result: a burgher who's gone astray in art, a bohemian who feels homesick for his good upbringing, an artist with a bad conscience. For after all, my bourgeois conscience is what makes me regard all artistry, all genius, indeed all exceptional things, as deeply ambiguous, deeply unsavory, deeply questionable, and that same bourgeois conscience fills me with a lovelorn weakness for simplicity, candor, and pleasant normality, for nongenius and respectability.

I stand between two worlds, I am at home in neither, and this makes things a bit difficult for me. You artists call me a burgher, and the burghers feel tempted to arrest me. . . . I don't know which of the two hurts me more. The burghers are stupid; but you worshipers of beauty, who call me phlegmatic and devoid of yearning, ought to remember that there is an artistry that is so deep, by birth and by destiny, that no yearning makes it seem sweeter and more worth feeling than the yearning for the bliss of normality.

I admire those proud, cold people who venture along the paths of great, demonic beauty and scorn "human beings"—but I do not envy them. For if anything can turn a litterateur into a true writer, it is my bourgeois love for what is human, alive, and normal. All warmth, all goodness, all humor, come from that love, and it almost strikes me as being the love with which, it is written, one can speak with the tongues of men and angels and without which one is merely a piece of low-grade ore, a jingly bell.

What I have accomplished so far is nothing, not much, as good as nothing. I will do better, Lisaveta—that's a promise. As I write, the sea is roaring up to me, and I close my eyes. I look into an unborn, murky world that needs to be shaped and fashioned; I look into a teeming throng of human shadows, who beckon to me, wanting me to exorcise them and redeem them: tragic shadows and ludicrous ones and some that are both—and I am very fond of them. But my deepest and most furtive love is for the blond and blue-eyed people, the brightly living, the happy, lovable, and normal ones

Do not scold me for this love, Lisaveta; it is good and fruitful. It contains yearning and mournful envy and a wee bit of scorn and a very chaste bliss.

# THE WUNDERKIND

THE WUNDERKIND COMES IN, the hall hushes.

It hushes and then the people begin to applaud, because somewhere off to the side, a bellwether and born leader is the first to clap. They have heard nothing as yet, but they are expressing their acclaim; for a tremendous promotional apparatus has paved the way for the wunderkind, and the people are already beguiled, whether they know it or not.

The wunderkind emerges from behind a splendid screen that is embroidered with Empire wreaths and huge, legendary flowers; the child nimbly mounts the stairs to the platform and steps into the applause as if into a bath, shivering slightly, shuddering mildly, and yet as if entering a friendly element. He advances to the edge of the platform, smiles as though being photographed, and thanks the audience with a small, shy, and charming curtsy, even though the wunderkind is a boy.

He is dressed entirely in white silk, which stirs a number of hearts in the auditorium. He wears a small white silk jacket of a fanciful cut and with a sash underneath, and even his shoes are of white silk. However, his bare little legs, which are entirely brown, contrast sharply with the short white silk pants; for this boy is Greek.

Bibi Saccellaphylaccas is what he is called. That is simply his name. "Bibi" is a diminutive or a term of endearment, but no one knows what first name it is abbreviated from—except for the impresario, and he views it as a trade secret. Bibi has smooth black hair that, albeit shoulder length, is parted on the side, with a small silk bow tying it back from the narrow, domed, brownish forehead. He has the most innocent little juvenile face in the world, an incomplete little nose and ingenuous lips; however, the area under his pitch-black mouse eyes is already a bit dull and clearly delimited by two characteristic marks. He looks nine but is only eight years old and is claimed to be seven. The people themselves do not know whether to really believe it. Perhaps they know better but believe it all the same, as they are wont to do in certain cases. A lie or two, they think, are part of beauty. What, they think, would happen to edification and exaltation at the end of a commonplace day if we did not show a little good-will and stretch a little point? And they are quite correct in their all-too-human brains!

The wunderkind keeps thanking his audience, until the welcoming commotion subsides; then he goes over to the grand piano, and the people cast a final glance at their programs. First comes "Marche solennelle," then "Rêverie," and then "Le hibou et les moineaux"—all of them by Bibi Saccellaphylaccas. The entire program is by him; these are his compositions. He is unable to write them down, but he has them all in this small, unusual head, and their artistic significance must be acknowledged, as is noted earnestly and matter-of-factly on the impresario's posters. Apparently the impresario has had a hard struggle, wresting this concession from his critical nature.

The wunderkind sits down on the swivel stool, and his feet go fishing for the pedals, which an ingenious mechanism has raised to a much higher level than usual so that Bibi can reach them. This is his own private piano, which he takes along wherever he goes. It rests on wooden trestles, and its finish has been fairly battered by frequent transportation; but this simply makes it all the more interesting.

Bibi places his white silk feet on the pedals, then he makes a small, sophistic face, looks straight ahead, and raises his right hand. It is the naive and brownish little hand of a child, but the wrist is strong and unchildlike, revealing thoroughly developed bones.

Bibi makes his face for the benefit of the people, because he knows he has to entertain them a little. Yet he himself derives a certain furtive pleasure from this—a pleasure he could not describe to anyone. It consists of that tingly happiness, that secret blissful thrill running up and down his spine, the instant he sits at an open piano—and he will never lose that sensation. Once again the keyboard offers itself to him—those seven black-and-white octaves where he has so often lost himself in adventures, in deeply agitating destinies, and which once again appear as clean and intact as a washed slate. It is music, all music, that lies before him now! It lies spread out before him like a beckoning sea, and he can dive in and rapturously swim, float, and be carried away and go under completely in a tempest, and yet his hands will stay in control, will reign and rule. . . . His right hand is poised aloft.

The hall is breathlessly hushed. It is the suspense preceding the first note. . . . How will it begin? This is how it begins. And Bibi's forefinger draws the first note from the piano, a quite unexpectedly energetic note in the middle register, like a trumpet blast. It is joined by other notes, an introduction emerges—limbs relax.

It is a flamboyant hall, located in a fashionable four-star hotel, with rosy-fleshed paintings on the walls, with sumptuous columns, mirrors framed in curlicues, and a universe, a veritable infinity of lightbulbs, which sprout everywhere in clusters, in whole bundles, and their thin, golden, heavenly radiance quivers through the space far more brightly than the day. . . . No seat is empty—why, there are even people standing in the side aisles and at the back. In the front, where tickets cost twelve marks (the impresario reveres the principle of charging awe-inspiring prices), you find high society; for the highest circles are keenly interested in the wunderkind. You see many uniforms here, many exquisitely tasteful gowns. . . . There are even a number of children, their legs hanging demurely from their chairs, their shiny eyes beaming at their blessed little white-silk contemporary.

The wunderkind's mother, an extremely fat woman with a powdered double chin and a feather on her head, sits on the left side of the first row, next to the impresario, a gentleman of the Oriental type, with huge gold links on his blatantly exposed cuffs. And in the very center of the row sits the princess. This is a small, old, wrinkled, shriveled princess, but she is a patroness of the arts, so long as they are delicate. She sits in a deep velvet armchair, with Persian rugs spread out at her feet. She holds her hands together right under her chest, on her gray-striped silk gown, tilts her head to the side, and presents a picture of noble tranquillity as she watches the laboring wunderkind. Next to her sits her lady-in-waiting, who actually wears a green-striped silk dress. But then she is merely a lady-in-waiting after all and is not permitted even to lean against anything.

Bibi concludes with a gorgeous bravura. With what strength this little whippersnapper attacks the piano! You cannot believe your ears. The march theme, an impetuous, exuberant melody, erupts once again in a full harmonic fanfare, broad and boastful, and Bibi hurls his torso back at every beat as if he were triumphantly marching in the festive procession. Then he crashes to a close, bends over, pushes sideways from the stool, smiles, and waits impatiently for applause.

And the applause explodes, unanimous, heartfelt, enthusiastic: just look at what graceful hips the child has as he daintily curtsies! Clap, clap! Wait, let me take off my gloves. Bravo, little Saccophylax or whatever your name is! What a devil of a boy!

Bibi has to come out from behind the screen another three times before the audience quiets down. Several stragglers, latecomers, squeeze through from the back, arduously finding their places in the packed hall. Then the concert resumes.

Bibi murmurs his "Rêverie," which consists purely of arpeggios, with an occasional melodic strain rising over them with weak wings. And then he plays "Le hibou et les moineaux." This is a smash hit; it has a rousing effect. Truly a child's piece, marvelously vivid. In the bass you can see the owl perching and sullenly flapping its veiled eyes, while in the descant the both impudent and anxious sparrows are whirring around it, teasing and taunting it. Bibi has four curtain calls after that *pièce*. A bellhop with shiny buttons mounts the platform, carries the three laurel wreaths over, and offers them to Bibi from the side, while the boy curtsies gratefully. Even the princess participates in the applause, by very delicately moving her flat hands toward one another without producing any sort of sound.

How well this skillful manikin knows how to draw out the applause! Behind the screen he keeps the audience waiting, lingers briefly on the platform steps, and with childlike joy he studies the gaudy satin streamers of the wreaths even though for ages now he has been quite jaded about them; then he hesitantly executes a charming curtsy, giving the people time to exhaust themselves so that nothing is lost of the valuable noise of their palms. "Le hibou" is my big draw, he thinks, having learned that expression from the impresario. Next comes my fantasia, which is actually a lot better, especially the passage that shifts into C sharp. But you're crazy about my "hibou," you people, even though it was the first and stupidest thing I've ever done. And he thanks charmingly.

Then he plays a meditation and then an etude; it is a thoroughly comprehensive program. The meditation goes quite similarly to the "Rêverie" (which is not meant as criticism); and in the etude, Bibi shows off all his technical mastery, which, incidentally, is second only to his inventiveness. But then comes the fantasia. It is his favorite piece. He plays it a bit differently each time, handles it freely, and, on a good evening, is sometimes surprised by his own brainstorms and new variations.

He sits and plays, very small and shiny white against the big black piano, alone and elect on the platform above the blurry human throng, which has only a torpid, inflexible soul that he is supposed to affect with his singular and outstanding soul. . . .

236 • THOMAS MANN

His soft black hair has tumbled into his forehead, together with the white silk bow, his well-trained, strong-boned wrists are working, and you can see the muscles quivering in his brownish, childish cheeks.

Sometimes he has moments of oblivion and solitude, when his strange mouse eyes with their dull rings drift to the side, away from the audience, and he can see through the painted wall, losing himself in an eventful distance filled with vague life. But then, from the corners of his eyes, his gaze darts back to the hall, and he is once more in front of the people.

Lament and jubilation, soaring and plunging . . . My fantasia! Bibi thinks lovingly. Listen, here comes the C-sharp passage! And as he plays, the key shifts into C sharp. Are they noticing? Oh, no, heaven forfend, they do not notice! And that is why he flutters his pretty eyelashes at least once toward the ceiling, so as to give the people something to look at.

The people sit in long rows, watching the wunderkind. And they think all sorts of things in their all-too-human brains. An old gentleman with a white beard, a signet ring on his index finger, and a bulbous growth on his bald head—an excrescence, if you will—thinks to himself: I really should be ashamed of myself. I've never gotten beyond "Three Hunters from the Palatinate," and now here I sit, a white-haired old man, letting that little runt perform wonders. But one mustn't forget: it comes from above. God is chary with his gifts, we have no say in the matter, and there's no shame in being an ordinary person. It's like with the infant Jesus. You have to bow to a child without feeling abashed. How strangely beneficial this is! He does not dare think: How sweet this is! "Sweet" would be embarrassing for a feisty old gentleman. But he feels it! He does feel it!

Art . . . , thinks the businessman with the parrot nose. Yes, to be sure, it brings a little shimmer into your life, a little dingdong and white silk. Incidentally, he's not doing so badly. They've sold a good fifty seats at twelve marks apiece—that already adds up to six hundred marks—plus all the other tickets. Subtract the hall rental, the lighting, and the programs, and you've easily netted a thousand marks. A pretty penny.

Well, that's Chopin he's just regaled us with! thinks the piano teacher, a lady with a pointed nose and of an age when hopes are laid to rest and the mind gets sharper. One may say that he is not very spontaneous. I'll say afterward: "He is not spontaneous." That sounds good. Incidentally, the way he holds his hands shows wretched training. One should be able to put a plate on the back of the hand. . . . I would treat him with the ruler!

A young girl, who looks quite waxen and has reached that tense age when one can very readily have awkward thoughts, secretly thinks: Now, what's that? What's he playing? Why, that's passion he's playing! But he's just a child! If he kissed me, it would be like getting kissed by my little brother—it wouldn't be a kiss. Is there such a thing as an abstract passion, a passion in and of itself and with no earthly object, a passion that would only be fervent child's play? . . . Well, if I said that out loud, they'd feed me cod-liver oil. That's life.

An officer is leaning against a column. Gazing at the successful Bibi, he thinks: You're something, and I'm something, each in his own way! He clicks his heels, paying the wunderkind the tribute he pays to all the powers that be.

However, the critic, an aging man in a shiny black jacket and turned-up, splattered trousers, sits in his complimentary seat and thinks: Just look at him, that Bibi, that brat! As an individual he's still got a lot of growing-up to do, but as a type—the artist type—he's already complete. He has the artist's grandeur and his lack of dignity, his charlatanry and his holy spark, his scorn and his secret rapture. But I mustn't write that: it's too good. Ah, believe me, I'd have become an artist myself if I didn't see through all this so clearly. . . .

Now the wunderkind is finished, and a veritable storm arises in the hall. He has to emerge and reemerge from behind his screen. The man with the shiny buttons drags over more tributes: four laurel wreaths, a lyre of violets, a bouquet of roses. He doesn't have arms enough to hand the wunderkind all the homages; the impresario personally mounts the platform to help him out. He hangs a laurel wreath around Bibi's neck, he tenderly strokes his black hair. And suddenly, as if overwhelmed, he bends down and gives the wunderkind a kiss, a resounding kiss, right on the mouth. And now the storm swells into a hurricane. This kiss shoots through the hall like an electric shock, surges through the crowd like a nervous shudder. The people are swept away by a crazy need for noise. Loud bravos mingle with the wild banging of the applause. Down there, some of Bibi's normal little comrades wave their handkerchiefs. . . . However, the critic thinks: Of course, that impresario kiss had to come. An old and effective ploy. Yes, good Lord, if only I didn't see through everything so clearly!

And so the wunderkind's concert comes to an end. It began at seven-thirty; at eight-thirty it is over. The platform is groaning with wreaths, and two small flowerpots stand on the piano's music desk. Bibi's last number was his "Rhapsodie grecque," which ultimately turns into the Greek national anthem, and his compatriots in the audience would have strongly liked to sing along if this were not a genteel concert. But at the conclusion they make up for it with their a tremendous racket, a hot-blooded hullabaloo, a national demonstration. However, the aging critic thinks: Of course, the national anthem had to come. They carry the thing into another area. When it comes to inspiring enthusiasm, they leave no stone unturned. I will write that this is unartistic. But perhaps it's really utterly artistic. What is the artist? A buffoon. Criticism is the acme. But I can't write that. And he walks away in his splattered trousers.

After nine or ten curtain calls, the flushed wunderkind no longer goes back behind the screen; stepping down into the hall, he walks over to his mama and the impresario. The chairs have been pushed and pulled about, the people stand among them, applaud, press forward. Several also want to see the princess. Two clusters form in front of the platform—one around the wunderkind and one around the princess, and people cannot quite tell which of the two is actually holding court. However, the lady-in-waiting is ordered to go over to Bibi; she tugs a little on his silk jacket, smoothing it, to make him presentable, leads him by his arm to the princess, and solemnly instructs him to kiss Her Royal Highness's hand.

"How do you do it, child?" the princess asks. "Does it come to you spontaneously when you sit down?"

"*Oui, madame,*" Bibi replies. But on the inside he thinks: Oh, you stupid old princess!

Then he shyly and uncouthly turns away and goes back to his own people.

Outside, at the wardrobe, there is a dense crush. People brandish their tags, they open up their arms to receive furs, scarves, and galoshes across the tables. Somewhere the piano teacher is standing with acquaintances and critiquing. "He is not very spontaneous," she exclaims, and looks around.

At one of the large wall mirrors, an elegant young lady is helped into her evening coat and her fur shoes by her brothers, two lieutenants. She is gorgeous with her steel-blue eyes and her clear, purebred face—a true noblewoman. When she is ready, she waits for her brothers. "Don't spend so much time at the mirror, Adolf," she grumbles softly to one brother, who cannot tear himself away from his handsome and simple face. Well, what nerve! Lieutenant Adolf will most certainly be allowed to stay at the mirror long enough to button up his overcoat—with her kind permission! Then they leave, and out in the street the arc lamps are shimmering dimly through the snowy fog. As he walks along with his upturned collar and his hands in his slanting coat pockets, Lieutenant Adolf starts kicking out on the hard, frozen snow, performing a little African jazz dance because it's so cold.

A child! thinks the uncoiffed girl who, accompanied by a gloomy adolescent youth, walks behind them, her arms dangling freely. A charming child! That was worthy of admiration. And in a loud, monotonous voice, she says: "Each of us is a wunderkind—we creative people."

Well! thinks the old gentleman who has never gotten beyond "Three Hunters from the Palatinate" and whose excrescence is now covered by a top hat. Just what is that? A kind of Pythia, or so it seems.

But the gloomy adolescent, who knows exactly what the girl means, nods slowly.

Then they fall silent, and the uncoiffed girl gazes after the three aristocratic siblings. She despises them, but she gazes after them until they have vanished around a corner.

# *HARSH HOUR*

HARSH HOUR

HE STOOD UP FROM THE DESK, from the small, frail writing table; he stood up like a despairing man, and with his head drooping, he crossed over to the opposite corner of the room, to the
stove, which was as tall and slender as a column. He put his
hands on the tiles, but they were almost entirely cooled off, for
midnight was long past. And so, without the minor comfort he
was looking for, he leaned his back against the stove and
coughed as he pulled together the tails of his dressing gown,
with the faded lace jabot dangling from the lapels. He snorted
arduously, trying to get a little air, for as usual he had a cold.

It was a special and sinister cold, which seldom cleared up entirely. His eyelids were inflamed, the edges of his nostrils were
completely sore, and his illness lay in his head and limbs like a
heavy, painful drunkenness. Or was all this weakness and heaviness caused by the nasty house arrest to which the physician had
once again sentenced him weeks before? God only knew if this
confinement was the right remedy. It might be necessary for the
eternal catarrh and the convulsions in his chest and abdomen,
and Jena had been suffering bad weather for weeks now, for
weeks—that was true: a miserable and despicable weather that
you felt in all your nerves, wild, gloomy, and cold—and the De-
cember wind howled in the stovepipe, squalid and godforsaken,
sounding like a labyrinthal storm on a nocturnal heath, like a
dreadful spiritual sorrow. But it was not good, this cramped im-
prisonment, not good for his thoughts or for the rhythm of his
blood, from which his thoughts emerged. . . .

The hexagonal room was bare, sober, and uncomfortable,

with its whitewashed ceiling, the tobacco smoke hovering underneath, the obliquely checkered wallpaper on which oval-framed silhouettes hung, the four or five pieces of thin-legged furniture, and the two candles burning at the head of the manuscript on the writing table. Red curtains hung above the upper window frames—mere flags, symmetrically draped calico; but the curtains were red, a warm, sonorous red, and he loved them and refused to do without them, for they brought a touch of opulence and voluptuousness into the unsensual and abstemious squalor of his room.

He stood by the stove, and with a quick, strenuous, painful blinking of his eyes, he peered over at the work from which he had fled—that burden, that pleasure, that torment of the conscience, that ocean that he was forced to drink up, that horrible task that was his pride and his misery, his heaven and his damnation. It dragged, it jammed, it halted—once again, once again! The weather was to blame, and his catarrh and his fatigue. Or was it the piece, or the laboring itself—a sordid spawning doomed to despair?

He had stood up to gain a bit of detachment; spatial distance from the manuscript often provided an overview, a more general idea of the material, enabling him to take any necessary steps. Yes, at times he was profoundly inspired by the relief he felt at turning away from the site of the struggle. And this was a more innocent enthusiasm than sipping liqueur or strong black coffee. . . . The demitasse stood on the small table. Could it help him get past his block? No, no, not anymore! Not only the doctor but someone else, a more prestigious person, had cautioned him against it: the other man, that one in Weimar, whom he loved with both yearning and enmity. *He* was wise. *He* knew how to live, how to create; never abused himself; took good care of himself. . . .

The house was hushed. Only the wind could be heard, driving down Castle Street, and the rain, prickling and hurtling against the windows. Everyone was asleep: the landlord and his family, Lotte and the children. And here he stood, lonely and awake, by the cold stove, blinking torturously at the work, in which he believed because of his morbid dissatisfaction with himself. His white neck loomed high out of the necktie, and the parted skirts of his robe revealed his knock-kneed legs. His red hair was smoothed back from the high, delicate forehead, exposing pale-veined recesses over the temples and covering the ears with thin curls. At the root of the large, aquiline nose, which ended abruptly in a whitish tip, the thick eyebrows, darker than the hair on his head, were closely set, lending the sore and sunken eyes a tragic gaze. Forced to breathe through his mouth, he opened his thin lips, so that his freckled cheeks, wan for lack of fresh air, slackened and fell in.

No, it wasn't working, it was all in vain! The army! The army should have been brought in! The army was the basis of everything! Since it could not be shown directly—could he even conceive of mustering the tremendous skill to force it on the imagination? And the hero was no hero; he was cold and ignoble. The approach was wrong, and the language was wrong; it was a dry, drab history course, broad, sober, and useless for the stage!

Fine, so it was over. A defeat! A failure. Bankruptcy. He wanted to write Körner about it, good Körner, who believed in him, who clung to his genius like a trusting child. His friend would plead, scoff, scold him good-naturedly; would remind him of *Don Carlos,* which had likewise emerged from doubts and strains and profound revisions, and which ultimately, after all the torment, had proved to be an outstanding, a glorious achievement. But that had been different. Back then he had still been the man to attack something with a fortunate hand and fashion his victory out of it. Scruples and struggles? Oh, yes.

And he had been sick, probably sicker than now, a starveling, a fugitive who had fallen out with the world, depressed, and destitute of anything human. But young, still very young! Each time, no matter how deeply crushed, his mind and spirit had lithely rebounded, and the hours of grief had yielded to the hours of faith and inner triumph. Those hours came no more, came scarcely. A night could bring a blazing mood, a brilliant and passionate illumination of what might happen if you could always enjoy such grace; but such a night was paid for with a week of darkness and paralysis. He was tired, thirty-seven years old, and already at the end. Faith was no longer alive—faith in the future, which had been his lodestar in all misery. And this was so, this was the desperate truth: the years of need and nullity, which he had regarded as years of ordeals and afflictions—those had actually been rich and fruitful years; and now that a little happiness had settled here, now that he was no longer an intellectual freebooter, now that he had gained a bit of legitimacy and middle-class solidity, now that he had status and honor, a wife and children . . . he was exhausted, at the end of his rope. Failure and despair—they were all that was left.

He moaned, squeezed his hands against his eyes, and moved through the room as if hounded. What he had just thought was so dreadful that he could not remain where the thought had come to him. He sat down on a chair by the wall, dropping his folded hands between his knees, and stared dismally at the floor.

His conscience . . . How loudly his conscience shrieked! He had sinned through all those years, sinned against himself, against the delicate instrument of his body. The excesses of his youthful boldness, the white nights, the days of smoky indoor air, his extreme cerebrality, the heedless indifference to his own body, the narcotics goading him on—all those things were getting their revenge now, getting their revenge!

And if they got their revenge, then he would defy the gods, who sent guilt and then exacted punishment. He had lived as he had to live, with no time to be wise, no time to be watchful. Here, in this place in his chest, whenever he breathed, coughed, yawned, always in the same spot, that small, diabolical stabbing and drilling: a foreboding that had never kept silent since that time in Erfurt five years ago, when he had been attacked by a feverish cold, that acute ailment of the lungs—what was it trying to say? But he knew all too well what it was driving at, no matter what the doctor could or would do. He had no time to take care of himself wisely, to husband his resources with mild morality. He had to do what he wanted to do—soon, today, quickly. . . . Morality? Yet in the end, why was it that of all things, sin, the surrender to things that destroyed and devoured, struck him as more moral than any wisdom or cool discipline? It was not that and not the despicable art of maintaining a good conscience that were moral, but struggle and hardship, passion and pain!

Pain . . . How that word swelled his chest! He stretched, folded his arms; and his gaze, under the reddish, close-set eyebrows, was imbued with beautiful lament. He was not yet miserable, not entirely miserable yet, so long as it was possible to give his misery a proud and noble name. One thing was crucial: a good heart for giving his life grand and beautiful names! For not blaming his sufferings on indoor air and constipation! For being healthy enough to wax grandiloquent—in order to see beyond the physical, to feel beyond it! For being naive about this alone though knowledgeable about everything else! For believing in, for being able to believe in pain! . . . But he did believe in pain, so deeply, so fervently that according to this belief, anything occurring amid pain could be neither useless nor bad. His eyes swung over to the manuscript, and his arms tightened on his chest. . . .

Talent itself—was it not pain? And when *that* thing there, the wretched work, made him suffer, was that not as it should be and almost a good sign? It had never gushed, and if it did so, that would truly arouse his distrust. It gushed only for dabblers and bunglers, for the ignorant and the easily satisfied, who did not live under the pressure and discipline of talent. For talent, ladies and gentlemen down there, far away in the orchestra—talent is not facile, not frivolous, it is not mere ability. At its root it is a *need*, a critical knowing about the ideal, a dissatisfaction that cannot create, or increase its power, without torment. And for the greatest, the most dissatisfied, their talent is their sharpest scourge. . . . Do not lament! Do not brag! Be modest and patient when you think about what you have endured! And if not one day in the week, not one hour, was free of suffering—so what? Making light of the burdens and achievements, the demands, complaints, and exertions, trivializing them—that was what made a man great!

He stood up, pulled out the snuffbox, and snorted greedily, then he clasped his hands behind his back and charged so fiercely across the room that the candles flickered in the draft. . . . Greatness! Extraordinariness! Conquest of the world and immortality of the name! What good was all the happiness of people eternally unknown compared with this goal? To be known—known and loved by the nations of the world! Chatter away about egoism, you people, who know nothing about the sweetness of this dream and drive! All extraordinary men are egotistical insofar as they suffer. "See for yourselves," says Extraordinariness, "you people without a mission, you who have such an easier time on this earth!" And Ambition speaks: "Should my suffering have been in vain? No, it has to make me great!"

The nostrils of his large nose were flaring, his eyes glowered and darted. His right hand was vehemently thrust deep into his dressing gown, while his left fist dangled at his side. A hot flash of redness had spread into his haggard cheeks, a blaze whipped up from the fire of his artistic egoism, that passion for his self, burning unquenchably in his depths. He knew it well—the secret intoxication of this love. Sometimes all he needed to do was contemplate his hand in order to be filled with an enthusiastic affection for himself, determined to serve it with any weapons of talent and art that were his. He could do so, there was nothing ignoble about it. And even deeper than his egoism was his awareness that there was no virtue in devouring himself for a sublime ideal: his self-sacrifice was a necessity. And this was his jealousy: he wanted no one to be greater than he if that man had not also suffered more deeply to attain that height.

No one! . . . He stood still, his hand over his eyes, his upper body turned halfway to the side, shrinking, fleeing. Yet he already felt the sting of that inevitable thought in his heart, the thought of him, the other one, the clear, the blissfully active, the sensual, the divinely spontaneous man—the thought of *him,* there, in Weimar, whom he loved with yearning and enmity. . . . And once more, as always, deeply unsettled, with haste and zeal, he felt it beginning inside him—the work that followed this thought: to assert his own existence and stake off his artistry against those of the other man. . . . Was he greater? Wherein? Why? If he won, was it sheer obstinacy? If he lost, would his defeat ever be a tragic drama? He may have been a god perhaps— but no hero! Yet it was easier being a god than a hero! Easier . . . The other man had an easier time of it! He could wisely and skillfully distinguish between knowing and creating—this could leave you cheerful, free of torment, make you fertile and fruitful. But if creating was godly, then knowledge was heroism, and he was both a god and a hero, who created by knowing!

The will to brave difficulty . . . Did anyone sense how much discipline it cost him, how much self-control, to build a sentence, frame a rigorous idea? For ultimately he was ignorant and unschooled, a sluggish and rapturous dreamer. It was harder writing any of Caesar's letters than shaping the finest scene—and did not that alone make the latter the more sublime? From the first rhythmic urge of artistry for motif, material, possibility of effusion . . . to thought, to image, to words, to lines. What a struggle! What a calvary! His works were wonders of yearning, the yearning for shape, form, boundary, physicality, the yearning for the clear world of the other man, who, with his godly lips, immediately called the sunlit things by name.

Nevertheless, and despite that man: where was there an artist, a poet, like him? Who, like him, created ex nihilo, from his own breast? Was a poem not born in his soul as music, as a pure primal image of Being, long before borrowing metaphor and apparel from the world of appearances? History, philosophy, passion: means and pretexts, nothing more, for something that had little to do with them, that had its home in Orphic depths. Words, concepts: merely keys that his artistry struck in order to make hidden strings resound. Did people know that? They praised him greatly, those good people, for the strength of conviction with which he played this note or that. And his favorite word, his ultimate emotional eloquence, the great bell with which he summoned others to the loftiest feasts of the soul—it lured many people. . . . Freedom . . . He truly understood more and less by freedom than they did when cheering. Freedom— what did that mean? Certainly not a touch of civic dignity in front of princes and thrones. Do you people even dream just what a mind dares to mean with that word? Freedom from what? Ultimately from what else? Perhaps even from happiness, from human happiness, that silken fetter, that soft, sweet bond . . .

From happiness . . . His lips twitched; it was as if his gaze turned inward, and slowly his face sank into his hands. . . . He was in the next room. Bluish light flowed from the hanging lamp, and the flowery curtain shrouded the window in motionless folds. He stood by the bed, leaning over the sweet face on the pillow. A black ringlet curled over the cheek, which shone with the paleness of pearls, and the childlike lips were parted in slumber. . . . My wife! Beloved! Did you yield to my yearning and did you come to me to be my happiness? You are my happiness, lie still! And sleep. Do not open those sweet, long-shadowed lashes to look at me, sometimes as big and dark as if you were asking and seeking me! By God, by God, I love you so much! Only sometimes I can't find my feeling, because I'm often very tired from suffering and from struggling with the task that my self imposes on me. And I mustn't be yours all too much, never be fully happy in you, for the sake of my mission. . . .

He kissed her, pulled himself away from the loving warmth of her slumber, looked around, returned. The bell reminded him of how far the night had advanced, but it was also as if the bell were benignly announcing the end of a harsh hour. He took a deep breath, his lips closed tight; he went over and picked up the quill. . . . Do not brood! He was too deep down for brooding! Do not descend into the chaos, or at least do not linger there. Instead reach into the chaos, which is fullness, and lift to the light that which is fit and ripe enough to gain form. Do not brood: work! Limit, exclude, give shape, complete . . .

And complete it he did, the work of his suffering. It may not have been good, but complete it he did. And when it was completed, lo and behold, it was good. And from his soul, from Music and Idea, new works struggled upward, resonant and shimmering creations, which, in sacred form, wondrously hinted at their infinite homeland, just as the ocean, from which it is fished, roars in the seashell.

# THE BLOOD OF
## THE WALSUNGS

SINCE IT WAS SEVEN MINUTES TO TWELVE, Wendelin came into the second-floor vestibule and beat the gong. Broad-legged, in his violet knee breeches, he stood on an old, faded prayer rug as he belabored the metal with his club. The brass clanging, savage, cannibalistic, and far too excessive for its purpose, penetrated everywhere: the parlors to the right and to the left, the billiard room, the library, the winter garden. The racket filled the entire house, whose evenly warmed atmosphere was thoroughly imbued with a sweet and exotic perfume. Finally the banging stopped, and for another seven minutes Wendelin attended to other business, while Florian, in the dining room, put the last touches on the luncheon table. But at the stroke of twelve the martial warning blasted a second time. And now everyone appeared.

Herr Aarenhold shuffled in from the library, where he had been absorbed in his old editions. He constantly acquired literary antiques, first editions in all languages, costly and moldy volumes. Quietly rubbing his hands, he asked in his subdued and slightly painful manner: "Isn't Beckerath here yet?"

"Oh, he'll come. How could he not come? He's saving himself a lunch in a restaurant," replied Frau Aarenhold, soundlessly descending the thickly carpeted stairs, passing the small, ancient church organ on the landing.

Herr Aarenhold blinked. His wife was impossible. She was small, ugly, prematurely aged, and looked as if she had withered under a torrid foreign sun. A diamond necklace lay on her sunken bosom. With its many curlicues and overhangs, her gray hair was arranged in an intricate and high-built coiffure, and attached somewhere on the side was a huge, iridescent diamond clasp, itself adorned with a tuft of white aigrettes. With tactful words, Herr Aarenhold and the children had reprimanded her more than once. But Frau Aarenhold tenaciously stuck to her taste.

The children came: Kunz and Märit, Siegmund and Sieglinde. Kunz, wearing a braided uniform, was a dark, handsome man with pouting lips and a dangerous-looking scar. He was training with his hussar regiment for six weeks. Märit showed up without a corset. She was ash blond, a stern girl of twenty-eight with a hooked nose, the gray eyes of a raptorial bird, and a bitter mouth. She was studying law and always went her own way, with an expression of scorn.

Siegmund and Sieglinde came last, hand in hand, from the third floor. They were twins, and the youngest children: gracile and willowy, their bodies childlike despite their nineteen years. She wore a Bordeaux velvet dress, too heavy for her figure and close in its cut to the fashion of the Florentine cinquecento. He wore a gray suit, with a raspberry tie of raw silk, patent-leather shoes on his slender feet, and cuff links with tiny diamonds. His heavy black beard was shaven, so that his thin, wan face with the joining black eyebrows likewise preserved the ephebic quality of his physique. His head was covered with thick black curls that were vehemently parted on the side and grew far into his temples. She had dark-brown hair, combed in a deep, smooth part over her ears and sporting a gold circlet from which a large pearl hung into her forehead; the circlet was a present from him. On one of his boyish wrists he had a heavy gold chain—a present from her. The twins looked very much alike. They had the same slightly downpressed nose, the same lips resting full and soft on each other, the same prominent cheekbones and shiny black eyes. But they resembled each other most in their long, slender hands—his being no more masculine than hers but simply more reddish. And they constantly held hands, unfazed by the fact that their hands tended to moisten. . . .

The family stood awhile on the rugs in the hall, barely speaking. Finally von Beckerath arrived—Sieglinde's fiancé. Wendelin opened the foyer door for him, and he entered in a black frock coat, apologizing to all and sundry for his tardiness. He was a civil servant and of a fine family—short, canary-yellow, goateed, and zealously well-mannered. Before starting a sentence, he would quickly inhale the air through his open mouth while squeezing his chin into his chest.

He kissed Sieglinde's hand and said:

"Yes, you forgive me too, Sieglinde! It's such a long way from the ministry to the Tiergarten." He could not yet use the familiar pronoun with her; she did not care for that. Without hesitating, she replied:

"A very long way. And by the by, considering how long it is, what if you left your ministry a wee bit earlier?"

Kunz added, and his eyes narrowed into flashing slits:

"That would have a decidedly stimulating effect on our household schedule."

"Yes, my goodness . . . Urgent matters . . . ," said von Beckerath dully. He was thirty-five years old.

The children had spoken with quick, sharp tongues. They seemed aggressive, but perhaps it was only an inborn defensiveness, and they probably enjoyed their own glibness, however hurtful it might be, so that only a nitpicker would have been annoyed. They shrugged off von Beckerath's feeble response as if finding that it fitted his character and that any witty retort would be wasted on him.

They went to the table, led by Herr Aarenhold, who wanted to show Herr von Beckerath that he was hungry. They sat down, they unfolded their stiff napkins. In the tremendous dining room, with its rugs, its eighteenth-century boiserie, and the three electric lusters on the ceiling, the family table with the seven diners was utterly forlorn. The table had been moved over to the huge floor-length window, beneath which the delicate silvery jet of a fountain capered beyond a lattice; the panes offered a wide view of the still wintry garden. The upper portions of the dining-room walls were decked out with Gobelins of pastoral idylls, which, like the wainscoting, had long ago decorated a French château. The diners sat in deep chairs, whose wide and yielding cushions were covered with Gobelins. On the strong, dazzling white, and sharply ironed damask, each place setting featured a tapering glass vase holding two orchids. With his haggard and cautious hand, Herr Aarenhold wedged his pince-nez halfway up his nose and distrustfully read the menu, which lay threefold on the table. He suffered from a weakness of the solar plexis, that sheaf of nerves which, located in the pit of the stomach, can be a source of serious travail. He was therefore obliged to watch what he ate.

There was consommé with beef marrow, sole au vin blanc, pheasant, and pineapple. Nothing else. It was a simple family luncheon. But Herr Aarenhold was satisfied: this was good, wholesome food. The soup came. A dumbwaiter soundlessly brought it down from the kitchen to the buffet, and the servants handed it around the table, leaning over with their faces concentrated in a kind of passion for serving. The soup was consumed from tiny cups made of the most delicate, translucent porcelain. Whitish clumps of marrow floated in the hot, golden-yellow liquid.

Warmed by the soup, Herr Aarenhold was stimulated to bring up a little air. With fastidious fingers, he put the napkin to his mouth, seeking some outlet for what was stirring his mind.

"Do have another cup, Beckerath," he said. "It's nourishing. A man who works has the right to indulge himself, and with gusto at that. . . . Do you actually enjoy eating? Is eating a pleasure for you? If not, then too bad. For me, every meal is a small feast. Someone once said that life is indeed beautiful, since it is structured in such a way that we can eat four times a day. He took the words right out of my mouth. To appreciate such an arrangement, though, we have to remain somewhat youthful and grateful, but not everyone knows how. People grow old—fine, there's nothing we can do about that. But the point is that things have to remain fresh and you should never get accustomed to anything. . . . Now," he went on, bedding a little beef marrow on a piece of roll and salting it, "your circumstances are about to change; the level of your existence will rise, not unessentially." Von Beckerath smiled. "If you want to enjoy your life, truly enjoy it, consciously, artistically, then try not to get accustomed to the new circumstances. Habit is death. It dulls the mind. Do not get acclimated, do not take anything for granted, maintain a child's sweet tooth for the delights of prosperity. Look—for some years now I have been in a position to indulge in some of life's amenities"—von Beckerath smiled—"but I assure you that every morning that God grants me, when I wake up, my heart still pounds a little because my bedcover is made of silk. That is youthfulness. . . . I do know how I did it; and yet I can look around me and feel like an enchanted prince. . . ."

The children all exchanged glances, and so recklessly that Herr Aarenhold could not help but notice, much to his obvious embarrassment. He knew that they were united against him and that they despised him: for his origins, for the blood that flowed in his veins and that they had received from him; for the way he had acquired his wealth; for his hobbies, which they thought unbecoming; for the way he took care of himself, to which, they felt, he likewise had no right; for his weak, poetic garrulousness, which ignored the boundaries of good taste. . . . He knew all this and, in a way, agreed; he was not without a sense of guilt toward them. But ultimately he had to assert his personality, he had to live his life and also be able to talk about it—namely, say these things. He had the right, he had demonstrated that he was worthy of consideration. He had been a worm, a louse, yes indeed; but the very ability to feel this with such fervor and self-contempt had become the cause of that tenacious and insatiable striving that had made him great. . . . Herr Aarenhold had been born in some far-flung backwater in Eastern Europe, had married the daughter of a well-to-do shopkeeper, and by means of bold and shrewd enterprise and extensive machinations in regard to a mine, the exposure of a coal seam, he had steered a tremendous and inexhaustible stream of gold into his bank account.

The fish course arrived. The servants quickly carried it from the buffet across the vastness of the room. They also brought the creamy sauce accompanying the fish and poured Rhine wine, which made the tongue prickle softly. The diners talked about Sieglinde's and Beckerath's wedding.

It was right around the corner, scheduled to take place in one week. They mentioned the trousseau, they outlined the honeymoon trip to Spain. Actually these matters were discussed by Herr Aarenhold alone, supported by von Beckerath's well-mannered compliance. Frau Aarenhold ate greedily, responding to questions, as was her way, with new questions, which were anything but useful. Her speech was larded with bizarre and richly guttural words—expressions from her childhood dialect. Märit was full of implicit opposition to the planned church wedding, which offended her thoroughly enlightened convictions. Incidentally, Herr Aarenhold likewise felt cool toward this ceremony, since von Beckerath was a Protestant. Protestant nuptials, he said, were devoid of beauty. It would have been different had von Beckerath been of the Catholic faith.

Kunz held his tongue, because in von Beckerath's presence he was always annoyed at his mother. And neither Siegmund nor Sieglinde revealed any interest in the subject. Between their chairs, they held each other's damp, slender hands. Now and then their eyes met, melted, formed a rapport to which no one else had access or entry. Von Beckerath sat on Sieglinde's other side.

"Fifty hours," said Aarenhold, "and you'll be in Madrid if you like. They're making progress—the shortest way once took me sixty hours. I assume you would prefer the overland route to the maritime route from Rotterdam?"

Von Beckerath eagerly preferred the overland route.

"But you won't give Paris the cold shoulder. You do have the option of traveling directly via Lyons. . . . Sieglinde knows Paris; but you should not forgo the opportunity. . . . It's up to you whether you stop off beforehand. The choice of where the honeymoon should begin is entirely yours—it's only fair."

Sieglinde turned her head, turned it toward her fiancé for the first time: blunt and free, quite unconcerned about whether anyone noticed. She peered into the well-mannered face at her side, her big, dark eyes probing, expecting, inquiring—a shiny, earnest gaze, which, for those three seconds, spoke as mindlessly as the gaze of an animal. But between the chairs she held the slender hand of her twin, whose joining eyebrows formed two black creases at the root of his nose. . . .

The conversation drifted off into some unsteady bantering and then touched on a zinc-sealed consignment of fresh cigars, which had been sent to Herr Aarenhold personally from Havana. Next, the talk circled several times around a point—an issue of purely logical nature—casually tossed in by Kunz: if, namely, *a* is the necessary and sufficient condition for *b*, then is *b* similarly the necessary and sufficient condition for *a*? They argued, dissected astutely, cited examples, roamed and rambled, assaulted one another with abstract and ironclad dialectics, and snapped heatedly at each other. Märit had introduced a philosophical distinction into the debate—namely, the difference between the concrete and the causal principle. Kunz, talking down to them from his raised head, declared that "causal principle" was a pleonasm. Märit grumpily insisted that her terminology was valid. Herr Aarenhold adjusted himself in his chair, lifted a morsel of bread between thumb and index, and attempted to elucidate the entire matter. He suffered a complete fiasco. The children laughed their heads off. Even Frau Aarenhold reprimanded him. "What are you talking about?" she said. "Did you study that? You've studied almost nothing!" And by the time von Beckerath squeezed his chin into his chest and inhaled the air through his mouth in order to express his opinion, they had already changed the topic.

Siegmund was speaking. In an ironic tone, he described an acquaintance who was getting more and more simpleminded and closer to nature, so that he could no longer tell the difference between a regular jacket and a dinner jacket. This Parsifal even talked about a checkered dinner jacket. . . . Kunz knew of an even more pathetic case of uncorrupted innocence: a man who went to low tea in a tuxedo.

"A tuxedo in the afternoon?" said Sieglinde, twisting her lips. "Why, only an animal would do that!"

Von Beckerath laughed assiduously, particularly since a tweak of his conscience reminded him that he himself had attended teas in a tuxedo.

While partaking of the fowl, they began discussing questions of an all-around cultural nature: the fine arts (von Beckerath was a devotee and a connoisseur) as well as literature and theater, which enjoyed top priority in the Aarenhold house, although Siegmund did like to paint.

The conversation grew animated and general, the children took a crucial part, they were well-spoken, their gestures nervous and arrogant. They marched in the vanguard of taste and demanded only the utmost. They ignored all vision, intention, and dreaming, all struggling will, they ruthlessly insisted on ability, achievement, success in the pitiless contest of forces; and it was the victorious piece of art that they acknowledged though never admired. Herr Aarenhold himself said to von Beckerath:

"You are very good-natured, my boy, you defend good inten-tions. But it's *results* that count, my friend! You say: 'What he does may not be all that good, but he was only a peasant before he switched to art, so that this is quite astonishing.' Not by a long shot! Achievement is absolute. There are no mitigating circum-stances. Let him do first-rate work, or he can haul manure. How far would I have ever gotten with your tolerant attitude? I could have told myself: 'You were born a nobody; it'll be great if you can work your way up to department head.' If I had thought along those lines, I wouldn't be sitting here now. I had to force the world to acknowledge me—well, now I want to be forced to acknowledge something. Here is Rhodes; be so good as to dance!"

The children laughed. For a split second, they did not despise him. They sat in deep, soft cushions at the dining-room table, their postures casual, their faces pampered and capricious; they sat in sumptuous security, yet their words were barbed, as if brightness, hardness, and alert wit were crucial for their survival, as if their very lives hung on their defenses. Their praise was grudging assent; their censure quick, clever, and disrespectful: it could disarm you in an instant, blunt any enthusiasm, make it mute and stupid. They would call a work "very good" if a dreamless intellectuality shielded it against any grievance, and they scoffed at the faux pas of passion. Von Beckerath, with his bent for unarmed enthusiasm, had a hard time, especially since his age disqualified him. He kept shrinking in his chair, squeez-ing his chin into his chest and dazedly inhaling through his open mouth, bullied by their cheerful superiority. They disagreed no matter what, as if deeming it impossible, shameful, pitiful, not to disagree; they disagreed superbly, their eyes narrowing into flashing slits. They pounced on a word, a single word he had used, they tore it to shreds, rejected it, and dug up a different word, a dead certain one, which whizzed, struck, and quivered in the bull's-eye. . . . By the end of the luncheon, von Beckerath's eyes were red and he looked utterly deranged.

Suddenly (they were strewing sugar on the pineapple slices) Siegmund spoke, twisting his face like someone blinded by the sun:

"Oh, listen, Beckerath, before we forget, there's one more thing. . . . Sieglinde and I would like to approach you with a plea: They're doing *Die Walküre* tonight at the opera. Sieglinde and I would like to hear it together one more time. . . . May we? Naturally, it's all contingent on your grace and benevolence."

"How ingenious!" said Herr Aarenhold.

Kunz drummed the rhythm of the Hunding motif on the tablecloth.

Von Beckerath, stunned that anyone should be asking his permission for anything, eagerly replied: "But Siegmund, of course . . . And you, Sieglinde . . . I find that very reasonable. Do go, by all means. . . . I'll be able to join you. There's an excellent cast tonight. . . ."

The Aarenholds bent mirthfully over their plates. Von Beckerath, excluded, squinting, and struggling to orient himself, attempted, by hook or by crook, to share their mirth.

Siegmund promptly went on: "Oh, you know, I agree that it's really a good cast. But you misunderstood. Sieglinde and I would like to hear *Die Walküre* again *alone* with one another before the wedding. I don't know if you know . . ."

"But of course . . . I completely understand. Why, that's charming. You absolutely have to go."

"Thank you. We're very grateful to you. Well, then, I'll have Percy and Hurdy-Gurdy harnessed up for us."

"Permit me to remark," said Herr Aarenhold, "that your mother and I are having dinner at the Erlangers', and we're taking Percy and Hurdy-Gurdy. You must deign to make do with Baal and Zampa and the brown coupé."

"What about tickets?" asked Kunz.

"I got them long ago," said Siegmund, tossing back his head. They laughed and peered into the fiancée's eyes.

With sharp fingers, Herr Aarenhold undid a packet of belladonna powder and carefully shook it into his mouth. Then he lit a fat cigarette, which soon spread a delicious aroma. The servants sprang over and drew back the chairs behind him and Frau Aarenhold. They were ordered to serve coffee in the winter garden. In a sharp voice, Kunz demanded his dogcart to take him to the barracks.

Siegmund was dressing for the opera; he had been at it for an hour already. He had a constant and extraordinary need for cleanliness, so that he spent a considerable portion of each day at the washbasin. Now he stood in front of a huge, white-framed Empire mirror, dipping the powder puff into its embossed box and powdering his chin and cheeks, which were freshly shaved; for his beard growth was so heavy that if he went out in the evening, he was obliged to remove it yet again.

He stood there somewhat particolored: in pink silk socks and drawers, red Morocco slippers, and a padded house jacket with a dark pattern and light-gray fur lapels. And around him lay the huge bedroom, appointed entirely with elegantly practical white things, while the windows revealed the masses of naked and foggy treetops in the Tiergarten.

Since it was getting all too dark, he lit the lamps, which, arranged in a large glowing circle on the white ceiling, filled the room with a milky brightness, and he pulled the velvet curtains across the dusky panes. The light was taken up by the deep, watery-clear mirrors on the armoire, the washstand, and the vanity—and the small cut-glass bottles glittered on the tiled edges of the vanity. Siegmund continued working on himself. At times, when some thought flew through his mind, his joining eyebrows formed two black creases at the root of his nose.

His day had passed as his days always passed: vacant and swift. The opera began at six-thirty, and since he had started changing at four-thirty, he had not had much of an afternoon. He had rested on his chaise longue from two to three o'clock and then taken his tea, using the extra hour to stretch out in a deep leather easy chair in the study he shared with his brother, Kunz, and to read a few pages of several newly published novels. Although finding them all wretchedly feeble, he had nevertheless sent a few to his bookbinder in order to have them artistically bound for his library.

Incidentally, he had worked that morning. He had spent one hour, from ten to eleven o'clock, at his professor's studio. This professor, an artist of European fame, was shaping Siegmund's talent for drawing and painting, for which service he received two thousand marks a month from Herr Aarenhold. But nevertheless, what Siegmund painted was silly. He knew this himself and was far from placing any glowing expectations on his artistry. He was too astute not to realize that the circumstances of his existence were not exactly the most conducive for developing a creative gift.

The accoutrements of his life were so rich, so manifold, so overladen, that almost no room was left for life itself. Every last accessory was so costly and beautiful that it fastidiously transcended its designated purpose, confusing him, draining his attention. Siegmund had been born into this superfluousness; he was, no doubt, accustomed to it. And yet the fact was that this superfluousness never stopped occupying and exciting him, arousing him with constant sensuality. In this respect, like it or not, he resembled Herr Aarenhold, who practiced the art of getting accustomed to nothing.

Siegmund loved to read; he strove after language and intellect as if they were implements to which he was driven by a deep instinct. But never had he surrendered to a book, lost himself in it, such as happens when this one book becomes the most important one, the only one, the microcosm beyond which you cannot see, in which you are enclosed and absorbed, sucking nourishment from the very last syllable. Books and magazines poured in, he could buy them all, they piled up around him; and while trying to read, he was unsettled by the huge amount of reading still to be done. Yet the books got bound. And there they stood, in embossed leather, adorned with Siegmund Aarenhold's lovely insignia, sumptuous and self-sufficient, weighing down his life like a possession that he never managed to subjugate.

The day was his, was free, was given to him with all its hours from sunrise to sunset; and yet Siegmund found no time within himself to go after something, much less see it through. He was no hero, he had no vast powers. His preparations, his luxurious dispositions for the serious and authentic possibilities of life, used up whatever strength was his to commit. How much circumspection and introspection were depleted by dressing meticulously and impeccably, how much energy was focused on supervising his wardrobe, his supplies of cigarettes, soaps, and perfumes, how much initiative went into that moment that came two or three times a day, when he had to select a necktie! And he had to. It was crucial. Let the blond burghers of the land go about heedlessly in elasticized boots and Byron collars. He precisely, in his outer appearance, he had to be unassailable and irreproachable from head to foot. . . .

Ultimately, this was all that anyone expected of him. And in those occasional moments when he had vague qualms about "authenticity," he felt that this lack of expectation from other people lamed and loosened his sense of it. The household agenda was aimed at making the day go by swiftly and with no tangible blank periods. The next meal always came hurrying along. They dined before seven; the evening, the time of idling with a clear conscience, was long. The days melted away, and the seasons came and went just as hastily. Two summer months were spent in the lakeside château, with its vast, resplendent gardens, its tennis courts, cool park trails, and bronze statues on the manicured lawn; the third month was spent by the seashore or in the high mountains, at hotels that strove to outdo the extravagance back home. . . . On several recent winter days he had had himself driven to the university to attend a conveniently scheduled course in art history; he stopped going because, according to the verdict of his olfactory nerves, the other gentlemen in the class did not bathe anywhere near often enough. . . .

Instead he went strolling with Sieglinde. She had been at his side since their earliest beginnings, she had clung to him since they had both babbled their first sounds, taken their first steps. And he had no other friends, had never had any, aside from this girl who had been born with him: his preciously adorned, darkly beautiful likeness, whose moist and slender hand he held while the richly laden days glided past them with vacant eyes. They brought fresh flowers along on their walks, a nosegay of violets or lilies of the valley, taking turns sniffing them, sometimes smelling them together. As they sauntered, they inhaled the lovely fragrance with languid and luscious abandon, tending themselves like self-absorbed invalids, drugging themselves like people without hope, mentally shooing away the foul-reeking world and loving each other for their exquisite uselessness. Their language, however, was sharp and sparkling; it captured the people they encountered, the things they had seen, heard, read, things made by others, by those who were meant to expose a work to language, designation, witty disagreement. . . .

Then von Beckerath had come: employed at the ministry and of a fine family. He had courted Sieglinde, enjoying benevolent neutrality from Herr Aarenhold, endorsement from Frau Aarenhold, and zealous support from Kunz, the hussar. The suitor had been patient, solicitous, and infinitely well-mannered. And eventually, after telling him often enough that she did not love him, Sieglinde had started looking at him, probing him, wordless and expectant, with a shiny, earnest gaze that spoke as mindlessly as the gaze of an animal—and she had said yes. And Siegmund himself, whose word was her law, shared the responsibility; though he despised himself for his acquiescence, he had not opposed the match, because von Beckerath was employed at the ministry and was of a fine family. . . . Sometimes, while Siegmund was occupied with dressing, his joining eyebrows formed two black creases over the root of his nose. . . .

Siegmund stood there, his feet vanishing in the hair of the polar-bear rug that stretched out its paws in front of the bed. Having washed his entire body with cologne, he took the pleated dress shirt and let the starched and shimmering linen glide over his sallow torso, which was as scrawny as a boy's and yet shaggy with black hair. He then slipped into a pair of black silk drawers, socks of black silk, and black garters with silver clasps, and he pulled on the well-pressed trousers, whose black cloth shimmered like silk. Then he fastened the white silk suspenders over his narrow shoulders, and propping his foot on a stool, he started buttoning his patent-leather boots. Someone knocked.

"May I come in, Gigi?" asked Sieglinde outside.

"Yes, come in," he replied.

She entered, fully dressed, in a gown of shiny, sea-green silk, its rectangular décolletage lined with a wide band of embroidered ecru. Two embroidered peacocks, facing each other above the belt, held a garland in their beaks. Sieglinde's very dark hair was unadorned now, but a large oval jewel hung from a thin string of pearls on her bare throat, which had the color of slightly smoked meerschaum. A scarf heavily interwoven with silver was draped over one arm.

"I won't hide the fact," she said, "that the carriage is waiting."

"I won't hesitate to maintain," he parried, "that it will have to be patient for another two minutes." The two minutes became ten. She sat on the white velvet chaise longue, watching him work more zealously.

From a kaleidoscope of neckties, he chose a white piqué band and started looping it into a bow at the mirror.

"Beckerath," she said, "still wears colored ties crossed over— last year's fashion."

"Beckerath," he said, "leads the most trivial existence that I have ever caught a glimpse of." Then, turning to her, he added, twisting his face like someone blinded by the sun: "By the by, I'd like to ask you not to mention that Teuton again this evening."

She laughed briefly and answered: "You may rest assured that I can manage that without much difficulty."

He slipped into the low-cut piqué vest and then the tuxedo jacket, which he had tried on five times; its soft silk lining caressed his hands as they glided through the sleeves.

"Let me see your links and buttons," said Sieglinde, stepping over. It was the amethyst set. The shirt studs, the cuff links, the buttons on the white vest, all formed a matching group.

She beamed at him in proud admiration and devotion—a deep, dark tenderness in her shiny eyes. Her lips rested so softly on each other that he kissed them. The twins sat down on the chaise longue to cuddle for a moment, as they liked to do.

"You're very, very soft again," she said, stroking his shaven cheeks.

"Your little arms feel like satin," he said, running his hand over her tender lower arm, while he breathed the violet scent of her hair.

She kissed him on the closed eyelids; he kissed her neck at the side of the jewel. They kissed each other's hands. With a sweet sensuality, they loved each other for their good fragrance, and for being pampered and precious and well groomed. Finally they played like little puppies, nipping at one another with their lips. Then he stood up.

"Let's not be late tonight," he said. He pressed the mouth of the perfume bottle to his handkerchief, rubbed a drop into his red, slender hands, picked up the gloves, and declared that he was ready.

He put out the light and they left, walking down the reddishly lit hallway, where old, dark paintings hung, and past the organ, and then down the stairs. In the ground-floor vestibule Wendelin was standing, waiting with their coats, gigantic in his own long yellow coat. They let him help them into their wraps. Sieglinde's dark little head half vanished in her silver-fox collar. They walked, followed by the butler, across the stone floor and stepped outside.

The air was mild; large, ragged snowflakes were falling slowly in the whitish light. The coupé stood right by the house. The coachman, his hand on his rosette hat, was leaning slightly forward from his seat while Wendelin handed the siblings into the vehicle. Then he shut its door. Wendelin swung himself up to the coachman, and the coupé, instantly speeding along, ground over the gravel of the front yard, glided through the high, wide-open barred gate, curved lithely to the right, and rolled away. . . .

The small, soft space they sat in was filled with gentle warmth. "Should I close up?" asked Siegmund. And since she nodded, he drew the brown silk curtains across the polished panes.

They were in the heart of the city. Lights whizzed past the curtains. Around the swift, steady thud of the horses' hooves, around the noiseless speed of the coupé, which carried them buoyantly over the bumpy streets, the machinery of metropolitan life roared and shrieked and boomed. And shut off from it, softly sheltered from it, they sat wordlessly in the wadded brown silk cushions, hand in hand.

The coupé drove up and halted. Wendelin was at the door to help them step down. In the brightness of the arc lamps, gray, freezing people watched their arrival, glaring at them with inquisitive hatred as they passed through the lobby, followed by the butler. It was already late, already still. They mounted the outside steps, threw their coats over Wendelin's arm, spent a moment side by side at a lofty mirror, and then passed through the small door into their box. They were greeted by the final clatter of seats, the final buzz of conversation before the hush. The instant the lackey pushed the velvet armchairs under them, the theater shrouded itself in darkness, and the prelude commenced with a wild pulsation.

Storm . . . storm . . . Reaching here, favored by an airy wafting and hovering, undisturbed, unperturbed by hindrances, by petty irritations, Siegmund and Sieglinde instantly gave it their all. Storm and thunderous rutting, wind whooshing wild in the woods. The raucous command of the god rumbled, recurred, wrenched by wrath, and the thunder obediently crashed. The curtain flew open as if blasted apart by the storm. There was the pagan hall, with the glow of the hearth in the dark, the looming outline of the ash tree in the middle.

Siegmund, a rosy man with a wheat-colored beard, appeared in the wooden doorway and leaned driven and drained, against the jamb. Then his powerful legs, wrapped in skins and straps, tragically shuffled forward. Under the blond brows, under the blond forelock of his wig, his blue eyes were broken, imploring the kapellmeister; and at last the music died down, died out, to let his voice be heard, and his voice sounded clear and brazen, though mellowed into a gasp. He sang briefly, explaining that he had to rest, no matter whose hearth it might be; and with the final word he collapsed heavily on the bearskin and lay there, bedding his head on his fleshy arm. His chest heaved in his slumber.

A minute wore by, filled with the singing, speaking, heralding flow of the music, rolling its tide at the foot of the events. . . . Then came Sieglinde from the left. She had an alabaster bosom, which swayed marvelously in the décolletage of her muslin robe and her mantle of fur. She was shocked at the sight of the stranger; and so she squeezed her doubling chin into her chest, shaped her lips, and uttered her shock in notes that rose, soft and warm, from her white larynx as she formed the sounds with her tongue, her mobile mouth. . . .

She tended him. Bending over him, so that her breasts blossomed toward him from the wild fur, she held out the horn with both hands. He drank. Poignantly the music spoke of refreshment, cool kindness. Then they gazed at each other in a first ecstasy, a first dim recognition, silently yielding to the moment, which sang underneath, a deep and drawing song. . . .

She brought him mead, first touching the horn with her lips, then watched him drinking and drinking. And again their eyes met and melted, and again the deep melody drew and yearned underneath. . . . Then he got up to go; gloomy, turning painfully away, with his naked arms dangling, he went to the door, to carry everything from her, bear it all back to the wilderness: his suffering, his loneliness, his hated, harried life. She called to him, and since he did not hear, she, recklessly, with raised hands, let slip the confession of her own disaster. He halted. She lowered her eyes. At their feet the music spoke darkly of sorrow that both understood. He stayed. With folded arms, he stood at the hearth, awaiting fate.

Hunding came, knock-kneed and big-bellied like a cow. His beard was black, with many dark tufts. He was announced by his defiant motif, and he stood there, dark and coarse, leaning on his spear, glaring with buffalo eyes at the guest, whom he then, in a sort of savage civility, greeted and welcomed. His bass was like rust and colossal.

Sieglinde set the table for supper; and while she worked, Hunding's slow and suspicious gaze lumbered between her and the stranger. This oaf very clearly saw their resemblance; they were of one breed, that independent, uncontrollable, and extraordinary breed that he hated, that made him feel inadequate. . . .

Then they sat down, and Hunding introduced himself, explained simply and tersely his simple and orderly existence, based on general respect. He thus forced Siegmund to reveal himself, which was incomparably harder. But Siegmund sang— sang brightly, beautifully, about his life and woe, and how he had been born as one of two, with a twin sister, and, like people who must be a bit cautious, he used a false name and spoke eloquently about the hatred, the envy, the persecution of him and his strange father, about the burning of the hall, the disappearance of his sister, the harried and notorious outlaw existence of the son and the father, and how in the end he mysteriously lost his father. . . .

And then Siegmund sang of his foremost sorrow: his craving to be with others, his longing and his endless loneliness. He had wooed men and women, he sang, had courted friendship and love, and yet he had always been spurned. A curse had lain upon him; he was branded by his strange origin. His language was not the language of others, nor was theirs his. The things he liked offended most others, the ancient things they venerated made his blood boil. He was caught in strife and struggle always and everywhere, scorn and hatred and contempt at his heels, and all because he was of a foreign breed, a hopelessly different race. . . .

Hunding's reaction to all this was utterly typical of him. No sympathy and no understanding were revealed by his responses: only repulsion and dark distrust toward Siegmund's dubious, adventurous, and irregular existence. And now it dawned on him: here, in his own house, was the fugitive he was called on to hunt, had set out to hound; and Hunding acted as might be expected of his foursquare pedantry. With ill-befitting civility, he declared again that his house was holy and would harbor the stranger tonight, but tomorrow he would have the honor of felling Siegmund in a fight. He then snapped gruffly at Sieglinde, ordering her to mull his nocturnal beverage and wait for him in bed; he spewed out two or three more threats and then stomped off, taking all his weapons along, leaving Siegmund alone, in deepest despair.

Siegmund, in his chair, bending over the velvet-covered balustrade, leaned his dark, boyish head on his red and slender hand. His eyebrows formed two black creases, and one of his feet, resting only on the heel of the patent-leather boot, kept nervously moving, restlessly twitching and turning. It stopped when he heard the whisper at his side: "Gigi . . ."

And as he looked around, his lips had an insolent twist.

Sieglinde was offering him a mother-of-pearl box of cognac cherries.

"The maraschino chocolates are on the bottom," she whispered. But he took only a cherry, and while he removed the tissue wrapping, she leaned over again and whispered into his ear: "She's coming right back to him."

"I am not totally unaware of that," he said, so loudly that several hateful faces jerked toward them.

Down below, in the dark, the huge Siegmund sang to himself, from the depths of his breast he called for his sword, the lustrous blade that he could swing if someday, in blazing uproar, the angry emotions erupted—the hatred and yearning locked up in his heart. He saw the sword hilt shining in the tree, saw the glow and the hearth fire fade, he sank back into desperate slumber—and propped himself up on his hands in delicious dismay when Sieglinde stole over to him in the darkness.

Hunding slept like a log, dazed and drunk. Siegmund and Sieglinde were delighted that the cloddish boor was outfoxed—and their eyes had the same way of shrinking when smiling. But then Sieglinde peeked at the kapellmeister and received her cue, shaped and formed her lips and sang in detail about her plight—sang heartbreakingly about how they had caught the lonesome woman, who had grown up wild and foreign, how they had given her, without asking, to the gloomy and loutish man, and how they had even demanded that she deem herself lucky for the honorable marriage that would make others forget her obscure origins. . . . She sang deep and comfortingly about the old man in the hat and how he had plunged the sword into the trunk of the ash tree—for the One who alone was destined to draw it from its restraint. She sang in ecstasy that he might be the one she meant and she knew and so grievously longed for, the friend who was more than her friend, the consoler in her distress, the avenger of her dishonor, he whom she had lost long ago and whom she wept for in disgrace, her brother in suffering, her savior, her rescuer. . . .

But now Siegmund flung both his rosy, fleshy arms around her, pressed her cheek to the fur on his chest, and sang beyond her head, sang with an unleashed voice, a silvery shattering, sang his exultation into all the winds. His breast was hot with the oath that bound him to her, the lovely mate. All longing of his outlaw life was quenched in her—and he found everything healed in her: the hurtful spurning when he had approached men and women, when he had courted friendship and love with the insolence that was timidity and the awareness of his stigma. She lay in shame as he in sorrow, dishonored she as he an outlaw—and now their sibling love would be vengeance, vengeance!

A gust whistled, the huge wooden door flew open, a flood of white electric light engulfed the theater, and, suddenly exposed in the darkness, they stood there and sang the song of Spring and Spring's sister, Love.

They crouched on the bearskin, each looked at the other in the light and sang sweet things to him, to her. Their naked arms grazed one another, their hands were on the other's temples, each peered into the other's eyes, and their mouths were close together in their singing. Eyes and temples, foreheads and voices, they compared them and found them alike. The urging, growing recognition wrested forth the father's name; she called him by his name: Siegmund! Siegmund! He swung the freed sword over his head, blissful she sang to him, said who she was: his twin sister, Sieglinde. . . . Enthralled, he held out his arms to her, his bride, she sank against his heart, the curtain rustled to a close, the music whirled in a raging, roaring, foaming maelstrom of sweeping passion, whirled, whirled, and stood still with a violent stroke!

Lively applause. The lights went on. A thousand people stood up, stretched inconspicuously, and applauded, their bodies already facing the exits, their heads still turned toward the stage, toward the singers, who lined up in front of the curtain, like masks in a booth at the county fair. Hunding also emerged, with a well-mannered smile despite all that had happened. . . .

Siegmund pushed back his chair and got to his feet. He felt hot; a redness gleamed on his cheekbones, above the wan, scrawny, shaven cheeks.

"If I count at all," he said, "I would like to seek some better air. By the by, Siegmund was downright feeble."

"Also," said Sieglinde, "the orchestra saw fit to drag terribly during the 'Spring Song.'"

"Sentimental," said Siegmund, shrugging his narrow shoulders in his tuxedo. "Are you coming?"

She lingered for a moment, sat leaning on her hands, staring at the stage. He looked at her as she got up, took her silver scarf, and went along with him. Her twitching lips rested full and soft on each other.

They entered the foyer, moved through the sluggish crowd, greeted acquaintances, walked down the stairs, at times hand in hand.

"I would get an ice," she said, "if I were not convinced that it would be so inferior."

"Forget about it!" he said. And so they ate her bonbons—the cognac cherries and bean-shaped maraschino chocolates.

When the bell rang, they looked askance and scornfully at the hurrying, hampering throng until the corridors grew still, and they entered their box in the last moment, when the light was already receding, the sinking darkness soothing and silencing the confused agitation of the audience. The bell rang softly, the conductor stretched his arms, and again the sublime sounds that he commanded filled the ears that had rested a little.

Siegmund peered at the musicians. The deep pit was bright in the listening house and filled with labor—with fingering hands, fiddling arms, bloated blowing cheeks; simple and zealous people, serving the Work of a great and suffering force—this Work that appeared up there in childishly lofty visions. . . . A Work! How did one do a Work? A pain was in Siegmund's breast, a burning or rending, something like a sweet distress—for what purpose, what end? It was so dark, so shamefully unclear. He felt two words: Creation . . . Passion. And while the heat throbbed in his temples, he had something like a yearning insight that Creation came from Passion and then in turn assumed the shape of Passion. He saw the white, exhausted woman clinging on the lap of the fugitive man, to whom she had surrendered; he saw her love and agony and felt that life must be like that to be creative. He looked at his own life, this life made up of softness and wit, of pampering and denial, luxury and disagreement, lavishness and lucidity, rich security and dallying hatred—this life that had no experience, only logical games; no sensation, only lethal designation—and his breast felt a burning and rending, something like a sweet distress . . . for what purpose, what end? For the Work? Experience? Passion?

The rustling of the curtain and a grand conclusion! Light, applause, and haste toward the doors. Siegmund and Sieglinde spent this intermission like the last. They said little, walked slowly through corridors and stairways, sometimes hand in hand. She offered him cognac cherries, but he took no more. She looked at him, and when he stared at her, she looked away, walked softly and somewhat tensely at his side and allowed him to contemplate her. Her childlike shoulders under the silver embroidery were a bit too high and horizontal, like the shoulders of Egyptian statues. On her cheeks she felt the same heat that he felt on his.

They waited again until the huge throng had melted, and they settled in their armchairs at the last moment. Storm wind and cloud ride and distorted pagan exulting. On the rocky stage, eight ladies, of a slightly inferior appearance, were laughing in their virginal wildness. Brünnhilde's terror dreadfully disrupted their merriment. Wotan's wrath, fearfully approaching, swept the sisters away, confronted Brünnhilde alone, nearly annihilated her, but then roared itself out and subsided slowly, slowly into mildness and melancholy. It came to an end. A vast and far-off vista opened up, a sublime intention. All was epic consecration. Brünnhilde slept; the god climbed over the rocks. Thick-bodied flames, flaring and faltering, blazed round the boards. In sparks and red smoke, ringed by the flickering and fluttering, the enchanting and intoxicating singsong and lullaby of the fire, the Valkyrie lay under shield and armor, stretched out on her mossy couch. But in the womb of the woman whom she had managed to rescue, the seed was tenaciously sprouting—the hated, disrespectful, and god-chosen breed, from which a pair of twins united their anguish and agony in such free bliss.

When Siegmund and Sieglinde emerged from their box, Wendelin was standing outside, gigantic in his yellow overcoat, holding their wraps. Behind the pair of them, bundled up so warmly and delicately, the two strange, dark creatures, he strode down the stairs, a towering slave.

The coupé was ready. The two horses, high, noble, and utterly identical, waited on their slender legs, silent and glossy in the foggy winter night, now and then haughtily tossing their heads. The small, warmed, silk-cushioned interior ensconced the twins. Behind them the door closed. Lightly shaken by

Wendelin's practiced swing up to the coachman's seat, the coupé lingered for an instant, a split second. Then a soft and quick forward gliding, and the theater portal was left behind.

And again the noiselessly rolling speed and the swift, regular thud of the horses' hooves, that sense of being carried gently, buoyantly over the bumpy streets, that delicate sheltering from the shrill life all around. They were silent, closed off from the commonplace, as if still sitting in their velvet chairs, facing the stage, and still in that same atmosphere. There was nothing that could have brought them away from the wild, rutting, and rapturous world that had cast a spell on them, drawing them over, drawing them into itself. . . . They did not immediately grasp why the carriage had stopped; they thought some hindrance stood in its way. But they were already at their parental home, and Wendelin appeared at the coupé door.

The concierge had emerged from his lodge to let them in.

"Are Herr and Frau Aarenhold back already?" Siegmund asked him, gazing over the concierge's head, twisting his face like someone blinded by the sun.

They were not yet back from their dinner at the Erlangers'.

Nor was Kunz at home. As for Märit, she was likewise out, no one knew where, for she usually went her own way.

In the ground-floor vestibule, the butler took off their coats, and then they walked up the steps, through the second-floor vestibule, and into the dining room, which lay, tremendous, in semidark splendor. The only light came from a luster above the other end of the set table, and there Florian was waiting. They walked, swift and soundless, through the vast, carpeted space. Florian pushed the chairs under them as they sat down. Then a sign from Siegmund informed him that he was no longer needed.

A plate of sandwiches, a centerpiece heaped with fruit, and a carafe of wine were on the table. Surrounded by its paraphernalia, the electric teakettle hummed on a huge silver tray.

Siegmund ate a caviar sandwich and gulped down some wine, which glowed darkly in the delicate glass. Then, in an irritated voice, he complained that the pairing of caviar and red wine was utterly uncivilized. With staccato gestures he took a cigarette from his silver case, and leaning back, with his hands in his trouser pockets, he began to smoke, twisting his face while sliding the cigarette from one corner of his mouth to the other. His cheeks, under the prominent cheekbones, were already darkening because of his beard growth. His eyebrows formed two black creases at the root of his nose.

Sieglinde had prepared tea for herself, adding a drop of burgundy. Her full, soft lips embraced the thin edge of the cup, and as she drank, her big, moist black eyes gazed over at Siegmund.

She set down the cup and leaned her dark, sweet, exotic head on her slender reddish hand. Her eyes remained on him, so revealing, with such fluent and penetrating eloquence, that the words she spoke seemed less than nothing by comparison.

"Don't you want to eat anything more, Gigi?"

"Since I'm smoking," he answered, "one may assume that I do not plan to eat anything more."

"But you've had nothing since tea, except for some bonbons. Have a peach, at least. . . ."

He shrugged his shoulders, heaving them in his tuxedo like an obstinate child.

"No; that's boring. I'm going upstairs. Good night!"

He drank up his red wine, tossed the napkin away, and vanished, with his cigarette in his mouth, his hands in his trouser pockets, sauntering grumpily through the twilight of the room.

He went into his bedroom and turned on the light—not much, just two or three of the lamps forming a big circle on the ceiling; after switching them on, he stood still, unsure of what to do next. His good-night had not been definitive. That was not how they normally ended the day. She was bound to come here, he was certain. He threw off his tuxedo jacket, donned his fur-trimmed house jacket, and took another cigarette. Then he stretched out on the chaise longue, sat up, tried to lie on his side, with his cheek in the silk cushion, rolled over on his back again, and stayed like that awhile, his hands under his head.

The fine and pungent tobacco aroma blended with the scent of his cosmetics, the soaps, the colognes. Siegmund inhaled these fragrances that were drifting through the lukewarm air of the heated room; he was aware of them and found them sweeter than usual. Shutting his eyes, he surrendered to them like someone painfully enjoying a little bliss and tender happiness of the senses amid the harshness of his extraordinary destiny.

Suddenly he got up, tossed away the cigarette, and went over to the white armoire, which had enormous mirrors mounted in its three sections. He stood in front of the middle one, very close, eye-to-eye with himself, gazing at his face. Curious and meticulous, he examined every feature, opened the two side wings of the armoire and viewed himself in profile between the three mirrors. He stood and stood, examining the marks of his blood, the slightly downpressed nose, the lips resting full and soft on each other, the very prominent cheekbones, his thick black curly hair that was vehemently parted on the side and grew far into his temples, and his eyes themselves under the dense, joining eyebrows—those big, black, shiny-moist eyes, which he filled with lament and weary suffering.

In the mirror he spotted the polar-bear rug that stretched out its paws in front of the bed. He turned around, tragically shuffled over, and after a moment's hesitation, he collapsed full-length on the fur, bedding his head on his arm.

For a time he lay quite still; then he propped up his elbow, leaned his cheek on his slender and reddish hand, and remained in that posture, absorbed in his mirror image over there, in the armoire. Someone knocked. He winced, reddened, tried to get up. But then he sank back, dropping his head on his outstretched arm, and stayed silent.

Sieglinde came in. Her eyes hunted him in the room without finding him right away. Finally she spied him on the bearskin and was horrified.

"Gigi . . . what are you doing? Are you ill?" She ran to him, leaned over him, and, stroking his forehead and his hair, she said: "You're not ill, are you?"

He shook his head and peered up at her as he lay on his arm, caressed by her.

Half ready for bed, she had come in small slippers from her room across the hallway. Her loosened hair tumbled down on her open white dressing jacket. Under the lace of her bodice, Siegmund could see her little breasts, the color of slightly smoked meerschaum.

"You were so bad," she said, "you went away so nastily, I didn't want to come at all. But I *have* come anyway, because that wasn't a decent good-night before. . . ."

"I've been waiting for you," he said.

She still stood there, leaning over him, but her face twisted in pain, drastically emphasizing the physiognomic peculiarities of her race.

"Which doesn't prevent my present posture," she said in her usual tone, "from causing a rather notable discomfort in my back."

He writhed to and fro, warding her off.

"Don't, don't. . . . Not that, not that . . . It doesn't have to be this way, Sieglinde, do you understand?" His voice was strange; he could hear it himself. His head was dry and hot, his hands and feet were clammy. She was kneeling beside him on the fur, her fingers in his hair. Half up, he wound an arm around her neck and looked at her, contemplated her just as he had contemplated himself earlier, peered at her eyes and temples, her cheeks and forehead.

"You're totally like me," he said with lame lips, swallowing because his throat was parched. "Everything is like me . . . and for that . . . with the experience . . . with me . . . the Beckerath stuff with you . . . it balances out, Sieglinde, and altogether it's . . . the same . . . especially regarding this . . . to get even, Sieglinde."

His words strove to cloak themselves in logic, and yet they emerged bold and bizarre, as if from a tangled dream.

But to her they did not sound strange, not peculiar. She was not ashamed to hear him saying such unpolished things, such turbid and incoherent things. His words settled like a fog around her mind, drew her down, to where they came from, to a deep realm that she had never reached, but ever since her engagement, several expectant dreams had carried her to its borders.

She kissed him on his closed eyelids, he kissed her on the throat under the lace. They kissed each other's hands. With a sweet sensuality, they loved each other for their good fragrance, for being pampered and precious and well groomed. They breathed that fragrance with languid and luscious abandon, tending themselves like self-absorbed invalids, drugging themselves like people without hope, forgetting themselves in encroaching caresses that turned into a hasty tumult and finally were nothing but sobs. . . .

She still sat on the fur, with open lips, propped on one hand, brushing the hair from her eyes. With his hands on his back, he leaned against the white dresser, rocking to and fro on his hips as he stared into space.

"But Beckerath . . . ," she said, trying to put some order in her thoughts. "Beckerath, Gigi . . . What about him?"

"Well," he said, and for a moment the marks of his race stood out very sharply on his face. "He ought to be grateful to us. He will lead a less trivial existence from now on."

# DEATH IN VENICE

# CHAPTER ONE

ON A SPRING AFTERNOON IN 19—, a year that had been glowering so ominously at our continent for months, Gustav Aschenbach (or von Aschenbach, as he had been officially called since his fiftieth birthday) left his home on Prince Regent Street in Munich in order to take a rather long walk by himself. During this period in particular, the difficult and debilitating work that he did every morning demanded utmost caution and prudence, urgency and precision from his willpower; but even after lunch, the writer, overwrought from his labor, had failed to halt the forward thrust of the engine producing, inside him, that *motus animi continuus* that Cicero views as the essence of eloquence; nor had Aschenbach managed to fall asleep, even though he so badly needed his daily nap to counteract the growing depletion of his strength. And so, shortly after tea, he had sought the outdoors, hoping that fresh air and exercise would restore his energy so that he might enjoy a fruitful evening.

It was early May, and after several cold and clammy weeks, a mock summer had set in. The English Garden, though sprouting only tender leaves as yet, had been as muggy as in August, and the area near the city had been full of vehicles and strollers. Led by stiller and stiller paths to Aumeister, Aschenbach had gazed briefly at the lively, crowded restaurant garden with a few hansoms and carriages parked at its edge; from there he had headed back at sunset, leaving the park and crossing the open meadows. Feeling tired and noticing that a storm was brewing over Föhring, he went to North Cemetery, where he waited for the streetcar that would convey him straight back to town.

The trolley stop and its surroundings happened to be deserted. No vehicle was in sight on Föhringer Chaussee or on Ungerer Street, a paved avenue with lonesome, shiny tracks running toward Schwabing. Nothing stirred behind the fences of the stonecutters, where the crosses, monuments, and commemorative tablets, all of them for sale, made up a second, unintentional burial field; while across the road, the mortuary chapel, a Byzantine edifice, stood silently in the glow of the waning day. On the facade, which was decorated with Greek crosses and brightly colored hieratic designs, a few symmetrically arranged gold letters spelled out select inscriptions about the afterlife, such as: "They are entering the Dwelling of God" or "May Light Everlasting shine for them." For several minutes Aschenbach had found an earnest distraction in reading those formulas and losing himself in the mysticism showing through. But then, upon surfacing from his reveries, he noticed a man standing in the portico, above the two apocalyptic beasts guarding the stairs; with his not quite ordinary appearance, the man sent Aschenbach's thoughts in an entirely different direction.

There was no telling whether the stranger had emerged from inside the chapel and through the bronze gates or had inconspicuously mounted the steps from the outside. Aschenbach, without dwelling on the issue, leaned toward the former assumption. Medium in height, thin, beardless, and blatantly snubnosed, the man was of the red-haired type and had its milky, freckled skin. He was obviously not of Bavarian stock: at the very least, the broad, straight-brimmed bast hat covering his head lent him the exotic look of someone from far away. Granted, the customary local rucksack was strapped to his shoulders, and his yellowish belted suit was, apparently, made of loden; a gray rain cape was slung over his left forearm, which was supported on his waist; in his right hand he held an iron-tipped stick, which was propped obliquely on the ground, and, with crossed legs, he braced his hip against the crook. His head was raised, exposing the strong, naked Adam's apple on his throat, which loomed gaunt from the loose sport shirt, while his colorless, red-lashed eyes gaped sharply into space, flanking two energetic vertical furrows, which, strangely enough, fitted in with his short, upturned nose.

Because of all these features—and his heightened and heightening position may have contributed to this impression—he appeared to be surveying his surroundings, lording it over them, boldly or even savagely; for whether he was grimacing because of the blinding sunset or because of some permanent physiognomical deformity, his lips seemed too short: they curled back, completely baring even the gums, so that the long, white teeth glistened between them.

Perhaps Aschenbach, half absently, half inquisitively, had shown a want of tact when scrutinizing the stranger; for suddenly he realized that the man was glaring back at him so directly and belligerently, so blatantly intent on having it out with him and forcing his retreat, that the writer squeamishly turned away and began walking along the fences, vaguely determined to pay the man no further heed. He had forgotten him a minute later. Now, whether Aschenbach's imagination was stirred by the stranger's air of wandering or by some other physical or mental influence, he quite surprisingly felt an expansion of his psyche, a kind of roving disquiet, a youthful craving and yearning for faraway places. And indeed, these sensations were so vivid, so novel, or at least so long outgrown and forgotten, that, with his hands behind his back, his eyes on the ground, he halted, spellbound, trying to examine the essence and purpose of these emotions.

It was wanderlust, nothing more; but it pounced on him as a seizure, intensifying into a burst of passion, even a hallucination.

His desire could virtually see, his ability to fantasize, unlulled since his hours of working, conjured up all the wonders and terrors, all the variety of the earth, which he strove to envision. He saw, saw a landscape, a tropical quagmire under a steamy sky, muggy, luxuriant, and monstrous, a primordial jungle of islands, morasses, and alluvial inlets; saw hairy palm shafts near and far striving upward out of rank and rampant ferns, realms of fat, swollen plants with fantastic blossoms; saw eccentrically misshapen trees plunging their roots through the air and into the ground, into stagnant waters reflecting green shadows; saw bowl-sized, milky white flowers drifting on surfaces and outlandish species of birds, with hunched shoulders and deformed beaks, standing in shallow liquids and inertly ogling sideways; saw the sparkling eyes of a crouching tiger between the knotty canes of the bamboo thicket—and he felt his heart pounding with horror and enigmatic longing. Then the vision faded; and shaking his head, Aschenbach resumed his promenade along the fences of the gravestone yards.

By the time he had gained the wherewithal to enjoy the advantages of taking trips at will, he had started viewing travel as nothing but a health measure to be endured now and then, no matter what he might think or feel. Too preoccupied with the tasks that he himself and the European soul imposed on him, too overburdened by the obligation to produce, too averse to any distraction, he was no lover of the outer world and its rich variety; quite satisfied with whatever anyone can observe of the earth's surface without stirring far from his immediate turf, he had never so much as been tempted to leave Europe. Now his life was slowly waning, and his fear of not completing his artistic mission, his concern that the clock might run down before he had done his bit and given fully of himself, could no longer be waved off as an idle quirk. His external life was therefore confined almost exclusively to the beautiful city that had become his home and to the crude rustic cottage that he had built in the mountains and where he spent the rainy summers.

So this sudden and tardy impulse was quickly restrained and rectified by his common sense and by the self-discipline he had been practicing since his youth. His intention had been to head for the country only after reaching a certain point in the work he lived for; and the thought of abandoning his labors for several months of globe-trotting seemed like an all-too-reckless disruption of his schedule—it was entirely out of the question and not to be taken seriously. And yet he knew only too well the source of this unexpected temptation. His yearning for new and faraway places, his desire for freedom, relief, and oblivion was, as he admitted to himself, an urge to flee—an urge to get away from his work, from the everyday site of a cold, rigid, and passionate servitude. He certainly loved this servitude and almost loved the enervating conflict that recurred every day, the struggle between his proud, tenacious, so often tested willpower and this growing fatigue that no one must know about, that was not to betray the results in any way, with any hint of laxity or failure.

Then again, it clearly made sense not to exaggerate, not to obstinately throttle such a vitally erupting need. He thought about his work, thought about the passage that he had once more been forced to abandon today, like yesterday, since it would yield neither to patient application nor to surprise attack. He reexamined that passage, tried to smash through or dissolve his block, and, with a shudder of repugnance, he abandoned the assault. No extraordinary difficulty was involved; what paralyzed him were the scruples of his aversion, which manifested itself as an incapacity to satisfy his own insatiable demands. The adolescent, of course, had viewed his insatiability as the inmost nature, the very essence of talent; and because of these demands he had reined in his feelings, letting them cool off, because he knew that emotion tends to be satisfied with cheerful approximation and less than perfection. Were his enslaved feelings now getting their revenge by deserting him, by refusing to carry his art any further or lend it wings, by taking along all his pleasure, all his delight in form and expression?

Not that he was doing bad work: the advantage of his years was that he at least felt calm and certain about his mastery at every moment. But he himself, though his mastery was honored by the nation, was not happy with it: his work struck him as lacking those aspects of fiery and playful caprice—those products of joy—which, more than any intrinsic substance, any weightier merit, brought joy to the savoring readership. He dreaded the summer in the country, where he would be alone in the small cottage with the maid, who prepared his meals, and the domestic, who served them; he dreaded the familiar countenances of the mountain peaks and mountain walls that would again surround his sluggish dissatisfaction. And so he needed a breather, a change of air, some spontaneity, idleness, and new blood, to make the summer endurable and fruitful. A trip—that would do it. Not too far, not all the way to the tigers. A night in a sleeping car and a "siesta" of three or four weeks at some cosmopolitan resort in the charming south . . .

Those were his reflections as the streetcar came rattling down Ungerer Street, and, climbing aboard, he decided to spend the evening poring over maps and timetables. Standing on the trolley platform, he thought of looking for the man in the bast hat, his companion during that brief yet fertile recess. But Aschenbach was unable to determine his whereabouts since the stranger was neither at his previous location nor farther down the stop nor even inside the trolley.

# CHAPTER TWO

GUSTAV ASCHENBACH was the author of the lucid and mighty prose epic about the life of Frederick the Great of Prussia; he was the patient artist who had devoted so much time and diligence to weaving *Maia*, the crowded tapestry of a novel that gathers so many human destinies in the service of an idea; the creator of that powerful tale "A Wretched Man," which showed an entire generation of grateful youths that ethical resoluteness is still possible even after a man has plumbed the utmost depths of knowledge; and, last but not least (and exemplifying his mature works), the writer who had penned the passionate discourse *Mind and Art*, which, because of its logical strength and eloquent antitheses, had led serious critics to rank it with Schiller's cogitations on naive and reflective literature.

Born in L., an administrative seat of the province of Silesia, Aschenbach was the son of a senior judicial functionary. His forebears had been army officers, judges, bureaucrats—men who had led their austere and decently frugal lives serving king and state. A more inward spirituality had been embodied among them once, in the person of a clergyman; in the previous generation, swifter, more sensual blood had come into the family through the writer's mother, the daughter of a Bohemian orchestra conductor. It was from her that Aschenbach had inherited the foreign racial features of his exterior. The marriage of sober, official punctiliousness with darker, more fiery impulses brought forth an artist—and this specific artist.

Since his entire being was geared to fame, he proved to be, if not exactly precocious, then ripe and ready for the public at an early age, thanks to the lean and decisive quality of his personal voice. He had already made a name for himself when barely out of high school. Within another ten years he had learned to maintain his prestige and supervise his renown from his desk, to be kind and meaningful in letters that had to be terse—for many claims are made on a successful and trustworthy man. The forty-year-old, worn out by the strain and stress of his own writing, also had to cope with a daily load of mail bearing stamps from all over the world.

With a talent as remote from the banal as it was from the eccentric, he had the knack of gaining both the faith of the broader public and the admiring and demanding sympathy of the more fastidious readers. In his adolescence, he had already been pushed on all sides to achieve—achieve extraordinary things— and so he had never known idleness, never known the carefree heedlessness of youth. Once, around the age of thirty-five, when he fell ill in Vienna, an astute observer made a comment about him at a social gathering: "You know, Aschenbach has always lived like this"—the speaker made a tight fist with his left hand— "but never like *this*"—and he let his open hand dangle comfortably from the arm of his chair. This remark was apt; and Aschenbach's stance was all the more valiant and ethical for his nature was such that his anything but robust constitution was only called upon for constant exertion, but not truly born for it.

Medical consultants had kept the boy out of school and insisted on private tutoring. He had grown up solitary, without friends, and yet had been forced to realize early on that he was part of a lineage that had no shortage of talent but lacked the physical basis for the fulfillment of talent. However, his favorite word was *Durchhalten* (see it through); and he viewed his novel about Frederick the Great as nothing less than the apotheosis of this command, which struck him as the epitome of active virtue in the teeth of suffering. He also eagerly looked forward to growing old, for he had always believed that an artistry can be called truly great, universal, indeed truly admirable and honorable, only if it is fortunate enough to be characteristically fertile on all levels of human experience.

Charged by his talent with tasks that he wished to bear on his frail shoulders and intent on going far, he so greatly needed discipline—and discipline, luckily, was an innate quality he had inherited from his father's side. At forty, at fifty, an age at which others waste time, rhapsodize, and have no qualms about putting off their great plans, the early riser would start each day with torrents of cold water on his chest and back. Then, after placing a pair of tall wax candles in silver holders at the head of his manuscript, he would spend two or three fervently conscientious morning hours tapping the strength gathered in sleep and sacrificing his energy to art. It was forgivable, indeed it betokened a genuine victory for his mortality, when the uninitiated assumed that his works were the result of concentrated pressure and a long, single breath. In reality, however, his *Maia* world or the mammoth epic that unrolled the life of Frederick of Prussia had been gradually built up into greatness, layer by layer, through small daily installments as well as hundreds upon hundreds of individual spurts of inspiration; and each work was so excellent both as a whole and in every detail because its creator exerted the same persistence and tenacity with which Frederick had conquered Aschenbach's native province. The writer had endured years of stressful absorption in one and the same work, devoting only his strongest and worthiest hours to its actual composition.

For an important product of the intellect to make a wide and deep impact on the spot, a secret kinship, indeed a congruence, must exist between the personal destiny of the author and the overall destiny of his generation. People do not know why they grant fame to a given work of art. Far from being connoisseurs, they believe they can justify so much sympathy by pinpointing a hundred virtues; but the real basis of their acclaim is an imponderable, a nonrational bond. Once, in an inconspicuous place, Aschenbach had stated outright that almost every great opus that exists has come into existence despite everything—despite grief and torment, poverty, abandonment, physical weakness, vice, passion, and a thousand other hindrances. But that was more than an observation, it was his own experience—it was quite simply the formula for his life and his fame, the key to his oeuvre; so was it any wonder that it was also the ethical nature, the outer conduct of his most peculiar dramatis personae?

The new type of hero favored by this writer and recurring in a variety of his characterizations had been analyzed quite early on: a shrewd critic had explained that this protagonist was the embodiment of "an intellectual and adolescent manliness that, in proud modesty, clenches its teeth and calmly stands there while its flesh is skewered by swords and spears." That was sharp, glorious, and exact, despite the plainly far-too-passive image. After all, confronting destiny, maintaining grace under torture—these do not betoken merely passive endurance; they are active achievement, positive triumph, and the figure of Saint Sebastian is the finest symbol, if not of art as a whole, then certainly of the art under discussion here.

Anyone who looked at this narrative world saw a number of features in it. He saw the elegant self-possession with which an inner undermining, a biological decay, is concealed from the eyes of the world until the very last moment; he saw the sallow and thoroughly unappealing ugliness that can fan the smoldering in its breast into a pure flame, that can even come to rule the kingdom of beauty. He saw the pale impotence that reaches into the glowing depths of the mind and draws forth the strength to hurl an entire arrogant nation to the foot of the cross, to the feet of that impotence itself; he saw the gracious stance in the empty and rigorous service to form; the false and dangerous life, the swiftly enervating lust and art of the born deceiver.

If anyone contemplated all these destinies and so many like them in this narrative world, he could doubt the existence of any heroism but that of weakness. And yet, what other kind of heroism would be more suitable to these times? Gustav Aschenbach was the literary spokesman for all those who labor on the verge of exhaustion, those who are overburdened, already ground down, barely managing to stay upright—all those moralists of accomplishment who, puny of body and chary of means, husband their resources, and apply exaltation of the will so that they may attain, at least for a while, the effects of greatness. There are many such people; they are the heroes of the age. And they all recognized themselves in Aschenbach's writings, they felt validated, celebrated, glorified; they were grateful to him, they proclaimed his name.

He had been young and raw with the times, and ill advised by them, he had stumbled publicly, and made false moves, compromised himself, flouted tact and common sense in both words and works. But he had then gained the dignity that, he asserted, every great talent has an innate urge and impulse to achieve; in fact, one may say that his entire development, abandoning all constraints caused by doubt and irony, was nothing but a deliberate and defiant rise to this dignity.

Lively and tangible depictions with no intellectual demands are the delight of the bourgeois masses; but the younger generation, passionate and unconditional, is fascinated only by problems; and Aschenbach had been as problematic, as unconditional, as any adolescent. He had been a thrall to intellect, depleted the soil through overanalysis, ground up seed grain, divulged secrets, impugned talent, betrayed and exposed art—yes, even while his opuses diverted, elevated, and animated his credulous followers, he, the young artist, had kept the twenty-year-olds on tenterhooks with his cynicism about the questionable nature of art and the artistic life.

Yet apparently a noble and proficient mind is dulled by

nothing so swiftly and thoroughly as the sharp and bitter prod of knowledge; and it is certain that the adolescent's most melancholy and most conscientious thoroughness is shallow compared with the profound resoluteness of the adult master, who resolves to deny knowledge, to reject it, to transcend it with his head held high, insofar as knowledge is capable of even slightly paralyzing, discouraging, degrading willpower, action, emotion, and even passion. How else can we interpret the famous story "A Wretched Man" than as an outburst of disgust at the indecent psychologizing of our time—embodied in a silly, spineless rascal who fraudulently obtains a fate of sorts? Powerless, vice-ridden, and rather feckless in his ethics, he drives his wife into the arms of a beardless youth and then exploits his intellectual profundity as a rationale for committing sordid indignities.

The weight of words vilifying the vile ushered in the writer's rejection of any moral skepticism, any sympathy with the abyss, and they heralded his renunciation of the leniency summed up in the compassionate homily "To understand everything is to forgive everything." What was being prepared, indeed carried out, here was the "miraculous rebirth of naïveté"—and a short time later this miracle was explicitly discussed in one of the author's dialogues, though not without a certain mysterious intonation. Strange interconnections! Did this "rebirth," this new rigor and dignity, bear the intellectual responsibility for a simultaneous development that others observed in Aschenbach? People now noticed an almost excessive strengthening of his aesthetic sense, an aristocratic purity, simplicity, and harmony of form, which henceforth lent his works an obvious, indeed a calculated, stamp of mastery and classicism.

But if moral resoluteness transcends knowledge, transcends the hampering and disintegrative force of cognizance, then does not such tenacity simplify the world and the psyche, dumbing them ethically, while simplistically strengthening the wicked, the forbidden, the ethically impossible? And does not form have two faces? Is it not both ethical and unethical at once: ethical as the result and expression of discipline, yet unethical, even anti-ethical, insofar as, by its very nature, it is indifferent to all morality, indeed sedulously strives to make morality bow to form's proud and sovereign scepter.

Be that as it may! Development is destiny; and if it is accompanied by the sympathy, the mass confidence, of the general public, then shouldn't it run a different course than the kind that proceeds without the glamour and obligations of fame? It is only the eternal bohemians who are bored and sarcastic when a great talent outgrows its libertine cocoon: the genius then becomes accustomed to representing and expressing the dignity of the mind, and he adopts courtly manners to conceal the pains he suffered in isolation, the harsh struggles he waged on his own and with no counsel, until he finally attained power and honor in society. Incidentally, when talent shapes itself, how playful it is, how defiant and enjoyable! With time, there was something official and didactic about what Gustav Aschenbach had to offer; in later years, his style lost its unabashed boldness, its fresh and subtle shadings, it became fixed and exemplary, glib and conventional, conservative, formalistic, even formulaic, and, as tradition tells us about Louis XIV, the aging writer expunged every common word from his diction. It was at this point that the educational authorities began including selected pages from his works in the assigned readers. He also found it appropriate and did not refuse when a German prince, who had only just mounted the throne, knighted the author of *Frederick the Great* on his fiftieth birthday.

After several years of wandering, of trying out various places, he chose Munich as his permanent residence, living there in middle-class honor and enjoying the prestige that is awarded the intellect in certain special cases. At an early age he married a girl from an academic family, but she passed away after a short period of bliss. He had been left with a daughter, who was now married. He had never had a son.

Gustav von Aschenbach was somewhat below medium height, dark, and clean-shaven. His head looked a bit too large for his almost delicate physique. His hair, brushed back, thinning at the part, very thick and fairly gray at the temples, framed a high forehead so rugged that it looked scarred. His rimless gold spectacles cut into the root of his fleshy nose with its aristocratic curve. His lips were large, often slack, often unexpectedly narrow and clenched; his cheeks were lean and furrowed; the well-shaped chin had a soft cleft. Major destinies seemed to have swept across this head, which was usually tilted at a doleful angle; and yet it was art that had thoroughly molded these features—a labor normally performed by a hard and turbulent life. From behind that forehead had come the sparkling rapid-fire dialogues between Voltaire and King Frederick on the topic of war; those tired eyes, peering deeply through the lenses, had seen the gory inferno in the field hospitals of the Seven Years' War. But even on a personal level, art is, after all, a more sublime life. It delights more deeply, it consumes more swiftly. It carves the traces of imaginary, intellectual adventures into the features of its servant, and despite the monastic stillness of his outward life, it eventually brings about a fussiness and overrefinement, a weariness and nervous curiosity such as can scarcely evolve from a lifetime of dissolute passions and pleasures.

# CHAPTER THREE

SEVERAL MATTERS OF A practical or literary nature kept the eager traveler in Munich for some two weeks after that stroll. But finally he instructed his servants to prepare his mountain cottage for his arrival in four weeks, and on an evening between the middle and the end of May he boarded the night train to Trieste, spending only twenty-four hours there and then sailing to Pola the following morning.

What he sought was an exotic and unfamiliar locale that nevertheless could be reached quickly; and so he opted for an Adriatic island that people had been praising for several years: situated not far off the Istrian coast, it had beautifully jagged cliffs facing the open sea, and it was populated by rustics wearing colorful tatters and speaking a language full of outlandish sounds. However, it kept raining, the air was oppressive, and the hotel was filled with a self-contained group of Austrian provincials; furthermore, there was no way of establishing a peaceful and intimate rapport with the sea—the kind of relationship provided only by a gentle, sandy beach. All these annoyances were not conducive to making him feel that he had found what he was looking for; he was haunted by an anxious longing to move on, but he did not know where; he studied boat routes, he cast about for an idea.

And then all at once—it was both surprising and self-evident—he saw his destination before him. If you want to get to an incomparable place overnight, a place of fairy tales, a place like none you have ever known, where do you go? Why, that was obvious. What was he doing here? He had gone astray. *That* was where he had wished to be. He lost no time in announcing his departure from this wrong place. One hazy dawn some ten days after his arrival on the island, a swift motorboat ferried him and his luggage back across the water to the naval base, where he disembarked and then instantly walked up a gangplank to the wet deck of a steamship that was about to weigh anchor for Venice.

It was an ancient hulk of Italian registry, outmoded, sooty, and dingy. Upon boarding ship, Aschenbach was immediately approached by an unclean, hunchbacked sailor, who, with grinning courtesy, propelled him inside, to a cavernous, artificial illuminated cabin. Here, behind a table, sat a goateed man with the physiognomy of an old-time circus director, his hat askew over his forehead and a cigarette butt in the corner of his mouth; grimacing and gesturing easily and officiously, he recorded the personal data of the voyagers and made out their tickets.

"Venice!" he echoed Aschenbach's request, stretching out his arm and thrusting his pen into the mushy dregs in a slanting inkwell. "Venice, first class! Here you are, sir." And he scrawled something, bestrewed it with some blue sand from a box, poured the sand into a clay bowl, folded the paper with bony yellow fingers, and continued writing on the outside. "A wonderful choice!" he prattled. "Ah, Venice! A fabulous city! A city that's irresistible to a man of culture—both for its history and for its present-day appeal!" There was something numbing and distracting about his glib, swift motions and his empty chitchat, as if he were worried that the traveler might waver in his decision to go to Venice. The man quickly took the money, and with the nimbleness of a croupier, he dropped the change on the stained tablecloth. "Enjoy your visit, sir!" he said with a theatrical bow. "It's an honor to serve you. . . . Gentlemen!" he cried, beckoning with a raised arm as if business were booming, although there was no one else asking to be accommodated. Aschenbach returned to the upper deck.

With one arm propped on the railing, he gazed at the idlers loitering on the dock to watch the boat set sail, and then he looked at the other voyagers. On the foredeck, the second-class passengers, men and women, were squatting on their crates and bundles. A group of excited young men populated the main deck: clerks from Pola, apparently, on a group outing to Italy. They raised quite a fuss about themselves and their excursion, jabbering, laughing, and smugly enjoying their own gestures and movements; leaning over the railing, they yelled smug and sarcastic remarks at their fellow clerks, who came striding along the avenue on business, clutching their briefcases under their arms and shaking their slender canes at the vacationers.

One man aboard stood out: wearing an overly fashionable, pale-yellow summer suit, a red tie, and a flippantly uptilted panama hat encircled by a colorful scarf, he was outwhooping, outroistering everyone else. But no sooner did Aschenbach focus on him than, somewhat shocked, he realized that this was a bogus youth. The man was old, there was no doubting it. He had wrinkles around his mouth and eyes. The matte carmine of his cheeks was rouge, the brown hair under the straw hat was a toupee, his throat was stringy and scraggly, his thin, turned-up mustache and the imperial on his chin were dyed, his two full rows of yellow teeth, which he showed when he laughed, were cheap dentures, and his hands, sporting signet rings on both forefingers, were those of an old man. Horrified, Aschenbach watched him and the way he associated with his friends. Did they not know, not realize that he was old, that he had no right to wear their colorful, dandyish clothes, no right to pretend he was one of them? They clearly took him for granted, they were used to him, tolerated him in their midst, treated him as one of their own, gladly responded to his teasing, and returned his pokes in the ribs. How could they? Aschenbach cupped his forehead with his hand and closed his eyes, which were burning for lack of sleep. It was as if things were not quite normal, as if a dream-like alienation were spreading out, a bizarre warping of the world, which he might be able to halt if he could cover his eyes a little and then look around again. But at that instant, he began to feel he was floating, and glancing up in irrational alarm, he noticed that the bulky, gloomy boat was slowly easing away from the brick jetty. Amid the to-and-fro of the engine, the strip of dirty and iridescent water between dock and ship was widening inch by inch, and then, after some clumsy maneuvering, the steamer turned her bowsprit toward the open sea. Aschenbach crossed over to the starboard side, where the hunchback had set up a deck chair for him, and a steward in a spotted tuxedo asked if he wished to order anything.

The sky was gray, the wind damp. The harbor and the island had been left behind, and all land vanished quickly from the hazy field of vision. Flakes of coal dust, bloated with moisture, descended on the swabbed deck, which would not dry. Within an hour, a canvas shelter was put up because it was starting to rain.

Shrouded in his coat, a book in his lap, the voyager rested, and the hours slipped by him unnoticed. The rain had stopped; the awning was removed. The full circle of the horizon was visible. Under the dreary dome of the sky, the tremendous disk of the bleak sea stretched out all around. But in empty, unarticulated space, our senses lack the ability to measure time, and so we drowse in the immeasurable. Strange, shadowy figures—the elderly dandy, the goateed official from belowdecks—flashed through the mind of the resting man with vague gestures and tangled, dreamy murmurs, and he fell asleep.

At noon he was summoned to a light lunch down in the dining salon, which was virtually a corridor lined with the doors of the cabins; he ate at the head of the long table, at the foot of which the clerks, along with the old man, had been carousing with the jovial captain since ten A.M. The meal was pitiful, and Aschenbach quickly polished it off. He craved the open air, the sky; would the sky be brightening over Venice?

Nor had he imagined that it would not, for the city had always given him a radiant welcome. But sky and sea remained dreary and leaden, a misty rain came down at times, and he resigned himself to reaching a different Venice by water than he had ever found when approaching it by land. He stood at the foremast, gazing into the distance, watching for land. He remembered the melancholy yet enthusiastic poet for whom the turrets and cupolas of his dreams had once risen from these waves; he softly repeated the reverent words of joy and grief that had become a measured song; and moved effortlessly by sentiments already shaped, he examined his own earnest and weary heart, wondering if some new inspiration and confusion, some late adventure of the emotions, might not be lying in wait for the traveling idler.

Then, on the right, the flat coast hove into view, the sea bustling with fishing boats, the resort island, the Lido, floated by on the left as the ship slowed down and glided through the narrow harbor, which is named after that island. In the lagoon, facing poor and jumbled houses, the ship chugged to a halt, since it had to wait for the health department's *barca*.

It took the medical inspectors an hour to show up. The voyagers had arrived and not yet arrived; they were in no hurry and yet they were nervous and impatient. The young clerks from Pola, patriotically drawn, no doubt, to the blare of martial bugles from the Public Gardens across the water, had come on deck and, inflamed by the Asti, were yelling hurrahs at the drilling *bersaglieri*. But it was repulsive to see the state to which the dandified old man had been reduced by his sham association with youth. His old brain had not withstood the wine as resiliently as the frisky brains of his young companions: he was wretchedly drunk. With a moronic gape, a cigarette in his trembling fingers, he stood there lurching, laboriously keeping his balance, pulled forward and backward by his intoxication. Since he would have fallen down at his first step, he did not dare stir from the spot; but he was deplorably exuberant, buttonholed anyone drawing near, babbled, giggled, winked, raised a beringed and wrinkled forefinger in silly teasing, and the tip of his tongue licked the corners of his mouth in a revoltingly suggestive way. Aschenbach glared at him and was again overwhelmed with a sense of numbness, as if the world were showing an uncontrollable tendency to become bizarre and gargoylish; however, circumstances prevented him from indulging in that sensation, for the engine resumed its pounding, and the ship, whose course had been interrupted so close to its destination, continued through the Canale di San Marco.

And so he saw it once again, that most amazing of landing places, the dazzling composition of fantastic architecture that the Republic presented to the worshipful gazes of approaching mariners: the airy magnificence of the Doge's Palace and the Bridge of Sighs, the columns depicting lions and saints on the shore, the splendid and projecting flank of the fairy-tale temple, the view of the gateway and the gigantic clock. And while contemplating this scene, he mused that arriving at the Venice railroad station by land was like entering a palace through a back door and that one could only do as he had done: sail across the high seas in order to reach the most improbable of cities.

The engine stopped, gondolas thronged around the boat, the gangplank was lowered, customs officials climbed aboard and discharged their duties perfunctorily; the disembarking could begin. Aschenbach indicated that he needed a gondola to take him and his baggage to the pier of those small steamers that ply between the city and the Lido; for he planned to stay by the sea. His request was sanctioned, his wishes were hollered down to the surface of the water, where the gondoliers were squabbling in the local dialect. He was hindered from descending, impeded by his trunk, which was being arduously pulled and lugged down the runglike steps.

And so for a few minutes, he was unable to escape the obtrusiveness of the ghastly old man, who was dimly driven by liquor to do the honors of ushering the stranger out. "We wish you the happiest sojourn!" he bleated while bowing and scraping. "May you retain fond memories of us! *Au revoir, excusez* and *bonjour,* Your Excellency!" His mouth drooled, his eyes shut, he licked the corners of his mouth, and the dyed imperial below his senile lip bristled upward. "Our very best," he babbled, with two fingertips on his mouth, "our very best to your sweetheart, the sweetest, the loveliest sweetheart . . ." And suddenly his upper denture fell on his lower lip. Aschenbach was able to shake him

off. "Your sweetheart, your fine sweetheart," he heard the slurred
hollow cooing behind him as he clambered down the gangplank,
clutching the rope railing.

Who would not have to struggle against a fleeting thrill, a secret timidity and anxiety, upon boarding a Venetian gondola for
the first time or after a long deprivation. That strange vessel,
coming down intact from the days of troubadours and so peculiarly black, as only coffins can be, recalls hushed criminal adventures in a rippling night; and it recalls death even more, a bier
and a dismal burial, and the final, silent voyage. And have you
noticed that the seat in a gondola, the coffin-black armchair with
its dull black upholstery, is the softest, most sumptuous, the
most lulling seat in the world? Aschenbach realized this upon
settling down at the gondolier's feet, across from his ample luggage, which lay neatly arranged in the beak of the craft. The row-
ers were still squabbling: in raucous, unintelligible voices and
with ominous gestures. But the special hush of the water city
seemed to take their words up gently, disembody them, scatter
them across the sea. It was warm here in the harbor. Breathed on
by the tepid puff of the sirocco, the traveler leaned back into the
cushions, into the unresisting element, closing his eyes and delighting in this sweet and unusual indolence. The voyage will be
brief, he thought to himself. If only it could last forever! Swaying
quietly, he felt himself gliding away from the throng, from the
tangle of voices.

How still and stiller it became around him! Nothing could be
heard but the splashing of the oar, the hollow slapping of the
waves against the beak, which loomed over the water, steep and
black, its tip like a halberd. And something else was audible: a
murmuring, a muttering—the whispering of the gondolier, who
was talking to himself, through his teeth, in fits and starts, the
sounds squeezed out by the labor of his arms. Aschenbach
glanced up, a bit surprised to see that the lagoon was widening

about him and that they were heading toward the open sea. Plainly he could not relax all too much; he would have to make sure that his wishes were carried out.

"Take me to the steamboat pier," he said, turning halfway. The murmuring stopped. He received no answer.

"Take me to the steamboat pier!" he repeated, turning all the way around and peering up into the face of the gondolier, who stood behind him on the elevated stern, looming against the wan sky. He was a man with a disobliging, even brutal physiognomy, dressed in sailor blue, with a yellow sash; a shapeless straw hat, which was starting to unravel, perched flippantly askew on his head. His facial structure, his fluffy blond mustache, and his short, upturned nose made him look anything but Italian. Although his build was frail, so that you would not have thought him particularly suited for his job, he pulled the oar energetically, committing his entire body to each stroke. Now and then the terrible strain made him curl back his lips, baring his white teeth. Puckering his reddish eyebrows, he gazed over his passenger's head as he retorted in a staunch, almost crude tone.

"You're going to the Lido."

Aschenbach countered: "Right. But I want to take the gondola only as far as San Marco. I wish to transfer to the vaporetto."

"You can't transfer to the vaporetto, signore."

"And why not?"

"Because the vaporetto doesn't carry luggage."

That was true; Aschenbach remembered. He fell silent. But he was quite offended by the man's gruff and presumptuous manner, so unlike the way his compatriots usually treated foreigners. Aschenbach said:

"That's my business. Perhaps I want to check my luggage. You will please turn around."

Silence. The oar splashed, the waves thudded against the prow. And the murmuring and muttering resumed: the gondolier was talking to himself through his teeth.

What could the traveler do? Alone on the water with this strangely defiant, eerily decisive man, he saw no chance of getting his way. Besides, how softly he could rest if he did not lose his temper! Had he not wished that the trip would last a long time, that it would last forever? It would be wisest to let things take their course, and above all, it was highly pleasant. A spell of indolence seemed to emanate from his seat, from this low armchair with its black upholstery, so gently cradled by the oar strokes of the high-handed gondolier behind him. The notion that he may have fallen into the hands of a criminal floated dreamily through Aschenbach's mind, but it failed to galvanize him into active resistance. More annoying was the possibility that the man was simply trying to squeeze extra money out of him. A sense of pride or duty, a memory, as it were, that this had to be prevented, enabled Aschenbach to pull himself together. He asked:

"How much do you charge for the ride?"

And looking beyond him, the gondolier replied: "You will pay."

There was an established rejoinder to this. Aschenbach said mechanically: "I will pay nothing, absolutely nothing, if you take me where I don't want to go."

"You want to go to the Lido."

"But not with you."

"I'm rowing you well."

That's true, thought Aschenbach, relaxing. "That's true, you're rowing me well. Even if you're after my cash and you hit me from behind with your oar and send me down to the House of Aides, you will have rowed me well."

But nothing of the sort happened. They even had company: a boatload of musical waylayers, male and female, singing to a guitar, a mandolin, riding obtrusively bow to bow with the gondola and filling the stillness of the waters with their mercenary poetry for foreigners. Aschenbach tossed money into the hat they held out. The buskers now fell silent and rowed away. And again he heard the disjointed whispering of the gondolier, who was talking to himself in fits and starts.

And so they arrived, lolloping in the wake of a steamer bound for the city. Two police officers, their hands on their backs, their faces toward the lagoon, were pacing to and fro on the shore. Aschenbach climbed on the jetty, helped by the old man who, armed with his grappling hook, is a fixture at every Venetian jetty; and since the traveler had no small bills, he went over to the hotel by the steamer pier to get change and pay the rower as he saw fit. He was taken care of in the lobby, he returned, he found his belongings in a cart on the dock, but the gondola and the gondolier had vanished.

"He took off," said the old man with the boat hook. "A bad man, a man without a license, signore. He is the only gondolier without a license. The others called up here. He saw that we were watching for him. So he took off."

Aschenbach shrugged.

"You rode for free, signore," said the old man, holding out his hat. Aschenbach threw in some coins. He directed his baggage to the Hôtel des Bains and followed the cart along the avenue, the white-blossoming avenue, which, flanked by booths, taverns, and rooming houses, cuts straight across the island to the beach.

He entered the spacious hotel through the back, from the garden terrace, strode through the enormous lobby and the vestibule, and stepped into the office. Since he had a reservation, he was received with officious courtesy. The manager, a short, quiet, polite, indeed flattering man with a black mustache and in a French frock coat, rode up with him to the third floor, where he showed the guest to his room, a pleasant room: furnished in cherrywood and decorated with strongly fragrant flowers, it had lofty windows offering a view of the open sea. When the manager withdrew, Aschenbach stepped over to one window, and while his luggage was being brought in and put away, he gazed out at the beach, which was deserted in the afternoon, and he peered at the sunless sea, which was at high tide now, sending long, low waves to the shore in a calm, even rhythm.

The observations and encounters of a loner who seldom speaks are both more nebulous and more penetrating than those of a gregarious man; his thoughts are more intense, more peculiar, and never without a touch of sadness. Images and perceptions, which might easily be brushed aside with a glance, a laugh, an exchange of opinions, occupy his mind unduly; they are deeper in silence, take on significance, become experience, adventure, emotion. Solitude ripens originality in us, bold and disconcerting beauty, poetry. But solitude also ripens the perverse, the asymmetrical, the absurd, the forbidden.

And so the traveler's mind was still unsettled by what he had encountered during his trip here: the horrible old dandy blabbering about the sweetheart, the outlawed gondolier who had been cheated of his fee. Without straining reason, without offering any real food for thought, these experiences nevertheless seemed utterly bizarre by their very nature, and it was this contradiction that was so upsetting. Amid his reflections he greeted the sea with his eyes and was delighted that Venice was so close, within grasp. He finally turned away, washed his face, gave the chambermaid some instructions for his greater comfort, and had the green-clad Swiss elevator operator take him down to the main floor.

He had his tea on the seaward terrace, then descended to the beach promenade and took a long stroll toward the Hotel Excelsior. When he returned, it was apparently time to change for dinner. He did it slowly and methodically, as was his way, for he normally worked while dressing; nevertheless, he reached the lobby a bit early, to find a large number of guests, strangers to one another, feigning mutual indifference but united in their expectation of their meal. He took a newspaper from a table, settled into a leather armchair and scrutinized the crowd, which differed pleasantly from the people at his first vacation stop.

A broad horizon opened up, encompassing and tolerating a wide gamut. The sounds of the major languages intermingled softly. The global evening attire, a uniform of civilization, outwardly fused the human variety in a decent homogeneity. He saw the dry, long face of an American, a multitudinous Russian family, British ladies, German children with French *bonnes*. The Slavic element seemed to dominate. Polish was being spoken nearby.

It was a group of adolescents, some not quite fully grown, gathered round a small wicker table, under the care of a governess or paid companion: three girls, whose ages seemed to range from fifteen to seventeen, and a long-haired boy of perhaps fourteen. Aschenbach was amazed to see that the boy was absolutely beautiful. His face, pale and of a graceful reserve, surrounded by honey-colored curls, with its straight nose, lovely lips, earnest expression, sweet and godly, all recalled Greek statues of the noblest era; but despite the pure and consummate form, his features exerted such a unique personal charm that the observer felt he had never encountered such perfection in nature or in the arts.

What struck him further was the way the clothing and treatment of the sisters contrasted sharply with that of their brother—an apparently basic gap between different standards of upbringing. The attire of the three girls, the eldest of whom could pass for an adult, were of a disfiguring modesty and austerity. They wore identical cloistral dresses, slate-colored, knee-length, and in a sober and deliberately unbecoming style, brightened only by white turndown collars and suppressing and stifling any grace in their figures. Their hair, plastered smooth and solid on their heads, made their faces as vacant and vacuous as a nun's.

Clearly a mother was behind this, and while she may have regarded pedagogical strictness as necessary for the girls, she never dreamed of applying it to the boy. His life was obviously ruled by softness and tenderness. They had been careful not to put any scissors to his beautiful hair; like that of *The Boy with the Thorn*, it curled into his forehead, over his ears, and down the back of his neck. The British sailor suit had puffy sleeves, narrowing snugly around the delicate wrists of his still childlike but slender hands, and with its loops, braids, and embroideries, it lent his delicate shape a rich and pampered look. He sat in half profile toward the viewer, one foot in front of the other in their black patent leathers, one elbow on the arm of his wicker chair, his cheek nestling on his closed hand, his overall posture showing casual decorum and entirely devoid of the almost submissive starchiness that appeared to be customary for his sisters. Was he ill? His ivory complexion stood out against the golden darkness of the framing locks. Or was he simply a coddled favorite, the pet of biased and capricious love? Aschenbach was inclined to go with the latter assumption. Innate in nearly every artistic nature is a luscious and treacherous penchant for acknowledging the injustice that creates beauty and for sympathizing with and paying homage to aristocratic privilege.

A waiter made the rounds, announcing in English that dinner was served. Little by little the crowd dispersed through the glass door into the dining room. Latecomers, emerging from the vestibule, from the elevators, strode past. The meal was already being served inside, but the young Poles lingered at their small wicker table; and Aschenbach, cozy and comfortable in his deep easy chair and, incidentally, with beauty before his eyes, waited with them.

The governess, short, red-faced, and corpulent, and something of a gentlewoman, finally signaled for them to rise. Lifting her eyebrows, she pushed back her chair and curtsied as a tall woman, dressed in grayish white and hung very lavishly with pearls, entered the lobby. Her demeanor was cool and measured, her lightly powdered coiffure and the cut of her gown were of the simplicity that determines good taste wherever piety is deemed a constituent of refinement. In Germany she could have been the wife of a high official. There was a fantastic luxury about her appearance if only because of her truly priceless jewels, consisting of earrings as well as a very long triple strand of softly shimmering pearls the size of cherries.

The children had stood up quickly. They bent over to kiss their mother's hand, and with a reserved smile on her well-cared-for but somewhat weary and sharp-nosed face, she peered over their heads, saying something in French to the governess. Then she walked toward the glass door. The children followed her: first the girls in order of age, then the governess, finally the boy. For some reason, he looked back before crossing the threshold, and since no one else was left in the lobby, his eyes, of a peculiar twilight gray, encountered those of Aschenbach, who, with his newspaper on his lap, was absorbed in watching the group.

There was, of course, nothing the least bit remarkable about what Aschenbach had seen. The children had not gone in to dinner before the mother; they had waited for her, greeted her respectfully, and observed customary protocol when entering the dining room. Yet it had all been done so explicitly, with such emphasis on duty, breeding, and dignified self-regard, that Aschenbach felt strangely moved. He hesitated for a few moments, then likewise went into the dining room and was shown to his small table, which, as he noted with a brief stir of regret, stood very far from that of the Polish family.

Tired and yet mentally alert, he spent the long and tedious meal pondering abstract, even transcendental matters, contemplating the mysterious rapport that the universal law must establish with the individual in order to produce human beauty. He then progressed to general problems of form and art, and eventually he concluded that his ideas and discoveries were like certain inspirations in a dream: they may appear felicitous, but once the mind is fully awake, they prove to be utterly vapid and useless. After dinner he dawdled in the park, smoking, sitting, roaming through the evening fragrance, then retired early, passing the night in a profound, unbroken sleep that was, however, repeatedly enlivened by dreams.

The weather was no more benign the following day. A land wind was blowing. Under a wan, overcast sky and with a close, sedate horizon, the sea lay dull and calm, virtually shrunken, retreating so far from the beach that it bared several rows of long sandbanks. Upon opening his window, Aschenbach thought he could smell the putrid stench of the lagoon.

Suddenly he felt disgruntled. He now considered leaving. Once, years ago, after weeks of cheerful springtime, such weather had afflicted him, wrecking his health so badly that he had been forced to abscond from Venice like a fugitive. Wasn't the same feverish weariness starting all over again, the pressure in his temples, the heaviness in his eyelids? Changing resorts yet again would be a nuisance; but if the wind did not shift, then this was no place for him. To be on the safe side, he did not unpack fully. At nine A.M. he breakfasted in the special buffet salon between the lobby and the dining room.

A solemn hush prevailed here—a mood that is the pride of the grand hotels. The waiters went about on quiet soles. All that could be heard was a clatter of tea paraphernalia, a half-whispered word. Two tables away from him, in a corner diagonally across from the door, Aschenbach noticed the Polish girls with their governess. Bolt upright, their eyes reddened, their ash-blond hair freshly plastered, they sat there in stiff blue linen frocks with small white cuffs and turndown collars, handing around a jar of preserves. They were almost finished with their breakfast. The boy was missing.

Aschenbach smiled. Well, little Phaeacian! he thought. Unlike your sisters, you seem to enjoy the privilege of sleeping as late as you like. And suddenly brightening up, he recited a verse to himself: " 'Frequently changed adornments and heated baths and rest.' "

He breakfasted in a leisurely manner; the porter, doffing his braided cap, came in and handed him some forwarded mail, whereupon Aschenbach, smoking a cigarette, opened a few letters. And so it happened that he witnessed the arrival of the sluggard, whom they were waiting for at the corner table.

The boy entered through the glass door and cut across the stillness of the room, toward his sisters. He was extraordinarily graceful in the way he held his upper body and moved his knees, the way he set down his white-shod feet; his bearing was very light, both delicate and proud, and its beauty was increased by the shy, childlike way he twice turned his head toward the interior of the room, glancing up and then lowering his eyes. Smiling, murmuring something in his soft, blurry language, he took his seat, and now that Aschenbach could see him in full profile, he was again astonished, indeed, alarmed by the truly godlike beauty of this mortal. Today the boy wore a washable cotton sailor suit: the tunic, with blue and white stripes and a red silk knot on the chest, was closed off at the neck by a plain white stand-up collar, which did not match the character of the outfit very elegantly. However, the head resting on the collar blossomed forth with incomparable seductive charm—the head of Eros, with the yellowish shimmer of Parian marble, the eyebrows fine and earnest, the ears and temples covered softly and darkly with the rectangular mass of recessed curls.

Good, good! thought Aschenbach, with the cool expertise in which artists sometimes cloak their delight, their rapture in front of a masterpiece. And he also thought: Really, if the sea and the beach weren't waiting for me, I'd stay here as long as you stayed! But then he did leave after all; he walked through the lobby past the obliging eyes of the personnel, went down the large terrace and straight along the boardwalk to the private beach reserved for the hotel guests. The beach attendant, a barefoot oldster in linen trousers, a sailor's tunic, and a straw hat, showed Aschenbach to his rented cabana and set up a table and a chair on the sandy wooden platform in front of it; and Aschenbach made himself comfortable in the deck chair after pulling it into the waxy yellow sand, closer to the water.

He was as thrilled and entertained as ever by the beach tableau, this vista of civilization enjoying its carefree, sensual pleasures on the edge of the liquid element. The gray and shallow sea was already bustling with swimmers and wading children, while colorful figures, their hands clasped under their heads, lay on the sandbanks. Others rowed small, keelless red-and-blue boats, laughing as they capsized. In front of the elongated line of cabanas, people sat on their decks as if on small verandas, playing animatedly or reclining lazily, visiting and chatting, sporting meticulous morning elegance next to the brash and relaxed enjoyment of the free-and-easy atmosphere of undress.

Farther out, on the wet, firm sand, individuals were strolling in white bathrobes or loose, gaudy tunics. To the right, a large, intricate sand castle, built by children, was ringed by flags in the colors of all nations. Vendors hawking fruit, pastries, and mussels were kneeling and spreading out their wares. To the left, a line of cabins, at a right angle to the others, ran down to the water, forming the boundary of the closed-off area; and outside one of the cabins, a Russian family was camping: men with beards and big teeth; listless, sluggish women; a Baltic Fräulein sitting at an easel and painting the sea amid her cries of despair; two homely but good-natured children; an old, kerchiefed domestic with tender and submissive serf-like manners. There they throve, in grateful enjoyment, indefatigably calling the names of the disobedient romping children, joking on and on in their broken Italian with the humorous old man from whom they bought candy, kissing one another on the cheeks, and utterly ignoring any observer of their human togetherness.

I think I'll stay on, Aschenbach thought to himself. Where would it be better? And folding his hands in his lap, he stared at the vastness of the sea, his eyes gliding, blurring, glassy in the monotonous mist of that endless wilderness. His love of the sea had profound roots: the hardworking artist's desire to rest, his longing to get away from the demanding diversity of phenomena and take shelter in the bosom of simplicity and immensity; a forbidden penchant that was entirely antithetical to his mission and, for that very reason, seductive—a proclivity for the unorganized, the immeasurable, the eternal: for nothingness. To rest in perfection: that is what the striver for excellence yearns for; and is not nothingness a form of perfection?

But as he dreamed into the distance, the horizontal waterline was suddenly intersected by a human shape, and when he gathered in his gaze, withdrawing it from the limitless void and refocusing it, the beautiful boy, coming from the left, passed him in the sand. He was barefoot, ready to wade, his slender legs exposed till over the knees; walking slowly, yet with a light, proud gait as if quite accustomed to sauntering without shoes, he peered over at the cabins in the perpendicular row. But no sooner did he spot the family of Russians, who were living their life here in grateful harmony, than a storm of angry disdain swept across his face. His forehead darkened, his lips curled up, one cheek was wrenched by a fierce twisting from the corner of his mouth, his frown was so severe that it seemed to push in his eyes, which were speaking the nasty and glowering language of hate. He looked at the ground, ominously glared back once more, then heaved it all off with a vehement and derogatory shrug and left his enemies behind.

A kind of affection or apprehension, something like deference and modesty, compelled Aschenbach to avert his head, as if he had seen nothing; for an earnest chance witness to passion is reluctant to make use of his observations even privately. But he was both amused and shocked at once—that is, thrilled. The childish fanaticism, aimed at that utterly good-natured segment of life, reduced a nonexpressive divinity to human terms; a precious masterpiece of nature, once a merely visual delight, now seemed worthy of deeper interest, and the adolescent, already outstanding because of his beauty, was given a foil that allowed him to be taken seriously beyond his years.

His head still averted, Aschenbach listened to the boy's voice, his clear if slightly weak voice, as he announced himself from far away, greeting his playmates, who were busy with the sand castle. They responded, yelling his name or nickname over and over; Aschenbach eavesdropped with a certain curiosity, unable to catch anything but two musical syllables like "Adgio" or, more often, "Adgiu," with a drawn-out *u* at the end. He enjoyed those sounds, he found them suitably melodious, repeated them to himself, and then contentedly turned to his letters and papers.

Holding his small portable writing case on his knees, he picked up his fountain pen and began attending to various demands of his correspondence. But within a quarter of an hour he decided it was a mistake to ignore this beach scene, the most enjoyable he had ever known, to lose out on it by mentally deserting it and concentrating on some indifferent activity. He tossed his pad and pen aside, he gazed out at the sea again; but in no time at all, distracted by the young voices at the sand construction, he turned his head, which was comfortably leaning against the back of his chair, to the right, so that he might see what the marvelous "Adgio" was up to.

He located him instantly; the red knot on his chest was not to be missed. The boy and his companions were busy laying an old plank as a bridge across the wet moat of the sand castle, and he kept calling out his orders, motioning with his head. There were some ten comrades—boys and girls—of his own age, and a few younger ones, chattering in a jumble of languages: Polish, French, and even some Balkan tongues. But it was his name that was heard most. He was obviously desired, admired, wooed. One playmate in particular, a Pole like him, named something like "Yashu," a husky teenager with slicked black hair and in a belted linen suit, appeared to be his chief vassal and closest friend. When the day's work on the sand structure was done, they walked along the beach with their arms around each other, and the youth called "Yashu" kissed the beautiful boy.

Aschenbach was tempted to wag his finger at him. But I advise you, Critobolus, he thought with a smile, to travel about for a year! For you will need at least that much time to recover! And then he snacked on large, fully ripened strawberries that he had bought from a vendor. The day had grown very warm, even though the sun was unable to penetrate the layer of mist in the sky. Aschenbach's mind was fettered by indolence, while his senses enjoyed the tremendous and numbing pleasure of the ocean's calm. The earnest man felt it was a suitable and utterly fulfilling objective and occupation to guess, to track down, the name that sounded roughly like "Adgio." And drawing on some recollections of Polish, he surmised that the name was Tadzio, short for Tadeusz, and that "Tadzio" became "Tadziu" in direct address.

Tadzio was swimming. Aschenbach, after losing sight of him, spotted his head, his arm, which swung out and paddled forward; he was far from shore: the sea was probably shallow a long way out. Yet people were already worried about him, several female voices were shouting from the cabanas, hollering that name, which dominated the beach almost like a watchword; and there was something both sweet and savage about it with its soft consonants, its drawn-out u at the end: "Tadziu! Tadziu!" He returned through the waves, he ran, his head flung back, his legs churning the resistant water into foam; the living figure with dripping curls, the sweet and acrid adolescent on the verge of masculinity, as beautiful as a tender deity, rising from the depths of sky and sea, emerging from the liquid element, absconding from it: this vision aroused mythical associations; it was like a poetic legend about primordial times, about the origins of form and the births of the gods. With closed eyes, Aschenbach listened to the anthem welling up within him, and once again he mused that it was good here and that he wanted to stay.

Later on, Tadzio, resting up from his swim, lay in the sand, his head pillowed on his bare arm, his body wrapped in his white sheet, which was pulled under the right shoulder; and even when Aschenbach, instead of gazing at him, was reading a few pages in his book, he seldom forgot that the boy was lying there and that he, Aschenbach, had only to turn his head a bit toward the right to see the object of admiration. He almost felt as if he were sitting there to guard the resting youngster—whereby Aschenbach, though preoccupied with his own affairs, was constantly alert to that noble human image nearby, at his right. And his heart was filled and moved by a fatherly benevolence, by a warm affection for the possessor of beauty—the emotions felt by someone who spiritually offers himself up to create beauty.

Past noon he left the beach, walked back to the hotel, and took the elevator up to his floor. Inside his room he lingered at the mirror for a long time, studying his gray hair, his pinched and tired face. He now thought about his fame, about the many people who recognized him on the street and gazed reverently at him because of his unerring and graceful language—he summoned up all the worldly achievements of his talent, all the successes he could remember, and he even reminisced about his knighthood. Then he went down to the dining room and had lunch at his small table. Afterward, as he entered the elevator, youngsters, likewise coming from their meal, crowded into the small, hovering compartment; and Tadzio stepped in too. He stood very close to Aschenbach—and for the first time he was so close that the writer, instead of peering at a distant image, could perceive him very carefully, scrutinize every detail of his human presence. Someone said something to the boy, and replying with an indescribably radiant smile, he got off on the second floor, backward, lowering his eyes. Beauty makes you bashful, thought Aschenbach, and he very astutely wondered why. He had noticed, however, that Tadzio's teeth were not very appealing: they were somewhat pale and jagged, without the sheen of health, and peculiarly brittle and translucent, like the teeth of certain people with anemia. He is very delicate, he is sickly, mused Aschenbach. He probably won't grow old. And he made no effort to understand why he felt satisfied and consoled by this thought.

He spent two hours in his room and then, in the afternoon, took the vaporetto to Venice, across the foul-smelling lagoon. He got off at San Marco, had tea in the square, and then, following his local agenda, he began ambling through the streets. And it was this walk that triggered a complete reversal of his mood, his decisions.

The narrow streets were sweltering repulsively; the air was so thick that the smells surging from homes, stores, chophouses, the oily billows, the haze of perfumes, the different vapors, hovered in clouds instead of dissipating. Cigarette smoke lingered in the air, drifting very sluggishly. The stroller felt exasperated rather than entertained by the crowds jostling through the streets. The farther he went, the more tortured he was by the dreadful alliance of sirocco and sea air—a condition that both agitates and enervates. He sweated painfully. His eyes blurred, his chest tightened, he was feverish, the blood pounded in his temples. He fled the packed shopping streets, hurried across bridges to the alleys of the slums. There he was pestered by beggars, and the horrible effluvia from the canals made it hard to breathe. On a silent square, one of those bedeviled and forgotten sites in the depths of Venice, he rested on the edge of a fountain; wiping his forehead, he realized he had to find a different vacation goal.

For the second time, and now definitively, this city had proved that it could be extremely harmful to him in such weather. Obstinately sticking it out would be unreasonable, and there was no telling whether the wind would shift. He had to make up his mind very quickly. Going home this soon was out of the question: neither his summer nor his winter quarters were ready to receive him. However, this was not the only place with sea and sand, and other shores would not have the nasty component of a lagoon and its feverish fumes. He remembered hearing the praises of a small beach resort near Trieste. Why not go there? And without further delay, so that it would still be worth his while to change yet again.

He made his decision and stood up. At the next dock he hired a gondola to San Marco and then glided through the dreary labyrinth of canals under delicate marble balconies flanked by effigies of lions; the *barca* curved around slithery corners of walls, along melancholy palazzo facades bearing huge commercial signs that were reflected in the water with its swaying garbage. He had a hard time reaching his destination, for the gondolier, being in league with lace factories and glass workshops, kept coaxing the visitor to stop everywhere so that he might view and buy; and while the bizarre passage through Venice began to cast its spell, the cutpurse bustling of the fallen queen did its bit to frazzle and disenchant him.

Back in the hotel, he went to the office even before dinner and explained that unforeseen circumstances made it necessary for him to leave early the next morning. The manager was very sorry and gave him his receipt. The visitor dined and then spent the lukewarm evening reading newspapers in a rocking chair on the rear terrace. Before retiring, he packed all his belongings and was ready to travel.

He did not sleep all that soundly, nervous as he was about his imminent departure. When he opened the windows in the morning, the sky was still overcast, but the air seemed fresher—

and he already began to regret his decision. Wasn't it a rash mistake, hadn't he been ill and not fully competent? If he had delayed giving notice instead of losing heart so quickly, if he had tried adjusting to the Venetian air or holding out for an improvement in the weather, he might have been able to take another morning stroll instead of coping with more stress and strain. Too late. Now he had to go on wanting what he had wanted yesterday. He dressed and, at eight, took the elevator down to breakfast.

When he entered the buffet room, there were no other guests. A few then arrived as he sat there, waiting for his order. With the teacup at his lips, he saw the Polish girls arriving with their chaperone; austere and fresh for the day, with reddish eyes, they headed toward their table in the window corner. Next, the doorman, his cap doffed, came over to Aschenbach and announced that it was time to leave. The automobile was ready, he said, to convey him and other travelers to the Hotel Excelsior, where the motorboat would carry them to the railroad station via the company's private canal. Time was pressing, said the man. But Aschenbach felt that it was doing nothing of the kind. His train would not be leaving for another hour or more. He was annoyed at this practice of whisking the departing guests out of the hotel prematurely, and he informed the doorman that he wished to breakfast in peace. The man hesitantly withdrew, only to return five minutes later. The automobile could not possibly wait any longer. Well, then let it leave and take his trunk along, Aschenbach snapped. He would board the public vaporetto at the appropriate time, and would they please leave any worrying about his departure to him. The employee bowed. Aschenbach, glad that he had fended off the galling admonitions, ended his long meal leisurely; in fact, he even asked the waiter for a newspaper. When he finally stood up, there was little time left. That very instant, Tadzio happened to come in through the glass door.

As he walked over to his family's table, he crossed the writer's path and modestly glanced down in front of this man with gray hair and a lofty brow; then he looked up again, opening his full, soft eyes in that charming way of his, and he was past. Farewell, Tadzio! thought Aschenbach. I saw you briefly. And contrary to his habit, his lips actually gave murmuring shape to his thoughts, and he added, "Bless you!"

Then, after the traveler went through the formalities of departure, doling out gratuities, the short, quiet manager in the French frock coat said goodbye to him, and Aschenbach left the hotel on foot, just as he had arrived, and followed by a bellboy carrying his hand luggage, he walked down the white-blossoming avenue, which cut straight across the island to the steamer dock. He reached it, sat down in the vaporetto—and what came next was a sorrowful Calvary through all the depths of remorse.

It was the familiar trip across the lagoon, past San Marco, and up the Grand Canal. Aschenbach sat on the round bench in the bow, his arm propped on the railing, his hand shading his eyes. The Public Gardens slipped back, the Piazzetta opened up again in its princely grace and was abandoned; then came the long sequence of palazzi, and when the waterway rounded a curve, the splendid and sweeping marble arch of the Rialto came into view. The traveler watched, and his heart was torn. The city's atmosphere, that faintly rotten odor of sea and swamp that had so urgently compelled him to flee—he now inhaled it in deep and delicately painful gulps. Was it possible that he had not known, had not considered, how deeply attached he was to all these things? What had been a halfhearted regret that morning, a vague doubt about the validity of his decision, now became grief, genuine affliction, anguish, and so bitter that tears kept coming to his eyes, and he told himself he could not possibly have foreseen it. What he found so intolerable, indeed at times so utterly excruciating, was, clearly, the thought that he would never see Venice again, that he was saying goodbye to it forever. For now that the city had twice shown that it made him ill, now that he had been twice forced to leave it helter-skelter, he would henceforth have to regard it as a prohibited and impossible place with which he could not cope and which it would make no sense to revisit. He even felt that if he retreated now, shame and pride must prevent him from ever returning to the beloved city, where his body had twice failed him; and all at once, this conflict between his spiritual inclination and his physical capability appeared so intense and important to the aging man, his bodily defeat so dishonorable and to be overcome at any price, that he could not understand his frivolous surrender on the previous day, when, without any serious struggle, he had decided to endure and acknowledge his rout.

Meanwhile, the steamer was approaching the train station, and his pain and helplessness turned into confusion. Departing struck the tortured man as out of the question and doubling back no less so. Torn apart by these cross-purposes, he entered the station. It was very late, he didn't have a moment to lose if he wanted to catch his train. He wanted to and did not want to. But time was pressing, it whipped him onward; hurrying to buy his ticket, he looked around for the hotel employee stationed somewhere in the tumult. The porter showed up and announced that the trunk had been dispatched. Already dispatched? Yes, in safe hands—to Como. To Como? And the hasty give-and-take, the angry questions and embarrassed answers, revealed that the trunk had been sent from the Hotel Excelsior's luggage office, together with other people's belongings, in an entirely wrong direction.

Aschenbach had trouble maintaining the only expression that was comprehensible in these circumstances. His heart was shaken almost convulsively by a fantastic joy, an unbelievable mirth. The employee dashed away, hoping to stop the trunk, and, as was to be expected, returned empty-handed. Aschenbach now declared that he did not wish to travel without his baggage, that he was determined to go back and wait for the

recovery of his trunk at the Hôtel des Bains. Was the hotel motorboat still docked by the railroad station? The man assured
him that it was right outside. In a torrent of Italian, he persuaded
the clerk to take back the train ticket; he swore to Aschenbach
that he would wire, that no effort, no expense, would be spared
to restore the trunk in no time at all—and so the bizarre thing
came to pass: twenty minutes after arriving at the railroad station, the traveler was once again steaming along the Grand
Canal, heading back to the Lido.

A peculiar and implausible, a humiliating, humorous, dream-
like adventure: he had just said goodbye forever to these places,
leaving them in deepest melancholy—and now was seeing them
again within that same hour after being whirled around by destiny and sent back! With foam at its prow, tacking with comical
agility between steamers and gondolas, the small, swift vessel
shot toward its goal, while its sole passenger concealed the anxious and rollicking excitement of a runaway boy behind a mask
of indignant resignation. From time to time, his chest still heaved
with laughter at this mishap, which, he told himself, could not
have afflicted even a lucky devil more agreeably. Explanations
had to be given, astonished faces endured—then, he told himself, everything would be fine once more, a misfortune would be
averted, a serious error rectified, and everything he had thought
he had left behind would open up to him again, would be his
again for as long as he liked. . . . Was he, incidentally, deceived
by the swiftness of the boat or, to top it all off, was the wind actually blowing in from the sea?

The waves slapped against the concrete walls of the narrow
canal that cut across the island to the Hotel Excelsior. A bus was
waiting for the returnee, and, driving straight above the rippling
water, it carried him to the Hôtel des Bains. The short, musta-
chioed manager in the tail coat came down the front steps to
greet him.

In soft, flattering words, he deplored the accident, said it was extremely embarrassing for him and the establishment but that he was convinced Aschenbach was doing the right thing by waiting here for his trunk. His room was already taken, alas, but another, in no way inferior, was available. *"Pas de chance, monsieur,"* said the Swiss elevator operator, smiling, as they glided up. And so the fugitive was lodged again, in a room almost identical with his earlier one in both location and furniture.

Dazed, worn out by the maelstrom of this strange morning, he settled in an armchair by the open window after distributing the contents of his overnight bag throughout the room. The sea had taken on a pale-green tinge, the air seemed thinner and purer, the beach with its boats and cabins more colorful, even though the sky was still gray. Aschenbach, with his hands folded in his lap, peered out, pleased to be here again, but displeased and shaking his head at his fickleness, his unawareness of his own wishes. He sat like that for roughly an hour, relaxing, daydreaming, without thinking. At noon he spotted Tadzio, who, in a striped linen suit with a red sailor knot, was coming from the sea, walking through the beach gate and along the boardwalk to the hotel. Aschenbach instantly recognized him even from this height before actually seeing him clearly, and he thought of saying, "Look, Tadzio, you're here again too!" But at that same moment, he felt the casual greeting faltering and fading before the truth of his heart—he felt the enthusiasm of his blood, the joy and pain of his soul, and he realized it was Tadzio who had made it so difficult for him to leave.

Aschenbach sat completely still, completely unseen on his high vantage point, and looked inside himself. His features were alert, his eyebrows rose, an attentive, inquisitive, intelligent smile drew out his lips. Then he lifted his head, while his hands, which were dangling limply over the sides of his chair, slowly circled upward, the palms turning forth, as if he were opening and spreading out his arms. It was an obliging gesture of welcome, of serene reception.

# CHAPTER FOUR

Now, DAY AFTER DAY, the naked god with the flaming cheeks drove his team of four fire-breathing horses through the expanses of heaven, and his yellow curls fluttered in the east wind that came blasting out at the same time.

A whitish, silken shimmer covered the vastness of the sluggishly rolling *pontos*. The sand burned. Under the flickering silvery blue of the ether, a rusty-red canvas stretched outside each cabana, and vacationers spent their morning hours in the sharply outlined shade created by the awning. However, the evening could also be delicious, when the plants in the park gave off a balmy fragrance, the constellations danced their rounds overhead, and the murmurs of the night-shrouded sea rose up softly, bewitching the soul. An evening like that could joyfully guarantee another sunny day of casually arranged idleness, densely adorned with countless charming and random possibilities.

The guest detained here by so convenient a mishap was far from viewing the recovery of his trunk as a reason for another departure. For two days he had been forced to put up with a few deprivations and don a travel suit for his meals in the main dining room. Then, when the stray freight was finally deposited in his room, he unpacked everything, filling the wardrobe and the drawers with his belongings—resolved as he was to stay on indefinitely, delighted that he could now spend his beach hours in a silk suit and wear the appropriate evening garb when showing up for dinner at his small table.

The pleasant monotony of this existence had already cast its spell on him, the soft and glossy mildness of this lifestyle had quickly beguiled him. And what a wonderful place it was, combining the charms of cultivated living on a south European beach with the familiar nearness of a wondrous and wonderful city! Aschenbach was no lover of pleasure. Whenever and wherever he began to skylark, to have fun, to enjoy himself—especially in his younger years—he soon felt restless and reluctant, and longed to go back to the sublime toil, the holy and austere service, of his normal agenda. Venice was the only place that could enchant him, relax his willpower, make him happy. He might be sitting under his cabana awning after breakfast, dreaming into the blueness of the southern sea; or, on a lukewarm night, after lingering awhile on Piazza San Marco, he might be leaning against the cushions in a gondola, under the vast and starry sky, gliding homeward to the Lido—with the colorful lights, the poignant strains of the serenade, fading behind him. And sometimes he would think of his mountain cottage, his struggles during the summer there, with the clouds drifting low through the garden, dreadful evening storms blowing the lights out in the cottage, and the ravens, fed by him, rocking in the crowns of the fir trees. He would then feel transported to the Elysian land, to the edges of the earth, where the easiest living is granted to human beings, where there is no snow and no winter, no storm and no downpour, but only the gently cooling breath of Okeanos, and the days flow by in blissful leisure, with no effort or conflict, devoted entirely to the sun and its festivities.

Aschenbach saw the boy Tadzio frequently, almost steadily; except for brief interruptions, the narrow confines and the uniform schedules of all these people kept the beautiful boy nearby throughout the day. He saw him, ran into him everywhere: in the ground-floor areas of the hotel, on the cool boat rides to and from the city, amid the splendor of the Piazza itself, and in any number of other places, if luck was with him. Chiefly, however, and with the most fortunate regularity, the mornings at the beach offered him lengthy opportunities to revere and scrutinize the sweet and lovely vision. Yes, this reliability of luck, this steady daily recurrence of favorable circumstances, were the very things that filled him with contentment and joie de vivre, that made his stay here so precious, that strung the sunny days so pleasantly together.

He rose early, as he normally did when driven by a throbbing urge to work, and he was one of the first on the beach, when the sun was still mild and the sea lay dazzling white in its morning dreams. He benevolently greeted the watchman at the gate, he also familiarly greeted the barefooted, white-bearded oldster who had prepared his place, had set up the brown awning and moved the chair and the table from the cabana to the platform, where Aschenbach then settled. Three or four hours were now his—hours in which the sun rose to its zenith, gaining dreadful might, in which the sea turned a deeper and deeper blue, and in which he could gaze at Tadzio.

He saw him coming from the left, along the waterline, or saw him emerging in the back, from between the cabins, or else he suddenly assumed, not without a certain joyful alarm, that he had missed the boy's arrival, that he was already here, already wearing the blue and white bathing suit that had become his sole garment on the beach. He feared that Tadzio was already immersed in his usual activities amid sun and sand—that charmingly idle, that unsteady and indolent life, playful and restful, that strolling, wading, digging, grabbing, lying, and swimming. The women watching him from the platform would shout for him, call his name in their high voices: "Tadziu! Tadziu!" and gesticulating at them, he would dash over to describe what he had experienced, to show them what he had found, had caught: mussels, sea horses, jellyfish, and sideways-scuttling crabs. Aschenbach did not understand anything he said, but no matter how banal his words might be, they formed blurry harmonies in the listener's ears. Their foreignness transformed them into music, an exuberant sun poured lavish brilliance over him, and the sublime vastness of the sea constantly served as his foil and background.

Soon the observer knew every line and pose of that body that presented itself so freely, so exaltedly; he joyously welcomed yet again every familiar trait of beauty, and there was no end to his admiration, to the tender delight of his senses. The boy might be summoned to say hello to a guest visiting the women at the cabin; Tadzio ran over, perhaps dripping wet from the sea, he tossed his curls, and holding out his hand, resting his weight on one leg, the other foot on tiptoe, he charmingly turned and twisted his body, gracefully in suspense, amiably bashful, anxious to please as an aristocratic obligation. Or he lay stretched out on the sand, his beach towel wrapped around his chest, his delicate chiseled arm propped on the ground, his chin on his high hand; the boy known as "Yashu" squatted by him, courting him, and nothing could be more enchanting than the smiling eyes and lips of the Chosen One as he peered up at his subaltern, his servant.

Or else, his hands clasped on the back of his neck, he might be standing by the water's edge, alone, aloof from his family, very near Aschenbach, erect, slowly rocking on the balls of his feet, dreaming into the blueness, while small waves lapped up and bathed his toes. His honey-colored curls snuggled against his temples and his neck, the sun illuminated the down on his upper spine, the fine lineation of the ribs, the symmetry of the chest emerged through the sheer skin on his torso; his armpits were still as smooth as a statue's, the hollows of his knees were shiny, and their bluish veins made his body look as if it were formed out of something more lucid than flesh. What breeding, what precision of thought were expressed in this elongated and youthfully perfect body! Yet wasn't the strict and pure will that had labored in obscurity to thrust this godly sculpture into the light—wasn't it known and familiar to him, the artist? Didn't that will operate within him too when, filled with sober passion, he worked on the marble mass of language and liberated the slender form that he had seen in spirit and that he presented to humanity as an idol and mirror of spiritual beauty?

Idol and mirror! His eyes enfolded the noble figure there, at the edge of the blue, and in sweeping, worshipful rapture he believed that with his gaze he could grasp beauty itself, form as a divine thought, the one and pure perfection, which lives in the mind, and of which a human effigy and metaphor had been put up here, light and lovely, to be revered. This was frenzy; and the aging artist welcomed it with no qualms, indeed greedily. His mind was in labor, his cultural foundation was heaving and seething, his memory cast up ancient thoughts that had been handed down to him in his youth and that had never, until now, been animated by his own fire. Was it not written that the sun diverts our attention from intellectual to sensual things? Supposedly, it so thoroughly benumbs and bewitches our reason and memory that the ecstatic soul completely forgets its own state of being and, with astonished admiration, dotes on the most beautiful of the sunlit objects; in fact, it is only with the help of a body that the soul can then rise to a more sublime contemplation. Amor truly emulated the mathematicians who show tangible pictures of ideal forms to children still unable to think abstractly: the god of love did likewise when, to make the spiritual visible to us, he used the shape and color of human youth, adorning it with all the reflected luster of beauty as an instrument for the memory, and making us burn with pain and hope at the mere sight of it.

Those were the enthusiast's thoughts; those were the things he could feel. And the intoxication of the sea and the brilliance of the sun wove into an enchanting tableau for him. There was the old plane tree not far from the walls of Athens—there was that holy and shady spot fragrant with chaste-tree blossoms and decorated with votive images and pious offerings in honor of the nymphs and Acheloos. Very clear was the brook tumbling over smooth pebbles at the foot of the spreading tree; the crickets fiddled. But on the grassy bank, which sloped down gently so that you could hold your head high while reclining, two men were resting, shielded from the heat of day: an elderly man and a young one, an ugly and a beautiful one, the wise man with the engaging one. And with courteous words and astutely wooing jests, Socrates taught Phaidros about desire and virtue.

He spoke to him about the burning shock that the feeling person suffers when laying eyes on an image of eternal Beauty; he spoke to him about the lust of the impious and evil man, who cannot conceive of Beauty upon seeing its effigy and who is incapable of awe; spoke about the sacred terror that overcomes the noble person when he beholds a godlike countenance, a perfect body. Such a man shudders and is beside himself and scarcely dares to peep, and he reveres the bearer of Beauty, would even sacrifice to him as to a statue if he did not fear being thought a madman. For Beauty, my Phaidros, Beauty alone, is both lovely and visible at once: Beauty—mark my words!—is the only form of the spiritual that we can receive with our senses, endure with our senses. What would become of us if godliness, if reason and virtue and truth, were to appear to our senses? Would we not be devastated and devoured by the flames of love as Semele by Zeus so long ago? Thus Beauty is the feeling man's way to the spirit— only the way, only a means, little Phaidros. . . . And then he uttered the very subtlest statement, the cunning wooer: he said that the lover is more divine than the beloved, because the god dwells in the one but not in the other—the tenderest, most sardonic thought, perhaps, that was ever thought, the wellspring of all the roguery and most secret voluptuousness of yearning.

The artist finds delight in thinking that can become sheer feeling and feeling that can become sheer thinking. At this time, such pulsative thinking, such precise feeling belonged to, obeyed the solitary man, who thought and felt that nature shudders with bliss when the spirit bows in homage to Beauty. He had a sudden urge to write. Now Eros, we are told, loves idleness, and that alone is why he was created. Yet at this point in the crisis, the stricken man's agitation focused on creativity. What prompted it scarcely mattered. A question, a challenge, about a certain great and burning issue of culture and taste had been raised as revelation in the intellectual world, and the query had reached the traveler. He was familiar with the subject, he had experienced it; and all at once, he could not resist a craving to make it glisten with his language. And he longed to work in Tadzio's presence, to model his writing after the boy's figure, to let his style follow the lines of that godly body and transform his beauty into the spiritual, the way the eagle once bore the Trojan shepherd to the ether.

Never had he felt the pleasure of words more sweetly, never had he known so deeply that Eros is in words as in the dangerously delicious hours when he sat at his crude table under the awning, with his idol in full view, the music of that voice in his ears; he was modeling his little essay on Tadzio's beauty, forming that page and a half of exquisite prose whose purity, nobility, and quivering emotional tension would shortly gain the admiration of many. It is most certainly a good thing that the world knows only the beautiful opus but not its origins, not the conditions of its creation; for if people knew the sources of the artist's inspiration, that knowledge would often confuse them, alarm them, and thereby destroy the effects of excellence. Strange hours! Strangely enervating labor! Bizarrely fertile intercourse of the mind with a body! By the time Aschenbach put away his work and abandoned the beach, he was exhausted, even shattered, and he felt his conscience lamenting as if after a debauchery.

It was on the following morning, when he was about to descend the outside stairs of the hotel, that he spotted Tadzio heading toward the beach, all alone, and already approaching the barrier gate. Aschenbach simply thought of using this opportunity to meet the boy who unknowingly aroused so much elation and emotion in him: he wished, almost urgently, to make his acquaintance, casually and serenely, to address him, to delight in his response, his gaze. The beauty was sauntering, he could be overtaken, and Aschenbach quickened his steps. He caught up with him on the boardwalk behind the cabins, he wanted to put his hand on the youngster's head, on his shoulder, and some words or other, an amiable French phrase, hovered on his lips. But then, perhaps partly because of his rapid stride, his heart was hammering, he was very short of breath, so that his voice would be quaking and strained. He hesitated, he tried to get hold of himself, he suddenly feared he had been trailing the beauty too long and too closely, he feared the boy would notice him, would look back quizzically; Aschenbach charged off faster, refrained, renounced, and, lowering his head, passed him by.

Too late! he thought at that moment. Too late! But was it too late? The step he had failed to take might readily have led to something light, something good and glad, to salutary sobering. But perhaps the aging man did not want any sobering; his rapture may have been too precious. Who can decipher the nature and character of artistry?! Who can grasp the profound instinctual merger of discipline and dissipation on which it is founded?! For inability to desire salutary sobering is in itself dissipation. Aschenbach no longer had a mind for self-criticism; given his taste and mental makeup at this point in his life, given his self-esteem, maturity, and late-won simplicity, he did not care to dissect his motives and determine whether his failure to carry out his plan was due to weakness or slovenliness. He was confused, he feared that someone, if only the beach guard, might have observed his dash, his defeat; he dreaded looking ridiculous. And yet he kept joking to himself about the funny and holy anxiety that had held him back. Bewildered, he thought; bewildered like a frightened rooster that droops its wings in a fight. This is truly the work of the god who, when we behold beauty, breaks our spirit and drastically crushes our pride. . . . He played with that idea, rhapsodized about it, and was much too arrogant to fear any feeling.

He failed to notice the end of the period of idleness that he had granted himself; he didn't even think of going home. He had assigned himself ample funds. His sole worry was that the Polish family might leave, but he had deviously learned—by casually asking the hotel barber—that they had arrived very shortly before him. The sun tanned his face and hands, the exhilarating salt air increased his emotional power. Normally, whatever refreshment he gained from sleep, food, or nature had been promptly expended on some work; but now, any daily strengthening by sun, sea air, and idleness was generously and inefficiently consumed in euphoria and sensation.

His sleep was fitful; the exquisitely uniform days were separated by brief nights of happy disquiet. True, he would retire early, since the day seemed to end for him at nine P.M., when Tadzio vanished from the scene. But at the crack of dawn, Aschenbach was awoken by a gently penetrating fear, his heart would recall his adventure, he could no longer stand being in bed, he got up, and lightly clad against the early-morning chill, he sat down at the open window to wait for the rising of the sun. His soul, already consecrated by sleep, was filled with awe at that miraculous event. Sky, earth, and sea were still lying in the ghostly and glassy pallor of daybreak; a fading star was still floating in unreality.

But then came a wafting, a winged tiding from inaccessible dwellings, the news that Eos was rising from her husband's side; and the farthest strips of sky and sea were tinged by the first sweet flush that heralds the sensory perception of Creation. The goddess was approaching, the seductress of adolescents—she who carried off Cleitos and Cephalos and, defying the envy of all the Olympians, enjoyed the love of the beautiful Orion. Roses were strewn at the edge of the earth, an ineffably lovely shining and flowering; infant clouds, transfigured, illumined, were hovering like attendant cupids in the rosy and bluish haze; purple radiance dropped on the sea, which surged and appeared to be heaving it forward; golden spears flashed from below to the height of the heavens, the glistening became a burning; soundlessly, with divine violence, the glow and the blaze and the flaring flames billowed upward; and with snatching hooves the brother's sacred steeds came galloping over the earth. Lit up by the god's splendor, the solitary waker sat there; he closed his eyes and let the magnificence kiss his lids. Long-lost feelings, early and precious sufferings of his heart, all of them having died in the severe servitude of his life, now returned, strangely transformed—he recognized them with a confused and astonished smile. He mused, he dreamed, and slowly his lips shaped a name, and still smiling, with his face turned up, his hands folded in his lap, he dozed off again in his chair.

But the day, which began so festive and fiery, was mysteriously exalted, was metamorphosed as in a myth. Where did it start, from where did it come—the breath, suddenly so soft and significant, that, like a whispering from loftier realms, played around his ears and temples? Hordes of white and wispy cloudlets were scattered widely across the sky like grazing herds owned by the gods. A stiffer wind arose, and Poseidon's horses came dashing and rearing, bulls, perhaps, that belonged to the one with the bluish curls, bulls that bellowed and charged with lowered horns. But between the rocks on the distant beach the waves came hopping up as leaping goats. A world disfigured by holiness, exalted by the existence of Pan, enveloped the spellbound human, and his heart dreamed of delicate fables. Often, when the sun was sinking behind Venice, he would sit on a bench in the park, watching Tadzio, who, clad in white with a colored belt, was joyfully playing ball on the rolled gravel court, and it was Hyacinth whom the viewer believed he saw, Hyacinth, who was doomed to die because he was loved by two gods. The viewer even felt Zephyr's painful jealousy of his rival, who forgot all about his bow, his oracle, and his cithara in order to play constantly with the beautiful youth; he saw the discus aimed by cruel jealousy and striking the lovely head; likewise turning pale, he received the buckled body, and the flower, blossoming from the sweet blood, bore the imprint of his endless lament. . . .

Nothing is more bizarre, more ticklish, than a relationship between two people who know each other only with their eyes—who encounter, observe each other daily, even hourly, never greeting, never speaking, constrained by convention or by caprice to keep acting the indifferent strangers. They experience discomfort and overwrought curiosity, the hysteria of an unsatisfied, unnaturally stifled need to recognize and to exchange, and they especially feel something like a tense mutual esteem. For people love and honor someone so long as they cannot judge him, and yearning is a product of defective knowledge.

Some kind of relationship, of acquaintanceship, was bound to develop between Aschenbach and young Tadzio, and the older man was deeply thrilled when he determined that his interest and attention were not entirely unrequited. What, for example, induced the beauty, when he appeared on the beach in the morning, to stop using the boardwalk behind the cabins and to walk only in front, over the sand, past Aschenbach's domicile, sometimes so unnecessarily close to the writer, almost brushing his table, his chair, as the boy sauntered toward his family's cabana? Was that how the attraction, the fascination of a superior feeling, affected its tender and heedless object? Aschenbach looked forward every day to Tadzio's arrival, and sometimes he pretended to be busy at that moment and to ignore the beauty strolling by. But at other times he did look up, and their eyes met. They were both deeply earnest whenever that happened. Nothing in the elderly man's cultivated and dignified expression so much as hinted at any emotion; but Tadzio's gaze was filled with questioning, with reflective wondering, and his feet faltered; he glanced at the ground, he charmingly glanced up again; and once he was past, a certain something in his posture appeared to be saying that only his upbringing kept him from turning his head.

One evening, however, things changed. The Polish family and its chaperon failed to show up for dinner—as Aschenbach anxiously noticed. He was worried about them, and after the meal, in evening attire and straw hat, he was strolling in front of the hotel, at the bottom of the terrace, when all at once he saw them emerging in the light of the arc lamps: the nunlike sisters with the governess and, four paces behind them, Tadzio. They were clearly coming from the steamer pier after dining in town for some reason. It must have been cooler out on the water; Tadzio wore a dark-blue peacoat with gold buttons and a matching cap. Sun and sea air never burned him; his skin had remained as yellowish as marble since the beginning; but tonight he seemed paler than usual, either because of the evening's coolness or because of the bleaching moonlight of the lamps. His symmetrical eyebrows stood out more sharply, his eyes darkened deeply. He was more beautiful than any words could say, and Aschenbach painfully felt, as so often before, that language can only praise, but not reproduce, the beauty that appeals to the senses.

He had not expected this precious appearance: it was unhoped for, he had no time to put on an expression of calm dignity. His face may have openly displayed his joy, surprise, admiration, when his eyes encountered those of the person he had missed—and at that instant it happened: Tadzio smiled; smiled at him; his lips slowly opened into an eloquent, intimate, charming, and candid smile. It was the smile of Narcissus leaning over the mirroring water, that deep, drawn-out, bewitching smile with which he stretched his arms toward the reflection of his own beauty—a very slightly distorted smile, distorted by the hopelessness of his striving to kiss the sweet lips of his image, coquettish, curious, and mildly tortured, beguiled and beguiling.

The man receiving this smile hurried away with it as with a

fateful gift. He was so deeply shaken that he was forced to flee the light of the terrace, the front gardens, and he hastily sought the darkness of the park behind the hotel. Strangely indignant and affectionate exhortations were wrung from him: "You mustn't smile like that! Listen, you mustn't smile at anyone like that!" He flung himself on a bench, he was beside himself, he breathed the nocturnal fragrance of the plants. And leaning back, with dangling arms, overwhelmed, and shuddering again and again, he whispered the standard formula of desire—impossible here, absurd, abject, ludicrous and yet sacred, and honorable even here: "I love you!"

# CHAPTER FIVE

DURING THE FOURTH WEEK of his sojourn on the Lido, Gustav von Aschenbach detected several eerie things in the world around him. First of all, it struck him that while the season was advancing, the number of guests at his hotel was going down rather than up; he felt especially that the German language here was waning and fading out, so that only foreign sounds reached his ears at meals and on the beach. Then one day, while conversing with the hotel barber, whom he now visited frequently, he heard something rather startling. The man had mentioned a German family that had just left after a brief visit, and he added, in a chatty and flattering tone: "You're staying on, signore! You're not scared of the illness."

Aschenbach looked at him. "Illness?" he echoed.

The prattler held his tongue, acted busy, ignored the question. And when the customer persisted, the barber said he knew nothing, and with an embarrassed babbling, he quickly tried to change the subject.

That was around noon. After lunch, in a dead calm and under a broiling sun, Aschenbach boarded a gondola to Venice, for he was driven by a mania: to follow the Polish siblings, who, with their chaperone, had set out for the steamer dock. He did not find his idol on Piazza di San Marco. But when Aschenbach was having his tea at a small, round iron table on the shady half of the square, he suddenly noticed a peculiar smell in the air, an aroma that he now felt he had been inhaling for days without realizing it: a cloying medicinal odor reminiscent of poverty and injury and dubious hygiene. He sniffed it and, after mulling, recognized it; he finished his snack and left the square on the side across from the cathedral. In the cramped alleys, the stench grew stronger. At corners, the city fathers had stuck up printed announcements to inform the inhabitants about certain gastric disorders common in this kind of weather, and to warn against the consumption of clams and oysters as well as canal water. These signs were obviously meant to gloss over an unpleasant situation. Groups of people clustered silently on the squares and bridges; and the stranger stood among them, probing and pondering.

A shopkeeper was leaning in his doorway, among coral necklaces and imitation-amethyst trinkets, and Aschenbach asked him about the obnoxious odor. The man scrutinized him with heavy eyes and hastily livened up: "A protective measure, signore!" he replied, gesticulating. "A police injunction that we can only approve of. This weather is oppressive, the sirocco is not conducive to good health. In short, you understand—a perhaps exaggerated precaution. . . ."

Aschenbach thanked him and walked on. And even on the steamer carrying him back to the Lido, he now caught the smell of the germicide.

Upon reentering the hotel, he headed straight for the periodicals table in the lobby and leafed through the various gazettes. He found nothing in the non-German ones. The German papers mentioned rumors, cited fluctuating figures, reported official denials, and doubted their veracity. That explained the departure of the German and Austrian contingents. Other nationals evidently knew nothing, sensed nothing, were not nervous as yet. They're trying to keep it quiet! thought Aschenbach, indignantly tossing the newspapers back on the table. They're trying to keep it quiet! But at the same time, he was happy about the adventure awaiting the world around him. For the established order and well-being of normal life run counter not only to crime but also to passion, which welcomes, and vaguely hopes to benefit from, any loosening of the bourgeois fabric, any confusion and affliction in the world. So Aschenbach felt a dark satisfaction about what was happening in the filthy alleys of Venice, about the official cover-up and the city's nasty secret—a secret that blended with his own most private secret and that he, too, was intent on guarding. For the lover had only one anxiety: that Tadzio might leave Venice; and Aschenbach realized, not without dismay, that he would not know how to go on living if that occurred.

By now he was no longer content to rely on the daily routine or on chance in order to see and be near the beauty; he followed him, he tracked him down. On Sundays, for instance, the Poles never showed up at the beach: he figured out that they were attending mass at San Marco; he hurried over and, passing from the torrid square into the golden twilight of the sanctuary, he found the youngster he had been deprived of: he was bowing over a prie-dieu. Aschenbach then stood in the back, on the fissured mosaic floor, amid worshipers, who were kneeling, murmuring, crossing themselves, and the crowded splendor of this Oriental temple weighed lusciously on his senses. In front, the heavily adorned priest was moving, gesturing, and singing; incense was billowing up, shrouding the small, limp flames of the altar candles, and the mawkish and mind-dulling sacrificial fragrance seemed to be mingling with a lesser smell: the odor of the sickened city. But through haze and sparkle Aschenbach saw the beauty turn his head, look for him, and sight him.

When the populace then streamed out through the opened portals and gathered in the lustrous square, which was teeming with pigeons, the infatuated fool hid in the vestibule, he lurked, he lay in wait. He saw the Poles leaving the church, saw the children ceremoniously saying goodbye to the mother, who now headed back to the Piazzetta; he determined that the beauty, the nunlike sisters, and the governess turned right, walked through the clock-tower gates and into the Merceria; and after giving them a head start, he followed them, followed them stealthily on their promenade through Venice. He had to halt whenever they lingered, he had to flee into restaurants and courtyards whenever they doubled back; he lost them, hunted them, feverish and fatigued, across bridges and through dirty dead ends, and he endured minutes of lethal anguish when he suddenly saw them coming toward him through a narrow passage from which there was no escape. Nevertheless, one cannot say that he suffered. His head and heart were intoxicated, and his steps obeyed the instructions of the demon who delights in trampling on human reason and dignity.

Tadzio and the others then boarded a gondola somewhere, while Aschenbach watched from behind a portico or fountain; next, after they pushed off, he likewise got into a gondola. Muttering hastily, he pointed to the one just rounding that corner there and he promised the oarsman a handsome gratuity if he trailed it inconspicuously, at a certain distance; and he shuddered when the man, with the roguish helpfulness of a panderer, assured him in the same tone of voice that he would be taken care of, conscientiously taken care of.

And so, leaning on soft black cushions, he swayed and glided along in the wake of the other black, beaked craft, to which he was fettered by passion. Sometimes the quarry eluded him: he would then feel anguish and disquiet. But as if well practiced in such affairs, his boatman, by maneuvering slyly, by shooting crisscross and taking shortcuts, always managed to sight the cov-

eted object again. The air was still and smelly, the sun burned
heavily through the haze that turned the sky the color of slate.
Gurgling water slapped against wood and stone. Thanks to
some bizarre convention, the gondolier's cry, half warning, half
greeting, was answered from deep within the hush of the
labyrinth. From small, high-lying gardens, white and purple
blossoms with an almond scent were dangling over crumbling
walls. Moorish window frames stood out in the dreary light. The
marble steps of a church descended into the canal; a beggar,
squatting there, proclaiming his poverty, held out his hat and
showed the whites of his eyes as if he were blind; an antiques
dealer, outside his dumpy booth, groveled before the passenger,
inviting him to stop off, hoping to bilk him.

That was Venice, the cajoling and dubious beauty—this city,
half fairy tale, half tourist trap, where art had once voluptuously
run riot in the putrid air and which gave musicians sounds that
lull and lollop lasciviously. The adventurer felt as if his eyes were
drinking in this voluptuousness, as if his ears were being wooed
by such melodies; he also recalled that the city was ill, but concealing its illness out of greed, and he peered more wantonly after the gondola floating ahead of him.

All that the confused man knew and desired was to keep
ceaselessly pursuing the object that inflamed him, to dream
about him in his absence and, as lovers do, speak tenderly to his
mere phantom. Loneliness, foreignness, and the happiness of a
profound and belated intoxication encouraged him and persuaded him to experience the most astonishing things freely and
without blushing. Thus one night, returning from Venice, he
had halted on the second floor of the hotel, at the beauty's door:
utterly exhilarated, he had pressed his forehead against the hinge
for a long time, unable to tear himself away, running the risk of
being caught and snared in such an insane action.

But still, there were moments when he paused, half regaining
his sense. What am I doing? he would think in bewilderment.

What am I doing? As with any man whose native merits arouse an aristocratic interest in his ancestry, his achievements and successes always inspired him to recall his forebears, to assure himself mentally of their approval, their satisfaction, their mandatory respect. He thought of them here and now, entangled as he was in such an illicit experience, involved in such exotic emotional debauchery; he remembered their rigorous self-control, their respectable manliness, and he smiled dourly. What would they say? But then again, what would they have said about his entire life, which deviated from theirs to the point of degeneracy; what would they have said about this life lived under the sway of art? Once, with the bourgeois attitude of his forefathers, the adolescent had openly derided such an existence, which basically was so similar to theirs! He, too, had served in the military, had been a soldier and warrior, like a number of them—for art was a war, a grueling struggle that nowadays ground you down very quickly.

A life of defiance and strength of mind, a stern, staunch, and abstemious life that he had shaped into a symbol of the frail heroism that fitted in with the times—he had the right to call that life manly, to call it valiant; and it seemed to him as if the kind of eros that had overpowered him somehow fitted in with and favored such a life. Had not this eros been highly revered by the bravest nations; had it not, it was said, flourished in their cities because of bravery? Countless ancient war heroes had willingly borne its yoke, never viewing its commands as humiliations; and those heroes did things that would be condemned as cowardice if done for any other reasons: they knelt, vowed, begged, and slavishly groveled—and such actions never shamed the lover; why, he even reaped praise for them.

Those thoughts controlled Aschenbach's infatuated mind, they propped him up, they preserved his dignity. But at the same time, he kept stubbornly focusing on and investigating the shady events inside Venice, that adventure of the surrounding world, the adventure that darkly merged with his, nourishing his passion with vague, lawless hopes. Obsessed with obtaining reliable news about the status and progress of the disease, he went to the city's cafés and plowed through all the German newspapers, which had been missing from the hotel lobby during the past few days. Assertions alternated with retractions. The overall tally of patients, the number of deaths, supposedly ran to twenty, to forty, nay, one hundred and more; yet right after that, any occurrence of the epidemic was, if not roundly denied, at least waved off as sporadic, blamed on a few isolated cases among foreign tourists. Next came earnest warnings as well as protests against the dangerous game being played by the Italian authorities. But no certainty was to be had.

Nevertheless, the solitary man felt he had a special claim to be let in on the secret, and though excluded, he found a bizarre satisfaction in approaching the insiders and those who were allied in silence: by asking them embarrassing questions, he forced them to tell outright lies. One day, during lunch in the main dining room, he confronted the hotel manager, that short man in the French frock coat, who was walking softly among the guests, greeting them and supervising. When he paused at Aschenbach's small table to exchange a few inconsequential words, the guest asked casually, almost in passing, why in the world they had been disinfecting Venice for some time now.

"It's a police measure," the pussyfooter replied. "They are doing their duty and forestalling all kinds of unwholesome disturbances or disruptions that might assail the public health due to this unseasonably hot and stifling weather."

"The police deserve our praises," Aschenbach rejoined; and after a brief give-and-take of meteorological remarks, the manager excused himself.

That evening, after dinner, it so happened that a small troupe of buskers from the city were performing in the front garden of the hotel. They stood, two men and two women, by the iron post of an arc lamp, and their faces, whitened by the glow, were turned up toward the large terrace, where the guests, over their coffee and cooling drinks, were patronizing the folksy entertainment. The hotel personnel—bellhops, waiters, and office clerks—were listening from the lobby doorways. The members of the Russian family, eager and precise in their enjoyment, had their wicker chairs moved down into the garden, closer to the musicians, and they sat there gratefully in a half circle. Behind the mother stood her old serf, in her turbanlike headgear.

A mandolin, a guitar, a concertina, and a squealing fiddle were being strummed, scraped, or squeezed by the beggar virtuosi. Instrumental presentations alternated with vocal numbers, in which the younger woman, with her raspy, squawky voice, joined the sweetly falsettoing tenor in a yearning love duet. But the truly talented star and leader of the group proved incontestably to be the other man, a guitarist and a sort of baritone buffo, with no voice to speak of but with a gift for mimicry and with a remarkable comedic energy. Often, with his instrument on his arm, he would detach himself from the group and burlesque his way to the bottom of the terrace, the "footlights," where his antics were rewarded with buoyant laughter. The Russians, in their front-row seats, were particularly ecstatic about so much southern agility, and their clapping and cheering kept encouraging him to get bolder and brasher.

Aschenbach sat at the balustrade, occasionally cooling his lips with a blend of pomegranate juice and soda water, which sparkled ruby red in the glass. His nerves greedily lapped up the suffering sounds, the vulgar and languishing tunes, for passion paralyzes all sense of choosiness and succumbs quite earnestly to that which sobriety would take as a joke or reject indignantly. As he watched the prancing buffoon, Aschenbach's features froze into a painfully twisted grin. He sat there nonchalantly, but his mind was tense and totally absorbed in something else: for just six paces away from him Tadzio was leaning on the stone barrier.

He had on the white belted suit that he sometimes wore at

dinner, and he stood there, showing innate and inevitable grace, his lower left arm on the balustrade, his feet crossed, his right hand on his supporting hip; he looked down at the ballad-mongers with an expression that was not so much a smile as an aloof curiosity, a cordial acknowledgment. At times he would straighten up, toss out his chest, and with a lovely movement of both arms, he would draw his white jacket down through his leather belt. And at other times, as the aging man noted in tri-umph and dismay and with reeling senses, Tadzio would turn his head, and with cautious hesitancy or with sudden haste, as if to catch the lover off guard, he would peek at him over his left shoulder. Their eyes did not meet, for a mortifying uneasiness compelled the aberrant man to keep an anxious rein on his glances. The women in charge of Tadzio were sitting at the rear of the terrace, and matters had reached such a pass that the lover dreaded being conspicuous and arousing suspicion. Indeed, a few times, on the beach, in the hotel lobby, and on Piazza di San Marco, Aschenbach had noticed with a kind of numbness that they had called Tadzio back when he was near him, they were in-tent on keeping the boy away from him—and Aschenbach had been terribly offended, his pride had suffered unknown tortures, which his conscience had prevented him from forswearing.

Meanwhile, the guitarist, accompanying himself, had launched into a solo ditty, a smash hit throughout Italy, and while his en-tire group joined in with each refrain, singing and playing all their instruments, he devoted his full dramatic verve to deliver-ing the many stanzas. With his slight build and gaunt, emaciated face, he stood there on the gravel, separated from his compan-ions, a shabby felt hat on the back of his head, a shock of his red hair welling out from under the brim; with swaggering bravura, he twanged his guitar and belted out his parlando, hurling his banter up the terrace, so that his strenuous efforts made the veins bulge on his forehead.

He did not look like the Venetian type; he seemed to belong

to the race of Neapolitan comedians, half pimp, half actor, brutal and insolent, dangerous and entertaining. His lyrics were merely silly, but because of his expressions, his body movements, his leers, and the way his tongue played lasciviously in the corner of his mouth, the song became suggestive on his lips, vaguely scurrilous. From the soft collar of his sport shirt, which he wore with a more normal suit, his scraggy neck loomed up with a strikingly huge and naked-looking Adam's apple. There was no telling his age from his pale, stub-nosed, beardless face, which seemed thoroughly rumpled from grimaces and vices, and the two defiant, imperious, almost savage furrows between his reddish brows contrasted oddly with the grin on his mobile mouth. But what made the solitary traveler scrutinize the musician so thoroughly was that this suspicious figure appeared to bring along his own suspicious emanation. For at each refrain, the singer, twisting his features and shaking his hands, set off on a grotesque circular march, which took him directly beneath Aschenbach, and whenever this happened, the powerful stench of carbolic acid billowed up to the terrace from his clothes, his body.

After completing his song, the buffoon started collecting money. He began with the Russians, who were openly generous, and then he mounted the stairs. But insolent as he may have been during the performance, he was very obsequious up here: bowing and scraping, he skulked between the tables, baring his strong teeth in a smile of cunning servility, while the two menacing furrows remained between his red brows. As he gathered in his livelihood, the guests studied the exotic creature with a mingling of curiosity and some repugnance; they tossed coins into his felt hat with their fingertips, making sure not to touch it. The suspension of the physical distance between the performer—no matter how talented—and his respectable audience always creates a certain embarrassment. The musician felt this awkwardness and tried to apologize by groveling. He reached

Aschenbach and with him came that smell, which no one else seemed concerned about.

"Listen!" said the solitary man quietly, almost mechanically. "They're disinfecting Venice. Why?"

The jokester answered hoarsely, "On account of the police! It's the law, signore, because of the heat and the sirocco! The sirocco is oppressive. It's not conducive to good health." He spoke as if surprised that anyone could ask such a question, and with the flat of his hand he demonstrated how oppressive the sirocco was.

"So there's no illness in Venice?" Aschenbach murmured through his teeth.

The buffoon's facial muscles fell into a grimace of comical helplessness. "Illness? What sort of illness? Is the sirocco an illness? Could our police be an illness? You're joking! An illness! Not on your life! A preventive measure, you understand! A police action against the effects of the oppressive weather! . . ." He gesticulated.

"Fine," Aschenbach again murmured tersely, flinging an unduly large coin into the hat. Then he dismissed him with a glance. The man obeyed, grinning as he bowed several times. But before he even reached the steps, two hotel employees pounced on him and, their faces close to his, they cross-examined him in whispers. He shrugged, reassured them, swore that he been discreet—it was plain to see. When they released him, he went back down to the garden and, after briefly conferring with his colleagues under the arc lamp, stepped forward to express his gratitude in a farewell encore.

It was a song that the solitary man had, to his knowledge, never heard before: a brazen hit in an incomprehensible dialect, with a laughing refrain, which the group took up at regular intervals, roaring with mirth. The words would then stop, as would the instrumental accompaniment, leaving nothing but laughter arranged in some kind of rhythmic pattern, yet modulated in a very natural-sounding way; and the highly talented soloist in particular managed to produce the most deceptively lifelike guffaws. By restoring the artistic distance between him and his distinguished onlookers, he had regained all his impudence, so that his artificial laughter, insolently dispatched to the terrace, was a laughter of utter scorn. He sobbed, his voice faltered, he pressed his hand to his mouth, he contorted his shoulders, and at the right moment, his untamed laughter broke, burst, bellowed out of him, and with such verisimilitude that it became contagious, infecting the spectators, so that a groundless hilarity spread out, feeding purely on itself. But this seemed only to pump up the singer's merriment. He bent his knees, he slapped his thighs, he held his sides, he was ready to explode, he no longer laughed, he shrieked; he pointed his finger at the terrace as if there were nothing more hilarious in the world than that laughing audience, and finally everyone in the garden and on the veranda was laughing, even the waiters, bellhops, and porters in the doorways.

Aschenbach was no longer lounging in his chair; he sat erect as if about to fight or flee. But the laughter, the hospital smell wafting up to him, and the nearness of the beauty coalesced in a dreamlike spell that, indestructible and inescapable, held his head, his mind, captive. Amid the general commotion and amusement, he stole a glance at Tadzio, and in so doing, he noticed that when the beauty responded to his glimpse, he likewise remained serious, virtually attuning his own demeanor and expression to Aschenbach's, as if the general mood of the place had no hold on the boy because the adult stayed aloof. There was something so disarming, so overwhelming about that childlike and suggestive obedience that the gray-haired man barely resisted concealing his face in his hands. He also felt that when Tadzio occasionally sat up straight and drew a deep breath, it meant that his chest was constricted and he was heaving a sigh of relief.

"He is sickly, he probably won't grow old," Aschenbach mused again, with the neutrality that is sometimes the strange emancipation of euphoria and yearning; and his heart was filled with sheer concern but also reckless satisfaction.

Meanwhile, the Venetians had finished and were making their exit. Applause accompanied them, and their leader did not fail to spice up his departure with a few more pranks. The guests laughed at the way he bowed and scraped and blew kisses at them, and so he did twice as much. When his people were gone, he pretended to back into a lamppost, hurting himself badly, so that, doubled up in pain, he barely crept to the gate. Once there, he finally yanked off the mask of the comical unfortunate, straightened up, indeed elastically leaped up, impudently stuck out his tongue at the spectators on the terrace, and slipped into the darkness. The audience dispersed; Tadzio had long since left the balustrade. But to the annoyance of the waiters, the solitary man sat and sat at his small table, nursing the rest of his pomegranate beverage. Night wore on, time crumbled. Many years earlier, his parents had had an hourglass in their home: he could suddenly see the frail and meaningful little device as if it were standing before him. The fine, rusty-red sand dribbled soundlessly through the glassy narrowness, and as it ran low in the upper bulb, a small, raging vortex formed in the lower one.

The very next afternoon, the obstinate man took another step in baiting the outer world, and this time with all possible success. He entered the British travel bureau on Piazza di San Marco, where he changed some money, and then, playing the distrustful foreigner, he asked his irksome question. The clerk serving him was a young, tweedy Englishman with close-set eyes and hair parted down the middle, and with the sedate integrity that seems so alien, so bizarre, in the roguishly quick-witted south.

He began: "No reason to worry, sir. An almost meaningless formality. Such measures are often taken to forestall the unhealthy effects of the heat and the sirocco. . . ." But as he glanced up, his blue eyes met the stranger's bleak and somewhat weary scowl, which was focused on the clerk's lips. The Englishman reddened. "That," he then murmured somewhat emotionally, "is the official explanation, which they see fit to insist on here. But I can tell you that there's more to it than that." And now he told the truth in his sincere and comfortable way.

For several years now, Indian cholera had been showing a greater and greater tendency to spread and wander. Originating in the hot morasses of the Ganges Delta, the disease had risen with the mephitic breath of that lush and useless primordial island jungle, which people avoid and where the tiger crouches in the bamboo thickets. Next, the epidemic had raged and raged with unusual vehemence throughout Hindustan, spreading eastward to China and westward to Afghanistan and Persia; and then, following the main caravan routes, it had carried its horrors to Astrachan and even Moscow. But while Europe was terrified that the specter might travel there by land, it had been transported overseas by Syrian merchant ships, cropping up almost simultaneously in several Mediterranean ports. Next, it had reared its head in Toulon and Málaga, showed its mask at several points in Palermo and Naples, and apparently settled in for good throughout Calabria and Apulia. However, the northern part of the peninsula had been spared.

But in mid-May of this year, on one and the same day, Venice had discovered the dreadful vibrios in the blackened, emaciated corpses of a dockworker and a female grocer. These cases were covered up. Within a week, however, there were ten more, then twenty, then thirty, and in various neighborhoods to boot. An Austrian provincial, returning to his small town after a brief holiday in Venice, had died with all the unambiguous symptoms—and that was how the first rumors about the affliction in the lagoon city had gotten into the German newspapers. The Venetian authorities replied that the health conditions in the city had never been better, and they took the most necessary precautions to ward off any problems.

But the food supply must have gotten contaminated—meat, milk, or vegetables—for although denied and hushed up, death ate its way through the narrow lanes, and it was particularly encouraged by the premature summer heat, which warmed up the canal waters. Indeed, the pestilence seemed to have revived its strength, increasing the tenacity and productivity of its pathogens. Recovery was rare; eighty percent of the stricken died, and in the most horrible way, for the onslaught was extremely savage, with the illness often appearing in its most malignant form, known as the "dry" type. The diseased body could not even expel the masses of water secreted by the blood vessels. Within just hours, the patient shriveled up, hoarsely lamenting and convulsively choking on his pitch-like blood. The victim was fortunate, however, if, as sometimes occurred, a slight malaise was followed by a deep coma, from which he seldom if ever awoke.

By early June the quarantine barracks of the Ospedale Civile had quietly filled up, the two orphan asylums had a shortage of space, and there was a dreadful coming and going between the dock of the Fondamente Nuove and San Michele, the graveyard island. But the city fathers were concerned about overall damage to the vast tourist trade, about the painting exhibition that had recently opened in the Public Gardens; they were worried that a panic might break out, that the hotel might lose its reputation, that business would suffer if tourists kept away in droves. And these fears proved more powerful than love of truth and respect for international agreements; these fears compelled the authorities to uphold their obstinate policy of concealment and denial. Venice's chief medical official, a meritorious man, had indignantly resigned and had been surreptitiously replaced by a more compliant individual. The population knew about it; and this corruption in high places, together with the prevailing insecurity, the anxiety about the state of emergency caused by death as it stalked the city, had a certain demoralizing impact on the lower classes; these factors encouraged their unsavory and antisocial tendencies, which were manifested as indecency, shamelessness, and a rising crime rate. Contrary to the norm, one could see an abnormally high number of drunks in the evenings; nasty riffraff, it was said, made the streets unsafe at night; there were many muggings and even murders, for, allegedly, more victims were actually poisoned by their own relatives than carried off by the epidemic; and professional vice assumed more obnoxious and dissolute forms, which were otherwise unknown here and were at home only in southern Italy or in the Orient.

The Englishman had summed up the most important aspects of the situation. "You would do well," he concluded, "to leave today rather than tomorrow. The quarantine cannot be more than a day or two off."

"Thank you," said Aschenbach, and left the bureau. The Piazza was sunless and sweltering. Unaware foreigners sat on café terraces or, covered with pigeons, stood in front of the cathedral, watching the birds teeming, beating their wings, jostling one another, picking the corn kernels from cupped hands. Feverishly agitated, in triumphant possession of the truth, with a taste of nausea in his mouth and a fantastic horror in his heart, the solitary man paced up and down the flagstones of the magnificent courtyard. He weighed the possibility of a decent and purifying action. After dinner tonight, he could go to the lady with the pearls and say to her what he was already drafting word for word:

"Madame, permit a stranger to offer you a piece of advice, a warning, which self-interest is withholding from you. Leave Venice, immediately, with Tadzio and your daughters! Venice is infested." Then, after saying farewell by placing his hand on the head of that agent of a jeering deity, he could turn away and flee from this quagmire. But he also sensed that he was far from seriously desiring to take such a step. It would bring him back, would restore him to himself; but the man who is beside himself despises nothing more than becoming his old self again. He recalled a white building adorned with inscriptions that glistened in the sunset while his mind's eye had gotten lost in their translucent mysticism. Then he pictured that strange figure of a wanderer who had aroused the aging man's adolescent yearning, his roving desire for distant, foreign places; and the thought of going home, of regaining his prudence and sobriety, his strenuous self-mastery, was so repugnant that his face twisted into a grimace of physical disgust.

"They want us to keep quiet!" he whispered vehemently. And: "I will keep quiet!"

The awareness of his complicity, his connivance, intoxicated him the way small amounts of wine intoxicate a weary brain. He was haunted by the image of the afflicted and neglected city, a wild vision kindling his hopes, which were incomprehensible, utterly unreasonable, and tremendously sweet. For an instant he had dreamed of tender happiness, but what was that compared with these expectations? What use were art and virtue against the advantages of chaos? He kept quiet and stayed on.

That night he had an appalling dream—if "dream" is the right word for something both physical and mental that he endured in deepest slumber, an entirely self-contained experience that was concrete to his senses even though he did not see himself as present and moving through space beyond these events. Instead they took place in his own soul, they burst in from the outside, violently crushing his resistance—a profound resistance of his mind—and passed through him, devastating and annihilating his sheer existence, his cultured, civilized life.

Fear was the beginning, fear and pleasure and a horrified curiosity about what lay ahead. Night ruled, and his senses listened; for distant turmoil and tumult were approaching, a mixture of noises: rattling, shattering, and muffled thundering, shrill reveling and a certain howling in a drawn-out *u* sound—everything imbued and overtoned with ghastly sweetness by a deeply cooing, brutally insistent flute that, in a shamelessly intrusive way, bewitched the listener's entrails. But he knew a phrase, obscure yet naming what came: *"The alien god!"* A smoky fire glowed: he recognized a mountainous region like the one around his country home. And in the tattered light, from a wooded peak, there came plunging and rolling and tumbling, between trunks and mossy rock fragments: humans, animals, a swarm, a raging horde—flooding the slope with bodies, flames, pandemonium, and a reeling, rounding dance.

Women, tripping over lengthy hides that dangled from their belts, shook tambourines above their moaning, back-flung heads, brandished naked daggers and torches spewing trails of sparks, clutched tongue-darting serpents by the middle of their bodies or held up their breasts in both hands and shrieked. Men with horns above their foreheads, with shaggy skins, with furs draped around their loins, bent their necks and lifted their arms and thighs, pounded brass cymbals and furiously battered drums, while smooth boys with garlanded sticks prodded goats, clung to their horns, and yelled exultantly as they were dragged by the cavorting creatures. And the inspired carousers howled the call made of voiced consonants and ending in a drawn-out *u* sound, both sweet and savage, like no other that had ever been heard. And here it was blared and was bellowed into the air as if by stags, and there it was echoed by many wildly triumphant voices driving one another to dance, to fling their limbs about, and never letting that call fade.

However, permeating and dominating everything was that deep, enticing flute music. Did it not entice him too, though he tried to resist experience—did it not lure him shamelessly, persistently to the festival, the excessive rite of the ultimate immolation? Huge was his abhorrence, huge his terror, intense his desire to shield his own god to the very last, defend him against the stranger, the enemy of a calm and dignified intellect. But the uproar, the howling, multiplied by the reverberating mountain wall, grew, took control, swelled into entrancing madness. Vapors beset his mind, the pungent aroma of goats, the smell of panting bodies, and the stench of putrid water, plus another smell, a familiar one: of injuries and a rampant disease. His heart boomed with the beating drums, his brain whirled, rage grabbed him, blinded him, a numbing lust, and his soul ached to join the circling dance of the god.

The obscene symbol, gigantic, wooden, was bared and lifted: then they howled the watchword more wantonly. With foaming mouths, they stormed, egged one another on with lewd gestures and lecherous hands, laughing and groaning, thrust the prickle-prod goads into one another's flesh and licked the blood from their limbs. But now the dreamer was with them, one of them, and belonged to the alien god. Yes, they were he himself as they pounced on the beasts, ripping and killing, devouring shreds of steaming flesh, and on the churned-up mossy ground the promiscuous mating began—a sacrifice to the god. And his soul tasted the frenzy and fornication of doom.

The afflicted man awoke from this dream, unnerved, shattered, and powerless in the demon's grip. He no longer shunned the querying eyes of others; nor did he care whether he looked suspicious. They were leaving after all, fleeing: countless cabanas stood empty on the beach, there were many vacant tables in the dining room, and few foreigners were seen in the city. The truth seemed to have leaked out; the panic, despite the tenacious conspiracy, could no longer be halted. However, the woman with the pearls stayed on with her family, either because the rumors did not reach her or because she was too proud and fearless to give in to them: Tadzio stayed on. And at times the trapped man felt as if flight and death could remove all the interference around them, so that he might remain alone with the beauty on this island. In the mornings by the sea, his gaze lay fixed and heavy on the desired boy; in the waning day he skulked after him, undignified, through alleys secretly haunted by unacknowledged and disgusting death—and the monstrous appeared promising and the moral code null and void.

Like any lover, he wanted to please, and he was terrified that it might not be possible. He added cheerful, youthful touches to his suit, he wore jewels and used perfumes; several times a day he spent a long while getting dressed, and was adorned, excited, and anxious when he showed up for meals. Viewing the boy's sweet, bewitching youth, he was sickened by his own aging body: the sight of his gray hair, his pinched features, mortified him, left him hopeless. He felt an urge for physical revival and renewal; he frequented the hotel barber.

Wrapped in a smock, leaning back in the chair, under the prattler's grooming hands, Aschenbach peered tormentedly at his reflection.

"Gray," he said, twisting his lips.

"A little," replied the barber. "Due to a wee bit of neglect, indifference to external things, which is understandable in important people—but one cannot necessarily praise it, especially since such people should be above prejudice in matters of nature and artifice. If their strictures about cosmetic art were logically applied to their teeth, they would be quite offensive. After all, a man is as old as his mind and his heart may feel, and gray hair may be a greater untruth than any correction that people may scorn. In your case, sir, you have the right to your own natural hair color. Will you permit me simply to give you yours back again?"

"How?" asked Aschenbach.

The glib talker washed his customer's hair in two kinds of fluid, one clear and one dark, and his hair was as black as in his youth. Then, using the curling iron, the barber set the hair in soft waves, stepped back, and perused the treated head.

"All we have to do now," he said, "is freshen up your complexion a little."

And like someone who cannot stop, who cannot do enough,

he moved more and more briskly from one challenge to the next. Aschenbach, resting comfortably, unable to resist, more and more excited and hopeful about what was happening, studied his reflection, and he saw that his eyebrows arched more evenly and decisively, his eyes were elongated, their glow brought out by a slight application on the lids. Farther down, he saw a delicate carmine awakening on what had been brownish and leathery; his lips, anemic only a moment before, swelled in a raspberry tint; his crow's-feet and the furrows of his cheeks and mouth had vanished under cream and a youthful bloom. . . . His heart throbbing, Aschenbach saw a radiant young man in the mirror. At last the makeup man was satisfied and showed it, as his kind do, by abjectly thanking the person he had served.

"Some insignificant assistance," he said, adding a final detail to Aschenbach's appearance. "Now the signore will have no qualms about falling in love."

The enchanted man left, as joyful as in a dream, confused and fearful. His necktie was red, a gaudily striped band was slung around his wide-brimmed straw hat.

A tepid storm wind had sprung up; though the drizzle was light and fitful, the air remained thick, humid, and heavy with foul vapors. The man was feverish under his rouge, and his ears were besieged by whirring, flapping, fluttering; it sounded as if the most evil wind spirits were haunting the area—unhallowed ocean birds that attack a condemned man's last meal, clawing it, gnawing it, defiling it with filth. For the sultriness ruined his appetite, and he imagined that the food here was contaminated, infected.

One afternoon Aschenbach had followed the beauty into the tangled core of the stricken city. He was getting more and more disoriented, for the alleys, bridges, canals, and small squares in the labyrinth looked much too much alike, and since he could no longer tell north from south, he was especially intent on not losing sight of the ardently tracked image. Forced to exercise ignoble caution, he kept hugging walls, seeking refuge behind people's backs, so that for a long time he was unaware of his fatigue, his exhaustion, which emotion and persistent tension had inflicted on his mind and body. Tadzio walked behind his family; he usually let the governess and the nunlike sisters go first through narrow lanes; and, sauntering alone, he would peek back over his shoulder with his peculiar, twilight-gray eyes to make sure his lover was trailing him. He saw him, and he did not betray him. Heady with this realization, lured forward by those eyes, pulled along on the ludicrous leash of passion, the lover stole after his unsuitable hope—and was eventually cheated of the sight. The Poles had crossed a small, vaulted bridge, whose high arch concealed them from the pursuer, and by the time he reached the bridge, they were gone. He looked for them in three directions, straight ahead and to the right and left along the narrow, dirty quay; but it was no use. Feeling frail and enervated, he finally had to give up his search.

His head burned, his body was covered with sticky sweat, his neck trembled, he was plagued by unbearable thirst, he peered around for any kind of immediate refreshment. Outside a small produce shop he bought some fruit, strawberries, soft and overripe, and he ate them while trudging along. A small deserted square that felt hexed opened up before him; he recognized it: he had been here weeks before when devising his abortive plan to escape. He sank down on the steps of the well at the center of the square, leaning his head against the stone rim. It was still, grass was growing between the cobblestones, garbage lay scattered about. The weather-beaten houses surrounding him were of different heights, and one looked rather palatial, with small balconies flanked by lions and with pointed Gothic windows that led into emptiness. Another house had a pharmacy on the ground floor. Now and then the smell of carbolic acid came wafting on a warm gust of wind.

He sat there, the master, the artist who had achieved dignity, the author of "A Wretched Man," who, employing a form of exemplary purity, had renounced bohemianism and the dismal chasm, had broken with the abyss and reviled all vileness. He had risen high, transcending his knowledge and outgrowing all irony, he had adjusted to his responsibilities toward the public and its trust in him—he, whose fame was official, whose name was ennobled, and whose style was a model for schoolboys. He sat there with closed eyes, but at times a quick sidelong glance, mocking and sheepish, glided out and was instantly concealed again, and his rouged and droopy lips shaped isolated words from the strange, dreamy logic produced by his half-dozing brain.

"For Beauty, Phaidros—mark my words!—Beauty alone is divine and visible at once, and so it is the path of the senses, young Phaidros, the artist's path to the spirit. But do you actually believe, my friend, that he can ever find wisdom and true manhood if he takes the path of the senses to reach the spiritual? Or do you instead assume (I leave the decision up to you) that this is a path of perilous charm, truly a path of sin, a path that is bound to lead you astray? For you must know that we poets cannot take the path of Beauty unless Eros joins us and sets himself up as our guide; indeed, though we may be heroes after our fashion and virtuous warriors, we are nevertheless like women, for passion is our exaltation, and our longing must remain love—that is our bliss and our shame.

"Do you now see that we poets cannot be wise or dignified? That we are bound to go astray, bound to remain wanton adventurers of the emotions? Our masterful style is falsehood and folly, our renown and prestige are a farce, the public faith in us is utterly ludicrous, and educating the populace, the younger generation, through art is a hazardous enterprise that should be outlawed. For how can a man be a fit educator if he has an inborn, natural, and incorrigible preference for the abyss? We can certainly shun it and gain our status, but no matter where we turn, we are still drawn to the abyss. And so we renounce knowledge, which disintegrates things, for knowledge, Phaidros, has no dignity or severity; knowledge is all-knowing, understanding, forgiving, devoid of composure, of form; it sympathizes with the abyss, it *is* the abyss. And so we firmly reject knowledge, and henceforth our sole concern is Beauty—that is, simplicity, grandeur, and new severity, a new innocence and form. But form and innocence, Phaidros, lead to euphoria and desire, may lead the noble person to a horrid emotional blasphemy, which his own beautiful severity will reject as disgraceful—and they lead to the abyss, they, too, lead to the abyss. They lead us poets there, I tell you, for we cannot soar, we can only be wanton. And now I shall leave, Phaidros, and you shall remain, and do not leave until you can no longer see me."

Several mornings thereafter, Gustav von Aschenbach left the Hôtel des Bains later than usual because he felt under the weather. He was suffering from certain only partly physical dizzy spells, which were accompanied by an intensely mounting anxiety, a sense of hopelessness and helplessness, and there was no telling whether his fears had to do with the surrounding world or his own existence. Down in the lobby he noticed a huge amount of luggage ready to be dispatched; wondering which guests were leaving, he asked a doorman, who pronounced the aristocratic Polish name that Aschenbach had secretly expected. He received his answer without so much as a twitch of his sunken features; he merely lifted his head for a second—the gesture with which we casually register something that we do not need to know. He then asked, "When?" and was told, "After lunch." He nodded and walked to the sea.

The beach was desolate. Shivers curled across the wide stretch of shallow water separating the coast from the first long sandbank. An autumnal atmosphere, a sense that it had outlived its usefulness, seemed to press down on the once so bustling and colorful pleasure haunt, which was now almost deserted, its sand no longer kept clean. A camera, seemingly abandoned, perched on its tripod by the waterline, and the black cloth covering the apparatus snapped and fluttered in the chilly wind.

Tadzio, with three or four remaining playmates, was moving to the right of his family's cabana. With a blanket drawn up over his knees, Aschenbach, resting in his deck chair, roughly halfway between the sea and the row of cabins, watched the boy once again. The game, which was unsupervised (the women must have been making their final preparations), seemed to have no rules and was getting out of hand. The husky boy, the one called "Yashu," was there, with his slicked black hair and his belted suit; annoyed and blinded by sand thrown in his face, he forced Tadzio into a wrestling match that swiftly ended with the downfall of the weaker boy, the beauty. But in this time of departure, the subaltern apparently wanted to overcome his sense of inferiority and, through a cruel action, get even for a long enslavement; the winner refused to let go of the loser; kneeling on his back, he kept pushing the loser's face into the sand, on and on, so that Tadzio, already breathless from the struggle, was on the point of suffocating. His attempts to shake off the weighty victor were convulsive, they kept stopping altogether for several moments, then resumed as a mere twitching.

Horrified, Aschenbach was about to jump up and rescue him when the violent wrestler released his victim at last. Tadzio, very pale, straightened halfway, sat there motionless for a few minutes, leaning on one arm, his hair disheveled, his eyes darkening. Then he got to his feet and slowly trudged away. The others called to him, first cheerfully, then pleading anxiously; but he ignored them. The black-haired boy, who must have felt instant remorse about his outrageous conduct, caught up with him and tried to make peace. But with a heave of his shoulders, Tadzio rebuffed him. He veered down toward the water. His feet were bare, and he was wearing his striped linen suit with the red knot.

His head drooping, he lingered at the edge of the water, drawing figures in the wet sand with the tip of one foot; and then he stepped into the shallow water, which did not go up to his knees even in its deepest part; walking across it, casually advancing, he reached the sandbank. There he paused for a moment, facing the open vista, then turned left, slowly moving along the narrow, lengthy strip of exposed sand. Separated from the mainland by the wide water, separated from his comrades by his proud mood, he walked, an extremely isolated and dissociated figure, his hair fluttering out there in the sea, in the wind, in front of the hazy boundlessness. Once again he halted and looked around. And suddenly, as if recollecting something, as if obeying an impulse, he put his hand on his hip, turned his upper body in a beautiful contraposto and peered over his shoulder at the shore.

The watcher there sat as he had sat long ago, when those twilight-gray eyes had first gazed at him from the doorway to the dining room. Aschenbach's head, on the back of the chair, had slowly followed the movements of the figure walking out there; now his head lifted up, virtually toward that gaze, and sank on his chest, so that his eyes looked from below, while his face showed that slack, heartfelt absorption of profound slumber. It was as if the pale and charming psychagogue, the guide of the spirits, was smiling at him from out there, beckoning to him; as if he were taking his hand from his hip, pointing outward, floating ahead of him into a richly promising immensity. And, as so often before, the watcher proceeded to follow him.

Minutes passed before anyone dashed up to help the man who had slumped over the side of his chair. He was carried to his room. And that very same day a respectfully shocked world received the news of his death.